NO REASON TO DIE

Hilary Bonner is a former showbusiness editor of the *Mail on Sunday* and the *Daily Mirror*. She now writes full time and lives in the West Country where she was born and brought up and where all her books are based. She is the author of eight previous novels, *The Cruelty of Morning*, *A Fancy to Kill For*, *A Passion So Deadly*, *For Death Comes Softly*, *A Deep Deceit*, *A Kind of Wild Justice*, *A Moment of Madness* and *When the Dead Cry Out*. She also ghost-wrote *It's Not a Rehearsal*, the autobiography of Amanda Barrie. Hilary was the Chair of the Crime Writers' Association in 2003.

Also by Hilary Bonner

FICTION

The Cruelty of Morning
A Fancy to Kill For
A Passion So Deadly
For Death Comes Softly
A Deep Deceit
A Kind of Wild Justice
A Moment of Madness
When the Dead Cry Out

NON-FICTION

Heartbeat – The Real Life Story
Benny – A Biography of Benny Hill
René and Me (Gorden Kaye)
Journeyman (with Clive Gunnell)
It's Not a Rehearsal (with Amanda Barrie)

HILARY BONNER

NO REASON
TO DIE

WILLIAM HEINEMANN: LONDON

First published in the United Kingdom in 2004 by William Heinemann

1 3 5 7 9 10 8 6 4 2

Copyright © Hilary Bonner 2004

The right of Hilary Bonner to be identified as the author of this work has been
asserted by her in accordance with the Copyright, Designs and Patents Act, 1988

William Heinemann
The Random House Group Limited
20 Vauxhall Bridge Road, London SW1V 2SA

Random House Australia (Pty) Limited
20 Alfred Street, Milsons Point, Sydney,
New South Wales 2061, Australia

Random House New Zealand Limited
18 Poland Road, Glenfield
Auckland 10, New Zealand

Random House (Pty) Limited
Endulini, 5a Jubilee Road, Parktown, 2193, South Africa

The Random House Group Limited Reg. No. 954009

www.randomhouse.co.uk

A CIP catalogue record for this book is available from the British Library

Papers used by Random House are natural, recyclable products made from wood
grown in sustainable forests. The manufacturing processes conform to the
environmental regulations of the country of origin

Typeset in Plantin by SX Composing DTP, Rayleigh, Essex
Printed and bound in the United Kingdom by
Mackays of Chatham PLC, Chatham, Kent

ISBN 0 434 01112 6 (Hardback)
ISBN 0 434 01113 4 (Trade paperback)

This book is dedicated to the memory of Private James Collinson, aged 17, Private Geoff Gray, 17, Private Cheryl James, 18, and Private Sean Benton, 20; all of whom died suddenly and unexpectedly at the Princess Royal Barracks at Deepcut, headquarters of the Royal Logistics Corps.

And while this book is a work of fiction, and all the characters in it are fictional, the extraordinary events surrounding the death of those four young soldiers, and certain other of the 1,748 non combat deaths recorded within the British Army since 1990, provide its inspiration.

Acknowledgements

Geoff and Diane Gray, parents of Private Geoff Gray and Yvonne and Jim Collinson, parents of Private James Collinson, without whose generous assistance this book may not have been possible. Their dignity and quiet determination are awesome, and it was an honour and a private privilege to get to know them; Sergeant John Woods of the Devon and Cornwall Constabulary in Torquay; Police Constable Steve Mudge, of the Devon and Cornwall Constabulary, formerly a sergeant in the Royal Military Police; former Detective Sergeant Frank Waghorn of the Avon and Somerset Constabulary; former Parachute Regiment Colonel John Pullinger; and last but far from least, Major Rachel Grimes of the Royal Logistic Corps, currently employed in the Ministry of Defence Press Office, who freely helped me with all factual matters in spite of being aware of the inspiration for this book, leaving me to think that if the army had been as open from the beginning with the families of the young soldiers who died at Deepcut, then Geoff, Diane, Jim, Yvonne, and all the others who have formed the pressure group Deepcut and Beyond, may not have felt forced to campaign with every means at their disposal in order to, one day, be told the truth.

NO REASON TO DIE

One

The young man fell heavily. His right shoulder hit the floor first and the pain made him grunt. Then the rest of his body followed quite slowly. It was a bit like the final act of a very bad ballet. His head bounced just once on the ancient flagstones, while his arms flayed the air desperately searching for something to hang on to, until, after a final, ineffectually limp, kick of one leg, he lay spreadeagled, limbs outstretched, face up, eyes and mouth wide open in surprise.

There was a trickle of blood on his forehead where he had caught it against the edge of the bar on the way down. After the grunt he did not make a sound, but then the fall must have made it even harder for him to speak than it had been before. Neither did he attempt to move. But movement had also been pretty difficult before.

Kelly was sitting on a stool in the corner, as far away from the pool table as possible. Kelly didn't like pool in pubs. The cues, and the gyrating bottoms of those brandishing them, turned your average bar room into an obstacle course. There was nobody playing pool that evening, but there were some things in life which even Kelly would take no chances with.

There was actually hardly anybody in the pub at all. It was a wet Monday night in early November and the rain had been falling incessantly since early morning. It had been almost horizontal across the car park when Kelly had arrived a couple of hours earlier, and the driving easterly wind had been so strong that walking against it had not been easy. This had hardly been a day for a drive over the moors to The Wild Dog, an isolated eighteenth-century coaching inn, built alongside one of the handful of roads criss-crossing the heart of Dartmoor. Kelly, however, was prepared to undertake almost anything almost any time, except the things he should be doing with his life.

An elderly couple were sitting at a table at the far end of the bar, in the lounge area which Charlie Cooke, the landlord, a likeable but inadequate amateur from Birmingham, now used as a glorified dining room. Apart from the young man lying prostrate on the floor, they and Kelly were the only customers. In summer The Wild Dog was packed, and even in the winter, over weekends blessed with half-decent weather, the old inn attracted a quite respectable level of business with customers motoring out for lunch and dinner from the towns and cities on the edge of the moors, like Plymouth, Newton Abbot, and even Kelly's own home town of Torquay down on the coast. But The Dog had little or no local drinking trade and, in common with so many country pubs, had come to rely entirely on the provision of food and the seasonal influxes of tourists. Pubs just weren't pubs any more, thought Kelly morosely.

He had watched the young man's fall with a kind of detached fascination. It had been more of a slide really, head and shoulders first, as he had bent at the waist so far backwards that gravity had refused to allow his body to remain any longer on the stool. Then there had been that last almost lazy kick-out with one leg, as he had gradually descended to the floor, the weight of his lower body causing him to slide along the flagstones, worn slippery with age, until he lay full length, his head nearly inside the mighty old inglenook which dominated the room. He was, however, in no danger of burning. Only a small modern oil stove smouldered fitfully in the centre of the huge fireplace.

The elderly couple continued to concentrate very hard on finishing their microwaved frozen lasagne. Charlie's wife, who did most of the catering herself, didn't cook on out-of-season weekdays, but Charlie reckoned he was a dab hand with the microwave. Kelly didn't agree. He'd once eaten Charlie's micro-waved lasagne. It had been cool and soggy in the middle, dry and chewy round the edges, and totally and utterly tasteless. However, when the young man fell off his stool the elderly couple focused every bit of their attention on the sorry meal before them, as if it were a mouth-watering gourmet experience. And they gave absolutely no sign whatsoever of noticing the only bit of action The Wild Dog was likely to see that day.

Kelly noticed. But then Kelly noticed everything. It was his life's work really. One way or another, he had made a living since he was a boy out of watching and listening and then writing it all down. He had been a journalist for many years, at the very top in Fleet Street until he let the demons get to him, and then back to his local paper roots in South Devon. But that was all behind Kelly now. Kelly had had enough of destroying lives. He was no saintly philanthropist and he'd been a damned good investigative reporter, with a real nose for a story – the type of journalist who, by and large and with one or two notable exceptions, had achieved marginally more good than harm. It was the destruction of his own life Kelly had wanted to halt, far more than that of anybody else. He had decided he was going to be a novelist. Indeed he was already a novelist – in as much as that he had given up the day job and written half a treatment and almost two chapters of his first novel.

However, Kelly was at the displacement activity stage. It seemed to be lasting rather a long time and Kelly suspected that it would probably last throughout whatever passed for his writing career.

He put his pint glass down on the bar. It contained a couple of inches or so of warm, flat, Diet Coke. Kelly didn't drink alcohol any more, not because he didn't want to but because he knew, and this time round he really did know, that if he ever started drinking again it would kill him. Simple as that. But there was only so much Diet Coke a man could force down, and Kelly had been sitting in his corner of the bar for two hours, pretending to think. It had been a sorry pretence; his mind had remained more or less blank throughout. And the young man's fall had been the only real diversion of his day.

Kelly stared idly at the still prostrate figure on the floor. He supposed somebody should do something. He glanced towards the bar. On the other side of it he could just see the top edge of an open trap door, but there was no sign at all of the landlord. Charlie had disappeared into the cellar more than ten minutes previously, ostensibly to change a barrel. Kelly thought it likely he was bored rigid and wanted a change of scenery, and couldn't say he blamed him. Business was hardly brisk.

Kelly's back ached from sitting on the tall, angular, wooden stool for so long. He reached behind his head to rub his neck

3

muscles through the thick oily wool of his dark blue fisherman's sweater, then stretched his arms above his head. He didn't know what he was doing in a pub at all, to be honest. It was habit, he supposed. That morning he'd spent three hours at his screen playing computer games and periodically checking his email, which invariably consisted of unsolicited messages from suppliers of deeply sad soft porn and little else, before giving up even kidding himself that he was about to start writing at any moment. He'd made himself some scrambled eggs on toast for lunch and then gone through the same charade for most of the afternoon. By teatime he'd had enough. In a state of total frustration he'd taken off in his car and had made himself head for The Wild Dog, rather than a potentially cheerier hostelry nearer to home, so that he would be unlikely to find disruptive company. He was, after all, he told himself, merely looking for a change of scene, seeking out some new and convivial surroundings in which to plot his next chapter. Kelly sighed. Yet more self-deception. He had been just as unable to concentrate on the great novel in the pub as he had been at home, and The Dog was hardly convivial, as he had of course known it could not possibly be, in that weather, on a Monday evening in November. There was often just a touch of sackcloth and ashes about his behaviour, Kelly reflected.

He took a deep drag on his cigarette, then hastily removed it from his mouth. Kelly made his own roll-ups, and this one had burned so close to the end that it felt dangerously hot to his lips. He stubbed out the remains in an overflowing ashtray. Its contents were all Kelly's own work, an unedifying pile of tobacco waste produced entirely by his own appallingly abused lungs. Smoking was Kelly's sole remaining vice, although he'd only given up the others because he'd had no choice. He smoked a lot and he didn't care any more. The only thing about smoking he intended to give up was even pretending that he wanted to stop.

Automatically, he reached for the tobacco and the packet of Rizla papers in his pocket. Then the boy on the floor made a sort of half-strangled gurgling sound. The elderly couple bent their heads so close to their plates of lasagne it looked as if they might be about to disappear into them. Kelly glanced down at the boy without enthusiasm. Oh, shit, he thought.

'Charlie,' he called anxiously across the bar. 'Charlie.'

The young man rolled over onto his side and made an unsuccessful attempt to rise up on one shoulder.

'Charlie,' called Kelly again. There was no reply. Kelly leaned over the bar and peered down through the open trap door. There was a light shining up from below, but if Charlie was still in the cellar he made no response. The pub was built on the side of a hill and Kelly knew that there was a delivery door to one side of the cellar leading out into the yard and the beer garden beyond. If the night outside were not so bleak he might have suspected that Charlie had finally done a runner, for which Kelly would not have blamed him one bit. Charlie, a city boy who had previously been a motor insurance salesman, readily told the story of how throughout his adulthood he had dreamed the romantic dream of life as a country publican. But The Wild Dog, while being just the place for a writer who can't write to torture himself in, had given Charlie a rude awakening, Kelly reckoned. It was, in Kelly's opinion, a morgue in the winter and a tourists' hellhole in the summer.

Wondering what on earth he was doing in the place anyway, Kelly leaned a little further across the bar, until his attention was again demanded by more gurgling sounds from the floor. He swung round on the stool for another look. The young man's eyes were popping and his lower jaw drooped alarmingly. Kelly had a dreadful feeling he knew what was going to happen next. And he was right. The young man began to retch, great heaving motions racking his body.

'Oh, fuck,' said Kelly.

He'd always been able to move fast for a big man, and somewhat amazingly he still could. In a single smooth movement he was alongside and bending over the fallen drinker. With one hand, he caught hold of the collar of the boy's jacket at the back of his neck, while at the same time hooking the other beneath one of his arms.

'Right, sunshine, up!' he yelled.

The couple eating their supper shrunk further into their chairs, their heads buried even deeper into their lasagne. Meanwhile the young man, perhaps startled into something loosely resembling consciousness by Kelly's authoritative voice, began to at least come close to finding his feet, and, with Kelly's help, rose almost upright, still retching. Ducking to avoid the gnarled old beams laced across the pub's low ceiling, Kelly half dragged, half lifted him into the gents' toilet, kicking open the door with one foot. Once inside, he pushed the boy's head into the nearest latrine. He knew there wouldn't be time to get him into a cubicle.

They only just made it. The boy was at once resoundingly sick. Kelly leaned against the door breathing heavily. He might still be able to move fast, but all those years of self-abuse had left him monumentally short of breath nowadays whenever he took any form of exercise, however brief. And heaving a near dead-weight drunk into a toilet was actually a pretty demanding sort of exercise.

Kelly began to feel slightly nauseous himself. But he stood his ground. He told himself he didn't want the lad to choke on his own vomit, and that he was quite out of his head enough to do so. But there was also a further element of self-punishment about it. So-called writers who spend the best part of an entire day playing computer games don't deserve to have a good time. It seemed only right and proper to Kelly that he should suffer that day.

The boy remained slumped over the latrine for several seconds after he had finished vomiting, before lurching to one side and swinging himself around, leaning against the wall for support, so that he was looking directly towards Kelly. His face was flushed and blotchy, and he was of very average height and build, but through the drunkenness Kelly could see that this was an extremely fit young man. There was not an ounce of spare flesh on him, and his light reddish-brown hair was cut extremely short, shaven at the back and sides and only slightly longer on top. He could well be a boy soldier or a young wannabe marine out of Plymouth, thought Kelly idly as he turned away to bend over a washbasin in order to splash his own face with cold water.

'What's your name, mate?' he asked conversationally, straightening up and running the fingers of one hand through his thinning, once black hair.

The boy focused on him uncertainly, his eyes still glazed. He did not speak.

6

'Your name?' repeated Kelly, rather more loudly, and with exaggerated clarity.

'Whassit to you,' came the muttered reply.

'I was going to buy you a drink,' responded Kelly. 'And I only buy drinks for people whose names I know.'

Kelly spoke the language of drunks. He understood the logic. He was quite sure of the response he would get to that remark, and he was not disappointed.

'Oh, right, yeah. It'sh Alan, my name'sh Alan.' The young man spoke with a heavy Scottish accent which made it even more difficult to decipher his slurred tones. But Kelly managed it.

'OK Alan, time for a bath.'

Kelly moved quickly again, crossing the small room in two long strides and once more catching hold of the young man by the back of his jacket. Then he half dragged him, barely protesting at all, over to the basin, which he had already filled with water, and dunked his head in it. Alan spluttered a bit, but was uncomplaining when Kelly let go of his head and allowed him to stand upright again, or rather, as near to upright as he could manage. He was still very drunk and his eyes were glazed as, dripping water over himself, he propped himself uncertainly against the washbasin. Kelly threw him a handful of paper towels, then, reckoning he'd done quite enough thank you, and that it was time to leave the lad to it, he headed for the door back into the bar.

'Just clean yourself up, there's a good boy,' he said.

With the resilience of youth Alan seemed to recover almost immediately, enough to be able to walk, anyway, which in his case that night was a considerable improvement. He quickly followed Kelly into the bar, arriving just as the would-be writer was settling on his stool again and as Charlie emerged from the trap door.

The lad looked uncertainly around him. 'Where'sh my pint?' he asked, still barely able to get the words out, and equally unable to see that his half-full glass remained where he had left it further up the bar.

Charlie, perhaps indicating that he had been well enough aware of what was going on but had chosen to leave Kelly to deal with it, promptly removed the glass of beer, but was not quite quick enough. The young man, with perhaps surprising comprehension under the circumstances, both saw and grasped exactly what was happening.

''Ere, I want my pint,' he half growled, making a real attempt to appear aggressive.

'Now, now . . .' began Charlie.

Kelly sighed again. If there was one person in the world who knew all about dealing with drunks, it was John Kelly. After all, he'd been there. In spades.

'It's all right, mate,' he said. 'Come and sit down with me, and I'll get you another one.'

He steered the boy to a table by the wall and more or less pushed him into a chair. There was something about Kelly that allowed him to get away with it where another man might not. Perhaps even in his drunken state the lad could sense something of Kelly's chequered past.

At the bar he ordered a pint of ginger ale for the lad and another pint of Diet Coke for himself, resigned to the fact that he was going to do nothing constructive with the rest of that night, anyway, so he might just as well stay a little longer in The Dog. The ginger ale was warm, wet, pale brown and slightly fizzy. Kelly had a small bet with himself that the boy wouldn't even notice that it wasn't a pint of bitter.

He put the drink on the table next to the young Scotsman who picked it up and downed half of it in one swallow. Then he sat back in his seat and studied the glass in his hand with some puzzlement. For a moment it seemed he may not have been fooled and that he was about to comment on the true nature of its contents, but Kelly didn't give him chance to dwell on the matter.

'You a squaddie or something?' he asked.

Alan did not reply but looked directly at Kelly, obviously making a determined effort to focus. In his eyes there was just a glimpse of something beyond drunken incomprehension, but Kelly was not quite sure what it was.

'Well, are you?' Kelly repeated.

Alan nodded, reached for his glass again and, in doing so knocked it from the table so that it fell, sending a cascade of ginger ale over both Kelly and himself. The glass smashed into hundreds of small pieces on the flagstoned floor.

'Shit,' said Kelly.

Alan slumped back in his chair, eyes blank again, looking as if he was only vaguely aware of what was happening.

'Right,' said Charlie, finally playing the role of publican, as he approached from behind the bar with a cloth and a dustpan and brush. 'That's it. You're out of here, mate.'

The order was entirely wasted. Alan's eyes were closed and he seemed to have fallen asleep, or certainly slumped into drunken semi-consciousness.

'It's all right, Charlie, I'll sort him out,' said Kelly, who had been unceremoniously removed from more than his fair share of pubs in his time and saved from the same fate in numerous others thanks only to the assistance of various drinking companions.

Kelly shook the young man by the shoulders. Alan's eyes shot open, unnaturally wide.

'Look, I think you could do with a bit of a helping hand, old son,' he said gently. 'Where are you stationed? Why don't I call one of your mates. Somebody will come and pick you up, for certain.'

'No. No, I don't want that. No. You mushn't call anyone.' Alan shouted. He was still having difficulty getting his words out, but he had no difficulty whatsoever with his message. Kelly was mildly surprised by the strength of his reaction. He sounded quite alarmed at the prospect of being collected by his army mates.

'Well, you can't stay here, you know,' Kelly continued. 'Maybe I could drop you off.'

It wouldn't be such a bad idea. He might just as well, he thought. It would get him out of the pub anyway, and maybe on the road back to a late-night writing session after all.

'No.' The boy was adamant.

'Well, how else are you going to get back to your billet, Alan? Don't tell me you've got a vehicle parked outside? There's no way you could drive, anyway.'

Alan shook his head, in an almost dreamy sort of way. 'No, I walked here, didn't I?'

'Right.' Kelly thought for a moment, trying to remember an army base within anything like walking distance of The Wild Dog. He knew the moors, indeed that whole area of South Devon, extremely well, but could think of nowhere military nearby.

'So where did you walk from?' he asked casually.

'Hangridge,' replied the boy, and then seemed to realise that he'd divulged information he had not intended to. 'But I'm not bloody going back there, so don't even think about it,' he continued, so emphatically that for just a moment he sounded almost sober.

'Hangridge,' Kelly repeated. He knew about the place, of course. The isolated barracks built on a remote Dartmoor hilltop was the headquarters of the Devonshire Fusiliers and a major infantry training base. Farmers settled in moorland valleys, the army always chose hilltops. Hangridge was known not only for its bleakness, exposed by its geography to the most vicious of Dartmoor's elements, but also for the toughness of the regime endured by the young recruits stationed there. But the Devonshire Fusiliers was an elite regiment with a proud history, and Hangridge's training programme was designed to produce only top-notch professional soldiers. Idly, Kelly wondered how a Scots lad had come to join a regiment which he knew still drew around sixty per cent of its intake from Devon, its home county.

Kelly had been to Hangridge once, the previous year when his paper had sent him to cover an anniversary visit by the minor royal who was the regiment's colonel in chief, but for a moment he couldn't quite place its exact location in relation to The Wild Dog. He attempted to visualise a map of Dartmoor. The pub was on the south side of the moor, on one of the highest points of the road between the villages of Hexworthy and Buckfast, just forty-five minutes' or so drive out of Torquay. Hangridge was considerably further north, on the far side of the moor heading towards Okehampton. Kelly half closed his eyes, trying to measure the distances involved.

'Shit, Hangridge must be almost twenty miles away,' he said. 'And you say you walked here?'

'I yomped it,' muttered the boy, suddenly exhibiting just a flash of the military pride for which the Devonshire Fusiliers were famous. 'Came over the hills, didn't I? Not sho far that way.'

He slumped into his seat again, the moment of near-erudite diction behind him, his legs thrust out before him. For the first time, Kelly noticed that his jeans were stained with mud almost to the knees and that his boots were also caked in mud. A damp parka lay in a pile on the floor over by the bar.

'That's still quite a march for a pint,' said Kelly mildly.

Alan glanced around the bar before he replied. Kelly thought he seemed nervous.

'I was heading for the main road. I was going to hitch a ride. But I was wet through and so bloody cold . . .'

Alan interrupted himself with a sudden bout of hiccups.

Kelly finished his sentence for him.

'So you came in here. Where were you going on a night like this, anyway?'

'None of your fucking business,' Alan replied through his hiccups.

'Fine,' said Kelly, who had too much experience of drunks to be offended. 'But you've had a few now, so why don't I run you back to Hangridge. It won't take long in a car.'

He was unsure of why he was prepared to go so far out of his way. After all, the barracks were almost directly in the opposite direction to Torquay. Was he just being kind, or was his generous offer prompted rather more by the curiosity he was already beginning to feel about this young man? Something did not add up, and Kelly could never resist even the hint of a good human riddle.

However, he had no time for further introspection. Alan reacted almost as if Kelly had hit him. He shot upright in his chair and would no doubt have jumped to his feet had he been capable of such sudden movement.

'I'm not bloody going back there,' he yelled at the top of his voice. 'Nobody's bloody taking me back there.'

Out of the corner of his eye, Kelly noticed the elderly couple whose quiet supper had been so disrupted sidling towards the door, still averting their eyes from the cause of the disruption.

'For goodness sake, John,' said Charlie, this time from the

safety of behind the bar. 'Get that damned kid out of here, if you're going to. If not, I'm calling the filth.'

Kelly glanced at him balefully and did not bother to reply. The filth? Presumably, Charlie was referring to a possible visit from a patrol car out of Ashburton, which would now be highly unlikely to arrive before closing time. And, in any case, one drunken kid hardly warranted a 999 call. In pub-land terms, the landlord of The Wild Dog did not know he was born. Kelly turned to Alan.

'C'mon mate,' he said. 'You heard the man. You can't stay here. And if I don't take you back to Hangridge, where the hell else are you going to go?'

'Anywhere I can sh-shtay alive,' replied Alan, frowning with the effort of getting the words out. But at least he seemed to have stopped hiccupping.

Kelly chuckled. He was no stranger to alcoholic paranoia.

'Oh, come on,' he said gently. 'It can't be as bad as that?'

The young soldier made another huge effort to be lucid.

'Not that bad? If you don't fucking go along with everything out there, they fucking kill you.' Alan made a cutting motion across his throat with the side of his right hand. He then allowed his arm to fall loosely to his side as if the effort of keeping it in any other sort of position was too great.

'Sho, how bad's that, then?' he enquired.

Kelly grinned. He patted Alan on the shoulder and stood up. The boy really was out of it. Just a pub double or two away from the pink elephant and giant creepy insect stage, Kelly reckoned. Well, Kelly had never pretended to be a butch version of Mother Theresa. And he did have a novel to write. Or, at any rate, a date with his backgammon software.

'If you won't be helped, mate, then you won't be helped,' he said, picking up his glass and walking to the bar.

'Can't do anything with him, Charlie, short of carrying the little bugger out of here, and I'm too long in the tooth for that game,' he said. 'So, it's over to you. I'm off home.'

He raised his glass to drain the last of his final uninspiring pint of Coke when suddenly the young soldier rose unsteadily to his feet and with surprising swiftness crossed the bar and caught hold of Kelly's elbow, jerking his arm and causing him to spill some of his drink down the front of his sweater.

'Hey, steady on,' muttered Kelly, caught off balance.

The boy swayed slightly and perched himself precariously on a bar stool, giving Kelly a dangerous sense of *déjà vu*. This was getting boring. It really was time he left.

'You don't undershtand,' muttered Alan. 'Nobody does. That'sh the trouble. Nobody listens. I've tried to tell people, you see – tried to talk . . .'

'Yeah, yeah.' Kelly had heard it all before. Different background information, same message. The poor persecuted drunk. The boy still had a grip on his arm. He attempted to shake it off, but Alan hung on all the more tightly. He was a strong little bugger for a drunk.

'Don't leave me,' he said.

Dear God, thought Kelly. Don't leave me? He'd only just met the lad, for God's sake, and now he was on the receiving end of a line straight out of Mills & Boon. How did he always manage to get himself involved anywhere there was trouble?

'Look, just let go of me, Alan, you'll be fine,' he coaxed.

'No. No I won't. They'll get me. They will. And they'll do for me, jusht like the others.'

The boy's fingers were digging into Kelly's flesh. This really was getting to be too much.

'You've had a few drinks, mate, you don't know what you're saying,' Kelly began soothingly.

'Oh yes, I do.' The boy spat the words out angrily. 'I'm talking about Hangridge and why I'm never going back there. They've killed the others. They'll kill me, I'm sure of it . . .'

'Yeah, yeah, I know,' soothed Kelly, desperate to get away now. 'Just let go of my arm and we can talk properly, all right.'

The boy's grip began to slacken. Then the pub's ancient, oak, studded door burst open. Into the bar strode two men, one about Kelly's height and build, without the paunch, and the other not so tall but thickset, his broad shoulders almost filling the doorway as he stepped through. Both were wearing oilskin jackets with the collars turned up and woollen hats pulled down over their foreheads. Water was dripping off them onto the floor. The weather had obviously not improved. The two men stood very upright as they glanced around the bar. Kelly thought at once that they too were probably soldiers, but although he could not see their faces well, he was aware that they were both considerably older than Alan.

The taller man wiped raindrops off his forehead with the back of one hand and pointed to Kelly's companion with the other. 'Thank God for that, there he is,' he said.

Alan turned away from Kelly to face the two newcomers, so that Kelly could no longer see his face, only the back of his head. But he could sense him stiffen and saw his shoulders tensing, clenched shoulder blades suddenly prominent through his sweatshirt. At the same time his grip on Kelly's arm relaxed until his hand fell way, then the shoulders slumped and his whole body seemed to go limp. Kelly feared that recent history really was about to repeat itself and that Alan was going to fall off his bar stool again.

It was his turn to grab hold of the boy's arm. Instinctively, he reached out a steadying hand.

'You from Hangridge?' Kelly enquired of the two men. There was no verbal response, but four eyes rounded squarely on him. Neither man made any attempt to reply.

'Well, you're mates of his, yeah?' Kelly continued.

'We certainly are,' said the taller one. 'He was seen heading over the moor this way. We've been searching everywhere for him.'

'I'm glad you've found him, he needs looking after.'

'Yes. I can see that. And thanks for doing your bit.' The man's words were extremely friendly, and he was smiling. But there was no warmth in him. Kelly, who – for an old hack – was surprisingly sensitive to atmosphere and other people's feelings, felt that at once. They're sick to death of this one, he thought, taking his hand away from the young soldier as the tall man came alongside and began to help the boy upright. The second, shorter, broader man also approached and took the other arm. But it was the tall one who seemed to do all the talking. He turned to Kelly and spoke again.

'We'll take care of him now, mate. Had a right skinful, hasn't he? But don't worry, we'll soon sort him out.'

'A few hours' sleep, that's all he needs,' Kelly began, but stopped speaking when he realised no one was listening.

Alan seemed to have returned to the worst of his drunkenness

14

again and was dragging his legs behind him, barely even trying to walk, as he was more or less carried towards the door.

He made no further attempt to speak, but at the door he turned his head towards Kelly so that the older man could see his face for the first time since the arrival of the two newcomers.

The look in the boy's eyes, as he stared directly at him, cut through Kelly like a knife. As a reporter Kelly had dealt in abject misery, had seen more than anyone ought to of death, destruction and man's inhumanity to man. He had held on to weeping women who could not even bring themselves to talk about the beatings they had suffered at the hands of their husbands and lovers. He had watched men wage war all over the world, and commit appalling atrocities in the name of the various causes to which they were allegedly dedicated. He had seen what hunger, disease, and even just the daily drudgery of a mundane life, with no conceivable future, can do to people.

And he'd been launched many times himself into the terrifying heartlands of other people's mindless mayhem. In Northern Ireland in the 1970s, based at Belfast's famous Europa Hotel, which became the city's media centre right through the troubles, he'd on several occasions allowed himself to be blindfolded before being driven by the IRA to interview its more murderous leaders at unknown locations. He'd been caught in crossfire more times and in more places than he could remember, and had once been briefly kidnapped by revolutionaries in a remote part of Africa. That had been the worst of all. Kelly could still feel the parched dryness at the back of his throat along with the warm wetness between his legs when, confronted by machine gun-wielding thugs raging at him in languages he could not understand, he had involuntarily peed himself.

In fact, Kelly was as well equipped as any man alive to recognise what he could see in that young soldier's eyes.

It was fear. Total and utter, abject fear.

Two

Kelly continued to stare at the closed door of the pub for several seconds after the young squaddie and his unwelcome escort had left. In spite of the unexciting nature of his drink and the tedium of a pub which was now completely empty, apart from Charlie, he found himself rolling another cigarette and ordering another pint of Coke. The minor commotion caused by the arrival of the two men, and the extreme unease Kelly had experienced, had somehow destroyed his intention to make a move.

In addition, his stomach had begun to remind him that he had eaten nothing since his lunchtime scrambled eggs. Resolutely putting the incident of young Alan the squaddie out of his mind, after telling himself that he really had to stop letting his imagination run riot, Kelly concentrated his attention on The Wild Dog's out-of-season weekday menu. To his relief he found that bread, cheese and pickles still featured, so that at least he could be saved from Charlie's dubious microwaving skills.

The cheese was a decent enough Cheddar, and although the bread was definitely not as fresh as it could have been, Kelly wolfed the makeshift meal down.

One way and another, it was almost an hour later before Kelly finally decided to make his way home.

If anything the weather was even worse than when he had arrived at The Wild Dog. This was a truly filthy night. A lashing of horizontal rain hit him straight in the face as he stepped out of the old pub. It was cold as well as wet. The easterly wind continued to gust ferociously, and there was now a hill mist, whipped into flying wisps by the wind, swirling around the car park. Kelly hunched his shoulders beneath his inadequate suede bomber jacket, and wondered why on earth, as it had already been raining when he had left his house in Torquay, he had not worn a suitable coat. He broke into a trot, bowing his head against the weather, pulled open his car door and half dived inside, grateful that he never locked the little MG roadster. Kelly had driven an open MG for years and he knew from experience that there was no point in locking that kind of car. Anyone who wanted to break in merely slashed the soft top.

He started the engine, switched on the headlights and pulled out onto the main road. The visibility was dreadful. And when you drive an ancient MG in such conditions, you have an extra disadvantage. Kelly felt as if he were enclosed in a small black box. The windscreen was just a narrow slit between the dashboard and the hood, and in these conditions the headlights seemed to be no more effective than flickering gas lamps.

Kelly, who had only just got his licence back after three years off the road, following one of the more extreme acts of irresponsibility which littered his chequered past, drove with extreme care, concentrating every ounce of his being on the road ahead.

Even so, when, on a blind corner only about a mile or so away from The Wild Dog, a figure in a luminous orange waistcoat, waving a torch, materialised out of the gloom, Kelly thought he was going to hit it.

He slammed on the brakes and hoped for the best. The old car did not have the benefit of a modern anti-locking braking system, and its long low design had definitely not been conceived with emergency stops in mind. The tyres screeched in angry protest and Kelly felt the MG's rear end swing wildly from side to side, but somehow or other the little car shuddered to a halt just a few feet from the orange figure. Kelly slumped across the steering wheel in relief. He could see now that the orange figure was a police officer, and wondered what on earth was going on. Then, as the policeman approached, he wondered if he was about to be chastised for the erratic manner in which he had pulled to a halt.

He cranked down the driver's window and waited for the officer to speak first.

'You'll need to wait here for a moment, sir, afraid there's been an accident, and the road ahead is blocked.'

'I see. Right.'

There was no mention of Kelly's driving. It seemed the

policeman had other things on his mind. The MG's engine was still running and Kelly had yet to switch off the headlights and the windscreen wipers. He peered into the gloom, straining his eyes. Gradually, he became aware of a big black shape fifty yards or so away, and realised that a large articulated truck was indeed blocking the road. To one side of it he could also see a dimly flashing light, probably from this officer's police car parked beyond the truck, the bulk of which, even more than the poor visibility, prevented him from seeing what else was going on.

Well, Kelly reflected, at least he had a good excuse now for failing to visit Moira, his seriously ill partner. He was thoroughly ashamed of the thought as soon as it entered his head, but had, as so often seemed to be the case, been quite unable to prevent it doing so.

'Have you any idea how long it will be before the road will be cleared, Constable?' he asked.

The constable shook his head. 'Not at this stage, sir. Unfortunately, we have a casualty and we are waiting for the ambulance service to arrive.'

'Right.'

The policeman, shoulders hunched against the weather, walked away from the car and took up a position on the most acute angle of the corner which Kelly had just negotiated. Kelly suspected that having witnessed the way in which he and his little MG had so precariously slewed to a halt, the constable was probably trying to give himself a better chance of survival as he stopped any further traffic. He hadn't looked very happy. Kelly didn't blame him. He could just see the glimmer of the man's torch in the misty darkness.

He switched off his engine and settled down for a long wait. If there were casualties, the police would not be able to do anything about any of the vehicles involved until a medical team arrived on the scene. He could have turned and driven back to Two Bridges, then right across the high moorland to Moretonhampstead and on to Newton Abbot and Torquay, but that was a major detour which, in these conditions, Kelly didn't fancy at all. On balance, he preferred to wait. Automatically, he reached into his pocket for his tobacco and began to make himself yet another roll-up. He was adept at rolling cigarettes.

He didn't need to put a light on, which was all for the best as the MG's interior light was totally ineffectual.

After a bit, he was aware of another set of headlights coming round the corner and the policeman waving his warning torch in the air. The vehicle pulled to a halt directly behind his MG. The policeman approached it and, silhouetted by his torch, Kelly could see a figure in a raincoat stepping out, then leaning back into the car to retrieve what appeared to be a briefcase.

The policeman seemed to speak to him briefly, then began to escort the new arrival towards the scene of the accident, using his torch to light the way. As the two figures passed Kelly's car, the man with the briefcase turned his head towards the little MG, and was illuminated enough by the torchlight held in his companion's hand for Kelly to be able to recognise him. It was Audley Richards, the regional Home Office pathologist.

So, somebody's bought it, thought Kelly. That would seriously slow up any chances of the road being cleared in the near future. He sighed and, taking a long pull on his roll-up, settled down in his seat.

After just a minute or two the torch-bearing policeman returned to resume his sentry duty, and Kelly began to feel just a flickering of journalistic interest. He may have retired from the game in any sort of full-time capacity, but he had no objections to earning a few bob out of the odd freelance opportunity. In any case, under the circumstances it was probably an extremely good idea to keep his hand in. If he didn't very soon get to grips with the novel he was writing, which was, of course, destined to transform his life J.K. Rowling-style, he might well end up back on the road all over again. This time as an even more tired old hack.

Kelly knew that – particularly given the dreadful driving conditions – the odds were on this being merely a routine traffic accident involving people whose death would be of no interest to anyone other than their own family or friends. But, on the other hand, he also knew you could never be quite sure of that. Kelly had not so long ago made a few enquiries at the scene of a relatively minor road accident, only to discover that the driver of one of the vehicles involved was a senior Church of England bishop and that the woman who had been accompanying him, and who, in an apparent state of shock, was demanding rather demonstrative comfort from him, was not his wife. That one had brought in a nice few bob in lineage from the nationals.

And so, aware that his pay-off from his old job was close to running out and that his bank manager was unlikely to further fund his writing career without at least some indication of progress, Kelly, with slight reluctance, stepped out of his car. Within seconds he was drenched, his light suede jacket given yet another soaking from which, he felt, it was unlikely ever to fully recover. The lashing rain cut straight through his thinning hair and felt icy-cold against his scalp. None the less, he made himself join the policeman a little further up the road, his feet making unpleasant sloshing sounds on a road running with water. If Plod could cope with these conditions, then so could he, he told himself.

Out loud he said: 'What's happened, then? You've got a fatality, I presume.'

In the arc of the flashlight, the young policeman's eyes looked overly big.

'How do you know that?' he asked sharply.

Kelly shrugged. 'I saw Dr Richards arrive,' he said. 'I've known him for years.'

He smiled wryly and stretched out a hand. 'John Kelly,' he said. 'I've been, I mean I was, a journalist for more years than I care to remember. This was my patch.'

Kelly could see the policeman relaxing. In high places, the tension between police and press was considerable and led to all sorts of much publicised confrontation. On the road, the foot soldiers of both professions shared a natural affinity. More often than not they rather liked each other. Certainly, they understood each other's way of life and shared many of the same sort of experiences – standing around in the cold and wet, waiting for something to happen, being merely one example.

'So, some poor sod's bought it?' Kelly said questioningly, looking at the policeman sideways.

The constable paused only for a second. He was wet through and the night was yet young. It wasn't just struggling scribes who welcomed displacement activities.

'Yeah, only a kid too,' the police officer replied. 'We're not sure exactly what happened. The lorry driver's in total shock, can't tell us much at all. Apparently he should have been on the Okehampton bypass, on his way overnight down to Cornwall, but he took a wrong turning and got totally lost. He's miles out of his way. Not surprising in these conditions.'

The constable waved his arms at the murkiness around him and narrowed his eyes as if imagining what it would be like to drive a large, articulated truck over Dartmoor on such a terrible night.

'We've got the SOCOs coming out, and we're still waiting for the ambulance from Ashburton. It was a bit of a surprise, actually, that Dr Richards got here first.'

'Yes, well, he lives for his work,' said Kelly, a little caustically. He had clashed with Audley Richards, a doctor of the old school, very aware of his professional status and an extremely precise, taciturn character, more than once during his days on the *Evening Argus*.

The constable shot him a questioning glance, unsure how to take the remark. Kelly made his face expressionless.

'So, you don't know what happened, then?'

'Not really. It looks like the kid could have been drinking, though. He's still reeking of booze and all the lorry driver keeps saying is that he suddenly loomed up in front of him.'

'Loomed up in front of him,' Kelly repeated. 'You mean he was on foot?'

'Yeah, didn't I say? He was on foot. And you don't get many pedestrians out here on a road like this. Not at night, anyway. Bad luck, though. Not much traffic either . . . I mean, who'd want to drive over the moors in these conditions . . .'

Kelly stopped listening. A kid. A pedestrian. A drunken pedestrian involved in a road accident so close to The Wild Dog. Kelly had a quick brain, always had had, but he didn't need to be very quick at all for an obvious possibility to occur to him. His mind began to whirl. Could the casualty possibly be his young friend from The Wild Dog? On the one hand it seemed quite likely, but on the other, the Scottish squaddie had not left alone. He had been escorted out by two men, men whom Kelly had felt quite certain were army mates who had come looking for him in order to take him safely back to base. They wouldn't have let him come to harm in his drunken state, surely? And yet, and yet . . . Kelly didn't know what to think. Young Alan had looked frightened, after all, hadn't he?

'Look, Constable, I was in the pub back up the road – The Wild Dog – with this lad, just a kid, like you said . . . He'd had a real skinful. I wonder if it could be him?'

'Well, I've really no idea . . .'

'It might help if I could see him?' Kelly persisted.

'Well, I don't know,' hesitated the policeman. 'I'm not in charge.'

'Then perhaps I could speak to whoever is?'

'I suppose so.'

'It may be somebody I know,' ventured Kelly hopefully.

'Ron Smythe,' added the policeman. 'Sergeant Ron Smythe. The lorry driver called 999 on his mobile and the sarge and I were only down the road in Buckfastleigh on a domestic . . .'

'I really think I could help,' repeated Kelly. Being a displacement activity for a bored wet policeman was one thing, but Kelly himself was by now so wet he was afraid he might drown if he had to stand around in this downpour for much longer.

Without saying any more, the constable gestured for Kelly to follow and led the way through the narrow gap between the rear end of the articulated lorry and the stone wall to the right of the road. Kelly could see now that the big artic', which he guessed would have been travelling in the same direction from which he had arrived on the scene, had jackknifed and the wheels of the cab were dangling precariously over the ditch on the other side of the moorland road.

Beyond the artic' Kelly could just make out a figure laying in the middle of the road, limbs sprawled at unnatural angles, and another figure crouched by its side. That was Audley Richards, the pathologist. A third figure was silhouetted against the bright headlights of a parked police car, presumably left on to illuminate the scene. As Kelly and the police constable approached, the third figure, momentarily turned into a giant by the huge shadow he cast across the ground as he moved, strode towards them in an authoritative way.

'Who's this, Dave?' he asked.

'Name's John Kelly, says he's a journalist, Sarge.'

The sergeant, whose long bony face was now brightly lit up down one side, giving him a curiously skeletal appearance, studied Kelly with a complete lack of interest and no recognition, which in Kelly's case was a mixed blessing. He knew a lot of police officers, but had not necessarily made the acquaintance of all of them in the most desirable of manners. Kelly had had a varied relationship with the police over the years.

'No press,' said the sergeant sharply, looking directly at Kelly. 'The only information you're going to get is through the press office, mate.'

He turned on his heel, glancing towards the constable as he did so. 'And you should know that, Dave,' he finished.

'I'm not making a press enquiry,' Kelly interjected swiftly. 'There's just a chance I might be able to help. It's possible that I could have been with your victim earlier, in The Wild Dog.'

'Really.' Sergeant Smythe did not sound particularly interested, but he did pause as if considering what might be his next course of action. Then the wail of approaching emergency vehicles, rising above the noise of the wind and rain, demanded his attention. Smythe turned his back on Kelly as a second police car and an ambulance came into sight, sending showers of water into the night air as they pulled to a halt at the accident scene.

The two-man ambulance crew emerged swiftly from their vehicle and, carrying their medical equipment with them in boxes and bags, hurried towards the prostrate figure on the ground, slowing up when confronted by the crouched form of Audley Richards, whose presence indicated much the same to them as it had to Kelly earlier.

With rather less urgency, two officers carrying cases emerged from the police car. SOCOs, thought Kelly. Scenes of Crime Officers, whose attendance was standard procedure nowadays in the case of sudden death, even when there was little or no suggestion of any kind of foul play.

Sergeant Smythe promptly set off to join the various newcomers. 'You'll have to wait,' he called over his shoulder in a rather peremptory tone.

Kelly hunched his inadequately clad shoulders against the rain and did just that. Icy-cold droplets ran down his neck inside his collar. He shivered. One aspect of journalism that he had been looking forward to leaving behind was the waiting. Door-stepping, they called it. Waiting on the outside, looking in, waiting on the off-chance that somebody who knew something might give you a minute of their time, and, in so doing, enough information to make a story. Kelly was too old for door-stepping. Come to think of it, he reckoned he had always been too old for door-stepping. But here he was, at it again. And this time he wasn't even being paid for it, he grumbled silently to himself.

Eventually, Audley Richards stood up and stepped back from the body on the ground. Then the paramedics, by now looking as if they were quite satisfied that there was nothing they could do to help, began to load the dead man onto a stretcher.

The Home Office pathologist produced a packet of cigarettes from his pocket, removed one with one hand and put it in his mouth, and with his other hand raised an old Zippo lighter to the cigarette's end. Funny how many doctors smoked, thought Kelly idly. Indeed, doctors were probably leaders of the do what I say, not what I do brigade, he reflected.

The flame of Dr Richards' lighter flickered uncertainly for just a few seconds before dying out. Two further attempts to light up produced only the same result.

'Damn,' muttered Audley Richards, hunching his back against the wind and rain, as he tried to provide some sort of protection from the elements with his body's bulk.

'Allow me,' said Kelly, stepping smartly forward and cupping his hands around the pathologist's cigarette end.

'What the fuck are you doing here, Kelly?' asked the doctor conversationally, his small Hitler-like moustache bristling as he spoke. He and Kelly went back a long way. Kelly respected Audley Richards because of his reputation for professionalism, and was prepared to overlook his perennial grumpiness. Dr Richards, on the other hand, had always made it quite clear to Kelly that he saw no use whatsoever for journalists in general, and that he was particularly incensed merely by Kelly's presence on earth. This did not, however, prevent him from gratefully taking advantage of the shelter provided by Kelly's cupped hands in order to finally light up.

'Just driving by,' said Kelly. 'Or trying to.'

Richards grunted around his cigarette, which had finally begun to burn surprisingly well under the circumstances.

'I think I may know the victim,' Kelly continued.

'Poor sod,' said Audley Richards. Kelly eyed him quizzically. Poor sod because he was dead, or poor sod because he had been unlucky enough even to have met Kelly in passing? Kelly wasn't at all sure. But while he was still working it out, Sergeant Smythe approached and touched him lightly on one arm.

'Right, you can have a look now, if you wish.' Sergeant Smythe turned to the pathologist. 'Unless you have any objections, Dr Richards? Unorthodox, I know, but the lad doesn't seem to have any identification papers on him at all, and we do need to find out who he is.'

'No objections, Sergeant. Nothing more I can do. The whole thing's perfectly straightforward, if you ask me. One word of warning.' Audley Richards extended a thumb in the general direction of Kelly. 'It won't be if he gets involved.'

'You know this man, Doctor?'

'Oh, yes, I know him, Sergeant. Just make sure his coat button isn't a camera, that's all.'

The sergeant looked puzzled. Kelly stepped past him before he had time to change his mind and approached the paramedics who were now loading their stretcher into the ambulance.

'The sergeant says I can have a look,' he began.

The older of the two paramedics looked towards Sergeant Smythe, who nodded his assent, albeit a little uncertainly.

The body on the stretcher was entirely covered by a blanket. The second paramedic pulled it back, exposing the face of the dead young man.

There didn't seem to be a mark on him. Kelly had mentally prepared himself for a gruesome sight. But this lad just looked as if he were in a deep sleep. Whatever injuries he had sustained must have been solely to his body. His face remained untouched and Kelly had no problem at all identifying him.

Sergeant Smythe had followed him over to the ambulance. Kelly turned round to face him.

'Yes,' he said. 'Yes. It is the lad I met in the pub.'

'Right,' responded Smythe. 'You and I had better have a chat then, hadn't we, Mr Kelly.'

25

He led Kelly over to his patrol car and gestured to one of the paramedics to follow them. The interior light snapped on as the sergeant opened the nearside rear passenger door. There was already a man sitting in the back seat, and Kelly registered at once that this must be the lorry driver. He had a wide, plumpish face, etched with laughter lines around his eyes and mouth, indicating that he was probably a jovial good-humoured sort. At that moment, however, he appeared anything but jovial. His skin was so pale it looked almost as if all the blood had been drained from him, his eyes were red-rimmed and bright with shock, and he was trembling.

'OK, mate,' said the sergeant quite gently. 'The ambulance boys are going to look after you now. All right?'

Obediently, the lorry driver climbed out of the car. His legs buckled slightly as he tried to stand up. The paramedic put a supportive arm around him and steered him off in the direction of the ambulance. Sergeant Smythe and Kelly watched for only a second or two before getting into the car themselves, where, within its relative shelter, the sergeant produced his notebook and jotted down everything Kelly was able to tell him.

His attitude to Kelly seemed considerably less cool now, which was perhaps not surprising. After all, Kelly had done a large part of his job for him. He had been able to tell the sergeant that the victim was a soldier and that his name was Alan, and where he was stationed. One call to the barracks at Hangridge should be enough to sort out full identification. The accident seemed straightforward enough and Kelly guessed that Sergeant Smythe couldn't wait to get the scene cleared up so that he could return to the warm familiarity of Ashburton police station and a steaming hot cup of tea.

Kelly could well guess how the other man felt. He was shivering himself now, and it wasn't with shock. He had seen all too many dead bodies in his time. The cold and the wet had seeped right through his inadequate clothing and he felt chilled to the bone. But he was not yet quite finished.

'There's just one thing, Sergeant,' said Kelly. 'The two men who turned up in the pub looking for this lad. Two more soldiers, I'm sure. Where did they go? Has anybody seen them?'

26

'I don't know anything about any two men,' said Sergeant Smythe, reverting at once to his earlier attitude of near hostility. Smythe did not want any complications, thought Kelly. His body language defied Kelly to question him any further. However, Kelly had a thick skin. You grew one in the job he had done through most of his life.

'But didn't the lorry driver see them?' he persisted.

Smythe studied him for a few seconds without enthusiasm. Then, sighing exaggeratedly, he opened the driver's door and began to swing his long legs out onto the tarmac road, straight into an icy blast of windswept rain.

'Wait here,' he muttered to Kelly, who needed no encouragement whatsoever to remain exactly where he was, almost curled into the passenger seat of the police car, with his arms tightly wrapped round his chest in a futile bid to retain as much body warmth as possible.

The sergeant returned within only a couple of minutes, shaking droplets of icy water off his police issue waterproof jacket and all over Kelly as he climbed back into the car.

'The driver didn't see anybody else,' he said. 'He didn't see anyone at all apart from chummy, when it was too darned late.'

'But those two blokes must have been with the lad. They wouldn't have left him in that state, would they?'

'Who knows what a load of off-their-head soldiers will do,' responded Sergeant Smythe flatly.

Kelly opened his mouth to respond but found he didn't have the energy. He reached for the door handle. His fingers were so cold he had difficulty even grasping it. But the good news was that his body temperature was by now so low that when he eventually climbed out into the wind and rain he barely felt it any more. None the less, he began to sprint back to the MG, but his path was momentarily blocked by the ambulance containing the body of the dead squaddie, which was now slowly pulling away from the scene.

As Kelly watched it leave he could see again, all too clearly in his mind's eye, the lad's lifeless young face, and wondered fleetingly just how old he had been. Under twenty, definitely. Eighteen or nineteen, maximum, he thought. Little more than a child in the great scheme of things, and with so much life left to live. To his surprise Kelly, who was, after all, not unfamiliar with the spectacle of lives wasted and cut unnecessarily short, suddenly felt overwhelmed by a great sadness.

Three

Kelly had had enough. He wanted to get away from the scene, shut the dead boy's face out of his head and get warm as soon as possible.

He decided he wouldn't wait for the truck to be removed, after all. Instead, he would take that big detour, retracing his journey back along the road past The Wild Dog and swinging a right at Two Bridges. This would make his journey home at least half as long again as it should be, and he still wasn't looking forward to negotiating the top of the moor in thick mist, but he had now got to the point where he preferred the prospect of a long and difficult drive to merely waiting around getting colder and colder in such dreadful conditions. The rain was showing no signs whatsoever of easing. A fire engine and garage emergency vehicle had arrived just after Kelly had identified the boy, but they would not be allowed to even start their tricky manoeuvre until the SOCOs had finished measuring tyre marks on the road and generally checking out the accident scene.

Kelly started the little car's engine and proceeded to attempt to turn round so that he would be facing in the direction from which he had originally come – a feat accomplished not without difficulty in the poor visibility on one of the narrowest sections of the road, with a ditch on one side, a stone wall on the other, and a camber in the middle that could have been custom-built to wreck the low-slung exhaust system of an MGB.

He succeeded ultimately in executing something going on for a six- or seven-point turn and began to make his way back towards Two Bridges at little more than a crawl, as he struggled to see ahead through the mist and rain. But as he tentatively set out on the road over the highest section of the moor he would cross on his extended journey home, Dartmoor began to play one of its many tricks. The rain started to ease and the mist suddenly lifted. It was uncanny. A minute ago Kelly had hardly been able to see ten feet ahead, and now the road was totally clear.

Gratefully, he pressed his right foot down on the accelerator, the increased speed boosting the fairly meagre output of heat which was all the MG's heater ever seemed able to produce. However, Kelly had only recently acquired a new soft top which fitted more snugly than any he had previously endured, and the little car was now just about warm enough to allow his body temperature to return to what he thought might be an almost normal level.

In the much improved conditions he relaxed slightly, easing the tension from his shoulders, and began to reflect on the events of the evening. Once he was comfortable enough to think about anything other than his own sorry physical state, he found that all his journalistic antennae were waggling. He told himself he was being ridiculous, but he couldn't help it.

That lad in the pub had said that he was going to die. More than that. He had told Kelly he was going to be killed. And, probably only minutes later, he was dead. He had hinted at mysterious goings-on up at Hangridge. He had quite obviously been most unhappy to see the arrival of the two men who had been looking for him, and Kelly would not forget in a long while the look of abject fear in his eyes as he had stood in the doorway of The Wild Dog.

'Minutes later he was dead.' This time Kelly said the words out loud, as he motored through Newton Abbot, making himself abide by the speed limit, more or less, in spite of his eagerness to get home and dry. He didn't want any speeding points on his licence; he certainly couldn't afford to lose it again, that was for sure.

It was almost midnight by the time he arrived at his terraced home in St Marychurch, high above Torquay. He parked in the street outside and stepped out of the MG onto a dry pavement. The rain had obviously stopped here at least an hour or two hours earlier. He opened the little gate into his tiny front garden which – had he bothered to look he could have clearly seen, thanks to the illumination of the street lamp right outside – was almost completely overgrown by an impressive selection of weeds. Kelly did not look and, as usual, noticed nothing at all about his front garden until he stepped into it and a strand of bramble, blowing in the still strong wind, lashed him viciously across his left cheek.

'Fuck,' he said loudly, brushing it away. He touched his face cautiously. He felt sure the damned thing had drawn blood. He glanced at the garden then, taking in its sorry condition with mild disgust. He supposed it really was time he did something about it, but he couldn't afford to pay a gardener given the state his finances were in, and Kelly certainly wasn't much of a gardener himself. Before she'd been taken ill, his long-time partner Moira had always been in charge of the gardens, the tiny one at the front and the slightly bigger walled one at the back.

Moira. Kelly didn't like thinking about Moira. He really should have visited her that night. He hadn't. It was too late now, far too late, he told himself. Once inside he went straight to the bathroom, stripped off his damp clothes which he left in an untidy pile on the floor, and wrapped himself in his big towelling dressing gown. Then he headed for the kitchen, made himself a cup of strong sweet tea which he took into the living room, where he switched on the gas fire and settled gratefully in front of it in his favourite armchair. With his free hand he switched on the radio which was more or less permanently tuned to Classic FM, Kelly's writing and thinking music.

The journalist in him would not lie down. In his head, he went over again and again his meeting in the pub with the young man who had told him he was called Alan. The lad had been frightened. Genuinely frightened. There was no doubt about that. But on the other hand, he had also been drunk as a skunk. Alcoholic paranoia, Kelly told himself.

He sipped at his still scalding hot tea, deep in thought. Then his reverie was rudely interrupted by the phone. Kelly jumped in his chair. The telephone had a habit of making him jump at the moment, particularly if it rang late at night. Moira, he thought. Oh, shit. He reached out for the hands-free receiver which was sitting next to the radio on the table alongside his chair, its battery light flickering weakly. Naturally, he had failed to put it back in its charger when he had gone out earlier that day.

The low battery did not, however, cause him a problem. He

had no need to talk for long. The caller was Jennifer, Moira's youngest daughter.

'Mum's been expecting you all night,' said Jennifer, with only the slightest hint of reproach in her voice. At first, Kelly felt only relief. At least it didn't sound as if Moira were any worse. But as Jennifer continued to speak he became immersed in the all too familiar sense of guilt.

'You told Mum you'd be over tonight when you'd finished writing. She really wants to see you. Are you still coming?'

Kelly glanced at his watch. 'Well, it's so late. It's after midnight . . .'

'I know. But she can't sleep. We tried to call you earlier, at home and on your mobile . . .'

Kelly squeezed his eyes tightly shut for just a few seconds. Inside his head he could see his mobile phone sitting on his desk upstairs, where he had left it earlier, and he really had no idea whether or not he had deliberately failed to take it with him on his jaunt to The Wild Dog.

'I'm sorry,' he said, for what seemed like the umpteenth time, and automatically launched himself into a series of unconvincing lies. 'I seemed to manage to let all the batteries go . . .'

'You could still come over. She's wide awake . . .'

Kelly took a deep breath.

'Yes, of course,' he responded as brightly as he could. 'I'll be right there. I've been working late. I lost track of the time, that's all. The words were flowing for once.'

And that, of course, was the biggest lie of all. Kelly cursed himself roundly as he began the perennial hunt for his car keys, which he realised he must have put down somewhere only minutes earlier. But Kelly never ever knew where he'd put his car keys. He found them eventually on top of the cistern in the bathroom, and cursed himself and his various inadequacies all over again.

Back behind the wheel of the little MG – Moira's home, where she was being cared for by her three daughters, was only a couple of streets away – Kelly was suddenly in a real hurry to get there. He was hit by a major wave of guilt and remorse. This was not the first time he had promised to visit Moira and then failed to do so. But worse than ever on this occasion, by the time he had returned home he had more or less made himself forget that he had ever made the arrangement in the first place. His subconscious had been at work again, he feared.

Moira was terminally ill with cancer of the liver. And although the disease had only been diagnosed four months earlier, this notoriously fast-developing form of cancer had already brought her close to the end.

Kelly and Moira had never quite shared a home together, but they had none the less shared each other's lives for more than ten years. Throughout that time Moira had spent only limited periods in her own house, until the last few weeks in fact. By then Kelly had found himself quite unable to cope with his partner's illness. Almost before it began to really take a hold of her, he had realised that he could not possibly nurse her. Moira, who had been a nursing sister at Torbay Hospital, had, Kelly later realised, been aware of that from the beginning and had made it easy for him by telling him there was absolutely no way she was going to let him attempt to care for her and, in doing so, doubtless botch up whatever life she had left to live.

That had actually made Kelly feel even more of a worm. But Moira's daughters had promptly volunteered to share between them the task of caring for their mother in her own home until the end, and Kelly remained deeply grateful to them.

Paula, the eldest, drove down from London every week or so to spend several days with her mother, sometimes bringing her four-year-old son Dominic with her, and sometimes leaving him either with his dad, Ben, or with her mother-in-law. Lynne, the middle girl, came home each weekend from Bristol, where she was at university. And Jennifer, at barely nineteen the youngest of them, carried the biggest burden of all. She had returned to England after a gap year of travelling, following sixth form college, to find her mother in the grips of this terrible disease. Without appearing to pause for thought at all, she had promptly deferred a planned university course for another year and moved back into her mother's home announcing that she was going to take charge of caring for Moira, which she had continued to do uncomplainingly, helped as much as possible by her sisters. Kelly thought young Jennifer was a miracle on legs. Indeed, he thought all the girls were. And they really did put him to shame.

As he pulled up outside Moira's house, a three-bedroomed terraced job uncannily similar to his own home, even down to the angular style of the bay window at the front, Kelly leaned back in his seat and tried to prepare himself for the right sort of approach to a sick visit. He knew he had never got over the shock of Moira's diagnosis and the speed of her decline. Almost every day he intended to spend at least part of the evening with Moira, but one way and another, he actually seemed to be visiting her less and less. It wasn't that he didn't care. John Kelly cared about Moira probably as much as it was possible for him to care about anyone. It was just that he did not want to confront the grim reality of Moira's condition, so he refused to think about it. All too often that was Kelly's way. And it had probably been one of the main reasons why many years ago he had so casually embarked along the road that had led him to near-terminal drug and alcohol abuse. Kelly had spent far too much of his life looking for ways to obliterate reality.

He took a big, deep, long breath, stepped out of the car and made himself approach the front door, first walking through a little front garden, which was also pretty much like his own except that her knew there was not a single weed to be seen in the pristine-neat flowerbeds surrounding a rectangular patch of stone paving. On the doorstep he stood for a few seconds more, taking another deep breath, before ringing the bell. Kelly had his own key, of course, but since Moira had become ill and the girls had been there looking after her, he had stopped using it. He couldn't explain why exactly.

Jennifer opened the door. She was a slim, pretty girl with a shock of fair hair like her mother's, kind hazel-brown eyes, a big bright smile and long athletic limbs, who had absolutely no idea at all that she was attractive. John Kelly didn't really notice that any more either. All he saw was one of the bravest, strongest human beings he had ever met. She was so young and yet she was coping so well with her mother's illness. Certainly, she had taken it upon herself to ensure that her mother's last days were made as comfortable as was humanly possible.

She flashed her brightest smile when she saw Kelly on the doorstep. He didn't know how she could do it. He could see the strain around those hazel eyes, and he was sure her mother could too, but Jennifer was still putting on a front.

'I-I'm sorry,' he muttered in greeting.

Jennifer reached up and kissed him lightly on one cheek. She was quite tall, considerably taller than her petite mother, that was for sure, but Kelly, a good six foot two in his stockinged feet, still towered over her.

'You're here,' she said quietly. 'That's all that matters.'

'I did mean to come earlier, Jens . . .'

'I know.'

She did know too. Kelly and Jennifer had been friends from the start, from the moment he had first dated her mother. He supposed that even he was something of an improvement on her real father, a middle-class, middle England thug of a man who had systematically beaten his wife throughout their unhappy marriage. According to Moira none of the girls knew about their father's brutality, but Kelly had never been too sure about that. One way and another, he had come to treasure his relationship with all three of them every bit as much as his relationship with their mother. Perhaps more, if he was honest. Kelly had one son, Nick, now a grown man almost thirty years old, but he had somehow contrived to miss virtually all of Nick's childhood. Nick had been brought up almost entirely by his mother, not only after she and Kelly had separated but also before, because Kelly had spent so much time away on stories and in the pubs and clubs of Fleet Street that he had only rarely seemed to be at home. More recently, after Nick had actively sought out his father following years of estrangement, the two men had begun to build what Kelly regarded as a very special relationship. But ironically he had seen far more of the growing up of Moira's girls, as they moved from childhood into young womanhood, particularly Jennifer who had been only nine when her mother and Kelly had got together, than he had of his own son. And over the years they really had become like daughters to him. They had already forgiven him one hell of a lot, too.

Recently, however, he had become slightly embarrassed to be in the company of these girls he adored. He supposed that was just one manifestation of the guilt which seemed to consume his entire being throughout most of his waking hours, right now.

The girls accepted him, warts and all, always had done, and had never questioned his congenital inability to deal with their mother's illness.

Kelly followed Jennifer upstairs to Moira's bedroom, the pair of them moving almost soundlessly on the thick pile red carpet. He knew that Moira had not been downstairs for more than a week now, although she did still manage, with some difficulty he had been told, to struggle out of bed in order to use the bathroom next to her bedroom.

Moira's eldest daughter Paula, also a pretty, fair-haired young woman, but a little plumper than either of her sisters, was sitting by her bed. The two women were watching TV. Kelly found himself glancing towards the screen as he entered the room. Anything other than look at Moira. An old episode of *The Vicar of Dibley*, a programme which had always been one of Moira's favourites, flickered away on Plus. Kelly had once bought Moira the entire video set of the comedy featuring Dawn French as a village's first woman vicar as a birthday present, and the two of them had sat up in bed one night and watched virtually the whole lot straight through – something Kelly had, rather to his surprise, found that he had enjoyed every bit as much as Moira. It had been dawn before they had finally fallen asleep, his arm around her shoulders, her head resting on his chest, with the video still running. The memory hurt. Kelly concentrated hard on the flickering screen. In her bed by the window, Moira laughed weakly. She always had had a ready laugh, but it used to be a deep rip-roaring rumble of a laugh, which had always come as something of a surprise from such a small woman. A great hip-shaking eye-watering belter of a laugh. Kelly had teased her that she had the filthiest laugh in Devon, and that had always set her off all the more.

His eyes filled at the thought.

'Hello, John.' Moira's voice was even weaker than her laugh.

Shit, thought Kelly. How could anyone cope with this? What were they all supposed to do? Just sit around and wait for her to die?

Aloud he said: 'Hello, sweetheart.'

He made himself smile and walked over to the bed where he perched on the edge and took her hand. Moira had always been pretty and all three of her daughters had inherited their mother's looks. Her fluffy blonde hair still retained its original colour in spite of her age and illness, and she continued to look surprisingly good even though there were dark circles beneath her eyes and her skin was pale to the point of near translucence. In fact, she looked almost beautiful. Her face was drawn, thin skin taut over exposed cheekbones, while previously Moira's face had been quite plump, and although pretty, never beautiful. Not really. Her illness had added a sculpted look, and in the low light of the bedroom the yellowish tinge, which Kelly knew had been acquired due to liver deficiency, appeared only to give her skin a cream hue. Yes, she really had become quite tragically beautiful.

She had lost a lot of weight, of course, but she exhibited none of the usual signs of a body ravaged by cancer. That was because Moira, an experienced nurse who knew all about the illness she was bearing so gallantly, had, when she had been told the degree and extent of her cancer, opted to decline conventional treatment. Moira had believed that with her kind of cancer and the extent to which it had already destroyed her liver, her life expectancy would be much the same whether she put herself through the rigours of chemotherapy, and radiotherapy or whether she didn't.

And both Kelly and her daughters had accepted her decision that she would rather live out her last few months without having to cope with the cruelties she knew those treatments could inflict, instead choosing to allow her illness to take its course while striving to enjoy whatever of life was left to her. Her courage so far had been extraordinary, although Kelly was bewildered sometimes by the form it took. It was Moira's way to barely discuss her illness, and if she did ever mention it, to do so in such a manner that she gave no indication at all that it was terminal. She knew, though. Better than any of them, she knew.

'How are you doing, darling?' he muttered, cursing himself as he became aware of what he had said. How was she doing? What a stupid fucking question. Whether she chose to talk about it or not, the woman was dying. His woman was dying. How did he think she was doing, for fuck's sake. He glanced away, blinking rapidly.

37

'Oh, not so bad,' said Moira.

'Yes, we thought you were a little better today, Mum, didn't we?' interjected Paula.

'You know, I do believe I was,' continued Moira. 'I've not had a bad day at all, not at all.'

'You ate nearly all of that chicken broth I made you this evening, didn't you, Mum?'

'I did, dear. And, do you know, I really enjoyed it.'

Kelly felt his shoulders tensing. He wasn't sure how much of this he could listen to. It was the same every time. The imminence of Moira's death was never mentioned, and to Kelly the scene around her bed all too often resembled a cross between a Brian Rix farce and something out of Alan Bennett. If it weren't so fucking tragic, it really would be funny, he thought.

It was as if they all had parts in a play and were acting out their specific roles. Only Kelly wasn't very good at his. He sometimes thought he might do better if he were allowed to talk properly to Moira about her illness, about the death which was not far away and about how she felt, knowing that she would not be around for much longer. That was what he wanted to do, deep inside, but Moira had made it quite clear that was not her way. And in any case, if she suddenly did start to talk to him in that manner, he suspected he wouldn't be able to cope with that either. After all, Kelly was just as much of an ostrich as all of them. Worse really, he supposed. He did not even want to be in the same room as poor sick Moira, let alone make inconsequential small talk.

Moira squeezed his hand.

'So, come on, John, tell us how the book's going. What sort of day have you had?'

Kelly looked at her blankly. Once again, the truth did not seem quite the reply to make. What sort of day had he had? As seemed to be his habit, he had failed to write a single word. He had then gone to a pub, even though he dared not even have a beer, ostensibly to think, and more likely in a deliberate sub-conscious ploy both to avoid attempting to write and to evade seeing Moira. In the pub, he had met a frightened young man who had told him that he feared for his life. The young man had, however, been very drunk. None the less, a little later Kelly had watched his dead body being loaded into an ambulance, and his veteran reporter's brain had promptly begun to jerk into gear to such an extent that he had been able to shift his promised visit to Moira from the back of his mind straight out of his head altogether.

That was the sort of day he'd had.

'Pretty good, really,' he said. 'Another couple of thousand words done and dusted.'

Four

The next morning Kelly felt absolutely terrible. The alarm clock woke him at six and he managed to force himself out of bed within half an hour of being disturbed by its insistent shrill bleeping, which was pretty good for Kelly, who was not a man who had ever enjoyed mornings.

Whenever he had writing of any kind to do, he found that making an early start, before his brain became clogged up with other things, was the best and most efficient way to undertake the task. But lately, his enforced early rising had been a waste of energy and the pain inflicted had led absolutely nowhere, because Kelly seemed incapable of putting words onto paper whatever time he hauled himself out of bed, and early starts just made him feel tired and irritable throughout the day, more often than not.

Resolutely, he made his way downstairs to the kitchen and brewed himself a strong pot of English Breakfast tea. The steaming, hot, dark brown liquid, into which he ladled his customary three spoonfuls of sugar, hit the back of his throat like a blast of pure adrenaline. By God, sweet tea was the best reviver invented by mankind, he thought. Although, of course, it would never again taste quite so good to Kelly as it had during the many years when he had relied on it to cope with his regular morning hangovers. There was among certain people, non-drinkers, Kelly suspected, a theory that alcoholics didn't have hangovers. From extensive personal experience, Kelly did not agree with that. In fact, looking back, his drinking days had been more or less one long hangover, punctuated only by moments of total oblivion.

He put pot, milk bottle and sugar bowl, along with the mug of tea he had already poured and a packet of chocolate digestive biscuits, onto a tray and carried the lot upstairs to his third and

40

smallest bedroom, which he used as an office. Sitting down on his swivel-action black leather chair, he tried to make his body and mind relax as he switched on his computer. Perhaps this would be the morning, the morning when he would finally get it all together, when he would start to write at once and the words would continue to flow effortlessly and smoothly throughout the day.

Kelly took another long drink of the sweet, dark brown tea and wiped his mouth with the back of his hand. Writing, of course, was never like that. Not for John Kelly, anyway. It was instead a long drawn-out torture of inactivity. Kelly continued to find that his biggest problem in attempting to write a book was that he found the task ahead of him so overwhelmingly daunting that he barely saw the point in beginning it.

The screen before him shimmered into life and Kelly reached for his mouse, darting the cursor between the various icons before him. The documents containing the little of his book he had so far managed to compile were each called 'Untitled'. Kelly had never been very good at titles.

He moved the cursor until it settled neatly pointing at 'Untitled Chapter Three', and allowed it to rest there for a while. Kelly had written 'Untitled Chapter One' in one big glorious rush, within days of quitting his job on the *Argus* four months previously. Filled with enthusiasm for his chosen new career, he'd found that the words had really flowed.

But that seemed like a lifetime ago. His flow had quickly slowed to a dribble. He had struggled through a rough draft of chapter two and then stopped altogether, although only he knew that was as far as he had got. 'Untitled Chapter Three' had remained a totally blank new document in his computer for almost three months now. And this was seriously bad news, not least because his bank balance was beginning to look extremely thin.

Kelly had been able to take advantage of a voluntary redundancy scheme operated by the *Argus*, when he had decided he had had enough of journalism. And he had calculated that the money, quite a generous amount for a local paper to offer, could, if he was careful, last him the best part of a year, and that that would, of course, be plenty of time in which to complete his first novel. Which would be an instant best seller. Well, Kelly was too realistic about writing to have ever thought that, but he had been confident enough of his own ability as a professional scribe to believe that he would eventually acquire a publisher for almost any sort of writing that he put his hand to.

Kelly was, however, not naturally careful with money. And although he did not consider himself in any way extravagant, and he probably wasn't, he seemed to be getting through his pay-off at an alarming rate. Certainly, much faster than he had anticipated. Unfortunately, the speed of his writing achievement was not keeping pace at all with his spending. Indeed, not only did it look as if his money was not going to last a year, neither did it look as if a year was going to be nearly long enough for him to complete even the first draft of his novel.

'Fuck it,' muttered Kelly.

He flicked the cursor from 'Untitled Chapter Three' onto games, selected backgammon, his favourite, and began to play. Situation normal. He dreaded to think how many days of his life he'd totally wasted during these last four months playing computer games.

In the first game, Kelly achieved a shut-out with no less than two of his mechanical opponents' men on the bar. But he still managed to lose. He played three more games and lost all of them, too. Kelly was a good backgammon player, and well aware that one constant of playing against a computer is that there is always, as with anything automated and pre-programmed, a predictability factor. One way and another Kelly reckoned to beat his computer, at its highest level, something like seventy per cent of the time. Not today, it seemed. This really was not turning out to be a good morning.

Impatiently, Kelly closed the thing down. Not only did he feel as unable to write as he had done for weeks now, but it also seemed that he couldn't even play backgammon any more. He tossed his mouse to one side, tucked the keyboard into its home on a retractable shelf slotted beneath the top of his desk, and stared for several minutes at the empty black screen.

Then he made a decision. It wasn't much of a decision. He guessed he'd been intent, subconsciously at least, on this course of action since encountering that fatal accident the previous

42

night and discovering who the victim was. It had been just the kind of incident he could never resist delving into.

He reached for the phone to his left and pushed one button. A brisk female voice answered, a voice which always made Kelly smile. She had a way of answering the phone which, in itself, made it quite clear she had no time for prevarication.

'Karen Meadows.'

'Good morning, Detective Superintendent, and how are you this morning?'

'Instantly plunged into a state of nervous tension by the very sound of your voice, Kelly.'

'Now, that's not kind . . .'

'Probably not, but truthful. I don't think I've heard from you since you left the *Argus*, and it's been wonderfully peaceful, I can tell you.'

'Oh, come on, Karen, you know you've been missing me . . .'

'Really? I'm actually still coping with the flak from the last time you decided to meddle in police affairs—'

'So am I.' Kelly interrupted swiftly, and all the banter had gone from his voice.

When he and Karen had last had dealings together, the subsequent events had without doubt taken Kelly a step too far, and had more or less led directly both to him quitting journalism and for him and the high-ranking detective failing to be in touch with each other for an uncharacteristically long time.

He was well aware that under the circumstances it was going to be pretty hard for either him or Karen to slip back into the way things had once been between them.

'Yes, I'm sure you are, Kelly.'

There was no longer any inflection in Karen's voice. He realised that she had picked up at once on the flatness in his own voice. It seemed that they remained strangely good friends, beneath it all, these two. Just like always. He hoped so, anyway. He knew that she understood, and she was probably the only person in the world who did. But then, he and Karen had always been drawn to each other, although there had never been even the remotest suggestion of their friendship developing into anything more than that. As far as Kelly was concerned, if he had thought about it at all, he would probably have come to the conclusion that he so valued their relationship the way it was, that he would not want to risk changing it. But the truth was that he didn't think about it. He'd never thought about it. He and Karen were mates, that was all. They certainly had a great deal in common. They were both inclined to be loners by nature, and they shared a sometimes near-obsessional approach to their work. Kelly had been aware of some kind of bond between them virtually ever since he had first met Karen almost twenty years earlier, when she had been an ambitious young detective constable and he already a star of Fleet Street. Indeed, he had helped extricate her from the threat of a scandal which could have destroyed the high-flying career he had always believed she was destined for. Karen was not quite as much of a maverick as Kelly had always been, but she was certainly a free spirit, a talented and able police officer, fiercely independent, who quite frequently chose to rebel against the more petty restrictions the police force imposed upon its officers.

'You haven't called to ask after my health, though, have you, Kelly,' Karen continued in a perfectly normal sort of voice. 'That's never been your style.'

Kelly detected just a hint of edge there, but decided to ignore it. Instead he went straight to the point.

'Do you know about that fatal death on the Buckfast road last night?' he asked.

'Vaguely,' she responded. 'I have a report on it somewhere. Sent to CID as a matter of routine because somebody died, that's all. It seems straightforward enough . . .'

'No. I don't think it is.'

He heard Karen sigh down the line. 'And what, pray, do you know about it exactly, Kelly?'

'I was there. I don't think it was an accident.'

Kelly held his breath. He had no idea whether the young squaddie's death was an accident or not, but he did know that if he prevaricated at all he would lose her. Karen Meadows had always had a short attention span.

'Really?' The detective superintendent sounded as if she was trying for a mix of sarcasm and dismissal in her voice. Kelly knew her so well. Well enough to also be able to detect a distinct note of curiosity. She was interested. She wanted to know what he knew. He'd got her. He must not waste the opportunity.

'Look, have you got time for a pint at lunchtime.'

'Kelly, no . . .'

'Just for a few minutes, we could go to the Lansdowne.' He named the pub directly opposite Torquay police station.

'Kelly, I haven't got time to go to the toilet. I never have time to go to the toilet. And you want me to meet you in a pub?'

'They've got nice clean loos in the Lansdowne. We could chat in the ladies', if you like.'

'Very funny. All right. I'll see you there at one-thirty. Don't be late, I can spare half an hour, max.'

'As if . . .'

Kelly was smiling as he finished the call. It was funny how his conversations with Karen Meadows almost always left him smiling. She had that effect on him. He really shouldn't have left it so long to get in touch, while all the while hoping that she would contact him first. But, on the other hand, he supposed he had felt that he'd needed a reason, and maybe she had felt the same. After the last time. When Kelly had decided to actively intervene in a murder investigation gone wrong the previous year, the repercussions had been enormous, and had left him with death on his conscience. Kelly had acted honestly enough, as he almost always did, and his motives had, by and large, been good. But he had also behaved with reckless impulsiveness. He was not proud of the episode, and indeed it had led him to resign from the *Argus* on the grounds that he no longer wished to do a job which could lead him, however inadvertently, to cause such devastation.

And Karen Meadows, in spite of their long friendship, had made it quite clear at the time that she considered him to be a loose cannon with whom she no longer dared associate.

He supposed he was lucky that only six months later she was prepared, at least, to talk to him.

Kelly got to the pub first as Karen knew he probably would have done, even without her warning against being late. He was sitting in the corner by the window, his usual pint of Diet Coke on the table before him, when she arrived, throwing the pub door wide open so that it banged against the wall behind it.

Every head in the bar turned. Two CID men, sitting on tall stools, automatically lifted their pints and downed them. Karen knew they would not be comfortable to continue drinking in the same bar as their governor at lunchtime. It was raining again. Karen was wearing a long, white, caped mackintosh with a hood. She flung back the hood and tossed her bobbed dark hair. The pub lights enhanced its shine. The white cape fell open to display black sweater, black jeans and steel-tipped cowboy boots. She looked stunning. And her appearance was absolutely not what most people would expect of a policewoman. The jeans were just tight enough to show her shape, which remained pretty damned fine. But Karen had no idea how good she looked and totally failed to notice Kelly's admiring glance.

She had made quite an entrance, yet she was unaware of that, too.

She raised a hand towards Kelly, sitting in his corner, and strode across the bar to him. 'I'll join you in a pint of Coke,' she said by way of greeting. 'I've got a tricky meeting with the chief constable this afternoon, and I'm going to need all my remaining brain cells.'

'Right . . .' said Kelly, obediently rising from his seat and heading towards the bar.

'And I'll have a jacket potato with cheese, salad and a couple of sausages on the side. I'm absolutely fucking starving.'

'Right,' said Kelly again.

'That's all right, John, I'll bring it over to you,' called out Steve Jecks, the landlord.

'Thanks,' said Kelly. This was a copper's pub, and Steve, who had previously run another hostelry in Torquay which had also been a favourite haunt of local police, was a former copper. Karen was well aware that the waiter service was in her honour. Steve knew who she was well enough even though she was not a regular at the Lansdowne. She was head of regional CID and Steve knew all about keeping on the right side of the brass.

She turned abruptly to Kelly, who had quickly returned to his seat. 'So, let's get on with it,' she said.

'And it's lovely to see you, too.' Kelly grinned at her.

46

'Oh, stop it, Kelly. For a start, your boyish charm has never worked on me, and secondly, I've told you already, I don't have any time.' She glanced at her watch. 'Not even half an hour any more, twenty minutes max, now.'

'OK.' Kelly stopped playing games at once. 'OK. I met the lad who was killed by that truck. It was in The Wild Dog, probably only minutes before he died . . .'

He told Karen the whole story then, everything the young soldier had said about Hangridge, how frightened he'd seemed, the look in his eyes when he'd been escorted out of the pub by the two men who had come looking for him, and he put considerable emphasis on what had turned out to be not only the boy's last words to him, but for all that Kelly knew may well have been the last words he ever spoke.

'"They've killed the others. They'll kill me, I'm sure of it." That's what he said, Karen, and half an hour or so later he was dead. Now, it may be possible that we just have some kind of weird sort of coincidence here. But I think it's more than that. And, at the very least, surely it merits an investigation.'

Karen was thoughtful. She really had been extremely hungry, and while Kelly talked she had been tucking into the jacket potato and sausages, brought over to her by Steve, with some gusto and not a little haste. She was therefore reluctant to speak at all, muttering merely a grunt or two every so often during Kelly's discourse, until she had consumed enough of her meal to satisfy the worst of her hunger.

'The boy was drunk, Kelly,' she said eventually, narrowly avoiding spitting bits of half-chewed baked potato at him. 'I've made a point of looking into the case since we talked on the phone. The post-mortem examination was held early this morning and, in fact, with the amount of alcohol he had in his system, he would have had to be blind drunk. I'm sure you noticed just how pissed he was, Kelly. You've had enough experience.'

Kelly ignored the sarcasm, which Karen in any case felt had been rather beneath her, even though it was totally justified.

'Yes, I know,' he said. 'But, none the less, the lad was genuinely terrified. You could see it in his eyes.'

'Kelly, haven't you heard of alcoholic paranoia? You of all people.'

'Yes. Even suffered from it myself, Karen, just as you appear to be so kindly suggesting. Of course I know about alcoholic paranoia. But that wasn't it. I'm sure of it.'

'Really. You a psychiatrist now as well as a potential Booker prize-winner, are you?'

Karen didn't know quite why she was being so hard on him, but she didn't seem able to help herself. Perhaps it was because of what she had said to him as soon as he had phoned her that morning. Kelly always brought trouble. She watched him wince as she delivered her latest broadside, then shrug his shoulders. He didn't rise to the bait at all, and instead answered her in a level tone.

'Look, I can't explain it, Karen, but I really did think the lad was one hundred per cent genuine and, OK, I know I can't explain this either, but for some reason neither did I think he was suffering from alcoholic paranoia, or any other kind of paranoia, come to that.'

Karen finished the final mouthful of her meal before responding. She was an organised eater and had arranged her meal into little food parcels, a piece of sausage, some cheesy potato and a sprinkling of salad in each, which she had devoured quite systematically in spite of her haste.

'Look, Kelly, you saw the scene of the accident. You must have got some idea of what happened. There was one vehicle involved, a lorry being driven by a professional along a winding moorland road on a dark, rain-swept night, a pretty unsuitable road for a big artic', even under the best of conditions, and one pedestrian who was out of his brains. Now, if that doesn't add up to a straightforward, highly predictable scenario, I don't know what does.'

'Well, maybe, but you didn't hear the lad talking . . .'

'Let me tell you. Your squaddie, whose full name was Alan Connelly, by the way, and who shouldn't even have been getting boozed up in The Wild Dog as he was only seventeen, just lurched out across the road in front of this extremely large articulated lorry. That's what the driver said, and all the evidence, like tyre marks, etc, point to him having told the truth. There is absolutely no evidence to indicate any kind of foul play, and neither does there seem to have been any way the accident

48

could have been the driver's fault, not in that weather. The lad was out of his skull and the injuries that he received, according to the pathologist's report, back up the driver's claim that he seemed to virtually throw himself into the road. None the less, the poor bastard driver is totally traumatised and is still in hospital with shock. That's about the sum of it, one of life's minor tragedies. Nobody, but you, Kelly, has even suggested there could be anything more to it than that. So what are you really getting at?'

Kelly shrugged again. 'I don't know, Karen. Of course I don't know. But I do know this Alan Connelly was frightened silly and when I saw the pathetic little sod in a heap in that road, all I could think of was that he'd predicted his own death. And he'd been proven quite bloody right. There are some unanswered questions, Karen, you have to agree to that. What about those two men who turned up looking for him, for a start? And who were they? I asked them if they were from Hangridge, and come to think of it, they didn't answer, but I felt sure they were soldiers. They had that look. And I just assumed they were mates of his. At first, anyway. But where were they when the boy was killed? They weren't seen at the scene at all, and they haven't come forward since, have they?'

Karen finished her final food parcel, chewing appreciatively, and drained the last of her pint of Diet Coke.

'Maybe they were drunk too, Kelly, and they and your tragic young friend just all went their separate ways outside the pub. Simple as that.'

Kelly shook his head. 'No. They weren't drunk, no way. Not those two. And they wouldn't have parted company with that boy, surely? They'd come to get him. They made it quite clear they were looking for him. Plus Connelly was so damned drunk, I find it hard to believe he could have made it half a mile down the road unaided.'

'Oh, I dunno,' muttered Karen, rising to her feet and swinging her latest extravagance, an eccentrically decorated Voyage handbag made of blue denim, with lots of dangly bits and designed to look like the top of a pair of jeans, over one shoulder. 'It's amazing what drunks can do.'

'Yeah, all right, Karen, give it a break, will you.'

49

Karen's face broke into a grin. She had a really cheeky, yet extremely warm way of doing so. It was quite endearing, but she was unaware of that too. Kelly sat quietly waiting for her to speak again.

'OK, Kelly,' she said eventually. 'I'll at least see if we can find those two men. Do you remember what they looked like?'

'Sort of, but they were bundled up against the weather – woolly hats, coat collars turned up, that sort of thing.'

'Umm. Well, if you come across to the station with me, let's try to get as full a description as possible on record. Do you think you might remember enough to be able to help put together a computer image?'

Kelly nodded a little uncertainly.

'Right. Then I'll see what inquiries I can set in motion up at Hangridge. If your two men are soldiers stationed up there, and we can come up with good enough images, somebody out at the barracks might recognise them. Shouldn't hold your breath, though, Kelly, however good a likeness you come up with. The army doesn't take kindly to civilian plod poking about without a damned good reason.'

'Which is precisely my point,' said Kelly, rising to his feet, grabbing his jacket from the back of his chair, and setting off in pursuit of Karen, who was already half out of the door. 'They'll cover up anything they can to keep it in the family.'

Karen did not bother to reply. She knew he was right about that, though. Although the civilian police theoretically had jurisdiction over military establishments in almost all relevant matters, in practice the vast majority of non-combat deaths were investigated by the SIB, the Special Investigation Branch of the Royal Military Police, with no civilian police involvement at all. Civilian police forces were routinely notified of suicide and accidental deaths on military premises within their area, but only became actively involved when the RMP reported obvious foul play. And Karen was one of many senior officers who felt that all sudden non-combat deaths of military personnel should be investigated by civilian police forces in exactly the same way as all non-military sudden deaths were. Indeed, she believed it to be vital for such investigations to be independent as well as thorough.

Alan Connelly, of course, had died on a public highway, so his death was therefore automatically a CID matter should any further investigation be called for.

None the less, Karen had no illusions. Any enquiries she made up at Hangridge would be welcomed by the military about as much as a visit from Saddam Hussein during the period when he had still been Iraq's leader. And probably in much the same manner, at least as far as her career was concerned, she reflected glumly.

Five

Outside on the pavement, Karen paused to pull on her white mackintosh cape. It was still raining and she didn't like getting her hair wet. Kelly caught up then and was right behind her as, the steel tips on her boots making sharp ringing noises on the Tarmac, she hurried across South Street, past Torre Conservative Club, to the CID offices in their recently converted building opposite the entrance to the main police station yard. She heard Kelly start to laugh as he studied the sign outside the Lansdowne Dance Centre next door. It advertised tuition in everything from modern ballroom through Latin American disco, to rock and roll.

'I can just see Chris Tompkins doing the tango with a rose in his teeth,' he said.

In spite of herself, Karen laughed. Detective Sergeant Tompkins, one of Torquay CID's longest serving officers, who had only recently managed to finally achieve promotion from detective constable, was very tall, very thin, moved with a bony awkwardness and had a permanently morose hangdog sort of face. Karen always thought he looked like an anorexic bloodhound.

She punched the security code into the door ahead of her and led the way upstairs to her first-floor office. They had to pass through the open-plan incident room and Karen was aware of the eyes of every officer there focusing on Kelly. That last case still weighed heavily on all of them, and Kelly had been at the hub of it. Kelly might be a kindred spirit and someone for whom most of the team had considerable professional respect, but he did spell trouble, and she had known that bringing him, unannounced, into the CID offices would be bound to create something of a stir.

To hell with it, thought Karen. She had neither the time nor the inclination to pussyfoot around. Yes, Kelly did spell trouble, but that was because he had yet again encountered something troublesome, and being Kelly, he never seemed to learn to walk away. One thing Kelly didn't do was cry wolf. Karen may have given Kelly little or no indication of her true opinion, but in fact she reckoned that if John Kelly thought there was something fishy about that young squaddie's death, then there probably was. The only question was whether or not Karen wanted to take a potentially politically tricky matter further. And she was all too aware that she really wasn't so different from Kelly. Almost certainly, she would be unable to resist.

'Right, Farnsby,' she called to a young woman detective constable sitting at one of the computer stations by the wall. 'I want you to help Kelly build up an E-fit. We need to get a picture of two possible witnesses. Go on, Kelly, you know the form.'

'Your wish . . .' began Kelly, then let his voice trail away as he saw the look in Karen's eye.

Janet Farnsby, whose serious, rather humourless nature was somehow emphasised by the way she kept her straight, light brown hair tied back from her face and the round granny spectacles she affected, stood up and looked doubtfully around her. Torquay CID didn't run to providing a computer for every CID officer. Instead, they shared the bank of machines where DC Farnsby had been sitting. Karen knew what the young woman was thinking. Was she really supposed to work with John Kelly, of all people, in the middle of the incident room?

'You can use my office, I'm off to Middlemoor,' Karen announced, once more leading the way. Once inside her little glass cubicle, Karen busied herself picking up and sorting out the various papers she needed for her meeting with the chief constable at headquarters. There was just one item on the agenda: CID budget. Karen's favourite topic. No doubt, further economies were about to be demanded. Not only would her officers be sharing computers, Karen reckoned they'd be sharing notebooks and pencils if Harry Tomlinson had his way. She gritted her teeth and made herself concentrate on ensuring she had everything she needed for her unwelcome meeting.

Janet Farnsby, who had recently completed a course on

53

building E-fits, the modern computerised alternative to identikit, had settled in front of Karen's screen with Kelly by her side and was already typing in data and calling up various images for him to study.

Karen, still wearing the white cape, with an untidy bundle of papers tucked under one arm, the big denim Voyage bag under the other, watched them from the doorway for a few seconds.

Kelly glanced up at her and looked for a moment as if he might be about to say something clever. Karen didn't give him the chance.

'Right, I'm off,' she announced briskly. 'Good luck.'

As she crossed the incident room once more, heading for the stairs, she very nearly bumped into Chris Tompkins.

'Sorry, boss,' muttered the veteran detective in his familiarly flat tones.

Karen couldn't look at him. She really couldn't. But if she'd happened to have had a rose handy, she would definitely have at least attempted to put it between his teeth.

Once settled in her car for the forty-five-minute or so drive to the Devon and Cornwall force's HQ at Middlemoor, on the outskirts of Exeter, Karen immediately called the chief constable's office, ostensibly to confirm her appointment for later that afternoon.

The chief constable's secretary, Joan Lockharte, was her usual snooty self. Karen could just picture her, prim little face framed by an irritatingly geometric yellow haircut, sitting perfectly straight before her invariably immaculately tidy desk. Karen disliked the bloody woman almost as much as she did her boss, but she made herself remain courteous because she wanted something. She wanted information. She was far from ready to share any concerns she might have about Alan Connelly's death with Harry Tomlinson, but she was quite prepared to use his contacts.

'Oh, by the way, you know the commanding officer of the Devonshire Fusiliers, at Hangridge. He was at the CC's Oldway Mansions commendations bash last year,' she began. The chief constable traditionally threw an annual reception at Torbay Council's imposing offices at which he presented members of the local community with various awards for bravery and out-standing service, and Karen vaguely recalled the Fusiliers being commended for the part they played in searching for and rescuing a missing Dartmoor rambler.

Joan Lockharte muttered something that sounded vaguely affirmative. Or it may just have been a sniff. Karen wasn't sure.

'Could you remind me of his name?' she continued determinedly.

'Colonel Gerrard Parker-Brown.' The chief constable's secretary rattled off the name without hesitation. She was at least efficient, Karen had to give her that. And her memory was faultless. Karen knew that well enough. She had often had cause to wish that it wasn't quite so good.

Her next call was to Hangridge. She had decided to make her initial inquiries informal – which was in any case all she could reasonably do under the circumstances – hence her desire to know the name of the Fusiliers' commanding officer before contacting the barracks. She wanted to trade on her one and only social contact with Parker-Brown. That was, after all, how dealings between potentially immovable forces like the police and the army were more often than not conducted. Karen, as a relatively young woman with certain idiosyncrasies regarding her work, who had not only managed to survive but usually to triumph in a man's world, was not particularly good at these kind of tactics. It did not suit her either to prevaricate or to dissemble. But she reckoned that, in this case, her best chance of getting any real co-operation out of the army was to give it a go.

The sergeant who answered the phone put her straight through to the colonel, whose double-barrelled name, while so traditionally appropriate for a senior army officer, did not fit at all with her brief memory of him. Certainly she was not surprised when he so promptly came on the line. He hadn't seemed the type who would hide behind minions under any circumstances.

'Parker-Brown.' He spoke crisply, not quite with the aristo-cratic intonation of previous generations of army officer, but Karen suspected that upper-crust vowels had probably been deliberately toned down.

She quickly introduced herself, at the same time reminding

the colonel that they had met once at the CC's party at Oldway Mansions.

'Yes, yes, I remember,' he responded at once, in such a way, however, that Karen was quite sure he didn't remember at all. 'How nice to hear from you, Detective Superintendent.'

His approach threw Karen a bit. She had expected the CO of the Devonshire Fusiliers to be rather more on his guard with a senior policewoman, albeit one who was playing the social card. She found herself pausing while she worked out exactly how to word what she wanted to say next. The colonel, still sounding helpful and friendly, filled the silence.

'So what can I do for you, Miss Meadows?'

Karen decided to get straight to the point.

'Look, I wondered if I might come up and see you. As soon as possible. Tomorrow morning, perhaps? It concerns one of your young soldiers, Alan Connelly, the lad killed on the road over the moors last night, near Buckfast. Certain matters have come to my attention that I'd very much like to talk through with you . . .'

'Ah, yes, Connelly. Tragic, quite tragic. He was only seventeen, you know. I'll help in any way I can, naturally. But his death is hardly a police matter, is it, Miss Meadows?'

'Any sudden violent death is a police matter, Colonel, at least in the initial stages. And that is the case even with serving military personnel when death occurs in a public place.'

Karen was determined to make that clear from the beginning.

'Yes, yes, of course. I do understand. Would you like to come up here for coffee tomorrow? Mid-morning? Would about eleven suit you?'

Karen agreed at once, reflecting on how civilised the modern army was, or at least how civilised it liked to be perceived as.

She ended the call and forced herself to concentrate for the last half-hour or so of her journey on the unwelcome meeting ahead. Karen reckoned that she was a good copper. She'd had her ups and downs, but, in reality, she knew darned well that she was a good copper. Paperwork, however, was her *bête noir*. She hated it. She loathed it. And managing a budget was the worst sort of paperwork in her opinion, and the most unsatisfactory aspect of her job. However, the chief constable was a paperwork

56

sort of policeman. If you considered him to be any kind of policeman, that is. Which Karen actually didn't.

It was one of those days when Karen was extremely pleased eventually to get home. Her meeting with the chief constable had gone much as she had expected. It had been a bit like a visit to an accountant, really. Only an accountant who was not so much on your side as that of the tax authorities. As usual when finances were under discussion, Karen had found herself forced to duck and dive quite spectacularly. It had been one of her trickiest sessions with Harry Tomlinson, and by the time it was finally over Karen had felt uncharacteristically drained of energy.

As soon as she entered her apartment in West Beach Heights, an old Victorian block to the west of Torquay seafront, she headed straight to the small kitchen at the back to make herself a large gin and tonic. Plymouth gin poured over lots of ice and a slice of lime, in a decent tall glass filled to the brim with Schweppes tonic – her favourite tipple, and the kind of G and T that was still hard to find in British bars of any kind, and virtually non-existent in pubs.

As she took a long, deep drink she became aware of a small furry creature rubbing itself against her legs. Sophie, the handsome brown and white cat with which Karen shared her home, was inclined to scratch, claw and deliver impatient love bites if she did not receive enough attention. So Karen, wondering why she was quite so fond of such a self-centred pet, dutifully bent down to tickle Sophie's ears, as she knew was required. Then she carried the remains of her drink into the sitting room. It was a rather lovely room, decorated in pale creams and white, and furnished with the various antique pieces Karen so much liked to collect. Two huge windows along one wall, stretching almost from floor to ceiling, gave sweeping views of the bay. Karen was by nature congenitally untidy, but she more or less kept her untidiness to the bedroom, making a real effort to keep the living room in at least reasonable order. She slumped gratefully onto the sofa, deliberately omitting to switch on the lights so that she could savour the view outside. Almost at once, Sophie took a flying leap onto her lap and demanded attention again.

Karen grumbled at her in good-humoured fashion. She was actually grateful for Sophie's company. It wasn't that she was short of friends, or certainly acquaintances, eager to spend time with her. But she rarely seemed to have time in her head to arrange anything, even if she did have the inclination. And since her affair with the man she had believed to be the love of her life had ended the previous year, she seemed to have no interest whatsoever in starting a new relationship with anyone. Or certainly not with anyone she had so far met.

She sighed, and trying not to disturb Sophie – who now appeared to be asleep, after digging her claws into Karen's legs for at least a minute while making herself a suitable bed in her mistress's lap – she reached for the telephone on the little table next to the sofa. She pushed the appropriate buttons to check for messages.

The first was from her elderly neighbour Ethel, whose spirited attitude to life and apparently perpetual good humour put Karen to shame, she sometimes felt.

'I've taken in a parcel for you, dear. Pop round any time. I've got a nice bottle of port that fell off the back of a lorry. Only I shouldn't be telling you that, should I? Still, if you arrest me and put me inside, at least I won't have to spend Christmas with that blessed sister of mine.'

Karen grinned and waited for the next message.

'Darling, where are you? It's Alison. Didn't you get my message at the weekend? George and I would really love you to come to dinner on Saturday. Our new neighbours will be there, and Sally Sturgis and her husband are down from London. Sally Court that was, do you remember her? She's dying to see you again . . .'

Karen pulled a face. She and Alison Barker had once, a million years ago, been good friends, when they were at police training college together. Since then their paths had diverged dramatically. While Karen had concentrated on her career, and had only once even come close to marriage, Alison had quickly abandoned the police force to become a wife and mother of four. The two women had absolutely nothing in common any more, in Karen's opinion, but, none the less, Alison had been wooing Karen constantly since she and her husband had moved to Torquay from the Midlands several months earlier. Twice now Karen had accepted invitations from Alison, primarily, if perversely, in an attempt to make her phone calls go away, and each time she had regretted it. On the second occasion, Sunday lunch a few weeks previously, Karen had been obliged to spend her entire visit cooing over Alison's first grandchild. Apart from anything else, that had made her feel dreadfully old, as she knew she was almost exactly the same age as Alison. And now Alison wanted her to meet another police cadet from their ancient past. Someone else she would no doubt have absolutely nothing in common with. She could barely even remember Sally Court.

Resolutely, she pressed delete. Just hearing Alison's voice had somehow made her even wearier than she had been before, and she knew that she would have to be at her desk by seven, at the latest, in the morning if she wanted to keep her appointment at Hangridge. First, she had to sort out a load more paperwork to send off to Harry Tomlinson, in a desperate effort to back up some of the claims of financial diligence which she had made that afternoon.

Carefully, she lifted a purring Sophie off her lap and lay her on the sofa by her side. The cat stretched sensuously, but otherwise didn't stir. Lascivious little beast, thought Karen, as she wandered into the kitchen to pour herself another drink. She was vaguely hungry, but not sure that she had the energy to make herself something to eat. Missing supper would, in any case, do her no harm, she reflected. She had consumed that rather large lunch in the Lansdowne, after all.

All she really wanted to do now was to fall into bed and watch TV for the rest of the evening.

Ethel would have to wait until tomorrow. And Alison Barker could wait for ever.

In the morning, Karen succeeded in making her early start as planned. And by around ten she was able to throw a bundle of papers at a somewhat bemused DC Farnsby, along with instructions to send them to the chief constable's office. Then she set off for Hangridge. In spite of his apparently relaxed manner, Gerrard Parker-Brown was still a soldier, and a high-ranking one at that. Karen doubted he would have much truck with unpunctuality.

She had decided that in order to keep up the appearance of informality she would make the trip in her own car, a modern MG convertible, which she thought was a great little motor, even though Kelly, an MG purist, had looked down on it from the start.

She took the coast road to Paignton, then on through Dartington, and on to the moors via Buckfastleigh, so that she would pass the spot where Alan Connelly had been killed. The incessant rain which had fallen barely without pause through the first week of November had finally cleared up, and this was a beautiful day for a drive over Dartmoor. She slowed down as she approached the stretch of road where the accident had happened. It was not difficult to pinpoint. Karen had been told that part of the drystone wall on the north side of the road had been demolished by the rear end of the big articulated lorry, and angry black tyre marks criss-crossed the Tarmac, which had paled with age. Today, driving conditions were perfect. Everything was bathed in the orange glow of autumn sunshine. But Karen knew Dartmoor. She could imagine well enough how different it would have been on a dark wet night, with a swirling mist cutting down visibility to just a few feet.

Thoughtfully, she continued on to Two Bridges, turned right towards Moretonhampstead, just as Kelly had done two days previously in such very different driving conditions, and then, a couple of miles before Moreton, swung north through the pretty village of Chagford and up on to the remote part of the moor along the narrow winding road, which she knew led to Hangridge. All around her, vaguely purple hills, each topped with a tor, a distinctive irregular pile of granite, jaggedly dissected the skyline. Hangridge was relatively new. It had been built on MoD land in the 1970s. Karen knew almost exactly where the barracks were situated, built on a hillside in a particularly remote and unforgiving part of the moor, not far from Okehampton. But she had never actually been there before. The camp was quite isolated, the last two or three miles reached only by its own specially constructed approach road, so even the most tenacious of tourists exploring the moor would be unlikely to pass it by chance. And, in any case, Karen, who had loved Dartmoor since she was a child, rarely had time any more to play tourist. In addition, with every promotion her job had become more and more that of a manager and less and less what she regarded to be that of a police officer. She was desk-bound far too much of the time. No doubt about that. Karen didn't think that was healthy for any police officer, whatever their rank and job description. And at least one bonus of this so far unofficial inquiry was that it had already given her the excuse to get out of her office and back on the beat, as it were, even if only fleetingly.

She was mulling over these thoughts as a dip in the hills took her through a ragged patch of dark conifers. The road swung sharply to the right as it rose steeply upwards again and, as she turned the corner, quite suddenly she was confronted for the first time by Hangridge barracks, headquarters of the Devonshire Fusiliers and a crack infantry training depot. Karen was completely taken by surprise.

She didn't know quite what she had expected, and indeed had been unaware of any particular expectations, but she had not been prepared at all for what lay directly before her, built in such a way that she could see almost the entire layout on the bleakly exposed hillside.

Karen was well aware of Hangridge's reputation for housing one of the army's toughest training centres, a place designed to turn out elite fighting forces, or so she had been told, and she supposed that in her imagination she had conjured up a picture of some grim, moorland reincarnation of Colditz. Certainly, she admitted to herself, her extremely limited knowledge of the army was probably stuck in a time warp. Somewhere inside her head lurked an image of squat, black Nissen huts surrounded by unassailably tall walls or fences, topped by tangled rolls of potentially lethal barbed wire.

The reality of Hangridge could not have been more different. A neat cluster of conventionally built buildings, one or two storeys high, lay surrounded by playing fields which had been levelled out of the hillside. A rugby game was in process on one such field and groundsmen were at work on another. Karen realised that this was the kind of glorious moorland day which would even brighten the dark bleakness of Dartmoor Prison at Princetown, about as grim a building as you could get. But there was definitely nothing grim or at all forbidding about Hangridge. There was a perimeter fence, of course, made of wire netting, and even a strand or two of barbed wire here and there, but the whole impression of the place was open and pleasant.

Indeed, thought Karen, the place looked more like a comprehensive school than a barracks. Or her idea of a barracks, anyway. Of course, she reflected, as she drove very slowly towards the gates, Hangridge had been built in the '70s when new comprehensive schools were popping up all over Britain. Obscurely, she wondered if the same architects had been used by the army.

The gates to Hangridge stood open, and only the presence of two young men on sentry duty, both carrying automatic rifles, detracted from the notion that the camp was as likely to be a centre of education for young civilians as a military establishment.

Karen pulled to a halt at the sentry point and wound down her window. One of the sentries stepped smartly forward. Every inch the soldier. But his dark blue beret, with its distinctive Fusiliers' red and white feathered hackle, seemed too big for his head and Karen was struck at once by how young he looked. At first sight he could have been an overgrown fourteen-year-old. God, she must be getting old. This was boy-soldier land, but she knew the fresh-faced sentry had to be at least seventeen, probably more.

The young sentry saluted as he approached. He was of mixed race and rather gorgeous. His smooth olive skin gleamed with good health and he had big, beautiful, black eyes. There was something boyishly cheeky about him, and Karen could not help thinking how nice it would be to see him smile. She swiftly dismissed the thought from her mind and made an effort to pull herself together. She began to introduce herself, but it seemed she did not need to.

'Good afternoon, miss,' said the boy soldier respectfully, and Karen couldn't help enjoying the moment. It had been a long time since anyone had called her 'miss', let alone an attractive young lad. Unmarried as she remained, she was none the less much more of a 'madam' nowadays than a 'miss'.

'The CO is expecting you,' the sentry continued.

'Thank you very much. Now, where do I go exactly?'

'Just a minute, miss,' interrupted the second sentry, who looked equally boyish in spite of the stern expression he had adopted. 'Your ID, please.'

The first soldier flushed slightly. Karen was reminded that these young men probably still had their L-plates on. They may have been primed by their commanding officers about her visit, but they were still supposed to go through the motions of correct sentry duty.

She produced her warrant card which was duly inspected almost to the point of unnecessary diligence, she thought, by the second sentry. Finally, she was directed to the largest and most centrally positioned of the cluster of buildings where, after she had parked her car in one of several spaces reserved for visitors, a third sentry led her directly to the CO's office.

Gerrard Parker-Brown was exactly as she had remembered him from their previous brief meeting: warm, affable and almost disturbingly unmilitary.

He rose from his desk as she was shown into his room, and stared at her in undisguised surprise.

'Oh, it's you,' he said. 'I didn't realise. Terrible with names, always have been. But I remember you now. And I remember thinking when we met at that do, how unlike a police officer you were.'

He stepped forward and enclosed her right hand in both of his.

'Splendid to see you again, absolutely splendid,' he went on. 'Now, coffee, tea? Something stronger?'

He grinned broadly, flashing big strong white teeth. He had sandy hair, cropped short around the sides, and somewhat unruly at the front, where it had been allowed to grow a little longer over a broad, open face heavily sprinkled with freckles. His square-jawed, rather old-fashioned, kind of boy's comic, good looks could only properly be described as handsome. There were prominent laughter lines around his dark brown eyes, which were framed by unusually long thick eyelashes. Karen couldn't help registering that they were rather exceptional eyes, more like a woman's than a man's, although she didn't remember noticing that before.

'Coffee, please,' she said, and found herself smiling at him involuntarily. He was quite disarming. 'And I remember thinking how unlike an army officer you were.'

He positively beamed back at her. 'That's only because everybody still thinks in clichés,' he said, gesturing for her to sit in one of the two low armchairs to one side of his desk, and lowering himself into the other. 'But things have changed, about time too in many respects, but not all for the good, unfortunately. Army officers, police officers, we're all the same nowadays, aren't we? Bloody managers. Don't know about you, it's the endless paperwork that gets me down.'

'Absolutely,' smiled Karen.

She had not expected to meet this kind of kindred spirit in the British army, that was for certain. She studied Parker-Brown carefully for a moment. He was tall and slim, looked extremely fit, and she suspected that his almost excessively casual manner involved more than just a little bit of front. None the less, you couldn't help responding to him. She had to make a conscious effort to remember that this was an extremely senior military man, commanding officer of a major infantry regiment, and she was a senior police officer with a job to do, which might yet prove to be extremely tricky.

'So, what exactly can I do for you, Detective Superintendent?'

'As I indicated to you on the phone, Colonel, I have one or two anxieties concerning the death of Alan Connelly.'

'But I understood it was perfectly straightforward. A tragedy, of course, but there's no mystery, is there? Private Connelly had left base without permission and was, unfortunately, extremely drunk. He more or less threw himself in front of an articulated truck, didn't he, in conditions that made it almost impossible for the driver to have avoided hitting him? That's what I understood, anyway.'

'We have no evidence to the contrary, Colonel, but there are one or two so far unexplained aspects of the case, and as I was quite sure you would be as anxious as we are to clear everything up, I decided it might be helpful for you and I to have an informal chat.'

Karen was aware of the colonel studying her quizzically. The corners of his mouth twitched. Had she said something to amuse him? Karen was pretty certain that he had not been entirely taken in by her allegedly informal approach, and probably suspected that she had good reason for being there and that she would have some serious questions to ask. Indeed, she was becoming increasingly more determined to find out everything there was to know about Alan Connelly's death.

'Of course,' he said. And then he waited.

Karen told him about the two men, believed to be soldiers, who had come to find Alan Connelly in the pub, and then more or less disappeared, and about how Connelly had earlier claimed that he was likely to be killed and that his death would not be the first at Hangridge.

'We have a reliable witness to all of that,' she concluded, trying not to think too much about Kelly and the trouble he had got himself and her into over the years.

The colonel's reaction surprised Karen. He burst out laughing. She observed in silence, more than a little thrown. Then he stopped laughing as abruptly as he had begun.

'I'm so sorry, Detective Superintendent,' he said. 'That was absolutely appalling of me. A young man has lost his life in a tragic accident and I really shouldn't have laughed. It's just that, well, of course, you didn't know Alan Connelly . . .'

He paused and it seemed some sort of response was called for. Karen obliged with a slight shake of her head.

'No,' continued Colonel Parker-Brown. 'Well, to put it short, sharp and sweet, Connelly was a complete Walter Mitty. He damned near lived in a fantasy world. He was always making up stories. It was as if he couldn't stop himself.'

'What sort of stories, Colonel?'

The colonel flashed her the quickest of smiles. 'Gerry, please.' he said.

She nodded.

'They varied. Some were quite funny, and the majority pretty harmless, but some were disruptive. Most were absurd, like saying he had a date with Kylie Minogue, and not just mentioning it in passing, you understand, but giving the lads an allegedly detailed account when he came back from a weekend pass. Oh, and he would claim that his father was a millionaire and he'd only joined the army because it was a condition of his inheritance.'

The colonel paused again.

'No truth in that either, I don't suppose,' commented Karen.

'Indeed not, Detective Superintendent.' Parker-Brown flashed her yet another of his grins. 'Or may I call you Karen?'

'Yes, of course,' she responded automatically, while reflecting that this meeting was not going quite the way she had planned. One way or another the colonel seemed to be taking control. She supposed he was trained to do just that, and made a mental note to watch him in future. If indeed she ever had cause to meet with him again, she reminded herself.

'No,' continued Parker-Brown. 'Connelly's father was a shipbuilder in Glasgow, who lost his job some years ago when so many of the shipyards on the Clyde were closed down. He has never worked since and is apparently a manic depressive and an alcoholic, inclined to take out his own disappointment with life on his family. Violently, sometimes, I'm told. No wonder the boy took to fantasy—'

'You're extremely well informed,' interrupted Karen.

'We operate a major training programme here, with upwards of two hundred young people going through our infantry course at any given time. We take in soldiers from other regiments for specialist infantry training, and some of it is pretty demanding stuff. My staff give me a weekly report in writing on every young man and woman we have here. Our job is to train soldiers, and an intrinsic part of that, I'm afraid, is to weed out those who should not be in the army, or certainly not attached to infantry units. Therefore, all of us in charge need to know about our young people. And that includes as much as possible about their backgrounds, as that can have considerable bearing on their behaviour and progress. I'm the boss. I need to be aware of everything, Karen. Past and present.'

He held out both hands in a gesture that could have been supplication or maybe just resignation. 'I'm not, of course, but I do my best. And naturally, as soon as I heard about Fusilier Connelly's death, I not only studied his file thoroughly but also went over everything with his training sergeant.'

'You said Alan Connelly's fantasies were sometimes disruptive, Colonel?' Karen was determined to regain a little of the high ground and quite deliberately avoided addressing the

66

Hangridge commandant by his Christian name as he had requested, even though he was now using hers.

'Yes. We have young women undergoing infantry training here as well as young men. There are a lot of senior people in the army who still disapprove of mixing the sexes in this way, and I have to say that my tour of duty here has, on occasions, made me think they might sometimes be right.' He shot her a sideways look. 'I don't really mean that, Karen. I do believe in a thoroughly modern integrated army. But, by God, it brings its problems along with it. Particularly when you have a young man like Connelly aboard. He used to invent relationships with the female soldiers—'

'I didn't actually realise that you had women in infantry regiments,' Karen interrupted.

'We don't, not as such,' Parker-Brown replied. 'But women from other regiments are stationed here for infantry training if they are going into certain situations, in particular in preparation for a posting to Northern Ireland, for example. Anyway, there was one young woman, in particular, whom Alan Connelly focused his attentions on in ways which were quite unacceptable. He referred to her as his girlfriend, even though she patently wasn't, he plagued her with thoroughly inappropriate love letters and followed her around the place . . .'

The colonel took a cigarette from a packet on his desk and offered Karen one. She shook her head. Karen had been a heavy smoker for most of her life since her late teens. She had given up for the umpteenth time just a couple of weeks earlier and this time she was determined to stick it out.

Parker-Brown nodded. 'Filthy habit,' he muttered, in a manner which left little doubt that the remark itself was also a habit and not something he gave any thought to whatsoever.

'You have probably gathered, Karen, that Alan Connelly was one of those chaps who was just not going to make it here. Strangely enough, he wasn't actually bad at the job – I think it was like another fantasy game to him, really, playing soldiers.'

Parker-Brown tapped a file on his desk. 'It's all here. I've had the computer data printed out and final reports put together by the training staff.

'Connelly was a fit, athletic young man who was quite

67

organised and able in his work, and certainly extremely willing. But his state of mind gave us a great deal of concern and there was little doubt that we were going to have to let him go. He had actually been disciplined only a couple of days before his death for pestering the young woman recruit I told you about. He knew his days were numbered here. He'd been warned often enough. To be honest, Karen, I imagine that is why he took off from here and went on such a God-almighty bender.'

'So your opinion is that when Alan Connelly told our witness that he feared he would be killed, that this was a figment of his imagination?'

'Most definitely.' Parker-Brown made the open-handed gesture again. 'That would have been Connelly all over. He watched too many bad action movies, then made up his own script as he went along.'

'What about his claim that there had been other deaths at Hangridge? "They killed the others, now they'll kill me," he told our witness. Have there been any other deaths here recently?'

Parker-Brown looked thoughtful, as if he was trying desperately to help but didn't quite know how to.

'Well, we did have a tragedy earlier in the year, about six months ago it would have been. One of our recruits died in a training accident on the firing range. They happen, I'm afraid. The first thing we try to teach them when we give them guns is elementary safety. And still they manage to shoot themselves.'

'This soldier shot himself?'

'Yes. Accidentally, of course. We have our own range about a mile away from the barracks. The recruits were simulating an attack on an enemy position, running forwards, throwing themselves on the ground, that sort of thing, and this young soldier had his gun cocked, fell awkwardly and blew a hole in his chest. Our standard issue automatic, the SA80, is a formidable weapon and the results were not pretty. Got a bit of press coverage, particularly locally, you may have seen it. But these things do happen when you are training military personnel, however hard you try to avoid it.'

Karen nodded again, suddenly vaguely remembering seeing reports of the death of a soldier in an army training accident on Dartmoor. But it hadn't been a major story. As the colonel had said, accidents like that happen in military training, and, having occurred on army land and been summarily investigated by the SIB, neither did it ever become a police matter. So she had taken little notice. She had no recollection of even taking the details on board. Certainly, she hadn't registered that the soldier concerned had been stationed at Hangridge.

'And that has been the only other accidental death here at the camp in recent years.'

The colonel nodded back. 'Since I've been here, definitely, which is coming up to two years now. And I did study the records for several years before that.'

'How old was this soldier?'

'He was eighteen. Promising lad, too.'

'Can you supply me with a file on the incident, including all the young man's personal details? Family address, and so on?'

'Of course. Although I don't see the relevance.'

'I'm sure you're right, but I do need to be sure.'

Karen thought for a moment.

'We need to look at every aspect of this, Colonel. I am particularly interested in tracing these two men who went looking for Connelly?'

'Really?'

'Yes. After all, those men were definitely not figments of Connelly's imagination. As I think I have already explained, our witness saw them in the pub, The Wild Dog, just half a mile or so from the scene of the accident, Colonel—'

'Gerry,' he interrupted.

She studied him curiously. He gave the impression of being so eager to please and so anxious to be liked. What was going on behind those warm brown eyes, she wondered? Karen had had enough dealings with the military to know that you didn't become a colonel of a crack infantry regiment through being an ingenuous nice guy. And she thought that Gerrard Parker-Brown, whom she reckoned to be in his late thirties, was considerably younger than usual to be holding such a senior rank. In peacetime, at any rate.

'So, have you any idea who these two men might be, Gerry?' she enquired, putting only a light emphasis on his name.

He shrugged. 'I have no idea at all, Karen. We don't even

know for certain that they were soldiers, do we? Let alone stationed at Hangridge. If they were army chaps, I would imagine they were mates of Connelly's who went looking for him to try to stop him getting himself into more trouble . . .'

'A logical conclusion, and the same one our witness made. But I thought I'd explained that the witness also said Connelly didn't react as if they were mates. Just the opposite. In fact, he seemed terrified of them.'

Gerry Parker-Brown shrugged. 'I can't comment on that, Karen. I wasn't there. But if they were his army mates and they were determined to bring him back to camp, and he didn't want to come back, well, he wouldn't have been pleased to see them exactly, would he? Even though they were almost certainly trying to do him a good turn.'

'Are you sure of that, Gerry?'

He flashed the easy grin again. 'How can I be? But I'd bet a month's pay on it. Soldiers look after their comrades, Karen. Indeed, it is part of their training that they do so.'

'So nobody at Hangridge officially sent anyone out looking for Connelly—'

'We didn't even know he was missing until we were contacted by the police after his death,' interrupted Parker-Brown. 'I'm more than a little embarrassed about that, to tell you the truth, Karen, but apparently his mates had been covering up for him. Again, that's what soldiers do.'

'All right. So, just assuming for a moment that your assumption is correct, and if these two men were soldiers that they were Connelly's mates, how easy would it be for you to find out who they are? I mean, would you know if Connelly had any special friends who would have wanted to bail him out from any trouble he'd got himself into?'

'I'm not sure, but most squaddies do have mates like that.' For the first time Karen thought that Gerry Parker-Brown looked a little wary. 'I'd have to make enquiries.'

'I wish you would, Gerry.' She paused. 'There's something else. Our witness reckoned that both men were quite a bit older than Connelly. That indicates to me either that they are instructors or more senior soldiers from another company here at Hangridge, rather than the training unit. And if so, they

70

aren't likely to have been *mates* of Alan Connelly's, are they?'

Gerry smiled. 'I really wouldn't know, Karen, and as we have already established that you have no real idea whether or not these men even were soldiers, I wouldn't like to guess.'

For a moment Karen thought there might be a slightly patronising note in Gerry Parker-Brown's voice. But only for a moment. When the colonel continued to speak, he still appeared to be trying to be as helpful as ever.

'I will tell you this, though, Karen. Our instructor NCOs are inclined to be extremely protective towards their charges. Any one of them, knowing that Connelly was already in trouble with his career, could have taken it upon himself to seek him out and make one last attempt to get him back on the straight and narrow.'

'The straight and narrow?' queried Karen. 'At best, they left the lad to wander blind drunk along a dangerous road. At worst, I dread to think. I would really appreciate it, Gerry, if you would work on the assumption that these two mystery men are soldiers and do your best to seek them out.'

'Yes, of course. I'll put out an appeal for them to come forward. And as it is highly unlikely that they have done anything wrong or untoward, if they are soldiers stationed at Hangridge, I'm sure they will do so.'

'Maybe, Gerry, but we don't actually have to rely on them doing the right thing, as it were. Not entirely, anyway.' Karen felt in charge again now. 'I have computer images of them, compiled with the help of our witness.'

Parker-Brown passed no comment. Karen opened her bag and removed a cardboard-backed envelope. She dropped the contents onto the colonel's desk right in front of him. One E-fit landed the right way up, the other she had to turn over, and as she did so, she arranged both so that they were properly facing him.

'Do you recognise either of these two men?' she asked quietly.

He looked down then at the images before him. She had no idea how closely they resembled the men Kelly had seen, and doubted that Kelly did either. Certainly, the waterproof clothing they had both been wearing and their woolly hats pulled down almost to their eyes had not helped.

With his left hand Parker-Brown rubbed the back of his neck, and with his right he moved the E-fits slightly closer to him as if to make it easier for him to see them.

'Not from these, I don't,' he said casually. He was still looking down, and for a moment Karen thought he was not going to meet her eyes. But after a few seconds more of what appeared to be careful study, he suddenly looked up, leaned back in his chair and flashed her that grin again.

'Actually, they look a bit like Ant and Dec going skiing to me,' he said, and the laughter lines at the corner of his eyes crinkled, etching themselves even more deeply into his skin.

'This isn't a joke, Colonel,' said Karen. She was beginning to feel a little irritated now, and her reversion to addressing him by his rank was just part of her sudden determination to make it clear to Gerrard Parker-Brown that his boyish charm was not going to bowl her over. Absolutely not.

He changed his attitude at once. 'You're absolutely right, Detective Superintendent Meadows,' he responded with such elaborate correctness, that she once more wondered fleetingly if he were patronising her. But when he spoke again there was no such inflection in his voice and he seemed absolutely sincere and straightforward.

'A young soldier has died and it was quite wrong of me even to appear to be making light of it,' he continued. 'I do, however, assure you that I do not recognise either of these men. Certainly not from the pictures you have shown me, anyway. However, I also realise that this does not rule out their being part of our complement here. And I assure you that I will take this immensely seriously and that I will commence enquiries immediately. If these are our chaps, Karen,' he tapped the two computer images before him, 'we'll find them, have no fear.'

'Thank you,' said Karen. And she couldn't have begun to explain why she was so convinced that Colonel Gerrard Parker-Brown's inquiries would be of no help to her whatsoever.

Six

Kelly was sitting in front of his computer when she called around lunchtime the following day. He had been in front of his computer all morning. Since six. He had just checked the machine's memory and it seemed that he had so far played ten games of backgammon and eleven games of hearts.

The bleep of his telephone was a welcome displacement activity. At least it would relieve him, albeit briefly, from even having to pretend that he was writing.

'Good morning, Detective Superintendent,' he said.

'Yeah.'

Karen Meadows rarely had time for life's niceties, Kelly reflected. He saw no point in speaking further until she had told him whatever it was she wanted to tell him. Karen was not the sort of person who used the telephone for small talk.

'I've been out to Hangridge,' she began. 'Had a long talk with the CO. It has to be said that he did give me a rather better reception than I expected.'

She paused. Kelly continued to wait.

'In fact, Colonel Parker-Brown was not what I expected in any way at all.'

There was a note in her voice that Kelly couldn't quite make out. He was unable to resist butting in with what was, no doubt, a totally inappropriate quip.

'Really. Drag queen or something, is she?'

'Hilarious, Kelly. No, Gerrard Parker-Brown is the acceptable, accessible, personable face of the modern army. Helpful, friendly and highly co-operative. At least, that's what he appears to be. So why do I think the result of our meeting will be much the same as it would have been had I spent yesterday morning with Colonel Blimp?'

'Ah.'

73

'Look, to tell the truth, Kelly, I am not at all sure there is much else I can do without something hard to go on. The colonel has promised to try to find those two soldiers you encountered. I gave him the E-fits. But, I wouldn't hold your breath, if I were you.'

'So, you think he's hiding something?'

'Kelly, why do you always take everything in life a step too far? I have absolutely no reason to believe he's hiding anything. Indeed, to all intents and purposes, he was very open and honest with me. He said he did not recognise the two men from the E-fits, that certainly nobody was sent officially from Hangridge to search for Connelly, and that if they were soldiers they were probably mates of Con—'

'Oh, no, they bloody well weren't. I'd stake my life on that.' Kelly interrupted. He wasn't going to let that go by.

'Kelly, I had no reason to argue with the man about anything. And no reason to probe any further into army affairs. I just wanted to call you and tell you that I had tried. Oh, and I also had the SOCOs out at the accident scene again today. Made them go over the ground there with an effing toothcomb. So far, zilch, and I don't have very high expectations.'

'There must be something,' interjected Kelly. 'There has to be.'

'No, Kelly, there does not have to be. It is of course possible that there is something in this which we have yet to discover, and it is also possible that you are totally mistaken and that the death of Alan Connelly was merely the tragic accident it appeared to be from the start.'

Just occasionally, Kelly got extremely fed up with the way Karen Meadows was inclined to talk down to him. He knew he'd probably given her good reason to do so over the years, because of his tendency, on occasion, to behave with a recklessness bordering on gross stupidity. None the less, it grated sometimes, and this was one of those times.

'This isn't about me, Karen,' he responded curtly. 'It's about a young man who was frightened half out of his wits. You didn't meet him. I did. Had you done so, I suspect you might have taken this whole matter more seriously. '

'Don't get stroppy with me, Kelly,' she said. 'I have taken it

74

seriously. And I am still taking it seriously. More so than I should be doing, I suspect, with the caseload of crimes I have on my books right now. That is why I have phoned you.'

Kelly relented slightly.

'OK,' he said. 'I'm sorry. I appreciate what you've done, really I do. Did you get anything at all out of this Colonel Parker-Brown? Alan Connelly said there had been other deaths at the camp. What about that? Did you ask about other deaths? What did he say?'

'Whoa, Kelly. One question at a time. I was coming to that. Of course I asked.'

She told him then, very briefly, about the recruit who had been killed on a training exercise.

'Shot?' Kelly responded eagerly. 'Did you say shot? So that makes two violent deaths in six months. Jesus, surely that's enough to warrant taking this further, isn't it?'

'No, Kelly, I don't think it is. And I bloody well know the chief constable wouldn't think so. There was an inquest of course. Even the military has always been bound by that procedure – in peacetime, anyway. I did a quick check with the coroner's office and the verdict was, quite properly, accidental death. As I am sure it will be ultimately with Alan Connelly. Yes, there have been two deaths, but both, although tragic, were hardly earth-shattering. A soldier dies in a training incident. Well, when you play with loaded guns, every so often some poor bastard gets shot.'

'Look, Karen, Connelly said: "Like they killed the others." It could all fit . . .'

'Not really, Kelly. There's more. Not only was he drunk out of his skull the night he died, but apparently Connelly was considered to be a real Walter Mitty. The colonel says he was always making up unlikely stories . . .'

'"The colonel says,"' repeated Kelly in a mocking voice. 'Of course he would, Karen. Surely you are not going to be taken in by some sort of military whitewash? You of all people, Karen.'

'Kelly, don't be so bloody insulting or I'm going to finish this call.'

'Sorry, sorry. It's just that, as you know, I really think there is a strong possibility that that poor little sod was pushed under the lorry which killed him, and I reckon you must agree with me or you wouldn't even have got this involved.'

'Kelly, I did consider that after what you told me, of course I did. But I also considered suicide . . .'

'Oh no, oh no. For a start, why would a young chap like Connelly kill himself in that way, even if he did want to take his own life? He was a boy soldier, for goodness sake. He had access to guns . . .'

'Maybe he didn't like guns that much, in spite of his job. I don't know. I do know we can't rule out suicide. The lorry driver's description of the way the accident happened would be totally consistent with someone deliberately throwing them-selves into the path of an oncoming vehicle—'

'Or being pushed,' Kelly interrupted.

'Kelly, please, will you listen. Apparently, Connelly was on the brink of being chucked out of the army because of his story-telling, and, rather more seriously, he'd been fantasising about a woman soldier and had been more or less stalking her. He'd been warned about his behaviour and the possible consequences several times. He knew he was on the way out, and yet other than this Walter Mitty side to him he was a good soldier, it seems. He would not have wanted to be made to leave the army. And apparently his family life was pretty terrible. According to the colonel, his father is a drunken bully, who hasn't worked in years, and a manic depressive. So if you put all that together, suicide has to be a possibility, if we are being sensible about this, which I am desperately trying to be.'

Kelly took on board the note of criticism in her voice and decided he'd better accept it. It was probably justified. Kelly was not noted for being sensible. Karen didn't need to spell that one out. He waited for her to continue.

'There's something else, Kelly. A witness has come forward, just this morning, after noticing a report of the accident in an old copy of the *Argus*. A passing motorist who saw a young man, almost certainly Connelly, walking along the side of the road a couple of hundred yards or so away from The Wild Dog, just minutes before the accident. He was weaving erratically. The witness said he nearly hit him. And, apparently, Connelly seemed to be quite alone.'

'All right,' said Kelly. 'But if he really was alone, where did those two men go to so suddenly, right after having found someone they had been searching for? And why? Why did they leave him alone? If indeed they did. If I'm right and they were soldiers, they probably know all about keeping themselves out of sight when they want to. Are you sure Parker-Brown doesn't know a hell of a lot more than he's telling you, Karen?'

'Look, I've no doubt he's as reluctant as any other army officer to let the police force meddle in army affairs, in spite of trying to give the opposite impression,' responded Karen. 'But I have absolutely no reason to believe that he is hiding anything that is in any way pertinent to this case.'

'Come on, Karen. How many soldiers are there up at Hangridge? I bet your colonel knows them all. So why can't he lead you to those two who came to the pub, eh? I bet he knows bloody well who they are.'

'Kelly, you're running away with yourself. How many times do we have to go over this ground. We don't even know that these men were soldiers, for God's sake. And for your information the total complement at Hangridge, including the training unit, is well over a thousand men and women. I very much doubt that Parker-Brown could recognise and name all of them.'

'I bet he's got a fair idea, from the way you describe him.'

'Oh, Kelly. In any case, you only saw the two men briefly in the pub. Sometimes E-fit images are terrific and sometimes they're a bad joke. How the hell do I know how good yours were, when I doubt you do yourself. The two guys you created looked pretty damned peculiar, I know that, especially in those silly hats. Look, closing ranks against the meddling of the civilian police force is one thing, Kelly, but I really don't think the commanding officer of the Devonshire Fusiliers would tell me a deliberate lie. Come on. Do you, Kelly?'

'Only if he thought he could get away with it,' muttered Kelly.

'What?' Kelly knew that Karen had heard him perfectly well. You could tell that from the way she had snapped her reply.

'I don't know, Karen,' Kelly replied in a more conversational tone of voice. 'I expect he would, if he were privy to murders. Most people in that situation don't find lying too difficult.'

77

'Now you're talking nonsense.' Karen snapped the words again. For a moment Kelly thought she was going to hang up on him. And he wasn't going to let her do that until he had extracted all the information he possibly could from her.

'Look, just tell me one thing,' he asked quickly. 'Do you have the name of the recruit who was killed on the range.'

'Yes, I do.'

'Well?'

'C'mon, Kelly. I know you. You're always bloody trouble. I've made further enquiries and, to be honest, I'm pretty well satisfied now that Alan Connelly's death was a tragic accident and no more.'

'No you're not, Karen, or you wouldn't even have phoned me today.'

Kelly was quite certain he was right. He knew Karen Meadows every bit as well as she knew him.

'Apart from anything else, Kelly, I'm not sure that you of all people should be getting any further involved. You'll start poking around and causing mayhem as usual. It's not even your territory any more, is it? You're supposed to be a novelist now.'

'Yeah, and Hangridge is just a displacement activity, that's all. And maybe a way of earning a bit of lineage which I could certainly do with. Look, if everything is as above board as you say it is, what harm can there be in giving me that name?'

He could hear Karen sigh.

'I know I'm going to regret this . . .' she muttered.

Kelly waited. He still wasn't sure whether or not Karen was going to give him the information he had asked for, but he knew well enough when to stop pushing her.

'OK,' she said eventually. 'It's Foster. Fusilier Craig Foster. Actually, I'm a bit surprised you don't remember anything about his death. Though I must admit, I didn't. But apparently it did get some press coverage, and you were actually working for the *Argus* at the time.'

'Six months ago? I think I probably had other things on my mind.'

Six months previously, Kelly had still been deeply involved with another case. And as always with him, his involvement had bordered on obsession and he had taken little notice of anything much else happening in the world.

Karen didn't respond. But he knew she would be well enough aware of what he was referring to.

'Is there anything else you can tell me?' he asked.

'No, Kelly. No doubt I've told you too much already. Situation normal.'

She hung up then without saying goodbye. Situation normal, indeed, thought Kelly.

He replaced the receiver slowly and forced himself to turn his attention back to his computer screen.

The phone rang again almost at once. It was Moira's daughter Jennifer.

'I just thought I'd call, John, to remind you that Mum's expecting you over tonight.'

Kelly knew what she meant. Could hear the unspoken words inside his head. Please don't forget, or pretend to forget, or whatever it is that you do to avoid seeing Mum. Please don't let her down again.

The awful truth was that he didn't want to visit Moira ever again. Not for as long as she was ill. And it was a tragic fact that she was not going to get better. Even if nobody was ever allowed to say the words. But he knew that this time he would visit, if only to make some amends for his many shortcomings.

'I'll be there,' he promised. 'You just give her all my love and tell her I'll see if I can't find a couple of hot new videos for her.'

He put the phone down again, held his head in his hands for a few minutes, and then, with a great effort of will, reverted his attention yet again to the computer screen and made himself exit his games programme.

'Right,' he said, as he resolutely clicked on 'My Documents' and called up that empty document 'Untitled Chapter Three'. For a good ten minutes he stared at the blank white screen, moving barely a muscle. Then, very suddenly he grabbed his mouse, quit Word and called up his games programme again.

Halfway through being beaten rotten in his third back-gammon game, he accepted that he was unable even to concentrate on that, let alone on writing. His thoughts were somewhere else. On a moorland road, late on a wet foggy night.

And within the confines of an isolated barracks where young soldiers learned their trade well away from prying eyes. A place where almost anything could happen, and yet, even in the high-tech communications era of the twenty-first century, in a country which retained an allegedly free and probing press, it remained quite likely that nobody outside its sentry-posted perimeters would ever know.

'Damn,' Kelly muttered to himself. 'There's something going on up there, something big. I can just feel it.'

Just an hour or so later, Karen Meadows received a totally unexpected phone call. Her head was buried in the inevitable piles of paper on her desk when it came, and Karen welcomed distractions from her paperwork every bit as much as Kelly did from his alleged writing.

This call, however, was more than that, and, in addition to being merely unexpected, was also, she had to admit to herself, surprisingly welcome.

'Good afternoon, Karen, it's Gerry Parker-Brown here.'

Good Lord, she thought. It had not really occurred to her that he would contact her. Indeed she had automatically assumed, under the circumstances, that she would have to chase him if she considered it necessary to follow up their meeting at Hangridge. Out loud she merely said: 'Oh, hello.'

'I just called to tell you that I'm afraid the results of my preliminary inquiries at the camp have not so far been helpful at all,' the colonel continued. 'Nobody I've shown your pictures to has recognised either of the chaps from the pub, not from those images anyway, and neither have any of my men come forward to say that they were there.'

Now that was not a surprise, thought Karen. She did wonder, however, why the colonel was calling to tell her nothing at all, and so soon.

'It won't stop here, though, I can assure you, Karen,' Parker-Brown went on. 'I will set up an internal inquiry and I'm sure we'll be able to come up with something . . .'

Karen remained unconvinced, but said nothing.

'Even if they were soldiers, they could have been friends of young Connelly from another regiment, who knows? But I haven't given up yet, Karen, and as soon as we get anything, anything at all, I'll be right on to you, I promise.'

'Thank you very much,' said Karen. She couldn't think of anything else to say. Indeed, she didn't think there was much else to say. And she was still wondering what had motivated Gerry Parker-Brown to call her so quickly in order to give her no information. She did not think, somehow, that he was the kind of man to do anything much without a reason.

'Meanwhile, I wondered how you felt about a drink and a spot of dinner,' Parker-Brown went on smoothly.

Karen nearly fell off her chair. Whatever had been flitting through her mind concerning this call, Colonel Gerrard Parker-Brown asking her out on a date had not figured at all. But that did seem to be what was happening. And she was so confused that she found herself unable to respond properly.

'Um, well . . . I'm not sure . . . uh . . .'

He interrupted her stumblings. 'I know it's a frightful cheek, but all too many of my evenings seem to get filled up with army business of one kind or another, and tonight I happen to be free. So I just wondered how you were fixed? I'm sick and tired of spending my free time on my own, if you want the truth.'

The last bit was not particularly flattering, but the colonel – or Gerry, as Karen supposed she really must start thinking of him after this approach – had also managed to indicate pretty clearly that he was unattached. And she suspected that he had done so quite deliberately.

'Well, I don't know . . .' she continued hesitantly, while at the same time feeling quite angry with herself. What on earth was the matter with her? Why was she so thrown at being asked out by a man? She knew the answer to that, of course. Her last thoroughly unwise love affair, which had been so important to her, had been with a married junior police officer, Detective Sergeant Phil Cooper, and it had left her totally disillusioned with men generally. When Cooper's wife had found out, he had ended the affair at once. He had later tried to start it all again, of course, but Karen's heart had by then been broken. It really had. And since that sorry episode, which apart from anything else had threatened to wreck her career, Karen had totally shut down her emotions. For almost a year now, both her head and heart had been closed to even the notion of romance. She had also shut down sexually, too. When Cooper had stepped out of her life, so her libido had also departed, and she had not felt so much as a flicker in that direction since.

Parker-Brown interrupted her again, for which she was grateful, as she suspected that he may have stopped her causing both of them considerable embarrassment with her dithering.

'Look, nothing special,' he said reassuringly. 'Just two people, who I suspect may have a great deal in common and who I hope may become friends, sharing a drink and a spot of supper. That's all.'

He had a pretty good turn of phrase, Karen had to give him that.

'Well, I am free tonight . . .' she began. She was free, in fact, virtually every night. Except when she was working. And that, at least, she suspected, might be one thing they had in common.

'And?'

She took a deep breath. 'I'd be delighted,' she heard herself saying. And she realised that she meant it too. Which was yet another surprise.

He called for at her flat at eight-thirty, just as he had said he would. He was wearing blue jeans, a black jacket and a bright white T-shirt. It was an extremely classy black jacket. Karen knew about clothes. She thought it was probably Paul Smith. And she was glad he had dressed casually. Karen only did casual. She spent a disproportionate part of her salary on very special designer numbers, but she preferred a DKNY track suit or an Armani bomber jacket to more formal wear.

She was wearing khaki combat trousers from Replay, and a big, loose, white cotton Comme des Garçons shirt with an elaborately embroidered red abstract relief down one side of its front. She thought their styles matched rather well.

He looked good, she had to admit it. And very young. She had already guessed that he was probably four or five years younger than her forty-three years, but out of uniform he appeared even more youthful. And rather more dishy, Karen thought. But then she had never been into uniforms. In her opinion, they were a necessary evil in certain professions, and she had been delighted to discard her own permanently when she had moved into CID.

Covertly, she looked him up and down. With his shock of sandy hair, those crinkly eyes and that ready smile, he was an extremely attractive man. She would just have to overlook the fact that he looked so much like a square-jawed hero out of the *Eagle* or *Boys' Own*, that was all.

He was carrying a bunch of white roses which he handed over with a small bow.

'Sorry to be so old-fashioned, it's the way I was brought up,' he said with a wide grin.

He both looked and sounded as if he was trying to make a weak joke, but she suspected he was probably just telling the truth. After all, if ever a man had public school and Sandhurst written all over him, it was Gerrard Parker-Brown. Even his name spoke for itself. Karen could only imagine what sort of family he came from.

'I thought this was just a drink between friends,' she said, but softened the words by smiling back at him.

'It is, but we passed a stall selling those roses and I couldn't resist.'

'Ah. You like flowers?'

'I do. Gardening is my passion. Or it used to be . . .'

He seemed about to tell her something, then stopped. Which was reasonable. They were, after all, standing in the doorway to her flat, and it was not quite the place for exchanging confidences.

'Funny sort of hobby for a soldier, isn't it?' she enquired casually, as she gestured for him to step inside.

'Not so much as you may think,' he replied. 'Some of the greatest generals in history were gardeners.'

'Name two,' she said.

'Do you know, my mind has gone completely blank and I can't think of one,' he responded. 'But it is true, honestly.'

Laughing, she reached for her white mackintosh cape. The weather had improved dramatically during the last couple of days, but Karen didn't trust it. It was still November. And she really did absolutely hate getting her hair wet. It went frizzy at the front and stuck out at an angle at the back and sides.

He grinned at her. 'If you're ready, the car is waiting,' he said.

She found that a rather curious turn of phrase, but he did not give her time to pass comment. He spoke again almost immediately, as she picked up her car keys from the little narrow console-table she kept next to the front door.

'Nice piece,' he remarked. 'Georgian?'

She nodded, mildly surprised yet again. Not only did she not see him as a gardener, but neither would she have put him down as a man with any interest at all in antiques.

In the car park, he steered her towards a black Range Rover. A uniformed soldier-chauffeur sat in the driver's seat. Suddenly, the phrase 'the car is waiting' made sense.

'One of the perks of the job,' said Parker-Brown quickly, yet again giving her little time to say anything. 'And it means I can have a drink.'

She still said nothing. Just go with the flow, girl, she told herself.

He took her to the Cott Inn at Dartington, where they drank bitter and ate piping hot steak-and-kidney pies. Conversation came easily, considerably more so than she would ever have expected.

'I much prefer this to eating formally, I do hope you agree,' he said, as they sat together by a raging fire.

Karen settled back in her chair, idly watching the flames. She did feel extremely relaxed in this man's company, that was for certain.

'I do, I love it,' she replied. 'But I would have put you down for a formal man. I mean, with your background I wouldn't have thought you'd ever had much experience of anything other than formal dining.'

'Well, that's pretty true of army life,' he said. 'Number one dress and the regimental silver and all of that—'

'I'm sure,' she interrupted. 'And one would assume that with your sort of family background, too . . .'

It was his turn to interrupt.

'Karen, what on earth sort of background do you think I have?' he asked.

She paused and studied him carefully. His face was giving nothing away.

'Well, public school and Sandhurst, I suppose,' she said. 'And

84

with a name like yours, a pretty upper-crust family, I should imagine.'

He grinned quickly, but was rather serious when he spoke again. 'My father was also a fusilier, another professional soldier, but he wasn't an officer,' he began. 'He was a corporal in the 1st Battalion of the Royal Regiment of Fusiliers. His name was Graham Parker and I can barely remember him. He was killed in Northern Ireland in 1968 when I was just four years old and I don't think we ever saw a lot of him at home . . .'

Karen found herself doing mental arithmetic. That made Gerry forty, at least a year or two older than she had judged him to be, but still young to be a full colonel, she was sure.

'It was only really the beginning of the troubles, not long after the civil rights march in Londonderry which is generally reckoned to have been the start of it all, and only weeks into the Royal Fusiliers' first tour of duty over there,' Parker-Brown continued. Karen noticed that his voice had acquired a far away note. 'He was actually very, very unlucky. But enough of that. It was all a long time ago.'

Parker-Brown flashed that grin again.

'Anyway, my mother remarried a couple of years later, a plumber named Martin Brown. He adopted me and brought me up, and did his best to be a father to me. But my mother never wanted me to forget my real father and she thought it was important that I retained his name, which is how I became Parker-Brown. That was her solution. And Martin went along with it.'

'I see,' said Karen. 'But what about your first name. Gerrard. I mean, isn't that a bit posh for a corporal's lad?'

'Ah.' Parker-Brown was smiling easily now. 'It seems that my mother had been watching a film shortly before I was born, in which Gerrard Street, in the West End of London, featured briefly. She's always suffered from occasional delusions of grandeur, my mum, and she so much liked the sound of Gerrard, which she did indeed think was suitably posh, that she decided that should be my name. Which is why I have two Rs in the middle, rather than the usual Gerard with one R. Unfortunately, she didn't realise until too late that it's actually a street full of Chinese restaurants and knocking shops, and not the tiniest bit posh.'

Karen laughed and shook her head.

'Not what you expected, eh?' he enquired.

She shook her head again.

'So, didn't you even go to public school, then?'

'Absolutely not. State primary and then a grammar school. Thank God for the eleven-plus. The system may not have been perfect, but it did give kids like me a real chance. I always wanted to go into the army, and more particularly I wanted to be a fusilier like my dad, and in spite of having lost her husband in action, my mother encouraged me. She has always said she knew it was what my father would have wanted. He'd been a dedicated career soldier, you see, although in the ranks. She was more than happy for me to chose a military career. I don't think she imagined that I'd be an officer, though – as you pointed out – she did give me the right name, I suppose. Anyway, grammar school gave me that opportunity. I passed the right exams and, yes, I did go to Sandhurst. That's the only bit you got right.'

'And now you're a full colonel. At what? Forty? That's quite young, isn't it?'

'Youngish. My promotion from lieutenant colonel only came through last month, but there you are. Life is full of little miracles, isn't it?'

'She must be very proud of you, your mum.'

'I think she is. It hasn't all been plain sailing, though. Certainly not in my personal life.'

'Ah.'

'Yes. Ah, indeed. My wife and I have been apart for some time. She seemed to prefer a chinless wonder with a title, which should not have been a huge surprise, really. I made the mistake of marrying into the army aristocracy, or what passes for it, and I don't think I was ever quite what she required. I thought I was head over heels in love, but sometimes now I think I was in love with my wife's family set-up more than anything else.'

She was surprised by his honesty. His directness. Indeed, he really was a thoroughly surprising man.

'Do you have children?'

He nodded. 'A boy and a girl, aged twelve and thirteen. They're both at boarding school. There is, of course, as far as their mother and her family are concerned, no alternative to a boarding-school education. I seem to see them less and less. Actually, I think that nearly always happens with fathers whose exes have custody of their children, whatever people tell you.'

'Maybe,' Karen said non-commitedly. 'I wouldn't know.'

'No children, then?'

'No.' Karen answered abruptly. She liked learning about other people's lives, but was never so keen on giving much away about her own. And she was, after all, at an age when she was fast having to accept that it was highly unlikely she would ever have any children, which was something, even though she had never been particularly maternal, that she did not like to dwell upon.

'And husbands, past or present?'

Karen studied him through narrowed eyes. She hadn't given it a thought, but, of course, Parker-Brown did not even know if she was married or not, because as usual she had said so little about herself. Yet he had still asked her out. Just for friendship, he had said. She wasn't so sure. Was he always this attentive to, and this interested in, his friends, she wondered. Or did he have an ulterior motive.

'No.' She was abrupt again, partly because more and more nowadays, when she met a man who interested her, she found herself wishing she wasn't always inclined to be so darned suspicious, which just seemed to come with the territory of her job, and partly because she remained determined not to talk about herself if she could possibly avoid it. But while she was still trying to think of a way to change the subject, he spoke again.

'I'm surprised. I would have thought you would be much in demand.'

She laughed. Smooth bastard, she thought. Aloud she said: 'Even if that were true, being in demand is not quite the same as getting married.'

He laughed with her then. She really was very easy in his company, and the rest of the evening passed extremely pleasantly. They continued to make small talk effortlessly and she discovered that they did indeed have a shared interest in collecting antiques.

'Actually, most of my stuff would generally be regarded as junk, I expect,' confessed Karen.

'The best sort,' said Parker-Brown. 'Anybody with a healthy bank balance can spend a fortune in Bond Street. It takes talent to seek out special pieces of junk.'

'Umm,' mused Karen. 'In my case, I don't have any choice. I certainly can't afford Bond Street on my salary.'

'Me neither,' said Parker-Brown. 'In spite of having a great deal of family money, my dearest ex insists on screwing the maximum possible maintenance out of me every month.'

She sympathised with him. The conversation moved on to holidays in the sun and to favourite restaurants, then circled back to antique fairs and to great finds in car boot sales.

Karen, invariably awkward at what might be the start of any kind of new relationship, found herself surprised both by how much she was enjoying herself and how much she was warming to Gerry Parker-Brown.

In fact, it would have been almost the perfect evening were it not for the shadow cast by the Alan Connelly affair. All evening it was in the back of her mind, and she was very tempted to bring it into the conversation. She wanted to know what Parker-Brown really thought and if his inquiries had made any progress. Indeed, she had wondered all along if at least a part of his purpose in arranging this occasion might be to talk about the matter.

But Parker-Brown didn't even mention it. And it was nearly time to leave before Karen managed to bring the subject up. Even then, she was aware that her interjection sat clumsily amid the evening's social chit-chat.

'I wondered if you had made any progress with your Alan Connelly inquiries, Gerry?' she asked quite bluntly, having failed to find any way at all of working the matter into the conversation.

Parker-Brown took a deep pull of his pint and stretched his long legs.

'Not really,' he replied. 'Are you sure you want to talk about it tonight?'

'Yes, quite sure.' She had no intention of letting him off the hook that easily.

'OK. Well, I'm pretty certain now that those two men your witness described are not in my lot. In fact, I can find no trace of anyone like them at all. Look, I know your witness was very sure in his own mind that they were soldiers, but he had no way of being certain, did he? It wasn't as if they were in uniform.'

'No.' She felt mildly irritated now. She suddenly had the feeling that she was being handled, that this whole evening may have been little more than a softening-up process, leading towards the moment when Parker-Brown would tell her, in effect, that he had no help to give her. And possibly no intention of trying to help either, she suspected, although he had been extremely careful from the start to avoid giving that impression.

'He couldn't be absolutely certain, but he got the clear impression that they were soldiers,' she continued resolutely. 'And, actually, our witness is, by coincidence, someone I have known for many years, someone whose judgement I trust.'

The absurdity of the situation struck her then. By and large, she did trust Kelly's judgement, but she didn't think she had ever let him know that.

Parker-Brown studied her thoughtfully, running the fingers of one hand over a chin that really could only be described as chiselled. 'Well, in that case, of course, I'll carry on making enquiries,' he said. 'I do want to assure you, Karen, that I will help all I can. One of my young men has died, and if there is anything suspicious about his death, then I want to know about it every bit as much as you do.'

'Thank you . . .' began Karen. He interrupted her before she had time to say anything else.

'And now, let's not spoil this evening with work things, eh? I really have enjoyed myself. You're great company, you know.' He paused. 'For a police officer,' he added mischievously.

'And you're not bad yourself – for a soldier,' she responded almost automatically.

But she was no longer quite so at ease, even though she could not deny to herself that she had thoroughly enjoyed the evening and Gerrard Parker-Brown's company. However, she still couldn't help wondering if the colonel was deliberately making a friend of her, and maybe even looking for more than that, in order to put her off the scent.

'C'mon, let's get you home,' he said, interrupting her train of thought. He grinned at her yet again, and it really was a disarming grin. He looked totally ingenuous, a big boyish man in a big boy's job, incapable surely, she told herself, of being so downright devious.

'Oh, and I really hope we can do this again some time.'

She hesitated, still battling with the feeling that there was a hidden agenda here. It was ridiculous, she told herself firmly. She was merely being fanciful, just like Alan Connelly. This wasn't some kind of Iraq-gate. Indeed, she had no information whatsoever concerning the death of Connelly or Craig Foster which indicated even the slightest need for any kind of cover-up.

There was no reason at all why she should not enjoy this man's company as often as she liked. He was attractive, charming and in every way great to be with. She really must control her tendency towards suspecting other peoples' motives all the time. And particularly the motives of anyone who seemed to show a special interest in her.

'I'd like that very much,' she said very deliberately, as he ushered her towards the door. And she meant it.

Seven

The following morning Kelly's mobile rang just as he was parking at Newton Abbot railway station. And, as was usual for him, he had barely a minute to spare if he was going to catch his intended train.

He had no intention of replying, particularly as it was not yet 8 a.m., but he did glance at the display panel of his phone, nestling in its dashboard cradle, just in case this was a call he could not miss. News of Moira, perhaps.

In fact the caller was his son Nick, who, of course, knew that his father was up early every morning and at his desk. Or allegedly so, anyway. Hastily Kelly pushed the receive button. Nick was one of the very few people in the world that he always had time for – even if in this case it would have to be little more than a few seconds.

'I just wondered how Moira was doing,' enquired Nick over the airwaves.

'Much the same, Nick.' Kelly paused. 'It's not good, not good at all. I saw her last night. They say it might not be long now . . .'

'Shit.'

Nick sounded both sad and angry. Kelly understood those emotions well enough. And he knew how fond Nick was of Moira, who had brought stability and more than a measure of happiness into Kelly's life, and had stood by him even when he had seemed determined to self-destruct.

'So how are you coping, Dad?'

'Oh, you know, bloody useless as ever. If it wasn't for those girls . . .'

'Don't put yourself down, Dad. I know how much you care, and Moira has always loved you for the man you are, not for the man you feel you should be.'

Kelly felt his eyes moisten and found rather to his surprise that he was also smiling, just a little. For a moment he forgot all about his train. Nick had a wonderful knack of knowing exactly what to say and when to say it, and Kelly was suddenly overwhelmed with a sense of gratitude that he had been given a second chance to get to know his only son. He felt proud too. Nick was a fine young man. And successful. As an ex-army officer, probably too independent to stay in uniform for too many years, or so Kelly had always thought, he had fitted back into civilian life admirably. For nearly four years now he had been working in the City as some kind of business and IT consultant, one of those jobs Kelly could never quite get his head round, but he was well aware of the rewards it had brought his bachelor son. Nick lived in a luxurious London Docklands apartment, holidayed in all the best places, usually accompanied by one of the string of glamorous girlfriends who seemed to drift in and out of his life in remarkably trouble-free fashion, and drove the kind of cars his father could only dream about.

'Thanks, Nick,' he said.

'You're kidding. Look, Dad, I can't get out of London this week, but I'll drive down as soon as I can. I'd really like to see Moira . . .'

'I know. And I'm sure she'd like to see you too.'

Kelly switched off the MG's engine and began to dismantle his phone from its hands-free system. Simultaneously, he checked the clock on the dashboard.

'Oh, Christ!'

'Sorry?'

'I've got about two minutes to catch a train. I'm sorry, Nick, I really have to go . . .'

'Sure, sure. I'll call you tomorrow. Where are you going, anyway?'

Automatically Kelly opened his mouth to tell Nick where he was going and why, then realised that would call for an explanation he had absolutely no time for.

'Research,' he said quickly. 'I'll tell you when I see you. Bye.'

Given the way he lived his life it was all for the best that Kelly could still move fast for a big, slightly paunchy man in his late forties. He arrived on the platform with seconds to spare. The

92

whole spur of the moment jaunt was absolutely typical Kelly, and had probably been inevitable from the beginning. Even though he had spent much of the previous night lying sleepless in his bed and telling himself that he would merely end up wasting both time and money.

The truth, however, was that he had probably made up his mind about what he was going to do the very moment that Karen told him about the second death at Hangridge.

Kelly was off to Scotland to see Alan Connelly's parents. He had driven to Newton Abbot in order to board one of the direct cross-country trains running virtually the entire length of Britain from Penzance to Glasgow. It was a damned good service when it worked. But, unfortunately, nowadays it seemed to work despairingly rarely.

On this occasion everything had begun well. The train arrived on time at Newton Abbot, departing on schedule, at 7.53 a.m. precisely, and remaining so until it reached Birmingham. There, in the dark cavernous hinterland of one of the city's network of cold black underground platforms, the red and grey Virgin Express sat for almost thirty minutes before anybody bothered to inform the passengers why.

Eventually the guard, or train manager as they were now called, muttered something about a mechanical fault. The passengers in Kelly's carriage shifted uneasily. With the number of accidents there had been on Britain's rail network recently, it had become almost as disturbing to be told your train had something wrong with it as to be told that an aircraft you were travelling on had developed a mechanical fault. Engineers were already working on the problem and we hope to be under way again shortly, continued the train manager in a flat, disinterested tone.

Kelly, wondering again, as he had done when he met Alan Connelly in The Wild Dog, what a Scotsman was doing in the Devonshire Fusiliers anyway, felt only bad vibes. He had been born impatient and he was, as ever, far more concerned with his personal timetable than his personal safety. And his pessimism in that respect was confirmed when, after another thirty minutes or so of complete lack of communication, the so-called train manager announced, with regret, that this particular train would be travelling no further that day. Would 'customers' make their way to platform eight and await the next train to Glasgow, which left at 13.51.

Kelly glanced at his watch. It was only just on midday. An already lengthy journey of around seven and a half hours was turning into a nightmare marathon. He was beginning to seriously wonder if the trip had been a good idea at all, particularly as he had embarked on it without making an appointment at the other end. But that, of course, had been deliberate. Kelly had been well trained in Fleet Street in the art of taking people by surprise. However, there were disadvantages, especially when you were paying your own fare and travelling second class on a saver ticket, instead of in the relative luxury of first class as provided by his former employers, and when the trip in question offered no reasonable chance, at least initially, of doing anything other than further depleting your already sorry bank balance.

On platform eight Kelly hunched his inadequate coat round his bony shoulders. It was a cold day and the platform seemed to have transformed itself into a wind tunnel. Things were not going well. At around 1.30, it was announced that the 13.51 was running half an hour late.

Kelly stamped his frozen feet on the unforgiving concrete and, wondering why he never seemed to remember to carry any gloves with him, rubbed his bare hands together in a vain attempt to warm them. There was quite a crowd on the platform awaiting the 13.51 to Glasgow, as was only to be expected when one Scotland train had been cancelled altogether. However, the proximity of so many bodies had done absolutely nothing to raise the air temperature. Kelly thought that might be because everybody's body temperature had already sunk to the same low.

The train eventually turned up at around 2.30 p.m., almost exactly an hour before Kelly should have been arriving in Glasgow. It drew to a halt with a kind of breathless weariness which may just have been Kelly's imagination – although, as he fought his way aboard along with all the other refugees from the earlier train, he began to think it wasn't his imagination at all. This new train had a definite aura of weariness about it. Every carriage seemed already to be packed. Younger, nimbler folk than him won the race for the few remaining seats. Kelly ended up leaning against a toilet door in the corridor. He was now convinced that his journey was pure unmitigated folly.

After, with extreme difficulty among the people and bags piled up in the corridor, moving away from the toilet for about the third time for passengers who wished to use it, Kelly had had enough.

'To hell with it,' he muttered. He slung his bag over his shoulder and began to push his way through the masses. He was moving into first class. After all, he still had a credit card that worked. Just.

Almost as soon as he sat down, the new train's manager was at his side waiting to check his ticket. Why was it, Kelly thought not for the first time, that the only thing which seemed to continually work well on Britain's beleaguered railway system was the checking of tickets? Particularly if he didn't happen to have the right one.

He handed over his credit card and tried not to wince as he signed a slip for more than a hundred pounds extra. He thought it was a disgrace that you couldn't have a decent journey across Britain, in reasonable comfort, without paying out that sort of money for first class, and was on the brink of telling the train manager so in no uncertain terms. After all, he had only moved into first class and been forced to fork out the extra dosh because of yet another breakdown in the rail system. He restrained himself, though, partly because he knew it would be a waste of time and partly because all he wanted to do was to shut himself off from the world for the rest of his journey. Naturally, he vowed to write to Richard Branson about it all when he got home. And, naturally, he knew that he'd never get around to doing it.

He settled back into his seat and closed his eyes. He had no desire to sleep. He just wanted to think. And he told himself that he really could not hope to arrive in Glasgow in any fit state to have even the remotest chance of succeeding in his mission, had he still been leaning against a toilet door.

It had not been difficult for Kelly to find out Alan Connelly's address. Karen Meadows was not his only police contact, which was just as well, because the way their last conversation had ended it had not seemed a good idea to ask her for any further information.

Instead Kelly had phoned George Salt, the retired policeman, now a civilian clerk at Torquay, who had been helping him out for years for a small consideration. Not cash, of course, that would have been open bribery and George Salt, in common with many of Kelly's contacts in all sorts of walks of life, would never have gone down that road, but was more than happy to take the odd pair of tickets to a hot soccer game or a voucher for a weekend away in a luxurious hotel.

Kelly sighed. The only problem was that when he had been in full employment as a journalist those sort of perks came his way from time to time and he had been quite content to pass them on in order to cultivate a contact. These days he had to dip into his own pocket.

And, with what had started off as very nearly an eight-hour journey now lengthened by at least three hours, Kelly had good reason to wonder whether or not the tickets to a hot boy-band concert in Exeter, acquired for George's eleven-year-old grand-daughter – teenage started early nowadays, apparently – had been even a halfway worthwhile investment.

The train seemed to make the correct progress through the North of England into Scotland, but then there was a twenty-minute wait outside Glasgow Central, caused, as the guard so helpfully explained, by being delayed in the first place which meant there was no platform available.

Ultimately, Kelly arrived just before 8 p.m., almost four and a half hours behind schedule.

It was raining heavily in Glasgow. Anxious not to arrive at the Connelly home too late in the evening, Kelly hurried to the taxi rank. There was a long queue, due partly to the bad weather, Kelly suspected, and to his immense frustration another fifteen minutes or so passed before he was able to climb into the back of a cab. The driver did not seem particularly enthusiastic when Kelly recited the address he had been given for Alan Connelly, and when, after twenty-five minutes or so, they approached the Belle View estate, Kelly could understand why.

Belle View was an extremely inappropriate name for one of the grimmest council estates Kelly had ever seen. The sprawling grey complex, a mix of rows of unappealing houses and tenement blocks, was spread over a surprisingly large area. Kelly guessed it had been built in the late sixties, a period of housing development all involved preferred to forget. The houses had small front gardens, almost all of which were totally uncared for, and the tenement blocks stood in rectangles of grass. Or what had once been grass. Broken bedsteads, old tyres and the twisted remains of abandoned bicycles were more in evidence than trees or flowers, and what grass there was had either grown tall and wild in ragged clumps, or more frequently had been worn to a powdery brownish sward. Connelly's family's address was 23 Primrose Close. As the taxi progressed further into the estate, Kelly noticed that every street seemed to be named after a flower. There was a Bluebell Close, a Gardenia Way and a Camellia Crescent, and the ill kept road which appeared to be the main drag through Belle View was called Cherry Blossom Avenue. Idly, Kelly wondered if cherry trees had originally been planted here. No sign of them survived, that was for certain.

Yet again Kelly questioned why he had even bothered to come to Glasgow. No wonder young Alan Connelly was a Walter Mitty. Anyone could be forgiven for developing an overactive imagination if this was what they came home to. Colonel Parker-Brown's description to Karen of a young man living out crazy fantasies, so much so that he could not be expected to succeed in the army, or anywhere else in life probably, began to make more sense with every second the cab passed through Belle View.

The driver slowed to a crawl as he entered Primrose Close. Number 23 was on the corner at the far end. Its garden was surrounded by a tall, neatly trimmed privet hedge, which stood out, spruce and vividly green in Belle View, where few house-holders had even attempted to bother with such niceties.

Kelly was able at once to ascertain that there was someone in. The lights were on both upstairs and down, an upstairs window was open, and as he opened the taxi door he could just make out the sound of voices – although it could have been a television – inside the house. Wondering if he would regret it, he paid the driver off, crossed the pavement, opened the freshly painted white gate ahead of him and walked up the short garden path.

Primrose Close was at least reasonably well lit and the lights from inside the house also illuminated the garden. Kelly could see clearly a square of tidy grass to either side of him, edged by a colourful border of winter bedding plants, mostly pansies, and a sprinkling of autumn crocuses.

He rang the shiny brass doorbell on the dark-stained front door. He seemed to wait a long time then, but eventually a boy of about fourteen or fifteen answered the door. Kelly guessed that this was probably Alan Connelly's younger brother. The boy was red-eyed, his hair dishevelled, his skin blotchy. He looked as if he had been crying.

Kelly felt like an intruder. It did not stop him. He was an old Fleet Street hand. He was used to intruding.

'Hi,' he said. 'Are either your dad or mum in?'

The boy nodded. He didn't even look interested. 'Dad, it's for you,' he called over his shoulder.

A small man, probably in his mid to late forties, came quickly to the door. He was slimly built and looked fit. He also looked remarkably like Alan Connelly.

'Hi,' said Kelly again. 'My name is John Kelly, I've come up from Devon. It's about Alan.'

The other man eyed him up and down, with only marginally more interest than had the boy who'd answered the door. And, like him, he looked as if he had recently been crying.

'Are ye from the army?' he asked eventually, in a voice with a heavy Glasgow accent.

Kelly dodged the question. 'I was with your son,' he said. 'I was with Alan the night he died.'

Connelly looked at him suspiciously.

'He was on his own. They told us he'd gone off on his own.'

Kelly nodded. 'Yes. That's right. He had. But I happened to meet him in a pub. We talked, and there were things that he said which still worry me.'

Kelly could see the curiosity flit across the man's face. I've cracked it, he thought. I've cracked it.

'You'd better come in.'

Kelly stepped into the hallway and pushed the door shut behind him. He already had something to think about. Colonel Parker-Brown had told Karen that Alan's father was a drunk, yet

98

not only was Mr Connelly totally sober, neither did he have the look of a drinker about him. And that was something Kelly knew about.

Connelly led the way into a living room which was both tastefully decorated and well furnished. A fair-haired woman, whom Kelly took to be Mrs Connelly, was sitting on the sofa. She was pretty, but there were dark shadows beneath her eyes and she looked pale to the point of illness. A girl of seven or eight sat on her lap, cuddling close. Kelly expressed his deepest sympathy for the loss of their son and succeeded in learning the Connellys' Christian names. They were Mary and Neil.

'All right, then, Mr Kelly,' said Neil Connelly, still formal, as he sat down on the sofa next to his wife and gestured for Kelly to take one of the room's two big easy chairs. 'What exactly have ye come all this way to tell us?'

Kelly went through it all then. Everything that had happened in The Wild Dog the night Alan had died, everything Alan had said to him, and how afraid the young man had seemed. Mary Connelly did not respond at all. It was almost as if she had not heard a word Kelly had said, so immersed was she in her own private grief. Neil Connelly seemed merely mildly puzzled.

'I wondered if your son had ever said anything like this to you,' continued Kelly. 'I wondered if, perhaps, what he had to say might mean any more to you than it would to me or to anyone else?'

'No,' said Neil Connelly, after a short pause. 'No. I do na understand it at all. Ma boy was very happy in the army, I'm sure of it. He was a good soldier. He liked the life. He was na unhappy. If he had been, he would have told us. We've always been a close family, Mr Kelly.'

'You hear about bullying in the army, Mr Connelly. Do you think Alan could have been the victim of bullying?'

'Ma boy could look after himself.'

'Of course. It's just that he seemed so frightened, and I think it might be important to find out why. He didn't seem like a young man who was happy in his life, not at all.'

Neil Connelly shrugged. 'He was drunk, wasn't he? They told me he was very drunk. And he wouldn't have been able to handle it. Our Al was na a drinker. He was only seventeen for Christ's sake. My wife and I have tried to bring our children up properly.'

'I'm sure you have, Neil.'

The other man frowned. 'Look, what are you? Army welfare? We've had someone from welfare here already—'

'I'm the man who's trying to find out exactly what happened to your son, Neil,' Kelly interrupted, dodging the question again. He looked around the room once more. Family photographs lined the wall. A picture of Alan, looking proud, in his army uniform, staring straight ahead from beneath his Fusiliers' blue beret with its distinctive red and white hackle, took pride of place. Next to it was a photograph of a second young man in similar uniform. They could have been twins.

'Another brother, I presume,' remarked Kelly casually.

Neil Connelly smiled for the first time. It was a weak smile but it lit up his face.

'No, that's me twenty years ago,' he said. 'We had a lot in common, my boy and me. I did fifteen years in the army, in the same regiment, the Devonshire Fusiliers, and they were some of the best years of my life.'

'Why the Devonshire Fusiliers?' Kelly asked. 'A regiment so far away from Scotland.'

'Ah, well, there's a bit of history in that,' Neil Connelly explained, coming to life a bit as he did so. 'My grandfather was a Devonian, from Plymouth, and he was called up to the Devonshires during the Second World War. Then, after the war, he stayed on as a regular. But my grandmother was a Scots lass, and when my grandfather retired from the army they moved up to Scotland. None the less, when my father decided to became a soldier, he wanted to join the same regiment as his da', even though it was based at the other end of the country. As for me, all I wanted was to be a Devonshire Fusilier from when I was just a scrap of a lad. Ma boy was just the same. We're a family of Fusiliers, Mr Kelly.'

Kelly studied the other man carefully. Neil Connelly, the way he described his family and the ordered, comfortable home in which they lived were not at all what he had been led to expect. Indeed, Connelly did not seem a bit like the picture of a bitter man, unemployed and probably unemployable, that Colonel Parker-Brown had painted to Karen.

'So, what've you been doing since you left the army?' Kelly asked conversationally.

'I came out to a good job, in the shipyard. I wanted to see my children grow up. I'd have stayed a fusilier till they kicked me out, but for that. It all went wrong in the end, of course, when they announced they were closing down my yard. We were just about to buy our own house, move out of this place. Then I was made redundant. Me and hundreds of others. We managed, though. Mary went back to nursing. She's an SRN and a good one.' He glanced at his wife, who still gave no indication that she was even listening to what was going on, with obvious pride. 'And I stayed at home to look after the kids for a bit.'

'So have you been out of work since then?'

'On and off. More off than on, I suppose. It's not easy to find work in Glasgow. But then last year I joined the post office. Postman. I like it. Doesn't pay great, but I like it.'

'So you're not out of work now.'

'No. I am na.'

Kelly thought about it. Had Parker-Brown been deliberately lying to Karen, he wondered? Or had he merely been misinformed.

'Look, what's this all about?' Connelly asked sharply.

'There may be things you should know about, Neil,' Kelly persisted. 'For a start, there was another alleged accidental death at Hangridge, only a few months ago.'

'Was there?' Kelly could detect a definite note of curiosity in Connelly's voice now.

'You didn't know, then?' Kelly was well aware that he was stating the obvious. He hadn't for one moment thought that the other man would know about the death of Craig Foster. He just wanted to stress the point.

'No.' There was a pause. Kelly waited. He wanted Connelly to be interested enough to come back at him, and was soon to be rewarded for his patience.

'What happened?'

'A young soldier was shot on a training exercise on the moors.'

Connelly shrugged. 'It happens,' he said. 'It's the army.'

'Yes, but it is another sudden death. And your son indicated that there were more.'

'My son was drunk. God bless him.'

Kelly had one last card to play.

'Mr Connelly, would you describe your son as a fantasist?'

'A what?'

'Did he live in a fantasy world, make up stories?'

'You have to be joking. You couldn't be more down to earth than our Alan. He was always a sensible lad.'

'So it would surprise you to know that his commanding officer told the police that Alan was a bit of a Walter Mitty?'

'Surprise me? It would bloody astonish me.'

'It's the truth, Mr Connelly.'

Neil Connelly narrowed his eyes, appearing to think hard.

'So you say,' he responded eventually. 'But how do I know that?'

'I promise you I'm telling the truth, Mr Connelly . . .'

'You're not from the army, are you? You're nothing to do with the army . . .' Connelly rose abruptly to his feet. His wife seemed to hold her daughter even more tightly to her, but did not look up. Kelly thought she must still be totally in shock. Neil Connelly looked angry now. 'You're a bloody journalist, aren't you? A vulture . . .'

Again Kelly avoided giving any information about himself. Instead he concentrated on trying to make Neil Connelly listen, on trying to convince the bereaved father that he had something to say that was worth listening to.

'Look, Neil. Colonel Parker-Brown even went so far as to say that Alan's days in the army were numbered because of his fantasising. He described him as a Walter Mitty.'

Neil Connelly sat down again on the sofa, as abruptly as he had risen from it. Kelly knew that he had at least succeeded in attracting the other man's attention again. He stared at Kelly long and hard before eventually making a reply.

'If my boy had been in any sort of trouble, he'd have told me,' he announced.

'Mr Connelly, I promise you, I'm telling you the truth,' Kelly repeated. 'I just think there are things that need looking into here. At the very least there's justification for doing a bit of digging, trying to find out if anything amiss did go on at Hangridge. Your son would have wanted that, I'm sure of it. Why else would he have talked to me the way he did? I need your help, Mr Connelly, if I'm going to take this any further. And I really think it should be taken further, don't you?'

Connelly stared at Kelly for a few moments longer, then he rose from his chair again and this time walked across the room to the mantelpiece, where he stood looking down at the pair of framed photographs taking pride of place. Two young men, proud and straight in the uniform of the Devonshire Fusiliers, looked back at him. One his own image from twenty years earlier, one that of an obviously cherished son.

After a few seconds he swung on his heel to face Kelly. His shoulders were back now, his jaw set and his gaze level and unblinking.

'This is an army family,' he announced. 'My grandfather went right through the Second World War with the Devonshires and was killed in the last push across Europe. My father served at Suez with the Devonshires. I did my fifteen years – Northern Ireland, the Falklands and, finally, the Gulf War. My boy was the fourth generation of Devonshire Fusiliers in this family. He was born to be a soldier, and he would have been a mighty fine one, whatever you or anyone else has to say.

'His death was a tragic accident. That's all. I'll not make trouble for the Devonshires. I'll not do it.

'I think you'd better leave, Mr Kelly.'

Eight

Kelly didn't wait to be told twice. He left at once. He had always known when to quit. Or, more exactly, when to back off. He didn't think somehow that his business with the Connellys was finished. His meeting with the father had in some ways not been as fruitful as he might have hoped, but, at the very least, he had learned that Colonel Parker-Brown may well have been deliberately misleading Karen.

He set off through the Belle View estate on foot until he spotted a pub which he thought it might just be possible for him to visit without having a broken glass thrust into his face, and then called the station taxi firm to come and pick him up.

Over a pint of his usual Diet Coke, he reflected on what he should do next. As he saw it, he had two choices. He could back off now. Dismiss Hangridge and young Alan Connelly from his mind and return to Torquay and to that novel. Or he could try to find Craig Foster's family and have one last crack at finding out if soldiers from the moorland barracks really were dying in mysterious circumstances.

Kelly had no doubt about what he should do. He told himself that he had no time to waste chasing fire engines any more. Not at his age and in his financial circumstances. He told himself that he could not afford a displacement activity on the scale that this one had already developed into.

In the taxi on the way back into the city centre, he reflected further. He ought to hightail it home and throw himself one hundred per cent into what passed for his work. Indeed, if he didn't do so, he dreaded to think what the future was likely to hold for him. He had taken a big gamble when he had decided to throw in his job at the *Argus* and take his chance as a novelist. And so far it was a gamble that didn't seem to be paying off.

He checked his watch. It was almost 10.30 p.m. He could not, however, go home that night – unless he took the sleeper, which he couldn't afford. Kelly reckoned he had been quite extravagant enough for one day. When he had finished the great novel and flogged it to a leading publisher for a cool half-million or so, everything would be different. Well, a man could dream. Only Kelly's dream was becoming less and less likely to become reality with every day that passed.

He booked into a cheap, downmarket but fairly clean-looking bed and breakfast establishment, about all he deserved, he thought, as he sat on the small divan bed with its once-white plastic headboard, and reflected on just how much he would like to visit the pub next door and have a real drink. No. Not *a* drink. Kelly would actually rather have liked to get blind drunk. The only problem was that he knew for certain, from thoroughly unpleasant past experience, that if he went out and got drunk that night, indeed if he went out and had just one alcoholic drink that night, then the next day he would do it again. And the next day. And the day after.

He settled for fish and chips from the still-open chippy he had noticed across the street, and, back in his room, tucked into the greasy contents of his paper-wrapped parcel which, as ever, smelled far more appetising than it tasted. He whiled away the rest of the evening watching repeats of old favourites like *Columbo* on Plus and *Absolutely Fabulous* on UK Gold. He congratulated himself on at least having managed to find a b & b with digital satellite TV. One way and another, Kelly, what with his near-addiction to computer games as well as spending more and more time, both day and night, watching TV, was in danger of growing square eyes, he reckoned.

It was gone midnight before he finally switched off the television. And he only did so then, because *The Vicar of Dibley* came on Gold after *Ab Fab*, and it reminded him of Moira and that he had yet again failed to contact her. It was too late now, and he had not even told her he was going away. In addition, if either she or the girls had tried to call him on his mobile, they would have found that it been switched off all day. It remained switched off. Kelly did not like, any more, having his life interrupted by something in his pocket ringing – even if he did find it difficult to recall what his life was exactly, at that point in time. And he knew he was playing an unpleasant sort of Russian roulette by not ensuring that Moira or the girls could always contact him, but there was no point, in even checking his messages now, he told himself, as he could do nothing constructive about anything until the morning.

He stripped off his clothes, crawled into the narrow bed and lay there awake for at least another couple of hours contemplating the mess he yet again seemed to be making of his life, and wondering what on earth had possessed him to travel the length of England on an off-chance, before finally, weighed down with his own inadequacies and troubled as ever by nagging guilt, he fell into a fitful sleep.

In the morning he woke feeling fresh enough, in spite of everything, which was one advantage, possibly the only advantage Kelly reckoned on a bad day, of not drinking.

He caught the first direct train to Newton Abbot, and once aboard, correctly seated in a second-class compartment this time, he tried not to think about Hangridge and the untimely death of Fusilier Connelly. It was, however, an extremely long journey back to Newton Abbot, even if this time the trip were to pass without any massive delay-causing incidents at all.

Kelly tried to sleep, but sleep wouldn't come. Once upon a time he would have wandered along to the buffet bar and downed a few large Scotches. That would have solved the problem. As it was, the prospect of yet another pint of Diet Coke left him cold.

He had bought several newspapers at the station and he made himself read them from cover to cover, even though he found them unusually uninteresting that day. He held out until just past Birmingham.

Then he switched on his mobile to make a call. Just the one call, he promised himself. He did not have any kind of address for Craig Foster, and he did not think he ought to push his luck with George Salt. So he decided that he would make one quick call to the *Evening Argus*, and ask Sally, the editor's secretary, with whom he had always had a good jokey relationship, to check out Craig Foster in the paper's cuttings library. He had no idea where Craig Foster came from – although he did hope that his home would turn out to be somewhere in the west rather than at the other end of the country – or how long he had been stationed at Hangridge. But Karen had said there had been stories written about the young man's death, and, at the very least, the *Argus* should have an inquest report on record.

Just as he started to dial the number, his mobile called him with a message from the previous day. It was Moira's daughter Jennifer, yet again wanting to know where he was. He promised himself he would phone to apologise as soon as he had made that call to the *Argus*.

Sally seemed genuinely pleased to hear from him.

'So, how are you, you old bugger,' she asked affectionately. Sally was a genuine Devon maid, born and bred in the South Hams, and, like all true Devonians, was inclined to use the word 'bugger' as a term of endearment.

Kelly had also been born and brought up in Devon, in Torquay, and he knew the form well enough, though he had often been amused by the reactions of foreigners.

'I'm fine, me lover,' he responded warmly. 'All the better for hearing your voice.'

'Yeah, yeah, me dear,' replied Sally sweetly. 'So, what do you want?'

'How do you know I want anything, me 'andsome?'

'Oh, I've always been able to read your mind, you bugger,' remarked Sally pleasantly. 'In any case, leopards don't change their spots. And, by the way, Kelly, I've got the afternoon off, so if you don't spit it out smartish you won't be getting it, whatever it is.'

Kelly grinned. He told her then about Craig Foster.

'As well as looking for him by name, you could try any cuts on the Devonshire Fusiliers, and Hangridge, too. It's some sort of address I'm after, most of all, or at least a town or a district. I do know there were stories, and there's bound to have been an inquest report, but goodness knows whether it would all have been filed or not, the way the library's been run down . . .'

They exchanged a few mutually comforting grumbles about how comprehensive the *Argus*' cuttings library had once been, and how, like most newspaper libraries, the culling of staff combined with switching to a computer database, without first loading it with back information, had caused standards to drop alarmingly. In spite of all that, Sally agreed to do the check as soon as she could and promised to call Kelly back when she had done so.

He settled into his seat. The sun was shining directly into his side of the train, which this time was mercifully only half full, and he suddenly felt extremely warm and comfortable. He would call Moira later, he decided, when he was a little nearer home. Within minutes the warmth and the gentle rocking movement of the train, combined perhaps with the satisfaction of having put something in motion, had lulled him off to sleep. And he woke with a start when his mobile rang half an hour or so later.

'I've found a few bits, Kelly,' came Sally's voice over the air waves. 'A page lead, back of the book, when Craig Foster died, the inquest report like you said, and a death notice. You're lucky. Deaths, marriages, and births, they still cut all of those. And he was a local lad, it seems—'

'That's great,' interjected Kelly excitedly. Death notices almost always gave full personal details including at least partial addresses. He loved getting a result like that, wherever it might lead, always had done. 'Will you read it to me.'

'Foster, Fusilier Craig Anthony. Aged seventeen. Much loved only son of Peter and Marcia Foster, of Grange Road, Babbacombe, Torquay. Killed in a military training accident. May 10th. Already greatly missed.'

A local lad and an address as well. Kelly could not have hoped for a better result. He told himself that this was fate, that he was destined to continue with his enquiries, at least until the next stage.

'Thanks a million, Sal,' he said. 'I can't believe you managed to find a death notice. That's bloody brilliant.'

'Yes, well, the computer system is actually extremely efficient, as long as the information has been pumped into it, you can always get it out easily enough,' said Sally. 'The problem is it can only tell you what somebody has already told it, if you see what I mean.'

'Ah, but nobody knows how to work the system better than you, Sal,' responded Kelly.

'I'll take that as a compliment, shall I?'

'Please do. It was meant as one. Well, very nearly . . .'

'If I were you Kelly, I'd quit while you're ahead.'

'I will. And thanks again, Sal.'

'Right. Do you want me to fax you the inquest report and the other story?'

'Yes, please.' He gave her his fax number.

'I owe you one, Sal, I really do,' he said.

'One? You owe me one? I'll send you an invoice, shall I?'

'Yeah, if you like, but you know better than most what I'm like at paper work . . .'

She was chuckling as he said a genuinely fond goodbye and ended the call. Sally, and the familiar banter between them, was one of the aspects of newspaper life which Kelly sorely missed. But there were even more which he was extremely glad to see the back of, he reminded himself.

He dialled directory enquiries. He knew, of course, that the service did not give out addresses. It was, however, an easy enough trick to ask for a P. Foster and pick a street number at random. Kelly asked for a P. Foster at number 7 Grange Road.

The reply came automatically, just as Kelly had hoped it would. 'I have a P. Foster at number 16, sir.'

Another result. Kelly switched off his phone, settled back into his seat, and within minutes was once more asleep.

He arrived back at Newton Abbot at around twenty past five, only a few minutes behind schedule. A miracle, he thought. With a bit of luck he could be at Babbacombe by around six, even in the rush-hour traffic, and he decided to go for it. Indeed, the truth was that he just couldn't resist.

He had automatically decided on the same surprise approach. It meant going in cold, but as an old Fleet Street hand Kelly knew well enough that the advantages of so doing almost always outweighed the disadvantages.

The traffic was reasonably light, with the bulk of it heading out of Torquay towards him as he made his way along the A380 through Kingskerswell and swung a left by the hospital out towards Babbacombe, which lay on the north side of the town, just a little nearer to Torquay town centre than his own district of St Marychurch.

Grange Road was a neat street of small pre-war semis in the heart of Babbacombe village, set back from the seafront. The whole area was in stark contrast to Belle View. Almost every house had a tidily manicured front garden and fresh paintwork.

It was already dark, and a reproduction Victorian carriage lamp attached to the wall next to the front door of number 16 caused Kelly to blink very rapidly. It shone directly into his eyes as he stood on the doorstep. He glanced over his shoulder. The street was very quiet. Yet again he had that feeling of being an intruder. Yet again he conquered any such misgivings, with the alacrity which came with years of experience as a professional intruder into other people's lives.

There was no doorbell. Instead, a brass ring doorknocker gleamed in the centre of the white painted door. However, Kelly did not need to use it. The door opened even before he had raised his right hand to the brass ring.

Before him stood a very thin, slightly unwell-looking woman, with unnaturally dark hair, dressed entirely in black from head to foot.

'Mr Stiles?' she enquired at once.

'Uh, no,' said Kelly hesitantly. He started to introduce himself.

'I'm—'

'But you are from Stiles & Merchant?' she interrupted swiftly.

'Uh, no,' Kelly repeated.

'Oh.' She looked puzzled.

'The undertakers,' she said, as if prompting him. 'Aren't you from the undertakers? I've been waiting all afternoon . . .'

It was Kelly's turn to look puzzled. Craig Foster had died more than six months ago, according to both Gerry Parker-Brown and the death notice in the *Argus*. Kelly didn't quite know what to say, so he merely shook his head.

'Oh,' the woman said again. 'I was expecting the undertakers . . .'

Her voice trailed away.

'I'm sorry,' said Kelly, making a conscious effort to regain both his brain and his voice. 'I didn't realise there had been a recent bereavement here. I wouldn't have come—'

She interrupted him then, staring at him curiously.

'Who are you, then? And what do you want?'

'I came about Craig. Your son. I'm so sorry. I'll come back another day.'

She stared a little longer, looking uncertain at first, and then appeared to make a decision.

'No,' she said. 'Don't go. Not if it's anything about Craig. Phillip wouldn't want that. I know he wouldn't. Please come in.'

Kelly was even more puzzled.

'I-I don't want to intrude,' he stumbled. He did, of course, but he didn't want to risk messing up the one and only opportunity he would probably have to get through to this woman.

'No, we've been wanting you to come,' she said, and opened the door wide for him to enter.

He did so at once. He realised that Mrs Foster must have mistaken him for someone else, but naturally he couldn't resist the invitation.

She led him into a small tidy kitchen and gestured for him to sit down at a very shiny, new, pine table. A black and white spaniel curled up on the mat by the back door, opened one eye and closed it again. Some house dog, thought Kelly, as he accepted Mrs Foster's offer of a cup of tea.

She poured from a teapot already on the table. The tea was a deep brown in colour, and Kelly could feel from the temperature of the mug she passed to him that it was only just warm. He reached for the sugar bowl and helped himself to four spoonfuls to be on the safe side, rather than his usual three. But the cool tea still tasted unpleasantly bitter and Kelly had to force himself to drink it.

'So, what have you come to tell us?' enquired Mrs Foster, and she sounded quite accusative.

'I was rather hoping you may have something to tell me,' responded Kelly.

She looked annoyed then.

'My husband spent the last six months of his life writing letters. All he wanted was to know exactly what happened to our Craig. That wasn't much to ask, surely? So far, we've not heard a word from the army since the first couple of weeks. And even then we got short shrift. My Phillip didn't want to make trouble, he wasn't that sort of man. He just wanted information, that's all. Somebody to talk to him properly.' Her voice softened. 'He worshipped our Craig, honestly, he did.'

Kelly thought quickly. Mrs Foster's attitude seemed very different to that of Neil Connelly, but, of course, six months later, she would at least have got over the initial shock of her son's death. He decided that he would almost certainly achieve more from this meeting if he was absolutely honest from the start.

'Mrs Foster, I'm not from the army,' he said.

'Not from the army?' Now, she looked more than puzzled. She looked alarmed. Kelly felt slightly guilty about even being in her home. But he had no intention of stopping.

'No, Mrs Foster.' He appraised the woman sitting opposite him. She looked drawn and worn out, as if life had dealt her one blow too many. Her eyes were dull. Kelly took a deep breath and started talking.

'Mrs Foster, I came to talk to you about how your son died. Look, I may be bothering you for nothing, and if so I apologise in advance, particularly at what is obviously a distressing time. But there has been another alleged accidental death at Hangridge—'

Kelly was about to tell the whole story, to explain how he had met Alan Connelly and what the young man had told him just minutes before he died. But Mrs Foster interrupted him.

'Another death?' she said, and her eyes were suddenly bright. 'That's three, then. Three in not much more than seven months, it must be.'

Kelly was completely taken aback.

'What do you mean, three?' he queried.

'Didn't you know?' Mrs Foster picked up the mug of tea on the table in front of her and sipped it gingerly, as if it were considerably hotter than Kelly knew it to be.

Kelly shook his head.

'Oh.' Mrs Foster took another sip of tea. She didn't seem to be in a hurry, but then, in spite of the instant spark of interest she exhibited when Kelly had begun to tell her about Alan Connelly, she didn't look like a woman who was capable of hurrying any more. Kelly realised that he must not put any pressure on her. He waited.

After a few seconds she started to speak again.

'Jossy was the first,' she said. 'The first we knew of, anyway. Jocelyn Slade, but they always called her Jossy. Craig did, anyway. She was Craig's girlfriend. Well, they hadn't known each other long and I've really no idea how serious they were about each other . . .'

'And she was stationed at Hangridge?' Kelly was puzzled and unwittingly echoed Karen's remark to Gerrard Parker-Brown. 'I didn't even know there were women in infantry regiments.'

'There aren't. Jossy was in the Adjutant General Corps. She was at Hangridge for infantry training before being sent to Northern Ireland with her own regiment. That's how she met our Craig—'

'Ah.' Kelly had interrupted Mrs Foster's flow and cursed himself. 'Please go on,' he encouraged. 'Will you tell me everything you know about Jossy's death.'

Mrs Foster nodded. 'That cut up about it, Craig was. She was eighteen, too, just a couple of months younger than our lad. She was shot. She died of gunshot wounds, just a few weeks before our Craig went. It wasn't right, you know. Craig always said it wasn't right. That's why my Phillip got on to it, you see. He was writing and phoning right up to when he died, wanting to know what happened. Exactly what happened, he said. But you know the army. They closed ranks on us, really, we never got told anything. That's what hurt, I think. Our boy dead and nobody even prepared to talk to us properly about it. He never got over it, Phillip, you know. He'd had a dodgy ticker for years, but he coped, did what the doctors told him. He'd learned to live with it, had Phillip. Till Craig went . . .'

Her voice tailed off. Kelly had a million questions and none of them were about Phillip Foster. But he knew that the moment had not yet come. If Marcia Foster was rambling, then it was because she needed to. Kelly had decades of experience of interviewing bereaved and distressed people. He knew better than to interrupt.

'. . . After our Craig died, well, Phil stopped taking care of himself, watching what he ate, taking regular exercise, like he'd been told. Stopped all of that. He began working all the hours God gave, to forget, I suppose, and he even took up smoking

113

again. Eventually his heart just gave out. So there you are. Six months ago I buried my only son, now I'm burying my husband.'

Kelly waited a few seconds before he spoke. 'Mrs Foster, how exactly did Jocelyn Slade die? Was her death also supposed to be a training accident?'

'No. She was on sentry duty. Standing outside the camp, by the main gates. They said she took her own life, shot herself. My Craig never believed it, you see. That was the thing. He said from the start that Jocelyn would never have killed herself. Not my Jossy, he used to say, not even after what they did to her. Not suicide. Not Jossy. But we took it all with a pinch of salt, to be honest, everything Craig said, because we knew he was that cut up, and, well, she was his girl. So if he accepted it was suicide, then he'd have blamed himself, wouldn't he. In some way. Bound to have done. And we'd never met Jocelyn, you see. But then when our Craig went too, no more than six weeks later, it was, well, you can't help wondering, can you? Something's not . . .'

'What did Craig think happened to Jossy? Did he think someone killed her? And if so, why?'

'He used to say Jossy hadn't committed suicide, that she'd been murdered because of things that had happened to her. We asked him what he meant, what had happened to her? And he just said there were some men in the army who wouldn't take no for an answer, and were untouchable. But he wouldn't say any more, and looking back, after he'd gone, we thought he might actually have been scared to say any more. But at the time, well. He liked to spin a bit of a yarn, did Craig, he liked a bit of drama, and we didn't take much notice at all, to tell the truth. Until he went too, that is. Looking back, Phil and I used to reckon there was something really important he hadn't told us. He kept going on about Jossy and him knowing things they shouldn't know. But he never said what, you see.'

Marcia Foster stopped abruptly. 'Look, who are you? If you're not army, who are you?'

Kelly did his best to enlighten her. It wasn't easy. He was a one-time journalist pretending to be a novelist, sticking his nose in where it didn't belong again. The story of his life, really, and now he no longer even did it for a living. It was actually quite tricky to make it halfway clear to Mrs Foster what he was doing getting involved in these deaths, not least because he wasn't quite sure himself.

Mrs Foster, however, did not seem to find it as bewildering as he did.

'Oh, a writer, are you?' she responded. 'That would explain it, then.'

'Yes,' said Kelly, who wasn't sure it explained anything, but was extremely pleased that she thought so. He told her then how his interest had been aroused, all about meeting Alan Connelly in the pub and what the boy had told him.

'I wish my Phil was here,' she said. 'He didn't have the strength to fight the way he would have done once. And nobody would listen to him. That's what finished him, I think. Do you know, we even had to fight to get Craig's belongings back, and we never got anything like all his stuff back, we were quite sure of that.'

'What about Jocelyn Slade's family? ' asked Kelly. 'What do they think about all of this?'

'We only ever knew of her mother, and Craig said she'd been ill for years. We wrote to her after Jossy died. My Phil was good at things like that. But we never heard back. And after Craig was killed, well, Phil wasn't interested in anything except that. Although Phil always did think there was a link between Craig and Jossy dying, but then he became so ill he just wasn't capable of following it through. And me, well, I hand my hands full looking after Phil. So, do you think their deaths were linked, Mr Kelly? Do you think our Craig and his Jossy were murdered?'

'I don't know, Mrs Foster. I don't know enough about anything yet. All I do know is that three young people have died suddenly and somewhat curiously, within a short period of time, and that the third one predicted his own death. "They killed the others, they'll kill me too," he said. What we do have here, Mrs Foster, is the makings of something extremely suspicious indeed. At the very least.'

Kelly felt quite excited as he climbed back into his car. Three deaths at Hangridge. What was going on in the barracks of the Devonshire Fusiliers?

It really did seem that he might have been right from the start, and that his gut instinct about Alan Connelly's death being suspicious had been spot on.

While he considered what steps he should take next, he reached in his pocket for his mobile phone and attempted to switch it on. The phone didn't seem to be working. He held it to the car's interior light and peered at the display panel. Damn. The battery was dead. He had forgotten to take his charger to Scotland the previous day and he supposed that he must have finally emptied the battery when he made his calls from the train. He hadn't switched it on since then. If Moira or the girls had been trying to call him, he wouldn't even know.

He checked his watch. It was almost 9.30 p.m. Still not too late to go round. They'd be pleased to see him.

It took Kelly less than fifteen minutes to drive from Babbacombe along the coast road, with its rows of pretty, flower-adorned private hotels, to Moira's St Marychurch street. He pulled to a halt outside her pale-blue-painted house and, as was almost customary, stayed in the car for a moment or two while he steeled himself for the visit. It was awful that he had to do that. But he couldn't help it.

After a couple of minutes he climbed out of the car, locked it, and then stepped across the pavement towards Moira's front gate. As he did so, he looked at the house properly for the first time. There were no lights on. No lights at all. Yet there were always lights on after dark, because Moira could no longer leave the house and one of the girls was always with her. And he knew that even when she was trying to sleep they left a low light on.

Kelly's heart sank into his belly. He rang the doorbell. He hammered on the door. He called through the letterbox. There was no response. There really was nobody in.

He turned his back on the house and leaned against the front door. It was a cool evening but he realised that he was sweating. The palms of his hands were damp and the brow of his head felt as if it was on fire. He closed his eyes. He was shaking.

'Oh, my God,' he muttered to himself. 'Oh, my God. It can't be. Not yet, surely. She can't have . . .'

Automatically, he reached into his pocket for his phone before remembering that it was not working. There was a phone box at the end of the road. He took off for it at a run. He didn't somehow trust himself to drive his car the short distance.

When he got there, he had to fish out his diary to look up Jennifer's mobile number. He fed pound coins into the phone and dialled.

'We've been trying to reach you since this morning, John,' she responded at once. 'Mum got so bad in the night that we called the doctor in the early hours. We were going to call you as well, but she wouldn't let us. You know what she's like. She said she'd be fine once the doctor had given her something, and she didn't want your night's sleep disturbed because you get up so early to write. Anyway, the doctor made her as comfortable as he could, but . . . but, I guess there's not much left that he can do. Not any more. And he rang later to say he'd got her a place in the hospice at Newton Abbot. We're all with her now . . .'

'I'm on my way,' said Kelly.

He walked briskly back to the MG, trying to calm down. Moira wasn't dead, but she was dying. That was the message, more or less, and was only what had been expected for some time. None the less, he was still trembling. It had really shaken him to arrive at Moira's house and find it locked up and dark. And, as ever, the guilt ate away at him in a totally physical fashion, as if some vicious alien creature was gradually devouring his internal organs. He hadn't been in touch for two days and Moira had refused to let him be disturbed in the night because he was writing. Which was actually a very bad joke.

Nine

The hospice was in a modern purpose-built building on the outskirts of Newton Abbot. Kelly had been there once before, to visit an old friend who had died in the hospice the previous year, and had hoped never to have cause to step foot in the place again.

When he had made his first visit, the atmosphere had not been what he had expected. The hospice was a calm and peaceful establishment where the nursing was both unobtrusive and highly efficient, as well as noticeably caring. Kelly thought the staff who worked there were remarkable. It was not a job he could do, that was for certain. However you dressed it up, people went into a hospice to die, and Kelly didn't think he could cope with that.

He tapped lightly on the door to Moira's room. Jennifer opened it, smiled and ushered him in. All three girls were gathered round Moira's bed. But they rose to leave almost as soon as Kelly arrived.

'You'll want to be alone with Mum,' said Jennifer. 'In any case, we could do with a cup of tea or something.'

Kelly nodded. As ever, none of the girls had uttered a word of criticism. They did not know, of course, that to his further shame, Kelly was not at all sure that he did want to be alone with Moira, but he could not possibly say so. He sat by the bed, very close to her, and put his hand over one of hers.

Moira smiled weakly at him. She looked terribly ill, but Kelly could see that she was genuinely pleased to see him.

'I'm so sorry . . .' he began.

Moira kept smiling. 'Aren't you always?' she said very quietly.

'I guess, I am,' he smiled back.

'You do love me, though, John, don't you?'

'Oh yes, my darling, I love you, I really do love you.'

118

That was easy. Seeing her lying there, so terribly poorly, he felt quite overwhelmed by love. But he also knew that the manner of his love for Moira had all too often been inadequate. A psychologist, who had seemed to Kelly to be blessed with far more common sense than most of his kind, had once told him that the trouble with love is that it means different things to different people. Kelly was all too aware that while it was the absolute truth that he loved Moira dearly, it did not necessarily mean that he loved her in the way she loved him. Moira was so much more steadfast than him, for a start. She had never let him down, not once in ten years, which was certainly more than Kelly could say.

'I love you, too, John.'

'I know that, darling. You don't have to tell me. Don't tire yourself . . .'

'No, I want to tell you. There's so much I want to say, John, you won't lose touch with the girls, will you?'

'No, of course not.'

'They'll be all right, all of them, I'm sure. I had good insurance, as you know, so there'll be a little bit of money for them each, and there's the house, of course. But Jennifer is only nineteen. It's very young to be left on your own. And Lynne's only a couple of years older. At least Paula is married and has a family of her own, and I know Lynne and Jennifer can visit her and Ben whenever they want, but none the less . . .'

Moira's voice tailed off. Kelly didn't know quite what to say.

'She looks upon you as her father, you know that, John,' Moira continued. 'You've been a damned sight better to her than her own father ever was, that's for sure.'

Jennifer's own father had beaten his wife and more or less ignored his daughters. Everything in life is relative. Kelly hoped to God that he had been better to all of Moira's girls than Peter Simmons had been. But he knew only too well that he had been a bloody lousy father to his own son. To Nick. It was funny how life paid little tricks like that.

'I look upon Jennifer as my daughter, Moira,' Kelly said. And that was almost true, too. But then, Jennifer had put few demands on him, which had made it all right. Kelly was never very good at coping with demands.

'So, you'll keep an eye on her, spend some time with her.' Moira's voice was little more than a whisper now. Kelly could see that even the smallest exertion drained her.

'Of course I will.'

Kelly was distinctly uncomfortable. Moira was giving him instructions about what she would like him to do after she was dead. That was perfectly clear. And yet, as ever, the 'd' word was never actually used. Kelly found himself once more wishing he wasn't at her bedside to hear this. Wasn't with her at all. It was dreadful, he knew, but he just wanted to be anywhere in the world, doing anything, absolutely anything at all, other than sitting at Moira's bedside watching her die, while knowing that the terrible reality of what was happening would never be addressed. Not ever. Moira had been a nurse, and yet in spite of that, or maybe because of that, she had never wanted to discuss any aspect of her illness and what it meant. Quite possibly, because she knew only too well exactly what it meant.

'Don't try to talk, darling,' he said. 'Don't tire yourself. You just rest and I'll stay here beside you.'

He squeezed her hand and felt her squeeze back. But it was almost imperceptible. Her eyes were closed. She seemed to be drifting off again. After a bit, he wasn't sure if she was sleeping or unconscious.

He rang the bell for a nurse. One came very quickly, leaning over Moira and gently taking her pulse.

'It's hard to say, really, exactly what's going on,' she said. 'But as long as she's peaceful, not in too much pain, not distressed, well . . .' She straightened up from the bed, just a young woman, a slip of a thing with long pale hair tied back in a ponytail, little more than a girl, and yet doing this extraordinary job. Kelly didn't know what to say to her.

The nurse turned to face him directly. 'Well, that's the best we can hope for now,' she said quietly.

Kelly nodded. Jennifer and Paula returned as the nurse left. Kelly saw that they both looked worn out.

'Look, I'll stay with your mother tonight,' he told them. 'Why don't you both go home, get some rest. Neither of you got much last night, did you?'

The girls, in particular Jennifer, protested at first but

eventually gave in to their obvious exhaustion and agreed to leave. At least this is something I can do for them, Kelly thought, at least I can give them the chance to rest.

One of the nurses brought him a cushion and a blanket, and he settled in the armchair by the bed, watching Moira for any change. Her breathing was shallow. Her eyes were closed. She lay very still. Kelly found the whole situation quite terrifying.

His chair was not particularly comfortable and his mind was in turmoil. He did not think there was a chance of him sleeping a wink, and indeed he did not want to sleep. He wanted to watch over Moira. That was, after all, what he was there for. He could hardly bear to think about what she must be going through, lying there just clinging on to life. Periodically a nurse visited to check on Moira. Once, she asked him if he would like a cup of tea, an offer he gratefully accepted. Midnight came and went, then one, two and three o'clock. But from then on, it seemed that he was not aware of very much until Jennifer returned in the morning. He was disturbed by the sound of a door opening and someone moving around in the room, and he opened his eyes to see her there, just as she gave Moira a kiss on her forehead.

'Hi,' he said, rubbing his fingers over his stubbled chin and his tongue across furry teeth. 'I-I must have dozed off.'

'That's allowed, John.' Jennifer smiled at him. She looked like a different person this morning from the exhausted young woman he had sent off home the previous night. Her skin glowed, her hair shone from an obviously recent shampoo, and her eyes were bright and clear. She seemed totally refreshed.

Kelly glanced at his watch. It was only 7.30 a.m. But Jennifer had obviously managed a good night's sleep. Kelly wondered at the resilience of youth.

'How's she been?' Jennifer asked.

Kelly hesitated for a moment. The bitter truth was that he hadn't a clue. Although he would not have believed it possible, he must have slept for at least four hours, and even based on the time he had been awake before that, just sitting and watching Moira, he did not know how to answer Jennifer's question.

How had Moira been? Asleep or unconscious? He did not know the answer to that. Waiting to die? That was the correct answer, he reckoned, but it was one you did not give. Not in this family, anyway. Maybe not in most. Kelly didn't know. He had never spent the night sitting beside the bed of a dying woman before. And he rather hoped he never would again.

'The same,' he said, eventually.

'Ah.' Jennifer smiled tenderly down at her near-comatose mother. Kelly stood up, stretching aching, cramped limbs. One leg had gone to sleep. He held on to the foot of the bed as he made his way clumsily over to where Jennifer was standing.

'Thank you for staying with Mum,' she said.

Kelly just nodded. He didn't reckon he deserved any thanks. Not with his track record.

He stared down at the recumbent figure on the bed. He couldn't explain quite what he felt. At that moment, he possibly loved Moira more than ever before. And yet, at the same time, he could barely recognise her as the woman he had shared his life with. She had changed quite dramatically since he had last seen her, only a couple of days earlier. She was so horribly thin, wasted really, and deathly pale. But it wasn't that. It was more that the very core of her no longer seemed to be there. As if her soul had somehow already left her. She just didn't seem to be Moira any more.

Then she opened her eyes.

Kelly felt a hot, sweet rush of shock course through his body. He realised then, that although he had not even formulated the thought, he hadn't ever expected Moira to open her eyes again. But her eyes brought her to life again. She was back. Perhaps not for long, but she was back.

'Good morning, darling,' said Jennifer, sounding wonderfully normal, if a little more gentle in her greeting than she would have been were her mother well. That was, however, the only difference.

Kelly tried to wish Moira good morning, too. The words stuck in his throat. He could not bring himself to wish for her to have another day in this life in the state she was in. He did not wish to see her suffer any more. He hadn't a clue what to say. He just couldn't speak. This whole bedside scene seemed like a kind of charade to him.

He leaned forward and took Moira's hand. The tears were pricking the backs of his eyes. He felt he did not have the right to cry, because he considered his behaviour throughout so much of Moira's illness to have been thoroughly tardy. And yet he did care. He really cared.

'You're still here, then.' Moira, quite incredibly, Kelly thought, managed a small wan smile. It seemed to him even more incredible that she had managed to speak, in an unreal hoarse whisper, forcing the words out as if they caused her real pain, which they almost certainly did. Then she winced and sank deeper back into the pillows. The effort of managing those few words, of making contact again with a world she had almost left behind, had obviously been extreme. She was awake, but she was even weaker than she had been the previous evening.

Kelly just nodded. He could feel his eyes filling up with tears. He was fighting to regain control. Jennifer turned to look at him.

'You can go home now, John,' she said, speaking to him almost as gently as she had addressed her mother. 'Lynne and Paula will be here any minute. They're just making some phone calls and sorting one or two things out, but they won't be long. You have to work, John. Mum wouldn't want you to stop.'

Kelly hesitated, ashamed of himself yet again when he realised how much he wanted to get out of that sickroom. But he mustn't let that show. He really mustn't.

'No, I'll s-stay, of course I'll stay,' he said.

Then he felt Moira squeeze his hand, and somehow she managed to find the strength to do so rather more forcefully than she had the previous night. Her eyes were closed again and, for a moment, he thought that the grip was just a reflex action. He squeezed back. It seemed all that he could do. Then Moira spoke again, eyes still shut, gripping his hand with more strength than he would have thought possible. The voice was even weaker than before, but the words were strong enough.

'Go home, John, get writing, you idle bastard,' Moira ordered. And she took her hand away from his.

Kelly's throat tightened involuntarily. It was almost as if he were choking. He was finding it hard to swallow and even harder to breathe normally. He was very close to breaking down. He feared that he was going to make a complete fool of himself and knew that he would only embarrass Moira, who had never been one for displays of emotion.

123

'I'll see you both later, then,' he muttered, as he headed gratefully for the door.

Once outside in the corridor, he could no longer control himself. The tears he had tried so hard to contain began to fall. The trembling and shaking he had experienced the previous night, when he had, for a moment, really thought that Moira was gone, overwhelmed him again.

He knew there was a gents' toilet at the end of the corridor and he headed for it in a hurry. The tears were falling freely, rolling down his face into his shirt collar, and he was no longer able even to attempt to stop their flow. He broke into a run, nearly knocking over a nurse coming out of the room next to Moira's. Afraid that she might try to speak to him, he did not pause to turn towards her, let alone apologise. Instead he ran all the faster, flinging open the door to the gents' and throwing himself in. Only when he had managed to lock himself into a cubicle, did he finally let go. And then he just cried and cried.

Great sobs wracked Kelly's body. All the pent-up emotions of the last few months poured out of him. He felt as if he was never ever going to stop weeping. And he wasn't even sure that he wanted to.

For several minutes, Kelly just gave in totally to despair.

Eventually he did stop weeping, of course.

He dried his tears, splashed cold water on his red, swollen eyes, then set off for the car park, keeping his head down. He didn't want anyone to see that he had been crying.

Once inside the little MG, he rummaged in the glove department for the battery-operated shaver he kept there. Kelly had been an on-the-road journalist for virtually the whole of his adult life, until just a few months ago. He always carried his passport and a major credit card in full working order. And he always had basic toiletries to hand. Old habits died hard.

As he ran the shaver over his stubbled jaw, he used his mobile to call Nick. He wanted to warn him of Moira's deterioration. But even though it was not yet quite eight o'clock, there was no reply either from Nick's home number or his mobile. However, Nick, unlike his father, was naturally an early riser and would already be well into his working day. He worked from home but,

124

even if he was in, was inclined, Kelly knew, to ignore his phone if he was busy on the computer, which seemed to demand so much of his time.

Kelly left a short, sad message explaining that Moira was now in a hospice, and then contemplated what to do next.

He needed a cup of tea, he reckoned, before he could even think straight. His mouth felt dry and his tongue and teeth were furry. He also wanted to clean his teeth and have a quick wash, and he knew exactly where to go to achieve all three aims.

He started the engine, saying a small prayer as he did so, because he had left his mobile phone plugged into the car charger all night. The battery seemed to have remained healthy enough. The car started on the second turn. Kelly headed on to the Torquay road but pulled into the first lay-by not far out of Newton Abbot, where a mobile, roadside snack bar was invariably to be found just yards away from a Portakabin public convenience. Kelly visited the loo first and quickly completed his toilet before buying two paper cartons of tea at the snack bar. He sniffed them appreciatively as he ambled back to his car. Bob, the owner, made good strong tea with proper tealeaves and was always generous with the sugar.

Kelly drank one of the cartons of tea almost straight down, scalding his tongue, which at least might take some of the fur off it, he reflected, because cleaning his teeth had only half done the job. Then he began to attempt to plan his day. He knew all too well that there was only one way for him to cope with emotional turmoil. He needed to bury himself in his work. And yet the thought of working on his novel held even less appeal than usual.

The Hangridge affair, on the other hand, was becoming quite fascinating.

He used his mobile to try to call Karen Meadows.

She was not in her office yet, which he supposed was not really surprising as it was still only twenty minutes past eight, and neither was she answering her mobile phone. He would have to try again later.

In any case, he now knew exactly what his next move was going to be. He wanted to talk to Jocelyn Slade's mother.

Mrs Foster had been able to supply him with an address for Mrs Slade, the mother of her son's girlfriend, although she had told Kelly she could not swear that it was current. Margaret Slade lived in Reading. Kelly thought for a moment before deciding to go home first. It might be helpful for him to log onto the Net and do a little research into the Devonshire Fusiliers before making any more Hangridge enquiries, and a shower and a change of clothes might also be a good idea, he reflected.

Then he would set off to drive to Reading, a journey he would expect to take between three and three and a half hours on a bad day, and yet again he would arrive unannounced. So far, his policy had provided plenty of results.

Kelly's brain was buzzing again. He had always so much more enjoyed looking into other people's lives rather than his own.

Ten

Karen had not answered her phone because she was on her way to Totnes with Gerrard Parker-Brown. He had phoned the previous afternoon to ask if she could sneak a morning off work to visit a rather special antiques fair that he had just heard about.

'I know it's short notice, but if we get there for the start we could both be back on parade by early afternoon,' he had said.

To her utter astonishment, she had heard herself agreeing almost without hesitation. And now she was sitting alongside Gerry in his black Range Rover, studiously avoiding all calls. Her excuse for, in effect, bunking off work had been an extremely vague muttering about an important community meeting. She could not remember when she had last done such a thing, if indeed she had ever done such a thing. And she knew perfectly well that it was the opportunity of spending time again with the man, as much as attending the event, which had caused her to behave in such an out of character manner.

He had picked her up, this time without an army driver, promptly at 8.15 a.m., and even at that hour of the morning conversation between them came alarmingly easily, she reckoned.

'I collect military memorabilia among other things, and this fair is allegedly going to have some really good stuff on sale,' he told her enthusiastically. He seemed to have an immense capacity for enthusiasm and it was a quality that Karen greatly appreciated.

They spent a couple of hours at the fair, which was in a huge barn on the outskirts of Totnes. Although it turned out to be rather disappointing in terms of the military memorabilia, Gerry did not seem unduly put out and Karen was impressed by the knowledgeable way in which he chatted to dealers.

As ever, she thoroughly enjoyed rummaging around at the

various stalls, and while she was negotiating to buy a rather beautiful, nineteenth-century, French candlestick she became aware of him drifting away from her side. But within little more than a couple of minutes he was back, beaming at her and triumphantly brandishing a small, but rather lovely, silver dagger brooch, which he promptly pinned to the lapel of her jacket.

'I thought a dagger was rather appropriate for a police detective,' he told her.

'Oh, Gerry, no, I couldn't possibly . . .' she began.

'Don't be silly, it cost nothing. Less than a tenner. And I want you to have it.'

She gave in gracefully, and he had another surprise for her as they prepared to leave the fair.

'Are you hungry?' he asked.

'Ravenous,' she replied, wishing, as she invariably did, that that were not so often the case. 'But we haven't really got time to go and eat somewhere, or I haven't, anyway.'

He nodded. 'Nor me. But, well, you see, I knew we were going to be pushed for time, so I took the liberty of preparing a bit of a picnic. Pretty rough and ready, I'm afraid.'

It turned out to be not so rough and ready at all. Back in the Range Rover, parked in a corner of the field allocated as car park for the antiques fair, he produced a Thermos flask of hot coffee and bacon sandwiches, which, made with really crispy bacon and fresh crusty bread, were wonderfully crunchy and quite delicious in spite of being cold.

'How did you know bacon sandwiches are my absolute favourite food?' she asked.

'I didn't, but they're mine, particularly when I make an early start.' He smiled at her. 'Something else we have in common.'

She smiled back. And it seemed perfectly natural for him to lean across the car and kiss her gently on the lips. It was a very brief kiss, but this time it was much more than merely a kiss of friendship, and she could sense the promise in it with her whole being. He tasted and smelt a little of bacon, but that just seemed to make him all the more attractive. And he had such absolutely beautiful eyes. Feelings she had denied for so long were beginning to make themselves known to her again, and she was not at all sure she could fight them off. Or that she wanted to any more.

128

He pulled away, touching her lightly on the cheek with the fingers of one hand as he did so, and settled back into the driver's seat, silently watching her. She did not try to speak. She had no wish to spoil the moment.

'Well, I suppose I'd better drop you off at Torquay police station or I expect the entire area will be overrun by a major crime wave,' he said.

She laughed and nodded her assent. She really did have to be back at work. None the less, she felt vaguely disappointed.

'Tell you what, how about lunch somewhere on Sunday, when we both have more time, hopefully?'

Her spirits rose at once. And she couldn't be bothered even to pretend to deliberate.

'That would be great,' she said.

She was in her office well before one o'clock, still in extremely high spirits. Yet again Gerry had not mentioned the Alan Connelly affair, and this time Karen had not felt inclined to do so either. In fact, rather to her surprise, she had managed to put any vague misgivings she had about either the colonel or his regiment completely out of her mind.

And, in spite of trying to tell herself that she must proceed with caution and remember past mistakes, she was still feeling immensely good-humoured when she finally returned Kelly's call more than an hour later.

'So, what have you been up to, you old bugger,' she enquired cheerily.

Kelly told her at once about the third death at Hangridge. And that was the end of her good humour.

'Shit,' she said. 'Shit!'

'I assume you weren't told about Jocelyn Slade.'

'No, I bloody wasn't,' she responded.

'But I thought you'd checked the records at the coroner's court.'

Karen cursed herself. It hadn't occurred to her that it would be necessary. Not at this stage, anyway. Even before their two social meetings, she hadn't really believed that the commanding officer of the Devonshire Fusiliers would deliberately mislead her, that he would fail to tell her about a death at his barracks.

Now, particularly since experiencing the closeness she had felt for Gerry Parker-Brown that morning and the promise of that kiss, she felt quite betrayed. She had to force herself to concentrate on her conversation with Kelly.

'I checked the records specifically on Craig Foster,' she said. I didn't ask the court to check for any other deaths at Hangridge.' She thought for a moment.

'They have a brand new clerk at the coroner's court. Old Reggie Lloyd remembered everything and would probably have volunteered the information.' She paused. Kelly didn't say anything.

'Oh shit,' she said again.

'Ah,' said Kelly.

Karen tried to sort out in her mind what she should do next.

'Look, where are you, Kelly?'

'I'm at home.'

'Right. I have to check out officially what you've told me, Kelly. It changes everything. Don't take this any further, will you? Please don't do anything at all until I get back to you, all right?'

'Sure,' said Kelly.

Kelly smiled as he drove slowly along a dull red-bricked street looking for Margaret Slade's address. He had lied to Karen, of course. He had already arrived in Reading when she called him, and he'd known she would not approve of him seeking out Jocelyn Slade's mother, so he had decided at once not to tell her. The lie had come quickly and easily enough, and he had absolutely no intention of heeding her plea for him to do nothing until he heard from her further.

Mrs Slade's home turned out to be a flat above a chip shop in what Kelly reckoned must surely be the most unattractive part of a town, which, with its towering central buildings and lack of any discernible sense of identity, he considered to be altogether thoroughly unappealing.

Kelly rang the bell four times before Margaret Slade finally answered. He had felt it in his bones that she was inside. And he would have stood leaning on the doorbell for the rest of the day, if necessary. He wasn't giving up. This was getting important.

The woman who eventually answered the door looked wan, pale and shaky, her wispy, obviously dyed, reddish-brown hair framing an unnaturally white face. It took Kelly five seconds to realise that she was drunk, even though it was still quite early in the day, not long after two in the afternoon. But this was not the sort of drunkenness you associate with closing time in a pub or the end of a wild party. This was the drunkenness of a seasoned alcoholic. And Kelly recognised it instantly. He'd had plenty of experience, after all. Alcoholism, he suddenly suspected, had been the mystery illness Craig Foster didn't tell his parents about, and quite possibly hadn't been told about himself by Jossy.

Margaret Slade looked at him with unseeing eyes, as he greeted her courteously.

'I don't buy or sell anything at the door and you've got no chance at all of converting me to any religion that's ever been invented,' she said. She stood holding onto the door and swaying very slightly along with it, as it moved on its hinges.

He grinned.

'I'm not buying or selling, and I'm certainly not preaching,' he replied.

'Ah.' He could see that she was finally focusing on him, albeit with some difficulty, as if considering the situation. She looked puzzled. 'I must have paid the rent,' she went on. 'It goes straight out of my social.'

She frowned at him, in considerable bewilderment, it seemed. Kelly didn't say anything.

'And Michael's just turned seventeen, he doesn't have to go to school.'

She leaned a little closer to Kelly and he was engulfed in a cloud of stale alcohol. But he didn't mind much. Kelly was a bit like a reformed smoker who gets at least some kind of kick out of inhaling other people's smoke. It was sad, he knew, but even old and second-hand alcoholic vapours were not totally repugnant to him.

'So, who the fuck are you?' she asked. And then, before giving him the chance to reply, continued with: 'I don't know you, do I?'

Kelly shook his head. 'It's about you daughter, Mrs Slade.'

'My daughter?' The eyes went blank again, her mouth tightened. 'I don't have a daughter. Not any more.'

'I know. I'd like to talk to you about her death—'

'You're from the army,' Margaret Slade interrupted. 'Well, you can fuck off. I hate the fucking army. I never wanted my Joss to join in the first place, and she'd still be alive too, if she hadn't. I reckon. So go on, then. I've told you, haven't I? Fuck off.'

She pushed the door as if she were about to shut it in his face.

'No, Mrs Slade, I'm not from the army.'

Margaret Slade wasn't listening. The door kept closing on him. Kelly put his foot in it. It was a total myth that journalists were always doing that. Kelly could only remember even attempting to do so just once before in his life, and as this time a small rather frail woman was leaning against the door trying to close it, rather than a large fit man, the process was at least not so painful as he remembered it being on the previous occasion.

He went for broke.

'Look, I think there is a possibility that your daughter was murdered, Mrs Slade,' he told her through the fast-closing gap between the door and its frame.

He knew he had no right to say that. Not yet, anyway. He had no hard evidence, just a hunch. But he was quite determined to get to talk to Mrs Slade properly. Or, as properly as her condition would allow. And he suspected that only shock tactics would work with her.

He felt the pressure on the door lessen. Margaret Slade eased away a little, releasing her hold on the door, and he took the opportunity to step inside, closing the door behind him.

'So who are you, then?' she asked.

'I'm just a man who doesn't like lies and cover-ups,' he said, realising that he sounded rather trite and pretentious, but he couldn't help it. And, strangely enough, it was pretty much the truth.

He explained to her straight away, and as best he could, exactly who he was and how he'd got involved.

'This Alan Connelly, when did you say he died?'

'Just four days ago.'

'Four days ago,' she repeated carefully.

'That's three, then,' she went on, after a small pause.

132

'I didn't realise that you knew about Craig Foster,' responded Kelly.

'Craig Foster, the lad Jossy was going out with? I don't know anything about him at all. What's happened to him, then?'

'He was killed just weeks after your Jocelyn. A training accident, allegedly. He died of gunshot wounds.'

'Oh, my God.' Margaret Slade sounded genuinely upset. 'He was ever such a nice kid. He and Jossy had only just started going out together. I never met him before . . . before she died. But he came to the funeral, you know. And he seemed ever so cut up.'

'Mrs Slade, if you didn't know about Craig, then what did you mean when you said: "That's three, then."'

'What?' Now, Margaret Slade just seemed bewildered. Kelly could almost see her brain cells fighting their way through the alcohol. 'Three? Yes. There was a lad who died at Hangridge a few months before Jossy, I think.'

She paused. Kelly was practically on the edge of his chair, but he said nothing. The news he had given Mrs Slade seemed to have sobered the woman up somewhat. But Kelly didn't dare push her.

'Neither Jossy nor Craig would have been there when it happened,' she continued. 'And, as far as I'm aware, neither of them even knew about it. The army tend to forget things like that, don't they? They're not likely to tell the new recruits about the ones who've come to a sticky end, are they?'

Kelly found himself sitting ever closer to the edge of his chair.

'So what happened to this boy, then?'

'He killed himself too. Or so they said. I didn't think anything about it at the time, but you begin to wonder . . .'

'And how exactly did he allegedly kill himself?'

'I don't know. Do you know, I don't think I ever asked. Now isn't that extraordinary.'

Kelly didn't think it was that extraordinary. He reckoned Mrs Slade's brain would turn on and off according to the amount of alcohol swimming around in her system. She had appeared to be surprisingly lucid through most of their conversation, but then, so did a lot of alcoholics. He doubted she was very often capable of stringing facts together and coming to a conclusion.

'Who are *they*? Who told you about him?'

She looked completely blank.

'I don't know, really I don't,' she said. 'It was after the funeral. Another soldier, I think. Not Craig. No, not Craig. Like I said, I doubt he ever knew. An older man. I made a bit of a fool of myself, you see. I'd had a couple, of course. But it wasn't that. I just broke down that day. I blamed myself . . .'

She gestured around the flat. Kelly had been so caught up in what she was saying that he had barely taken anything else in. She seemed to be inviting him to look around, so he did.

The place was a tip. The floors were covered in stained carpeting, the walls were so murky it was hard to see what colour they had started out, and there was very little furniture. Instead, boxes were piled against every wall alongside tottering heaps of old newspapers and magazines.

'I didn't give Jossy much of a childhood, nor much of a home either,' Margaret Slade continued. 'We always seemed to be in a mess. Mind you, I defy anyone married to my old man not to have got themselves into a mess. That bastard. But when they told me that my Joss had killed herself, well, I just blamed myself, you see. I thought it was all my fault.'

'You didn't question it?'

'No. I didn't.' She looked confused. 'Why would I have done? This officer came round and I just believed everything he said. He was that sort. And I felt so dreadful. I just wanted to kill myself, too.'

She picked up a glass from the top of one of the boxes. It looked as if it contained whisky. She drained most of it in one.

'And, in a way, that's what I've been doing ever since,' she said.

'But when you learned there'd been another suicide, did that really not make you think at all?'

Margaret Slade laughed in a dry, humourless sort of way.

'I don't do a lot of thinking, really,' she said. 'I prefer to have a drink. You may have noticed.'

She had a self-awareness, a knowledge of her own behaviour, which was unusual among alcoholics, who were more often than not in total denial, Kelly thought. He had been, anyway.

Kelly decided to ignore her response.

134

'Mrs Slade, did your daughter leave a suicide note of any kind?'

'No. Well, nothing was found, anyway, that's what they told me.'

'Umm.'

'Is that unusual?'

'Actually, no, it's not. The police would tell you that only around twenty-five per cent of suicides leave notes. But, obviously, it would make a huge difference if she had done.' Kelly thought for a moment. 'Tell me more about how you learned about the earlier suicide,' he said.

Mrs Slade put her glass down and sat upright. She was obviously concentrating hard. Kelly thought that somewhere beyond the alcoholic stupor she actually had rather intelligent eyes.

'It was strange, really,' she said. 'I do remember that the chap who told me, did so as if he was doing me a favour. Trying to reassure me, weird really. Like I said, I was in a dreadful state on the day of the funeral. I'd been a lousy mother, and Jossy didn't have a father worth mentioning. But I hadn't seen it coming or anything. And that made it worse. I didn't even know that my daughter was so unhappy that she had decided to do away with herself. And on the day of the funeral, it just got too much for me. Then this chap started trying to tell me that it wasn't my fault. At first I thought, what does he know? But he kept saying the army did that to people, that it wasn't so unusual for youngsters just not to be able to cope. He was older, like I said, several years older than Jossy. At the time, I sort of assumed that he was one of the instructors at Hangridge, I think. He said that he'd known this boy who'd been in the intake before Jossy's, who'd done the same thing.'

Mrs Slade paused. Kelly expected her to pick up her whisky glass again, but she didn't. She just sat looking at him in silence for several seconds. Kelly could see that she was concentrating, trying to sort things out in a mind more or less permanently addled by alcohol, but a mind which Kelly somehow suspected was actually pretty sharp in the rare moments when she was completely sober. If you caught her that day.

'It made me feel better,' she said suddenly. 'Him telling me that, made me feel better. But I never saw a link with Jossy's death. Never. Never thought, that's odd, two young people at the same barracks killing themselves like that. I never questioned it.'

She picked up the whisky then, but didn't take a drink, just held the glass in her hand and stared at the remaining contents.

'Not surprising, really. Alcohol stops you questioning things, you see. I guess that's what so good about it . . .'

Her voice tailed off.

'I know,' said Kelly gently.

She looked him in the eye properly for the first time. 'Ah,' she said.

He changed the subject then. He was there for a purpose, after all. And, as ever, he preferred not to talk about himself.

'Mrs Slade, did Jocelyn ever say anything to you about being bullied, or perhaps being sexually harassed. You do hear of that in the army. I just wondered?'

'No, she didn't. But then, looking back, she didn't say much to me about anything. And I can't say I blame her . . .'

Kelly thought for a moment.

'The soldier who told you about the other suicide, at Jocelyn's funeral,' he went on. 'I don't suppose he gave you a name, by any chance, did he?'

'He told me the lad's first name, yes, he did.'

'And do you remember it?'

She smiled wanly. 'Oh yes, I remember it all right. Same name as my bloody ex-husband, Jossy's rat of a father. Trevor. Young Trevor, he called him.'

'Thank you,' said Kelly. 'You've been a great help.'

He meant it too.

'What are you going to do next?' asked Mrs Slade.

'I'm going to do my level best to break through the red tape of the military and find out exactly why four presumably fit and healthy young people, stationed at Hangridge, have died in little more than a year, Mrs Slade, that's what I'm going to do,' said Kelly.

'Are you, indeed?'

Mrs Slade's control, rather admirable considering what she had drunk, Kelly thought, seemed to have slipped. She slurred

136

the words, her period of concentration and lucidity over, it seemed. Then she drained the dregs of her whisky in one.

'I don't know how you've got the strength,' she said, closing her eyes and slumping back in her seat.

Kelly reckoned he didn't have a chance of getting any more out of her that day, even if she knew anything more, which he doubted.

'Look, perhaps I could take your phone number?' he ventured.

Margaret Slade's eyes remained closed. For a moment or two Kelly did not think he was going to get a reply.

'I'm in the book,' she muttered eventually, still without opening her eyes.

Kelly rose to his feet, delved into his jacket pocket for a business card, which he propped against the whisky bottle, and headed for the door.

Karen had been left reeling by Kelly's news. It had shaken her rigid. And she just had to do something about it.

Almost immediately after ending her call to Kelly, she dialled the number of Hangridge. Gerry would be sure to have arrived back there by now. But just as an anonymous male voice answered, she replaced the receiver. No. The telephone wasn't good enough.

Impulsively, she switched off her computer, grabbed her coat and left the office, without explaining to anyone where she was going.

Her mind was racing as she embarked on the drive across the moors. And Gerry Parker-Brown and how fond she had been becoming of him figured all too much in her thoughts. She was both angry and upset. But she knew that she must do her best to dismiss any personal feelings, and smartish. So far, it seemed Kelly had run rings round both her and the colonel, which, she had to admit, was pretty typical when he got his investigating boots on, and she didn't like it. She felt she had been made to look like a fool. More specifically, she felt that Gerry Parker-Brown had been making a fool of her all along. It was not the first time in her life that she had been taken in by a personable and attractive man, and she hated that weakness in herself.

Karen got the impression that unannounced visitors at Hangridge were a rarity. This time, she barely glanced at the young man on sentry duty. She just about registered that this was not the same good-looking young soldier she had admired on her previous visit. But she wasn't interested either way. She was in a hurry to get on with it. She sat in her car, impatiently tapping her fingers on the steering wheel, while he retreated into his sentry box and made what seemed to be a series of phone calls.

He kept her waiting for an irritating four or five minutes before he eventually returned to the car and leaned down to speak to her through the open window.

'They say to go on through,' he told her, looking vaguely surprised. 'You're to head for the central admin building,' he went on, pointing in the appropriate direction.

'I know,' she said. 'I've been here before.'

'Yes, ma'am,' said the soldier, continuing as if she had not spoken at all. 'Visitors' car parking is to the right . . .'

'I know,' she said again, and jerked the car forward away from the jobsworth sentry who was beginning to annoy her. She wasn't in the mood for military red tape this afternoon.

She parked quickly and headed for the main entrance to the admin building. Another sentry gestured her straight in, and as she opened the door she saw a smiling Gerry Parker-Brown step out of his office and move forward to greet her.

'What a lovely surprise, my favourite policewoman twice in one day,' he began. 'Why don't we pop across to the mess—'

She interrupted abruptly.

'Cut it out, Gerry,' she fired at him. 'You've not been straight with me, have you?'

'I don't know what you mean,' he replied.

'I think you do. And if jolly little outings together are supposed to soften me up, I can assure you they do not.'

'What are you talking about, Karen?' he asked calmly, his expression slightly quizzical.

'I'm talking about whatever game it is you think you are playing. It stops. Now. This minute. All I want from you is the truth about what's going on here, at Hangridge.'

'So do I, Karen,' he replied lightly. 'Every day I tell myself, this will be the day when I get to grips with what each one of the little bastards is up to, but . . .'

'No, Gerry. I've told you. The game is over. No more feeble jokes. Please. I now know about the death of Jocelyn Slade. You lied to me, Gerry, and I would like to know exactly why?'

She was aware that the sergeant sitting at a desk, just inside the reception area, had stopped typing into his computer and was staring at her.

Gerry put his hand on her arm with a firmer than normal pressure, she thought, and ushered her towards his office.

'You'd better come in, then, hadn't you?' he said.

Once inside, he closed the door firmly and bade her sit down. She did so, choosing the only upright chair in the room except the one behind his desk. She did not intend to give him the psychological advantage of looking down at her, and she some-how suspected that had she chosen one of his two comfortably low armchairs, he would not have sat next to her as he had done the first time she visited Hangridge. Certainly, he headed straight for his swivel desk-chair and sat very upright. And, there was no banter at all in his voice, when he finally responded.

'I didn't lie to you, Karen,' he replied very quietly. 'As I recall, you asked me if any other of our soldiers had died in accidents at the camp. I told you about Craig Foster. And I believe I was perfectly frank about his death, and the manner of it, was I not? Jocelyn Slade's death was not an accident. Do you really regard suicide as an accident? I most certainly do not. Slade chose to take her own life. That was a private tragedy, which I did not see the need to share with you. I can only apologise if you felt that I misled you, because I can assure you that was not my intention.'

Smooth as ever, thought Karen. She could feel the anger rising in her and battled to keep control.

'Come off it, Gerry,' she snapped. 'You knew perfectly well that I was interested in any sudden death at Hangridge. I may have interviewed you informally but I did come to you in an official capacity, and you chose to keep information from me which would be vital to a police investigation. Apart from anything else, Colonel, that is an offence.'

Karen knew that she was pretty good at tough talking when the occasion called for it. After all, she'd had enough practice at deflating the bubble of arrogance all too often present in members of certain strata of society, who were inclined to give the impression that they thought they were above the law. And this time, her genuine anger and sense of personal outrage probably gave her an extra edge.

However, Gerry Parker-Brown did not seem much abashed.

'Oh, come on, Karen, we're a long way from a formal police investigation, surely,' he said, his voice calm and reassuring.

'As a matter of fact, Gerry, I think we're very close to a formal investigation, starting pretty much right now, unless you can find a way of reassuring me that there is no need, and I doubt that very much. You will recall that Alan Connelly's death occurred on a public road and I am perfectly within my rights to instigate an enquiry into that, which would then be sure to involve any other deaths of young people at Hangridge.'

'I thought you and I had a better relationship than that, Karen,' responded Parker-Brown. 'And just because we've had a minor misunderstanding, it doesn't mean we can't sort things out between us . . .'

Karen had the nasty feeling that their whole 'relationship', such as it was, may well have been based on nothing more than Gerry Parker-Brown soft-soaping her so that she would not delve any further into the affairs of the Devonshire Fusiliers. But she didn't want to go into that.

'I don't regard this as a minor misunderstanding, Gerry,' she said. 'And neither do I consider that you and I have any relationship at all worth mentioning, and certainly not one which is going to stand in the way of me launching a full-scale police investigation into these deaths, if I feel that is necessary, which I am increasingly beginning to do.

'So, do you have anything at all to say to me that might make me change my mind?'

'Well, I certainly know where I stand now, don't I, Detective Superintendent . . .' There was still a twinkle in his eye. Gerry Parker-Brown patently believed he could charm the world, and most certainly that he could charm a woman police officer from a seaside police force.

Karen really wasn't having it.

'Look, if you're absolutely determined not to take me

seriously, then I shall have to ask you to accompany me to Torquay police station where we can conduct this interview formally,' she snapped.

'You don't really mean that . . .'

'I mean it, absolutely. To start with, and this is really your last chance to do things the easy way, Gerry, I want to know exactly why you didn't tell me about Jocelyn Slade.'

Parker-Brown held out both hands, palms upwards, in what appeared to be a gesture of supplication.

'Jocelyn Slade shot herself while on sentry duty,' he began. 'It was a dreadful shock for all concerned. As far as I and my staff knew, she had no problems within the army at all. She was a good, young soldier with a promising career ahead of her. But I do understand that her personal life was not so good. There were certain family difficulties – a sick mother, I believe – although I don't know the details . . .'

'Gerry, Jocelyn Slade's family life is another matter entirely, and although, of course, it is most likely now that we will need sooner or later to involve her family in our enquiries, at this stage all I am interested in, and all I want to know from you, concerns the military,' said Karen firmly. 'And you have not answered my question, have you? You are obviously well aware of what happened to Jocelyn Slade. I do not accept that you did not think I would want to know about her death. So why didn't you tell me, Gerry?'

'I honestly didn't think it was relevant—'

'Please,' she interrupted sharply. 'Credit me with at least a modicum of intelligence.'

'Very well.' He leaned back in his chair, opened the top drawer of his desk and produced a large cigar.

'You don't mind?' he asked.

She shook her head impatiently and watched while he lit up, puffing perfectly formed balls of smoke into the air. When he started to speak again, his voice was conciliatory and his manner patient, bordering on condescending, she thought.

'Karen, you must remember that the army is a family,' he began. 'And, like most families, we do not like to display our dirty washing in public. Indeed, we owe that to all the splendid young men and women here, at Hangridge, who will no doubt go on to have wonderful careers serving their country. I genuinely did not think that you were asking me about suicides, and I genuinely do not believe that anything has happened at Hangridge, certainly not in my time here, which could possibly warrant a police investigation. In the army, we do like to put our own house in order, you know.'

He paused, puffing quite ferociously on the cigar, which did not seem to want to burn properly. Karen realised that she had never seen him smoke before and couldn't help wondering if that was in any way significant. He did seem different, or rather, perhaps, he had become different since she had gone into the attack. Before that, he had been his usual, affable, nonchalant self.

'I think you will find that your superiors already understand that,' he murmured casually, in between puffs.

She was startled. What was Parker-Brown inferring? That had not been a throwaway remark, she was quite sure. Indeed, she didn't think Gerry Parker-Brown went in for throwaway remarks. Could he possibly be suggesting some kind of cosy deal with the civilian law-enforcing agencies, a deal that would probably have been agreed in an oak-panelled gentlemens' club in Mayfair? Karen had encountered that sort of thing before, everybody halfway senior in the police force had at some time or other, and she had always hated it. All boys together, and, whatever happens, let's keep the hoi polloi at bay.

Karen felt her anger growing. She did not like being mnipulated, and she rather felt that that last remark had been yet another attempt by Gerry Parker-Brown to manage her – something she increasingly felt he had been doing his best to do from the moment they first met. And that was a depressing thought. However, if that was what he was trying to do, then he was going the wrong way about it. Karen thoroughly dis-approved of the old boys, network which she knew, damn well, from personal experience, operated not only within the police force and the military, but also in almost all corridors of power ranging from national government to the church.

She studied Gerry Parker-Brown carefully as he leaned back in his chair, drawing deeply on his fat cigar, which had begun to glow rather more healthily since his frantic puffing session. He still did not look at all like a traditional army officer, and she had, to her absolute fury now, thoroughly enjoyed his company. Indeed, she had been on the verge of allowing things to develop into much more than that. As well as being extremely attractive, the man was relaxed, funny and easy-going. Or that was how he appeared. But she was beginning to think it might all be an act, underneath which he was army brass through and through, and that he would do anything, absolutely anything at all, to prevent his particular military boat from being rocked.

He returned her stare without blinking. An old actor's trick. More and more she was beginning to think that he was probably rather a good actor. He might even be a bloody Freemason, she thought. Like so many of them. He didn't look the part, of course, not one little bit, but she was beginning to believe that was what Gerry Parker-Brown was all about. The acceptable face of the modern army on top, but, beneath the façade a dedicated career officer whose true attitudes had barely changed since the time of Wellington.

'And what makes you think that my superiors already understand what you are up to?' she enquired, struggling to keep her face expressionless.

He shrugged. 'Just a figure of speech, Karen, that's all. I was only trying to convince you that you really have no need to investigate Hangridge. We're the British army, Karen, and that puts us on the same side as you. The Devonshire Fusiliers is a wonderful regiment, with a proud history of defending queen and country, dating back to the Napoleonic wars. We're the good guys. And you'd surely be much better off chasing criminals, rather than wasting your time and the tax payer's money here. That's my advice and I really do suggest you take it.'

He grinned to soften his words, and there was nothing at all in his voice to suggest a threat. And yet, she felt threatened. Or, at the very least, she felt that she was being warned off.

'I never stop chasing criminals, Gerry,' she said, rising abruptly from her chair.

As she did so she removed the little silver dagger brooch from her jacket lapel, where he had pinned it earlier, and tossed it casually onto the desk before him.

'Yours, I think.'

'But Karen, we had such fun this morning.' He picked the brooch up and held it out to her. 'Surely you can keep this small memento?'

She ignored him and turned to leave. At the door she twisted around.

'And you can forget Sunday,' she told him over her shoulder. 'I don't think I'd better risk compromising myself any further, do you?'

His face was a picture of wide-eyed innocence.

'Oh, come on, Karen . . .'

She left the room quickly, opening the door and closing it with a bang. It gave her some satisfaction just to cut off the sound of his voice.

Eleven

The information Margaret Slade had given Kelly was dynamite. This was turning into a major story and Kelly had never stopped being excited about stories.

He felt he had now gathered together several parts of a jigsaw, but he knew that there were lots more still missing. In the case of each death, the families of the young soldiers concerned had certain information which alone amounted to very little. However, when you put all these little bits of information together, the possible implications were mind-boggling.

Could the culture of bullying, of which the army all too often stood accused, simply have gone too far at Hangridge? Could there even be a psychopath on the loose within the Devonshire Fusiliers? Or was he allowing his imagination to take him a step too far?

He sat in his car, parked outside Mrs Slade's flat, thinking it all through. Kelly felt considerable compassion for Margaret Slade, and for her daughter, just as he did for the Connellys in Glasgow and for Mrs Foster in Torquay. Somehow or other, these people had all been caught up in something that was beginning to look increasingly sinister. He was determined to do his best to solve the mystery.

He made himself a roll-up while he contemplated his next move. He might be able to find out more about this young soldier called Trevor, by getting Sally to troll through inquest reports in the *Argus'* library. But it would be much quicker to find out exactly who Trevor was and how he had died, if Karen Meadows would help. Although he had, not for the first time, ignored her entreaties for him to take no further action without her approval, he thought she might forgive him when he told her what he'd found out.

First he dialled her mobile, but it was switched to voicemail.

Then he tried her number at Torquay police station, but was told that she was out. He left messages for her to call him and then set off on the long drive back to Torquay. It was just after 6.30 p.m. when he arrived in the seaside town, and Karen had still not called him back. He tried both numbers again, with the same results as earlier. He wondered fleetingly if she was avoiding him. After all, he knew he was leading her, and himself, into deep water.

He made a decision then. If Karen wouldn't come to him, as it were, then he would go to Karen. He had, in any case, never had any intention of talking to her on the phone about what he had found out. He drove straight to Torquay police station and, remarkably, managed to find a parking space in Lansdowne Lane, just outside the dance school, from which he could see the entrance to the CID offices on his left and the big gateway leading into the car park at the back of Torquay police station, and the door to the custody suite, on his right. He got out of the car and walked towards the gateway. The actual gates that had once been there had disappeared years previously. Not for the first time, Kelly reflected on the apparent lack of security. There was closed-circuit TV in operation, of course, and the various doors leading into the station were all secure. It none the less amused Kelly to amble casually into the back yard of Torquay nick and have a snoop around. His purpose on this occasion was to check that Karen's car was there. It was. The distinctive blue MG was parked in its usual place. Kelly was not surprised that she was still working. Indeed, he did not think she ever left the station much before seven, and that was on a short day. He resolved to catch her when she left for home.

His mobile rang just as he was climbing back into his own MG. He checked the display panel, wondering if Karen had called him back at last. Instead, his caller turned out to be Nick.

'I've been out of touch all day, Dad. I just picked up your message about Moira,' Nick began. 'Any change?'

'I don't think so.'

Kelly was starkly aware that he didn't really know. He hadn't been in touch since leaving the hospice that morning. But nobody had called him. So he assumed that no news was good news.

146

'I can't get down to Torquay till the day after tomorrow at the earliest, do you think that will be all right?'

Kelly knew what he meant. Nick, too, did not want to put his true meaning into words. The question he was trying to ask was whether or not Moira would still be alive. And Kelly didn't have a clue.

'I'm sure it will,' he said automatically.

'Right, I'll see you then.'

'Yes.'

For once, the conversation between father and son was stilted. Impending death had that effect, Kelly reckoned.

For a moment he thought about discussing the Hangridge situation with his former soldier son, something he would certainly like to do at some stage. But definitely not on the phone, he thought. And not on the back of that awkward exchange about Moira. Indeed, it did not seem to be possible to talk about anything other than poor Moira. And when there was really nothing more that could be said about her, father and son ended the call in a kind of glum, mutual consent.

Not wishing to dwell further on Moira and her approaching death, Kelly fished in his pocket for his notebook and began to chronicle the events of the past few days, carefully assimilating the jottings he had made while talking to the various parents of the three dead soldiers whom he had so far met.

He was still a journalist at heart, however much he tried to fight against it. He told himself this would be his last story, and that it was going to be a huge one. He also told himself, that, for once, this would be a story which might do some good. This was going to be a classic example of true campaigning journalism, of the sort that he had gone into newspapers to pursue, in the days when he had still been young enough to believe in his own dreams.

As he wrote, he contemplated what he would do with the finished article. He was quite sure that he hadn't uncovered one half of it yet, but, on the other hand, there was enough of a story in what he had already – at least three, probably four, deaths of young soldiers at Hangridge in fifteen months, and one of them, to his certain first-hand knowledge, in suspicious circumstances – to guarantee him publication in almost any national

147

newspaper. However, if he went into print at this stage, the entire British press corps would then unleash its top investigative reporters onto the story.

The ramifications were, after all, enormous. At the very least, the army was surely guilty of a shocking lack of care at Hangridge. At worst, something very nasty was going on and, according to Karen Meadows, the army was already closing ranks.

One way and another, there was so much more that Kelly wanted to do, wanted to find out about, before he started to market the story. He needed to research some more military statistics for a start, like the number of alleged suicides and accidental deaths there had been in the army throughout the UK in recent years. He also wondered if finding the family of the fourth soldier would lead him to yet more surprises.

But, as he wrote, he became surprised at how much he already had to say. This could possibly be the biggest story of his life. Kelly could feel it in his bones.

As soon as she arrived back at her office from Hangridge, Karen Meadows attempted to contact the clerk to the coroner's court to ask him for the records of the inquest on Jocelyn Slade, something which, upon reflection, she probably should have done before taking off to confront Parker-Brown. But she just hadn't been able to wait.

A recorded message told her that the coroner's court was in session and that the clerk would return her call as soon as possible. She left a brief message.

It was hard for her to think about anything other than Hangridge. And she was still reflecting on her meeting with Gerry Parker-Brown and going over and over in her mind all that Kelly had so far told her, when to her utter amazement, just before six o'clock, she received an email from the CO of the Devonshire Fusiliers, repeating his invitation for her to join him for Sunday lunch.

'I know you were upset earlier and I do understand. But can't we at least try to keep our personal lives separate from our work? I have so enjoyed spending time with you, and I'd really love to see you on Sunday as we had planned. I do so hope we can still meet.'

Smooth, arrogant bastard, thought Karen.

She pushed delete at once. She couldn't believe the man's cheek. One thing was absolutely certain, she was risking no more unofficial meetings of any kind with Colonel Gerrard Parker-Brown. He was covering something up, she was quite convinced of that now. She also remained pretty sure that he had been using her all along. And, with his repeated Sunday invitation, was, quite incredibly she felt, actually still trying to use her. The very thought of it made her blazing mad.

And it was because of her state of mind that she did not want any further contact with John Kelly for a bit. Indeed, as soon as Kelly's name had flashed on her mobile earlier, she had not only deliberately ignored his call but also instructed the clerk who answered her office phone to field any further calls from him. She was not yet ready for Kelly. She had inquiries of her own to make and quite possibly a major investigation to launch, one that was not going to be easy. The sort of investigation that makes and breaks careers.

Karen was no coward, and certainly no jobsworth. She was not at all adverse to taking risks. And, by God, how she wanted to give Parker-Brown the shock of his smug smooth life! None the less, she was starkly aware that she had probably already taken quite enough risks in her career to last most senior police officers a lifetime. On more than one occasion she had put herself in a situation where her job had been on the line, and at least twice John Kelly had been involved.

And now, she realised, she was on the brink of diving into the deep end yet again. She knew that she should not make another move on this one until she had authorisation from the chief constable to delve further into military matters. However, if that authorisation did not come, Karen also knew, all too well, that she would probably not be able to stop herself taking some kind of action.

Her reflections were interrupted by having to attend a meeting concerning liaison between uniform and CID, and Karen, forcing herself to put Hangridge out of her mind, at least for the time being, made her way over to the main station about half an hour before Kelly had arrived outside.

When her meeting finally ended, shortly after 7.30, she left through the back door next to the custody suite. And only then did she remember that the coroner's clerk had not returned her call.

Kelly, who wished he was able to compile his novel with half the fluency he had found while attempting to write down the Hangridge story so far, was in mid-sentence when, out of the corner of his eye, he spotted Karen's MG pull out of the police station car park and turn left into Lansdowne Lane towards him. How the hell had she got across the road from CID without him noticing, he wondered. Then, with that surprising alacrity he so often displayed for a man of his size, years, and lifestyle he swung open his car door, jumped out and stepped smartly into the road in front of Karen's car, causing her to break sharply in order to avoid hitting him.

She lurched to a halt with a screeching of tyre rubber, wound down the window of her car and leaned out. Kelly continued to stand stoically in front of the little MG. He expected an earful and he got it.

'Exactly what the fuck do you think you are doing, you moron?' she yelled.

'I had to see you, Karen,' he began.

'OK, but is there any particular reason why you also wanted to kill yourself today?'

'Uh, I was afraid of missing you,' Kelly responded lamely. 'I've been trying to get you on the phone all afternoon. I thought you were deliberately dodging me . . .'

'And so you decided to doorstep me, did you, you arsehole? I don't suppose it occurred to you that I might just be busy?'

This was a blatant lie, of course. Karen most certainly had been avoiding him. But she was always inclined to be inventive when she was in full flow.

'I think you'll forgive me when I tell you everything I've found out.' Kelly gathered his courage, walked round to the side of Karen's car and leaned against it, looking down at her steadily. But Karen was not, it seemed, in an altogether forgiving mood.

'Listen, Kelly,' she countered. 'I haven't got time for you in my head, right now. You've handed me a potential atomic bomb. There are procedures . . .'

150

'Since when have you wasted time worrying about procedures?'

'Since I came close to losing my job, the last time I got involved with you and what you were up to, and the time before that.'

'Oh, come on, Karen . . .'

'No, this is serious stuff, Kelly, and this time I'm doing it by the book. We go through the chief constable, we go through the MoD, we go through the proper channels. There is a set procedure for police involvement in an army case, and I intend to stick to it. Now, thank you for drawing my attention to this matter, and please get the fuck out of my way.'

With that, Karen slammed the gearstick of the little MG into first, let go of the clutch with a deliberate jerk, and lurched forwards with another screech of her tyres. Kelly pulled away, stepping swiftly back in the nick of time. However, he still only just managed to avoid his left foot being run over by the rear nearside wheel of Karen's car. Keeping his balance with some difficulty, he cupped his hands around his mouth and yelled with all his might.

'I've found out about another one, Karen. There've been four deaths. At least, Karen . . . four deaths, at least.'

The car stopped with a bump again and yet more screeching rubber. Kelly winced. He was very fond of MGs and, although he rarely admitted it, he even had a certain limited affection for a modern imitation like Karen's.

There was a nasty crunching noise as she changed gear again and suddenly the little car lurched into reverse, roaring back alongside Kelly, only narrowly missing both his feet this time.

The driver's window was still open.

'Get in,' she snapped.

Kelly hurried around the back of Karen's car and quickly climbed into the passenger side. He wasn't giving her time to change her mind. No way.

'Right,' she said. 'What have you been up to, you bastard?'

He didn't prevaricate.

'I went to see Jocelyn Slade's mother.'

'Yeah, I might have guessed it. Even though I asked you not to.'

He shrugged. 'What did you expect, Karen? We both knew exactly what would happen if you started going down the red tape route, and it's already happening. You've been avoiding my calls all afternoon. Because you didn't know what to say to me, did you? Your hands are tied, aren't they, Karen? And if I hadn't gone to see Mrs Slade neither of us would be any further forward, and you know that's the truth . . .'

'So, thanks to you, we are now further forward, are we? You're sure of that?'

'Mrs Slade knows of another alleged suicide,' he said bluntly. 'A Hangridge soldier told her of a young male recruit who'd topped himself six months before her daughter died. He was trying to comfort her, to make her not blame herself . . .'

Kelly was interrupted by the horn of a white Transit van, the path of which was blocked by Karen's car, still stationary and parked at a crazy angle across the road.

Karen glowered at the driver, passed her left hand briefly across her forehead, slammed the car into first gear again and gunned it suddenly forwards to the main road junction, where she turned towards Kelly in a resigned sort of way.

'OK, Kelly. You can tell me everything over a fish supper. I haven't eaten all day.'

'Fine,' said Kelly, reflecting that this was just the way things always were between him and Karen Meadows. Naturally, she hadn't asked him if he wanted to eat. But, as it happened, the prospect was quite an appealing one. He suddenly remembered that he, too, had eaten little all day except a packet of plastic-wrapped sandwiches from a motorway service station and a couple of chocolate bars. And now he was heading for a fried fish supper, just to complete his healthy eating programme, he reflected wryly.

They ate cod and chips, accompanied by bread and butter and washed down with numerous cups of tea, in what both considered to be their favourite chippy, tucked away in a little backstreet not far from the railway station. Kelly told Karen all he knew.

Karen had lost her combative abrasiveness even before they reached the chip shop. She'd really, only been putting on an act, anyway. She sat quietly listening until Kelly had finished.

'Another death,' she murmured, almost to herself. 'And not only that, but another death bloody Gerry Parker-Brown avoided telling me about.'

'It's only second-hand so far, but we have an approximate date, and I assume it happened either at the barracks or thereabouts,' said Kelly. 'So I was hoping you could check it out with the coroner's court. The families of the dead soldiers have been the best leads so far. If this young man, Trevor, does turn out to have died under suspicious circumstances, then we need to get to his family.'

Karen looked thoughtful. 'Yes, well, let's see if he ever existed first, shall we?'

'Well, of course, but—'

'And if so,' Karen interrupted. 'What I want to do now is to put a formal investigation in place. Only that's easier said than done when the army is involved. However, I would hope that if we have four deaths like this, even our chief constable would be convinced.'

'Surely, he would be.'

'You never know with Harry Tomlinson.' Karen did not look happy. 'You should know that I went back to see Gerrard Parker-Brown this afternoon,' she continued, carefully avoiding mentioning that she had also spent the morning with the colonel.

'And?'

'And he was much the same as he was before, on the surface at any rate. Appearing to be helpful and co-operative and actually giving very little away. Denied having deliberately misled me, naturally.'

She then gave him a summary of her conversation with the colonel at Hangridge, still omitting, however, her personal relationship with the soldier, such as it was, and the way in which she felt that he had been deliberately trying to manipulate her. After all, that was none of Kelly's business.

It was Kelly's turn to listen quietly.

'And he didn't mention a dead soldier called Trevor, obviously?' he enquired eventually.

'Of course not. The more I find out, via you, mostly, it has to be said, the more aware I am of the wall Parker-Brown has put up around himself and his beloved Devonshire Fusiliers. Certainly, he does not seem willing to admit to any suicides out at Hangridge, nor anything else much, come to that, unless he has absolutely no alternative.'

'So what happens next from your point of view?' Kelly asked.

'I've told you what I want to do, but I really have to do it by the book this time,' said Karen. 'I have no choice. This could be a very hot potato, you know, Kelly. I'm going to have to be extremely careful with any information that comes my way from now on, too. I'm afraid I really am going to have to stick to the rules. And I know you'll find this unfair, but even if what Margaret Slade told you does check out, I'm not sure that I'll be able to give you a full ID on this chap, Trevor, let alone an address for his family . . .'

'Hmm.' Kelly grunted disapprovingly, through a large mouthful of cod. 'Damn right, I think it's unfair. I put you onto this in the first place and right along the line I've given you all the information I have. But you're not prepared to give me anything.'

Kelly was his usual animated self. He spoke so forcefully that he seemed to be having difficulty keeping the food he was trying at the same time to chew, inside his mouth. A flake or two of fish fell from his lips onto the plate before him. Impatiently, he took a big gulp of tea and swallowed. He then lapsed into baleful silence and sat glowering at her.

Karen sighed. However, Kelly was only reacting as she would have expected him to, and pretty much the same way she would have reacted in his place. They had always been kindred spirits, much as she tried to deny it to herself most of the time.

'I didn't say I wouldn't give you anything, Kelly,' she told him. 'I said I would have to be careful, and go by the book for once, that's all.'

'Much the same thing,' muttered Kelly, through a further mouthful of fish. He took another gulp of tea in order to wash down the food so that he could speak more easily.

'Oh, come on, Karen. If Margaret Slade's story checks out, then not only will there have been an inquest on this young chap, Trevor, but it will also have been reported in the press. So I can always get Sal at the *Argus* to troll through cuts, which is exactly

154

what I did to find Craig Foster's address. It would be tricky and time-consuming without a full name, but basically all you would do, would be to save me time.'

His mobile phone rang then, before Karen had the chance to reply, which was actually something of a relief to her. She was getting into deep water again with Kelly, and she knew it. She concentrated on her meal, while Kelly answered the phone with a belligerence which totally fitted the mood he seemed to have fallen into.

'Yes,' he snapped abruptly.

But almost at once his manner changed.

'I'll be there straight away,' he said, and his voice was quite shaky. 'I shouldn't be more than fifteen minutes.'

Karen studied him enquiringly as he finished the call. All the colour seemed to have drained from his face. She could not imagine what news he had just been given which would have had such an effect on him.

'It's Moira,' he said quietly. 'She's in the hospice at Newton Abbot. I-I have to go. Apparently she . . . she's very poorly. That was Jennifer. She said her mother . . . well . . .'

His voice tailed off.

'Moira?' queried Karen, who was genuinely shocked. 'I didn't even know she was ill.'

'No, well . . .'

His voice trailed away again.

'Why didn't you tell me you daft bugger. I like Moira a lot, you know how fond I am of her—'

'Yes,' Kelly interrupted. As ever, he didn't want to talk about emotions, didn't want to give anything away about his own feelings or learn about anybody else's, and neither did he want to talk about his partner's terminal illness to anyone apart from her and her family. And maybe he would not be able to talk about it to any of them either, even if they had been willing to do so. Maybe he was just kidding himself that he could ever have done that.

He rose abruptly and headed for the door.

'Kelly,' Karen called after him.

He turned in the doorway. He looked terrible. His head was down, and there was a haunted look in his eyes. Karen felt for him.

155

'I'm fond of you, too, Kelly,' she said with a softness that surprised even her. And then, with as much of her usual, edgy forcefulness in her voice as she could muster, she added: 'And don't you forget it.'

Kelly stared at her, as if not really seeing her, for several seconds. Then he managed a very small, very weak smile.

'You're the boss,' he said.

'Yeah, and don't you forget that, either,' she called after him.

All three of Moira's daughters were with her in her room at the hospice. They turned to look at Kelly as he made his entrance much more noisily than he had intended.

He had run all the way from the car park, through the front hall, right along the corridor on the first floor to the staircase at the far end, and then up three flights, much too anxious and impatient to take the lift. He was breathing heavily as he burst through the doorway, and he suspected that he looked red-faced and dishevelled.

'Uh, sorry,' he said automatically, realising as he spoke that his voice sounded high-pitched and squeaky.

He focused his gaze on the sick woman lying motionless on the bed. Her face was ashen, her eyes were shut tightly, and he could see no sign that she was even breathing.

'Is she . . . is she?' he began. And he could not, just could not get the words out, could not formulate the question. He could not even ask the girls if Moira was dead, and yet he had actually thought he had wanted to talk to them about their mother's impending death. Jesus! Why was he such a waste of space sometimes.

'She's unconscious, John,' responded Jennifer quietly. 'Why don't you pull up a chair. Come and sit with her.'

Not for the first time Kelly was amazed at the nineteen-year-old's composure and dignity. He thought she was one hell of a kid, and vowed to tell her so one day. But not now. It was neither the time nor the place. And, anyway, he didn't have the words. Again.

There was an orange plastic chair just to his left by the door. He carried it over to the bed and sat down, as Jennifer had suggested, alongside. There was a clock above Moira's bed. It said

9.23 p.m. He had left the hospice at half past seven that morning and he had not called once since then to find out how Moira was.

And yet – and yet – he loved her so. He touched Moira gently on one cheek. Her skin felt cool and clammy. He hoped she knew how much he had cared for her, really cared, even though he had not always shown it and had sometimes behaved very badly towards her. Now that it was too late, far too late, he wished he had behaved differently on so many occasions, looked after her better throughout their relationship, and been a much better all-round partner to her.

His mind began to wander over their time together. He felt the burden not only of grief but of guilt. He tried to concentrate on what was happening in the little room, tried to think of anything he could do that might help. But his eyelids seemed to be made of lead. It had, of course, been a long day and a short night previously. He blinked and shook his head furiously, glancing around him at Moira's three daughters – Jennifer on one side of the bed, her two sisters on the other, sitting quietly watching their mother. Jennifer was holding Moira's left hand, Paula her right, while Lynne every so often stroked her hair. Nobody was saying anything. Well, now there really was nothing to say. Kelly shifted on the hard plastic chair in an attempt to make himself more comfortable. It didn't seem to help much. The minutes ticked slowly by. The silence continued. Kelly's mouth felt dry. He licked his lips and thought about suggesting that he went in search of tea or coffee. He shifted on the chair again. He was very uncomfortable and extremely ill at ease. However, after a bit, his eyelids began to feel heavy, and then he had no further conscious memory until he felt his arm being gently shaken. He opened his eyes at once. It hurt to do so. They felt sore and were slightly stuck together. He must have fallen asleep again, and he had no idea how he had managed to do so under such circumstances, and seated so uncomfortably. Neither did he have any idea how long he had been asleep. Automatically, he checked the clock above the bed. It said 2 a.m. He must have slept, somehow, for at least three hours.

It was Jennifer who was shaking his arm. Calm, composed, dignified, wonderful Jennifer, who suddenly did not look calm at all. There were tears streaming down her cheeks.

'She's gone, John,' she cried. 'She's dead. Mum's dead.'

Kelly tried to stand up. It took more than one attempt. His left leg had gone to sleep and his spine seemed to have locked itself into a sitting position.

Eventually, if a little unsteadily, he struggled upright. He stared at Moira, lying on the bed before him. She actually looked much the same as she had the last time he had seen her, when she had still been desperately hanging on to life. But now she had let go. Kelly's first reaction took him by surprise and rather shocked him. He immediately felt a terrific sense of relief. For Moira. For her daughters. And, of course, for himself. Then he was overwhelmed by a dreadful emptiness.

He wrapped his arms around Jennifer and pulled her close to him. She leaned her head against his chest and sobbed her heart out.

Perversely, perhaps, it made Kelly feel a little better, not that Jennifer had broken down, but that she had wanted to turn to him as a shoulder to cry on. If he could at least give Jennifer a little comfort, then perhaps he wasn't quite such a hopelessly inadequate bugger, after all.

Twelve

In the morning Karen left home early again, not something she enjoyed but, none the less, she was actually quite glad to shut the door on her bedroom, which looked rather as if it had suffered a terrorist attack. In spite of her love of expensive designer clothes, she paid them little respect, which was one of the reasons why she preferred low-maintenance items, the sort that were not supposed to look freshly ironed. She was inclined to use the pretty, little, Victorian dressing chair at the foot of her bed as an alternative wardrobe, only when the pile of clothes upon it reached a certain level, they could do nothing other than fall onto the floor. She had not made her bed, either. Which wasn't entirely her fault, she told herself. Sophie had looked so comfortable curled up on the crumpled duvet that Karen had not had the heart to move her. In any case, the cat would probably have bitten her had she attempted to do so.

Making a mental note to blitz the bedroom at the weekend, she hurried along the corridor to West Beach Heights' famously rickety, ancient lift. In a nanny state increasingly governed by health and safety regulations, she found the ornate old lift, which moved both up and down only in a series of disconcerting jerks, rather reassuring.

For Karen, it was just another morning. She did think about Kelly and wondered whether she should call him or wait for him to call her, but she still had no idea that Moira was dead when she arrived at her office, in Torquay police station, just before 8 a.m. In any case, in spite of her genuine feelings for the woman and for Kelly, it would have made no difference whatsoever. Karen had a job to do and she just wanted to get on with it.

She was nearly ready to approach the chief constable, to ask for his authorisation to set up a formal police investigation at Hangridge. This was not something she could do of her own

159

volition. And it seemed pretty obvious that, in spite of trying to give every appearance of co-operating, Gerry Parker-Brown was not going to allow any kind of external investigation into the affairs of the Devonshire Fusiliers unless he was given little choice.

In terms of red tape there was a brick wall around Hangridge, Karen reckoned, much more impenetrable than the wire fence which was actually the army base's only physical perimeter barrier. And she intended to do her damnedest to knock that brick wall down.

But first, she needed all the information she could lay her hands on. Certainly enough to persuade the chief constable that a full police investigation of goings-on at Hangridge was not just advisable but necessary.

It was still too early to ring Mike Collins, the newly appointed clerk to the coroner's court, who had failed to return her call yesterday, so she decided to re-read the report he had already sent her of the inquest into the death of Craig Foster. This had actually contained few surprises except, perhaps, that the details of the military police investigation, conducted by the Special Investigation Branch of the RMP, the army's equivalent of the CID, were extremely sketchy. Their evidence had drawn the conclusion that Craig Foster had fallen on his own automatic rifle during a moorland training exercise, and in so doing had caused the gun to fire. He died from gunshot wounds to the chest. And although these did seem consistent with SIB's conclusions, Karen remained unimpressed. She knew that SIB investigations should be conducted in more or less exactly the same way as by the CID. Indeed, SIB officers, although soldiers, were trained in CID procedure at civilian police college. Yet there appeared not to have been any witness statements taken, even though Foster was on an exercise with the entire training company of around a hundred and twenty men and women. Instead, the SIB report, read out at the inquest by an NCO, had taken the form of little more than an assumption of the obvious. And the coroner had appeared to accept the army version of events without question and simply to declare a verdict of accidental death. In truth, it could well still be the case, she realised, that Craig Foster's death had been an accident.

Everything fitted, after all, and soldiers did die in training accidents of this kind, if not regularly, at least often enough for another one not to initially raise any suspicions. None the less, from the inquest report before her, Karen did not consider that Craig Foster's death had actually been proven to be an accident at all.

So engrossed was she in the report and her own thoughts that the time passed quickly and Mike Collins finally got back to her on virtually the dot of 9 a.m., before she'd made her planned second call to his office.

'I'm really sorry, Detective Superintendent,' he began. 'Court finished late yesterday and I didn't get your message until this morning because—'

Karen interrupted him there. She was neither interested in excuses nor incriminations. She just wanted to get on with it.

'Spare me you life story, please,' she said curtly. 'I just want the full report of an inquest into the death of a young soldier – by the name of Jocelyn Slade – about six months ago, and I want it straight away.'

She also asked Collins, too new in his job to even have a chance of being able to remember off the top of his head, to search records for an inquest on a soldier called Trevor, who had allegedly committed suicide at Hangridge a further six months or so earlier, and indeed to look for any other deaths connected with the barracks or the Devonshire Fusiliers.

Perhaps anxious now to prove his efficiency, the newly appointed coroner's clerk emailed her the requested report on Jocelyn Slade's inquest within minutes, and promised to get back to her as soon as possible on her other request.

The Jocelyn Slade inquest came as a bombshell to Karen. Unlike the inquest into Craig Foster's death, it did not just raise some procedural points and leave a few doubts hanging in the air. It was a revelation. Slade had allegedly shot herself with her SA80 rifle while on sentry duty at Hangridge main gates. Once again the coroner, now retired, seemed to have accepted the findings of the SIB investigation, that Jocelyn Slade had killed herself, without any discernible further inquiry. He pronounced a verdict of suicide in spite of evidence presented, which Karen, this time, considered to be highly questionable.

161

As she read, Karen could hardly believe her eyes. Jocelyn had been shot in the head five times. The SA80 was an automatic weapon. Karen had completed the obligatory police firearms courses and was, in fact, not at all a bad shot. She understood that an automatic used in a suicide attempt could continue to fire even after the first shot might well have done its job. But five hits? That was pushing it. And she noted that the investigation did not include any information on the angle of the shots, merely indicating that they had all been fired from close quarters, leading to the suicide verdict.

It was not satisfactory at all. And there was more. The second sentry on duty, at the entrance to the officers' mess a hundred yards or so away from where Jocelyn Slade had been on duty, Private John Gates, had been called to give evidence. He said that he had heard shots and called the duty sergeant, who ordered a search of the perimeter area of Hangridge. But at first no body had been found, even though more than one soldier had several times passed right by the spot where Jocelyn's body was eventually discovered.

Incompetence? Panic? All involved had, after all, been young and inexperienced. But Karen was not convinced. She considered the coroner's verdict to have been, at the very least, highly unsatisfactory.

She had, of course, known Torbay's former coroner, albeit only vaguely. And she was aware that Reginald Sykes had been an army officer himself, practising law within the military, before moving into civilian life as a solicitor in Torquay and ultimately becoming a coroner. Actually, even someone who did not know that would probably have guessed something of Sykes' military past. In total contrast to Gerrard Parker-Brown, she remembered Sykes as being something of a cliché on legs. With his small bristly moustache, accent you could cut with a knife and exaggeratedly upright bearing, he really had been a complete stereotype, old-style army officer.

She read the report several times, trying to imagine what could have happened to Jocelyn Slade. She wanted to call the chief constable straight away, but she made herself be patient, at least until she had heard back from the coroner's clerk concerning any other deaths connected with Hangridge.

162

Only a couple of hours later Mike Collins called. She didn't know him, but she knew the type. He had been a police officer, in common with many coroners' clerks, and he was the sort who liked to demonstrate the failings of others, particularly if he felt that he had been dealt with critically himself, as he might well after the way Karen had spoken to him earlier. One way and another, Mike Collins was not the kind of man Karen liked a bit. But the truth was that she couldn't have wished for a better person to be trolling through the court's records.

'Found him,' said Collins triumphantly. 'Fusilier Trevor Parsons, died just over a year ago. Verdict, suicide, like you said. Hard to believe that any coroner could have presided over three cases like this of young people from the same barracks, and not at least passed comment, isn't it?'

Collins was only voicing Karen's sentiments, but from him the comment sounded smug and self-satisfied. Quite deliberately, she did not respond. Instead she merely checked if he had unearthed any other Devonshire Fusilier cases. He hadn't.

'Fine, thank you,' she said curtly. 'So, just email me the report on Parsons, please.'

'Already done it,' said Collins, sounding even smugger.

Karen couldn't wait to hang up and read the records of Parsons' inquest. The similarities both with the death of Jocelyn Slade and the way in which such investigation as there was had been handled by the SIB, were immediately evident. Karen could feel the excitement coursing through her body.

Trevor Parsons, a seventeen-year-old recruit, had allegedly shot himself while on sentry duty at Hangridge and, like Jocelyn Slade, had died from multiple gunshot wounds, in his case three such wounds. The only witness called had been the young soldier he had been standing guard with, who had reported only hearing gunfire and then finding Parsons' body when he went to investigate.

Karen spent just a few minutes assimilating the information and rehearsing how she was going to present it, before eventually calling the chief constable. As ever, she did not relish any dealings at all with Harry Tomlinson.

He kept her waiting for almost five minutes before eventually coming on the line, something he quite often did with her and which she suspected was quite deliberate.

Telling herself that the most important thing with Tomlinson was never to let him get to you, she explained the events so far as calmly and as succinctly as she could. Tomlinson listened without interrupting, and continued to say nothing even when she deliberately paused to allow him the chance to chip in. He was, she thought, giving nothing away.

And when she finally got to the real aim of her call, she still had no idea at all of how he might react.

'I really do think we should initiate a police inquiry at Hangridge, now,' she said finally. 'I am not at all happy with the way the military investigations have been conducted, nor with at least one of the coroner's verdicts.'

'Karen, surely these are military matters, don't we have enough crime to deal with?'

Karen hesitated. This was the kind of response she had feared, but there was more. Tomlinson's attitude sounded so like that of Gerrard Parker-Brown, it was uncanny.

'Look, sir, it seems to me that there is a distinct possibility that these cases could be criminal in some way, and I think, at the very least, we should look into them,' she persisted. 'I am convinced there is justification for that. In my opinion, all four investigations should be reopened and this time conducted by the civilian police force.'

'Indeed, Detective Superintendent? And on what grounds exactly, prey, do you feel that we should take this course of action?'

Karen stifled her irritation with difficulty. The bastard was patronising her again. Surely, she'd given him grounds enough. Four deaths in just over a year, and at least two of them leaving a number of serious questions totally unanswered.

'I thought I had explained that, sir . . .'

'Nothing to warrant us meddling in legitimate army affairs, not as far as I can see. Gerry Parker-Brown is on the case, and he's going to have another look at it all, just to dot the Is and cross the Ts, you understand. Decent chap, Gerry. Does a job properly. Knows all about making sure we don't have any misunderstandings. You should be in no doubt, Karen, that I trust him to clear this up in no time. It's always been our procedure, as you well know, to let the SIB investigate these kind of deaths, which they have always done quite satisfactorily in my opinion, and I see no reason to start interfering now, stirring things up unnecessarily, that kind of thing.'

Karen found that she was becoming seriously irritated. No wonder the chief constable sounded like Gerry Parker-Brown. The Hangridge commander had obviously already got to him and done an excellent job of damage limitation, it would seem. As he would. She took a deep breath and fought to maintain control.

'It is, of course, quite in order for the civilian police to conduct a new investigation should we deem it necessary, sir,' she responded mildly.

If nothing else came out of this debacle, Karen reckoned that at least another step or two might be taken towards ensuring that all non-combat, sudden military deaths were subject to a civilian police inquiry as a matter of standard routine, like any other sudden death.

'I think you mean "if *I* deem it necessary," Detective Superintendent,' replied Tomlinson. Karen could almost see him bristling at the other end of the phone.

'And quite frankly, I don't,' he continued. 'I thought I had already made that abundantly clear. So now, if there's nothing else . . .'

Karen was really angry by the time the call ended – with the chief constable, with Gerry Parker-Brown, and with herself for ever having been taken in by the colonel's smooth-talking charms in the first place. Parker-Brown may have got the chief constable eating out of his hand, but not her. No way. Not any more.

She had another look at the reports of the two inquests. The home addresses of both the second sentry in the Jocelyn Slade case, John Gates, and the other young soldier to have allegedly committed suicide, Trevor Parsons, were listed in full, which was a result. It meant that with a bit of luck both Gates and members of Parsons' family could be contacted without going through military sources. On the other hand, assuming Gates was still a serving soldier, he may well already have been gagged.

Karen was beginning to go through conspiracy theories in her head. She told herself it was early days for that, and that she was getting as bad as John Kelly.

She also had to remind herself that she was still head of Torquay CID and, as such, had her normal heavy workload of cases to deal with – including a suspected major fraud, involving a well-known local councillor and former mayor, which promised to send shock waves around the entire West of England.

But throughout the day, whatever she was working on, she found her thoughts returning to Hangridge, and her feelings of anger and outrage mounting. She wasn't totally naive. She knew that there were those who believed that military secrets should sometimes be kept at the expense of justice. She understood that protecting national security could be a dirty business. She knew that cover-ups happened, and that occasionally they happened for the best of reasons. But she was damned if she was going to be part of one.

She was a police detective. And if she believed that crimes may have been committed, it was her job to investigate, regardless of the consequences.

It could be that she didn't dare to become directly involved herself, at least for the time being, but she did know a man who could do the job for her. If he chose.

Indeed, she had always suspected that she might have to rely on John Kelly, in the initial stages, at any rate. And knowing Kelly, as she did, she was quietly confident that he would effectively blow the whole thing wide open with or without her help.

Kelly was with his partner who, it seemed, was terminally ill. Perhaps dead. And Karen knew that even Kelly would need some time before launching himself again into the Hangridge mystery. But Karen could wait. For a few days, anyway.

She was, however, quite determined that the establishment was not going to cover this one up. No way.

They held the funeral five days later. Kelly helped the girls make the arrangements, and found during those four days that his mind was entirely taken up with that and with his grief. For once he did not seek a displacement activity. Moira was dead, so he

166

was no longer looking for any excuse to do anything other than deal with her being sick. The grim reality of her death had focused his feelings in a way which he sincerely wished could have happened much earlier.

He spent long hours walking alone along the beach, just gazing out to sea and thinking about his life, and about the life he had shared with Moira.

He did not attempt to contact any of the bereaved Hangridge families again. Neither did he contact Karen Meadows concerning Hangridge. And when she eventually called him to enquire after Moira, he told her the news briefly, gave her the funeral arrangements, and made it quite clear that he did not want to talk about anything else. Only very occasionally did he give Hangridge even a fleeting thought.

He did call Nick, of course, on the day of Moira's death.

'Oh shit, dad, I'm so bloody sorry,' Nick had responded. 'And I did want to see her. Damn it. Why didn't I just drop everything?'

'You weren't to know, son,' said Kelly. 'We didn't think it would be so quick.'

He had no idea whether that was true or not. He didn't remember at any stage ever discussing with anyone just how long Moira might have left. That had been one of those topics never to be broached.

'I'd just like to have seen her one more time, Dad, that's all . . .'

'I know, son.' Kelly did know too. Nick was another one who had always been extremely fond of Moira. She was a woman who had had in abundance the gift of making friends.

On the day, there must have been well over a hundred people, Kelly thought, crammed into the little crematorium chapel for the brief funeral service. It had been Moira's wish to be cremated. Kelly didn't like the idea of human bodies being burned, but, although he had known that her wish to be cremated was in her will, he had never tried to dissuade her. After all, if he was honest, neither did he much like the idea of human bodies rotting in a cemetery. At best, the way in which humans were disposed of, or laid to rest – the euphemism invariably preferred by those involved with the process – could only be the lesser of various evils in Kelly's opinion.

It was, however, gratifying to see such a good turn-out. Moira had been a gregarious woman at heart and Kelly knew she would have liked to think that so many people would attend her funeral.

Nick drove down from London to be there, as Kelly had known that he would, in his new, distinctively customised, silver Aston Martin, which on any other occasion Kelly would have demanded to be allowed to take for a drive. He and Nick shared a love of sports cars, particularly British sports cars in Kelly's case, and Kelly unashamedly envied his son for being in a position to buy himself almost any car he wanted.

There were various members of Moira's family present whom Kelly hadn't met before and there were all her friends from Torbay Hospital where she had worked on and off for most of her adult life, and where she had remained as a night sister in the children's ward until she had finally, just three months or so ago, become too ill to continue. One of the senior doctors, a long-time close friend, had given the address at the crematorium chapel, and he had done so with great warmth and affection. Kelly had been grateful for the way he had so accurately presented Moira's character, for the stories he told about her, and how he had praised her for her humour and practicality, for her kindness and generosity, and above all for her humanity.

Kelly's head was filled with his own memories. How he and Moira had first met, introduced by his matchmaking editor, and how they had first made love and he had been so nervous, after a long period of celibacy, and in such haste to remove his trousers, that he had actually fallen over because he had got them in such a tangle around his ankles. Like something out of a Brian Rix farce, Moira had said, and after that, all that followed had seemed totally natural.

He remembered as well her sense of humour, her willingness to laugh at even his most pathetic jokes, and, most of all, that great, big, rollicking roaring laugh of hers.

He also remembered Moira crying over the death of a child she and her colleagues at Torbay Hospital had fought so hard to save.

She had been a fine human being, and Kelly wished he had

told her how much he had valued and appreciated her far more often. Indeed, he wished he had told her at all, other than when he had done something crass and offensive, which was about the only time he remembered doing so.

He sat in the little chapel next to Jennifer. She held onto his hand tightly throughout the brief service. Nick was sitting behind them. Kelly reckoned they were both rather exceptional young people.

He had looked around as he had walked into the chapel behind Moira's coffin, but had somehow not been able to take a lot in. Certainly, he had recognised few faces that he knew among the congregation, but he had spotted Karen Meadows, sitting at the back near the door, and was glad to see her. She had been a good friend to Moira once, at a time when he had been anything but.

Moira's daughters had invited everyone back to their mother's house for a drink and a snack after the funeral was over; a tradition Kelly had never liked, but he did not even consider opting out because he knew that would upset the girls.

As they all made their way out into the crematorium car park, Karen Meadows approached Kelly and touched him lightly on the arm.

'I really am so very sorry, Kelly,' she said quietly.

'I know,' he said.

'Yes. She's going to be much missed, your Moira.'

'Yes.' These were just the usual platitudes, but Kelly knew she meant every word.

'Look, I won't be able to come back to the house, I'm up to my eyes, but I'll be thinking of you, OK?'

'Yes. Yes. Thank you.' Kelly turned quickly away. He hated people to see him being emotional. For that very reason, he had chosen to drive his own car rather than travel with Moira's daughters and other close family in the undertaker's limos, and as he headed for his car he was glad of that.

On the way back to Moira's house, he detoured to Babbacombe, and pulled off the coast road into a lay-by, where he sat quietly for a few minutes, looking out to sea, relieved to be alone. It was a beautiful day for the time of year. The sea sparkled. He thought about driving down the steep winding hill that led to The Cary Arms, one of his favourite pubs, right by Babbacombe beach. But he didn't really have the time. Had he still been drinking he would have found the time, of course. And, by God, he fancied a stiff drink. But that would have been the final insult to Moira, who had given him such support when he had last kicked the habit. So instead he settled for a roll-up, which he smoked gratefully as he sat in his little MG, looking out through the open window at the luminous navy blue of the Atlantic Ocean to his right and the rows of seaside hotels to his left, barely thinking, barely functioning, barely seeing. He did not break down and cry. It felt almost as if he was beyond that. He just wanted to be on his own for a bit, before rejoining the rest of the mourners.

By the time he arrived at Moira's house, just a few streets away from his own in St Marychurch, the place was packed solid with people. Kelly had no idea how many had turned up, as they were all in different rooms. A group of women, whom he vaguely recognised as nursing colleagues of Moira's, were giggling together over glasses of white wine. There was already that kind of hubbub you always get when large groups gather over a drink, regardless of the circumstances.

Kelly reflected not for the first time how strange it was that so many people seemed to have such a good time at funerals.

He struggled through the hall and living room, exchanging greetings and accepting condolences – mostly from folk he didn't know from Adam – until he reached the kitchen at the back of the house.

The girls had hired caterers for the occasion. None the less, all three of them were in the kitchen supervising the arrangements, as Kelly would have expected them to be. They took after their mother. Born organisers who liked to be in control. Poor Moira, thought Kelly for the umpteenth time. She had never been in control of him, not really. Not the way she would have liked to have been.

Jennifer pushed a tray of sausage rolls and sandwiches towards Kelly. He shook his head. He felt as if he would never eat again. Instead he touched Jennifer's hand, holding on to the rim of the tray, and forced a small smile. She still looked unnaturally pale, and dreadfully tired. He felt a great pang of compassion for her.

She had carried the burden of the last few months so magnificently. And she was so very young. It had been bound to take its toll.

'You should get some rest,' he told her.

'I can't sleep.'

'I know. Neither can I.'

She put the tray down then and came to him for a hug.

'You've been wonderful, you know,' he told her. 'Maybe you should get the doctor to give you something to make you sleep.'

'Maybe.'

She pulled away from him and picked up the tray of food again.

'I was just going to hand these around in the other room,' she said.

He watched her go, head high, back straight, and wished, as ever, that he could have found more words. The right words. Any that weren't trite and condescending, any that might make it all just a little easier. But then, there was no way to make it easier.

He decided to go out into the garden for another smoke, and had to push his way through yet more mourners to get to the back door. Once safely outside, he leaned against the wall of the house, swiftly made himself a roll-up and took a long drag, pulling at it as if it had been days or weeks since he'd had a cigarette rather than just minutes, holding the smoke in his lungs and closing his eyes tightly on the world.

The sun had shone brightly all day, but Moira's back garden faced north and the November air was crisp and chilly. However, Kelly barely noticed. He inhaled the nicotine gratefully and tried not to think about anything.

'Great minds, eh, Dad?'

Kelly opened his eyes abruptly. Nick, holding the collar of his suit jacket closed against the cold with one hand and a cigarette in the other, was standing alongside him. His son was about the only person in the world, Kelly thought, whom he could possibly have been pleased to see at that moment.

'Hello, Nick.'

'How are you doing, Dad?'

'Oh, you know. About how you'd expect, I suppose.'

Nick merely nodded and leaned against the wall alongside his father. For at least a minute they smoked together in companionable silence. Nick finished his cigarette first, threw the butt on the ground, pressed it into the concrete, then took the packet from his pocket and withdrew another one. When he had lit up, he passed the pack to his father who was now reaching the end of his roll-up. Kelly gratefully took one of the ready-made sort for a change, and lit it from his roll-up's glowing end.

'Not given up, then?' queried Nick with a smile.

'No bloody fear,' said Kelly. 'Anyway, you're supposed to be the fit one.'

He glanced towards his son, who still looked every bit as much in shape as he had done during his time in the army.

Nick grinned, flashing even white teeth. He really was a handsome bugger, thought Kelly, reflecting that he certainly didn't get his looks from his father.

'There is a limit,' said Nick. He stopped grinning and glanced at his father appraisingly.

'You sure you're OK, Dad?'

'Oh, yeah. Course I am.'

There was so much Kelly would like to say to Nick. He would like to tell him how much it meant to have his only son there that day, and, indeed, how much it meant to him to have found again this young man whose childhood he had almost totally missed, both when he was still married to Nick's mother, because he had been too busy playing newspapers – and playing around with other women too, if he was honest – and then later, after his marriage had ended, because he dared not look back. And he was so grateful to Nick for seeking him out after years of estrangement and making it so clear that he wanted to build a new relationship with him. The two men were now closer, Kelly sometimes thought, than many fathers and sons who had never had to deal with the disruption of families torn apart and trust destroyed. And Kelly couldn't believe his luck.

He thought Nick understood what he felt, but he was much the same with his son as he had been with his partner. He couldn't bring himself to tell Nick all that. Not properly, anyway. And neither could he bring himself to talk about Moira and just how totally devastated he felt. He had lost his greatest supporter, his rock, and he couldn't tell anyone how it felt, how it really felt, not even Nick.

'Perhaps you might like to come up to London and stay for a couple of days, in a week or two's time, maybe,' Nick began. 'We could take the Aston out for a proper test run somewhere. I'm sure you'd like to put her through her paces.'

Kelly smiled. He didn't think Nick had any idea quite how proud his father was of him. Kelly not only liked and respected Nick, but also admired him for the success he had made of his life, both as a career soldier and now as a business and IT consultant, even though he had never understood exactly what Nick did, except that his son was frequently employed by government departments and that his areas of expertise, particularly involving computers, came directly from his army training. Armies no long marched on their stomachs, but on their keyboards, Nick had once told him. And the secret of success in the modern world was to be multi-skilled, his son also maintained.

Kelly did understand that Nick's work earned him bucket-loads of money. He had actually helped Nick choose that special Aston he had only recently acquired, and the prospect of driving the Aston, coupled with the delight he always found in sharing Nick's company, would normally have caused Kelly to become boyishly excited. But that day he could manage little enthusiasm.

'Thanks, lad, I'll see,' he said.

As ever, Nick seemed to understand his feelings absolutely.

'Of course, Dad,' he said. 'You've got other things on your mind today. I'll call you from London. It's just that, well, I wanted you to know the offer was there, because I'm afraid I have to leave to drive back to town very soon. I'm really sorry, Dad. I had been hoping to stay over, at least for tonight, but I'm in the middle of this big project. I have to be at a meeting in the city first thing tomorrow morning and I just couldn't alter it.'

'That's all right son, don't worry about it. I do understand. I'm just so grateful to you for coming all this way, and I know Moira would have been too.'

'I couldn't do any other,' said Nick simply.

'I know.' Kelly studied him for a moment, so together and capable. Then, before he had really considered what he was going to say, he began to speak again.

'It's a pity, though, because there's something I wanted to talk to you about.'

Nick's eyes softened. Kelly realised at once that his son thought he wanted to touch on those areas he usually avoided, to talk about something concerning Moira, or maybe even about him. What Kelly actually wanted to talk about was Hangridge. Nick was a military man through and through, an ex-soldier who still had plenty of military contacts. He might be able to help considerably. After all, he had been at the cutting edge of the army and had even served with the SAS, possibly the most elite fighting regiment in the world.

Kelly reckoned that Nick might be able to shed all kinds of light on what could have been happening at the Dartmoor barracks. He was more than a little surprised at himself, however, for allowing his thoughts to wander along that road on the day of Moira's funeral. And he had the grace to feel ashamed. He hadn't intended to do this today, but now that the thought had suddenly shot into his mind, demanding his immediate attention, he couldn't quite stop himself, and he was about to launch into an account of the Hangridge affair and to start asking his son questions, when he was interrupted by Jennifer.

'John, Nick, will you come in?' she began. 'We thought we'd ask anyone who wanted to share their memories of Mum to say a few words. John, we wondered if you'd like to start?'

'Of course,' said Kelly automatically, even though his mind had immediately gone a complete blank.

He tossed his second cigarette onto the ground, and Nick did the same. He turned in silence to follow Jennifer, but Nick placed a big hand on his shoulder, momentarily restraining him.

'Look, Dad, I don't have to go straight away,' he said gently. 'I can stay at least another hour, maybe two. We can talk later.'

Kelly felt even more ashamed. He knew that to attempt to talk to Nick about Hangridge that day would be quite wrong, and he could hardly believe he had been about to do so. Nick, who was being so kind and considerate, and obviously making himself

174

ready to hear emotional outpourings from his father, would be more than a little shocked to learn what had been going on in his father's head on such a day.

'Thanks, son, you're a good man,' he said. 'But I don't think this is the time or the place.'

Nick did not even slacken his grip on his father's shoulder. My God, he had strong hands, Kelly thought obliquely.

'It's all right to talk, you know, Dad,' said Nick, and in stark contrast to the steel in his fingers his voice was very soft.

Kelly really did feel embarrassed then. Sometimes he wondered what was wrong with himself. He was genuinely overwhelmed with grief for a woman he really had loved, in his way, probably more than anyone else in his life, except his son, and yet Hangridge, his latest obsession, had, albeit briefly, taken over his head again.

He managed a small smile, one which he hoped was both appreciative and vaguely reassuring.

'Maybe when I come to visit you in London, OK?' he said.

Thirteen

Kelly went to bed very late, and even then he couldn't sleep. He lay tossing and turning for what seemed like an eternity, until he could stand it no more. Wearily he dragged himself out of bed and set off for the kitchen to make himself a cup of tea. On the way downstairs, he glanced at his watch. It was almost exactly 3.30 a.m.

His head ached and he really didn't think that was fair. After all, he was probably the only person at yesterday's wake who hadn't had an alcoholic drink. He felt totally disorientated and very ill at ease. Even though Moira had not been spending most of her time in his home for several months, the knowledge that she was there, with her family, just a couple of streets away, had seemed to make things all right. And, in spite of her being so dreadfully ill, maybe he had been half conning himself that one day she would return and everything would be back to normal. But now he knew she wasn't coming back. He felt empty. Bereft. Even the house felt different. Almost as if it had lost its soul.

While the kettle boiled, he rummaged in the kitchen cupboard where he kept the bulk of what passed for his medical supplies, and eventually found a packet of Nurofen with three pills left in it. He pushed two of the capsules through their silver-foil container and swallowed them dry, then he removed the third and swallowed that too.

To hell with it, he thought dejectedly. His head was throbbing for England.

He made the tea, ladled in the usual three spoonfuls of sugar and then headed for his favourite armchair in the living room, where he sat down and switched on the TV. His head began to ease a little as he drank the tea. An old episode of *Columbo* was being screened on Plus. Watching anything was better than struggling to sleep; in any case he rather liked the crumpled San

176

Francisco detective, and fervently wished that real-life investigators were able to come up with such neat endings so easily.

The last thing Kelly remembered was that Columbo was about to explain to the villain exactly how and why he was guilty of murder. Then he must have fallen asleep, and so would probably never know the denouement. He woke with a start. The phone was ringing. Immediately, he felt the familiar stab of panic which he had been experiencing for some weeks whenever the phone rang at an antisocial time. Moira. Had something happened to Moira? Then he remembered. Something had happened to Moira, all right. She was dead. That period of his life was over, and so was the constant, nagging anxiety that had recently been the major part of it. His eyes felt sore, but he registered that he no longer had a headache. He had not closed the curtains the previous night, and bright morning light was streaming into the east-facing room. However, that alone had not been enough to wake him. Automatically, he glanced at his watch. It was 7.45 a.m. Why did he seem able, even under the most stressful circumstances, to sleep in a chair when he couldn't do so in his own bed, he reflected obliquely as he reached for the phone. And, anyway, who the hell could be calling him at this time?

'Kelly,' he said abruptly.

'John, sorry if I'm calling you too early, it's just that I thought you might be leaving for work and I didn't want to miss you.'

Kelly didn't go to work any more, not in the way implied, and he had absolutely no idea who his caller was. It was a woman's voice – clear, intelligent and somehow rather determined-sounding. There was something vaguely familiar about the voice, but not enough for Kelly to come close to identifying it.

'It's Margaret Slade.'

Jesus, thought Kelly, she sounded a bit different to how she had been when he'd visited her in her sad little flat.

'Oh, hello,' he said.

'I just wondered if you'd managed to find out anything more about that other young soldier I told you about. The one called Trevor, the one I was told had also died at Hangridge.'

'Ah, no, not yet.' Kelly had made no further enquiries concerning Hangridge since Moira's death, and wasn't at all

177

sure when he'd feel able to do so again. He had felt so crass when he had almost started cross-examining Nick the previous day, that it had rather put him off the whole thing. But, naturally, he had no intention of sharing that with Margaret Slade.

'I've been a bit busy,' he finished lamely.

'Oh,' Margaret Slade sounded disappointed. 'Oh, well, it doesn't matter. I'm sorry I bothered you. I just thought . . .'

Her voice tailed off. She sounded more than disappointed. She sounded thoroughly let down. He knew exactly what she thought. Kelly had bounced in, full of confidence, appearing to be both capable and informed, and she had thought that he was committed to investigating the death of her daughter and the others. What he probably hadn't realised, based on that one meeting with her drunk out of her skull, was how much she still cared.

'No, no. It's not how it seems. Look . . .'

He considered for just a split second. He found he did not want to let this woman down, neither did he want to let down her daughter nor any of the other young people whose lives had been lost at Hangridge.

'Look,' he said again. 'My partner died right after I left you last week. It was the funeral yesterday. We'd been expecting it. She was very ill, but even so . . .'

He stopped and took a very deep breath. Margaret Slade, he thought, would have absolutely no idea what it cost Kelly to confide even as little as that to a total stranger. Somewhat to his surprise, however, he was immediately rather glad that he had done so.

'I'm so sorry, John,' said Mrs Slade, and her voice alone told him that she really meant it, even though she barely knew him and had not known Moira at all. But, of course, this was a woman who understood about grief and despair.

'And I'm so sorry for intruding at this sad time,' she went on, in a strangely formal sort of way. But then, thought Kelly, it is to the traditional and to the formal that we all cling in our grief. And, again, Margaret Slade would know about that.

'I'll call again in a week or two, if that's all right.'

'No, don't go, Margaret.' It seemed quite natural that they were now on Christian-name terms. 'Please. I'm fine, honestly.'

'If you're sure?'

'Absolutely sure. It will help me to think about something else.'

'Yes.' Only one word, but again Kelly was aware that Margaret Slade understood. 'It's just that, well, I've been in touch with Marcia Foster, Craig's mother. I found the letter she wrote after my Jossy died. I kept everything, you know. Put it all in a box. Anyway, we've decided we want to do something. We want all the families to get together, to form an organisation. An action group, I think they call it. I was hoping you might give me Alan Connelly's parents' address.'

Kelly was surprised and impressed. He thought for a moment. Apart from anything else, it was also a heaven-sent excuse to get in touch with the Connellys again. Neil Connelly hadn't been very receptive, but Kelly would now be able to tell him about two more deaths. That might change things.

'I'm not sure that I should do that, Margaret,' he said. 'But I'll tell you what I will do. I'll contact them again, tell them all about you and ask them to call you. How's that?'

'OK.' She paused. 'There's something else. Marcia Foster and I wondered if you would help us. We've no experience of doing anything like this. We wondered if you'd tell us what we should do, who we should write to, that sort of thing.'

'Well, yes,' Kelly begun. The journalist in him was beginning to think about what all this would mean in terms of his big story. Selfishly, the problem for him would be that this action group could mean that his exclusive might become public property sooner than he had bargained for. If the families started going straight to the TV and press, and there was little doubt that attracting the attention of the media would be a major part of any campaign, then Kelly's input would become virtually irrelevant – or, at least, it would be based solely on what he had so far.

'It's more than that, really, though,' Margaret Slade continued. 'We'd like you to conduct an investigation on our behalf. People hire private detectives for stuff like this, don't they? Well, we'd like to hire you. You're a professional investigator, after all, of a kind. And you've already told us much more than we knew before.'

'Well, I don't know—'

'We'll pay you,' interrupted Margaret Slade. 'I'd never expect anyone to work for nothing. We'll pay you the going rate. I don't have any money, but Marcia has her husband's life insurance, and she says she knows he wouldn't be able to think of a better way for her to spend it. We're going to start a fighting fund, too. I've read about that sort of thing. It's what people do when they're trying to achieve something, when they have a cause, isn't it?'

'Well, yes.' Kelly felt quite humbled. He was, however, still a journalist at heart. It occurred to him almost at once that Margaret Slade's suggestion could give him the solution to his exclusivity problem.

'There wouldn't be any need for you to pay me,' he said. 'Look, a big part of any campaign like this is getting the media on board and on your side. You realise that, I'm sure?'

'Yes, of course. That's one of the reasons we thought you would be the right person for us to employ.'

'You did?' Kelly was surprised. He was pretty sure he hadn't mentioned his journalistic past to either of the two women. He hadn't wanted to frighten them away, not at that stage. And, in any case, even if he had mentioned it to Margaret Slade, he very much doubted that she would have been in any condition to remember.

'Well, the thing is,' he continued. 'If you give me exclusive rights to place any stories and information that we come up with between us, I can make quite enough money directly from the media. You wouldn't need to pay me anything.'

'Better still.'

'Right.' Kelly paused. 'You seem to know that I was a journalist. How? I don't think I told you . . .'

'No, you said you were a writer, so I looked you up on the Net,' she said. 'Couldn't find any books, but then all these newspaper stories kept popping up, and I found a biog' on you when you'd been a speaker at a journalists' training seminar a few years ago.'

'Ah.' Kelly would have to rethink his opinion of Margaret Slade. When sober, she was very different to the image he had conjured up of her in his mind. He now detected a distinctly educated note in her voice, which he had totally missed when he first met her. But then, she had been so drunk it would have been difficult to detect anything. However, her memory of that afternoon seemed to be rather better than he would have considered possible, given the state she was in. None the less, his initial reaction had been to be surprised that she had a computer at all, let alone that she was able to surf the Net so effectively.

'It's a very old computer,' Margaret Slade continued, as if reading his mind. She really did seem to be an unusually perceptive woman. 'I bought it second-hand for Jossy when she was still at school. Before . . . before . . .'

She paused mid-sentence and Kelly was momentarily puzzled. She had already said she bought the computer when Jossy was still at school. She could have been about to say 'before Jossy died', but that was obvious. She wouldn't have bought her a computer afterwards, would she?'

'Before I started drinking again,' she continued eventually.

'Ah,' said Kelly.

'Yes. Look. I want you to know about my drinking before we go any further.'

'You sound sober enough, now,' said Kelly.

'It is ten to eight in the morning,' responded Margaret Slade, a light irony in her voice.

She had a sense of humour too, thought Kelly.

'Fair enough,' said Kelly. 'But you don't sound like someone who was drunk when they went to bed last night.'

'And you'd know that?'

'Oh, yes. First-hand knowledge. For many years. And I suspect I was probably much much worse than you've ever been.'

'You must have gone some, then,' retorted Margaret Slade.

Kelly was beginning to rather enjoy this conversation. 'I certainly did,' he replied.

'Well, it began in the usual way for me, as a young woman. Social drinking, that sort of thing. It was the seventies. Everybody I knew was drinking. About the only thing Jossy's father and I had in common was the booze. I think it's why I married him. My parents, well, they were already getting worried about my drinking, and they disapproved of Trevor from the start. Wish I'd listened to them. Then I might not be in this state.

'Anyway, after Trev left me, I very nearly hit rock bottom. But I managed to pull myself together, reckoned I had to, for the kids. I went to Alcoholics Anonymous, and somehow or other I kicked the drink. It was never easy for me, but I did it. Then my parents died suddenly one after the other, and they left me some money. We didn't always live in this crummy flat, you know. I had a nice little house.

'I wasn't such a bad mother, either, I don't think. Not all the time, anyway. I was dry for what – six, seven years. Then when Jossy was, oh, about fourteen, I started again. It was man trouble. Story of my life. I thought I'd found Mr Right, and he turned out to be an even bigger rat than my ex-husband. He conned me out of a lot of money. I took out a mortgage on our little house to invest in an office-cleaning business he was starting, and guess what, it went bust. If it ever bloody existed. And then, when he had milked me virtually dry, he took off. Gone. I was left bitter, twisted and broke. Naturally, I thought that alcohol was my only solace, and that was the final straw.

'We lost the house, ended up in this dump, and I don't think I've been sober for a day since. Until – until the day after you came calling.'

'Really?'

'I went to an AA meeting again that night. That very night. Half canned, still. First time in nearly five years. I thought I'd screwed my Jossy up. I thought I was the reason she was dead, and that made me not care about anything else at all, including myself. Now I know it may have been nothing to do with me. I need to find out the truth, for me and for my girl. She could have been murdered, John, that's what you're saying, isn't it?'

Kelly spoke carefully.

'It's possible,' he said. 'It has to be possible. But it isn't going to be an easy ride to find out what really happened. The army will block us all the way, I'm sure of it. They've already started doing just that.'

'I didn't imagine for one minute that it would be easy, John,' Margaret Slade responded. 'That's why I wanted you on board. I had an uncle who was a Fleet Street reporter. It was years ago

182

and he's dead now, but I still remember his stories from when I was a kid. If an old tabloid hack can't find a way through red tape and obstruction, I don't know who can.'

Kelly found that he was smiling when he put the phone down. The adrenaline was starting to pump. He couldn't wait to get on the case. He wanted to call Alan Connelly's father straight away, to try to persuade him that he should be prepared to question the army's version of events, and that he should get in touch with Margaret Slade.

He looked at his watch again. It was still not quite eight o'clock. He didn't dare ring the Connelly household yet, not before at least 8.30, he reckoned. He had not exactly been welcomed into their home with open arms, and he suspected that Neil Connelly was not going to be all that pleased to hear from him, let alone if he disturbed the family too early in the morning. Kelly had to persuade the man to listen and to think, and he had to be very careful in his approach.

He mulled all this over as he picked up the mug he had used in the early hours and made his way into the kitchen to make more tea. His right leg was still not functioning properly. He kicked it to and fro as he refilled the kettle, and while he waited for it to boil. Spending half the night in that chair had done him no good at all. He stretched his back and his arms. Everything ached.

He made tea in the same unwashed mug, pouring boiling water over a tea bag, and perched on one of the two stools alongside what Moira had called the breakfast bar. Moira. The service sheet from her funeral lay on the worktop next to the cooker. He hadn't noticed it in the night. But then, he had been in a kind of sleepless haze.

His mind was buzzing now. First of all there was Hangridge and the possibly immense significance of his conversation with Margaret Slade. Her approach to him presented something of a dream scenario. In his mind's eye, he could already see the avalanche of major stories with which he would bombard Fleet Street. Not to mention TV and radio. Then there would be the book, the real-life story of Hangridge, just an extension of the investigative journalism he had made a lifelong career of, something he was well qualified for – unlike attempting to be a novelist. And after that, the film . . .

Yes. There was all of that. But mixed up with it, somehow, were his feelings for Moira, his sense of loss, his compassion for her, and his guilt. He felt genuine compassion, too, for the young Hangridge soldiers who had died, and for their bereaved families.

Predictably enough, however, it was Hangridge that was dominating his thoughts. It wasn't just that the slowly unfolding drama was becoming so intriguing. He was also aware that his involvement in it would be sure to distract him from his pain. He told himself that Moira would have understood.

He checked his watch again. Quarter past eight. Still too early. There was a possibility, of course, that Neil Connelly had returned to his job as a postman, in which case he would probably have left his home hours earlier, but Kelly didn't think so. He reckoned it might be some time yet before Connelly would have recovered sufficiently from the shock of his son's death to return to work. He wandered into the living room and whiled away the next fifteen minutes watching breakfast TV. At 8.30 promptly he called the Connellys in Glasgow, which turned out to be something of an anticlimax. There was no reply. The family had an answering machine but Kelly did not leave a message. He needed to make a personal approach, and he needed it to be good. He would just have to keep calling until he could speak to Neil Connelly direct. Momentarily, he cursed himself for not phoning earlier, even though he knew really that he had done the right thing. He had no idea if Mrs Connelly still worked or not, but maybe Neil Connelly had returned to his job already, after all. If he had called earlier, he may have caught him. On the other hand, maybe the family were just not answering the phone. Maybe the whole lot of them – Alan Connelly's mother, father, younger brother and sister – had shut themselves away from the world in their neat little home, an oasis of order on that grim housing estate, isolated by their grief.

Kelly shivered. There was no physical reason for it. The room wasn't cold and he wasn't ill. He remembered his mother's old saying, that somebody had walked over his grave. Maybe they had. Kelly could think of one hell of a lot of folk who might like to.

Just before nine he called Karen Meadows. She was another one he had to use his best persuasion techniques on. He really needed her help. He also suddenly wanted very much to know what progress she had made, if any, during the six days since Moira had died.

'I didn't expect to hear from you today,' she said.

'No, well, I guess we all just try to carry on,' responded Kelly. He thought he sounded trite and pathetic at the same time.

'Yes, I guess we do.' At least he could rely on Karen Meadows not to be judgemental, thought Kelly. It was perhaps a strange asset for a police officer. Kelly was not sure that he had ever been aware of her passing any kind of personal judgement on anyone.

'I wanted to talk about Hangridge,' he said bluntly.

'Today? Are you sure?' She was being quite gentle with him. By her standards, certainly. He appreciated it.

'Absolutely sure,' he said.

'OK, I was going to call you tomorrow, anyway. I just didn't want to bother you the day after the funeral, but I do need to talk to you.'

That made Karen Meadows the second woman to surprise him that morning. And he had still not had breakfast. She had not been ready to give much away the last time they had met. All that stuff about procedure and protocol. Something must have happened. Something that had changed her mind, made her actually want to talk to him.

'I just wondered how you've been getting on with it, and if—' he began.

'No,' she interrupted swiftly. 'Not on the phone. Can you meet me this evening?'

'Of course. The pub? Or do you want to go for something to eat . . .'

'No. My place. About half past seven. We need to talk in private.'

Kelly felt a burst of adrenaline coursing through his veins. This was out of character. What did it mean? What was going on?

He agreed at once and Karen then ended the call with the

abruptness he was used to, which he was actually rather more comfortable with than her earlier gentle approach. He finished his tea, wolfed down a bowl of cornflakes and then tried the Connellys' number again. This time Neil Connelly himself answered promptly. Maybe the family had been having a lie-in. Kelly doubted they had been sleeping well. He knew all about not sleeping well.

The call was very nearly extremely short.

'I told ye, I didn't want to talk to ye,' said Connelly sharply, as soon as Kelly gave his name.

'I know, I just want to tell you something and then I'll go away.' Kelly spoke quickly, afraid the other man would hang up. 'I now know of at least two other suspicious deaths at Hangridge, a young man and a young woman, and a possible third. The parents of the other two are getting together, they want a proper investigation into the deaths—'

'You are a fucking journalist, aren't you, just like I thought.' Neil Connelly interrupted. Neither his tone of voice nor his language were encouraging.

'Not any more,' responded Kelly, more or less truthfully.

'Well, I don't fucking trust you—'

'You don't have to, Mr Connelly.' This time it was Kelly's turn to interrupt. Now he really was afraid that the Scotsman would hang up. 'But maybe you would trust the mother of a young woman soldier, called Jocelyn Slade, who died about six months before your lad. She wants to talk to you, and if you'd just make a note of her name and number, I promise you'll never hear from me again unless I know you want to.'

It seemed a very long time before Mr Connelly spoke again. And when he did, he was brief and to the point.

'Very well,' he said. 'That's a deal.'

Kelly gave him Margaret Slade's phone number and Neil Connelly ended the call at once. Kelly had no idea what the result might be. He thought Connelly was a stubborn man as well as a proud one, but there was little doubt that he had truly loved his son.

Kelly went over it all again in his head as he made his way upstairs to have a shower and dress. He was beginning to feel the familiar impatience. He wanted things to start happening. And he really wanted to talk to Karen Meadows. What was she going to tell him? What information was she going to give him? She hadn't summoned him to her home for nothing, that was for certain. He just couldn't wait for 7.30 that evening. And he had fat chance of doing any work on the great novel before then, he reflected wryly, as he stood under the hot jet of water and rubbed shampoo into his head with more energy than he had mustered in months.

Fourteen

After arranging to meet Kelly later, Karen then found herself battling with nagging doubts. Was she doing the right thing? After all, she had originally promised herself that this investigation, and the extent to which she was allowed to investigate it at all, would be strictly by the book.

She picked up the paper cup of coffee which she had extracted from the machine a little earlier, then half forgotten about, and took a mouthful which she promptly spat back into the cup. It was barely tepid, and the stuff was bad enough even when it was hot.

She poured the coffee into the pot of the rubber plant she kept in one corner, noticing as she did so that the plant no longer looked all that happy, which could, she reflected, be not unconnected with the many previous cups of highly questionable coffee which had been emptied into its container. None the less, she set off downstairs to fetch herself another one. There were all kinds of people in a CID office who could, without too much difficulty, be persuaded to fetch coffee for their boss, but somehow Karen was never comfortable asking people to do such menial tasks for her. In any case, running the errand herself gave her thinking time.

She didn't really have any doubts. Just some fears, she supposed. And that was only rational.

But by the time she reached her home that evening, only just before 7.30, she had conquered her fears and come to terms with her intentions.

He arrived on the dot of 7.30. She had barely had time to take off her coat and rush around her flat picking up the abandoned shoes and various other items of scattered clothing, which she then hurled indiscriminately into the bedroom. Sometimes her untidiness did spread from there into the living room and other parts of her flat, in spite of her best efforts not to let that happen.

She had only just shut the bedroom door on the mayhem within, even greater now than it had been that morning, when her front doorbell rang. As she hurried to open it, she ran the fingers of one hand through her hair, in a pathetic effort to bring it to order after her exertions. She thought her face was probably bright pink. But, in any case, it was only Kelly waiting outside in the corridor. And she forgot about herself when she saw him. His eyes were red-rimmed, his face pale and drawn. He did not look well at all, and she thought he had aged dramatically over the last few days.

'Come here,' she said, and, almost automatically, gave him a big hug. 'You look all in.'

'I've had better days,' he said. 'And better times in my life.' He paused. 'Mind you, I've had worst times, too.'

He grinned. Karen smiled. She knew all about his chequered past. Yes, he almost certainly had had worst times, she suspected.

Yet Kelly's sense of humour rarely failed him, even in the grimmest of situations, and it was, to Karen, one of his most endearing characteristics. He was acutely aware of his own shortcomings and had always used humour, often directed quite harshly against himself, to deal with the more unfortunate consequences of his frequently wayward behaviour.

'Come in,' she said, ushering him into the sitting room with one hand, as she closed the front door with the other.

She offered him tea and went to the kitchen to make it and to open a bottle of red wine for herself.

When she returned he was standing by a window, with his back to the room, looking out over the bay. She walked silently across to him and held out the mug of tea without speaking.

He turned and took it from her. 'You know, I think Moira enjoyed walking along Torquay seafront more than almost anything else. We had holidays together – even one or two quite flash ones – but I think the times when we both had an afternoon off and we walked together along the front, had an ice cream or a hot dog, and maybe a drink in the early evening and a fish supper, I think those may have been our happiest times together.'

He stopped abruptly and immediately looked as if he wished he had not said so much. Karen knew only too well that it did not come easily to John Kelly to share his feelings. And it was highly indicative of his state of mind for him to tell her a story about Moira, rather than jumping straight in to cross-examine her about any developments in the Hangridge case.

She waited for a moment, but he said nothing else. She also knew better than to try to prompt him. Instead, she squeezed his arm and invited him to sit down on the sofa.

She sat next to him and, without waiting for him to ask her anything, launched into an account of her problems with the hierarchy concerning any further investigation of Hangridge.

'At the moment, I cannot get the CC to agree to launch an official police investigation. I think that is wrong—'

'So do I.'

'Don't interrupt. This is tricky enough, and if you ever tell anyone a word of what I am about to say to you, I shall deny everything. OK?'

'Can I speak now?'

'Kelly!' There was a warning note in her voice, but she was actually mildly reassured. He might be in a bit of a state, but he was still the same old Kelly. And as sharp as ever.

'OK. I shall press delete immediately and wipe this meeting from my memory.'

'Very funny. This is no joke, though, Kelly, as you well know, and you really will have to do just that for both our sakes. You see, I actually want you to blow this thing wide open, because it's the only way, I'm afraid, that anyone is going to get even close to the truth.

'So, I'm prepared to give you every bit of information I can to help you investigate. And I'll be working with you behind the scenes. Officially I can do bugger all, not yet, anyway, but unofficially everything I can glean will be yours. However, in return, I do expect you to tell me everything you get. I don't want any holding back.'

Kelly looked doubtful. He really was a typical journalist, thought Karen, much better at acquiring information than giving any away. And that went for his personal life, too.

'That's the deal,' she said. 'Take it or leave it.'

190

'You're a hard woman,' he replied.

'Sometimes I think I'm soft as shit,' she replied.

'Never.'

She waited.

'OK, it's a deal,' he said.

He hesitated then. She saw through him at once. She knew Kelly well.

'Come on,' she instructed. 'Spit it out. You've something to tell me already, haven't you?'

'Yeah, I guess I have. The families are getting together. Margaret Slade called me this morning, sounding, much to my surprise, extremely switched on . . .'

He then gave her a précised version of the call.

'So, there you have it,' he said when he had finished. 'The families are going to form an action group, and they want me to be their official representative. Funny old world, isn't it?'

'It sure is. That could be extremely good news, though, Kelly. The authorities won't be able to ignore you if you're representing the families of the dead young soldiers, so you should be able to get access, certainly with a little persistence, to almost anyone you want to see. And it distances you from the media too.'

'Well, up to a point . . .' said Kelly cautiously.

Karen grinned. She was a realist. She would not even ask about whatever deal Kelly may have made with Margaret Slade, and indeed it was probably better that she didn't know. But she could imagine it well enough. And, deal or no deal, to imagine even for one moment that Kelly would investigate Hangridge without recording everything that happened and attempting to turn it into the story of his life would be completely unrealistic.

'Once a hack . . .' she said.

He grinned back.

'Thanks, anyway, Karen,' he said. 'You know, together we may even be able to crack this.'

'All I need from you is enough information, so that I can damned well force that arse-licking bastard Tomlinson to let me launch a proper police investigation. At least, that would be a start.'

'I'll do my best,' said Kelly. Karen felt his eyes on her.

'I have a feeling you may have some information for me first,' he continued.

'You're right,' she said, reaching for her Voyage denim bag which she had dumped on the floor next to the sofa. She opened it and retrieved a small sheaf of A4 paper print-outs from her office computer.

'Inquest reports,' she announced, and watched Kelly's eyes light up.

'Jocelyn Slade, whose death doesn't add up at all in my opinion, Craig Foster, and a young man called Trevor Parsons.'

She paused for dramatic effect and was not disappointed. Kelly was on the edge of his seat.

'And the death of Trevor Parsons is indeed another alleged suicide, even if it was much earlier.' She tapped the small pile of papers. 'Parsons' home address is on record and so is the address of another young soldier, who seems to me to be of considerable interest. Fusilier James Gates. He was called as a witness at Slade's inquest.'

'Wow,' said Kelly. 'That's a hell of a start, Karen. I'd better be off. I'll read the reports tonight and start following them up in the morning.'

He rose to his feet and held out one hand. She passed him the papers. He smiled at her, but it was a pretty wan attempt. Karen looked him up and down. His appearance was haggard. In spite of the enthusiasm he had displayed, she thought he might be close to total exhaustion.

'You're not sleeping, are you?' she enquired.

'No,' he said, then managing a smile, added: 'Well, not in a bed, anyway. Sit me upright in a chair and I go off like a light, only to wake up crippled with cramp and feeling a darned sight worse, I suspect, than if I hadn't slept at all.'

'And are you eating?'

'Eating?' Kelly sounded puzzled. 'Do you know, I can't really remember when I last ate anything. I felt sick all day yesterday, and today, eating just hasn't occurred to me.'

'Do you feel hungry now?'

'I honestly don't know.'

'How about staying here for a while, and I'll order us a pizza?'

192

She saw him hesitate, then he sat down again on the sofa, folding the papers and tucking them into his jacket pocket.

'I think I'd like that,' he said.

'Any particular sort?'

'I'll leave that to you.'

He may have recognised that he should eat, but he was obviously still uninterested in food. Karen was more than a little anxious about her old friend. Still watching him out of the corner of one eye, she reached for the phone and arranged for her local pizza takeaway to deliver a large Four Seasons.

Kelly started speaking again as soon as she finished the call. And it was almost as if he had forgotten all about the controversial case they had just been discussing and the plot the two of them had hatched.

'I know Moira and I never officially lived together,' he told her, his voice much softer and weaker than usual. 'But she was always in my house, and even when she wasn't, well, it felt like she was. Does that sound stupid? What I mean is, I could always feel her presence. She was there. In my life. Even when she wasn't actually within the same four walls. And now, well, she's gone. For good. Her presence is no longer there and the place just seems totally empty. And I . . . and I . . . I feel quite desolate.' He stumbled over the last few words.

'Does that make any sense at all?' he went on.

'Yes,' said Karen promptly. 'Of course it does. That's the way these things are, I think.'

It was the answer she thought that he needed, and she was also sure it must be the truth. But she realised, with a fleeting sadness, that she really had no idea whether that was actually the case, because she had never achieved a relationship which even approached what Kelly had described. There had been that disastrous early liaison with a man who turned out to be a con artist, which could have ended her career, had not Kelly, who was investigating the man, chosen to refrain from making it public. And her subsequent love life had been little more than a series of casual flings and one-night stands, until her recent, mind-numbing, soul-destroying affair with Detective Sergeant Phil Cooper. But she wasn't going to think about him and the devastating effect that relationship had had on her. Not tonight. Not ever again, if she could help it.

The ring of the doorbell saved her from having to come up with more of the right thing to say. After all, she was no better at soul-baring than Kelly. Indeed, quite possibly she was worse.

She opened the door, paid the pizza delivery boy, turning down Kelly's shouted-out offer to share the cost, and put the box on the coffee table in front of the sofa.

After going into the kitchen and fetching a roll of kitchen paper, another glass of red wine for herself and a Diet Coke from the fridge for Kelly, she returned to the living room to find Kelly staring into space, the box still unopened before him.

She did the honours and passed him a slice of pizza, precariously balanced on a piece of kitchen paper.

He ate without enthusiasm, but finished the slice apart from the edge of the crust, which he rolled up in the kitchen paper she had given him.

She persuaded him to take a second slice, which he ate half of. She was starving – as usual. Two slices disappeared at a rate of knots and she was well into the third before she felt her hunger even begin to abate.

Kelly, having finished, walked to the window again and once more stood, with his back to the room, looking out over the bay, while Karen continued to eat. When she eventually felt moderately full, she joined him there.

The room was dimly lit and they could see outside quite clearly, as the entire seafront was brightly illuminated by a mix of standard street lighting, strings of multicoloured fairy lights and the headlights of passing cars.

'Still thinking about those walks with Moira?' she ventured gently.

He did not reply, instead turning slightly more away from her.

She did not persist. She knew better. She stood quietly alongside him for a moment until she noticed that, although he had uttered absolutely no sound, his shoulders were shaking almost imperceptibly.

She put an arm around him and half turned him towards her. His body was strangely unresisting. She saw then that tears were streaming down his face. He was silently sobbing his heart out.

194

She put both arms around him then and held him very tightly, still saying nothing.

'It's all mixed up in my head,' he muttered through the tears. 'Moira's death, Hangridge, not being able to write. Did I tell you? Barely two fucking chapters, that's all I've managed. I didn't tell you that, did I?'

'No, Kelly, you didn't,' she said quietly.

'No. I haven't told anyone. I can't do it, Karen. So much for becoming the great bloody novelist. I can't fucking do it. You have to go into your head to write fiction. I don't like what's inside my head, and I can't cope with it either. Not now I can't. And as for Hangridge, well, I've been as absorbed with that over the last few weeks as I have with Moira. And that makes me feel guilty. I just feel so guilty. I can't sort myself out. It's all such a muddle . . . such a desperate, fucking muddle . . .'

He clung to her.

'I'm sorry, I'm so sorry.' He repeated the words over and over again, in between great wrenching sobs.

'It's all right, Kelly,' she said, in a way that she hoped was soothing. 'It's all right. It's allowed to show grief, you know. You're allowed to cry. So do so. Go on. Cry. As much and for as long as you like.'

After a bit, he stopped even attempting to weep quietly. He gave in to it and stopped trying to control the tears. It must have been fully two or three minutes before the sobs became less violent, but he still held onto her. Like a child, she thought. Then he said it again.

'I'm so sorry. Really.'

'Don't be, please don't be,' she said. 'I'm honoured.'

She took a paper tissue from the pocket of her jeans and gently wiped his face with it with one hand. With the other, she stroked his forehead. Suddenly she felt very tender towards him.

And then it happened. Something changed in his body, and to her surprise, and perhaps also to her dismay, she felt it change in her own body too. Maybe it was the display of tenderness that brought about the change, maybe it was something else, something beyond both their comprehension. She wasn't sure. But, suddenly, John Kelly was no longer a child seeking nothing more than comfort.

His arms tightened around her and he began to kiss her face, her forehead, her eyes, and then, finally, her mouth. His lips sought hers with a kind of desperation. She didn't mean to respond, but somehow could not stop herself. He pressed his lips against hers and his arms began to move over her body, stroking and caressing her. Then she found that she was doing that to him too. He eased her lips apart with his tongue. She did not resist, instead she opened her mouth for him. For several seconds they stood like that, wrapped around each other, straining to make the kiss deeper and deeper, more and more demanding.

Then, all of a sudden, a moment of sanity hit her. What they were doing was madness. Total and utter madness. And she had had enough of such madness in her life. Kelly had buried his partner only the day before. His emotions could not be trusted, and neither, she suspected, could her own. Also, this was, at the very least, totally crass behaviour. Worse than that, it was quite horrible behaviour. And she could not live with it, even if he could. In addition, this was John Kelly. Her old friend and sparring partner. He had never been, and never could be, her lover. Not under any circumstances, she told herself, and certainly not under these circumstances. She was disgusted with herself.

Immediately, she jerked her head back, pulling away from his kiss, and at the same time struggled to push him away. It wasn't much of a struggle. She felt his grip slacken and sensed him beginning to back off, even before she put both her hands on his shoulders and pushed. They both stepped back and stood, breathing heavily, looking at each other.

Kelly bowed his head slightly. She suspected he felt much the same way as she did.

'Now I really, really, am sorry,' he said eventually. 'I just don't know what came over me. That was a disgraceful thing to do. I'm just—'

'No,' she interrupted him. 'No. It takes two. I played my part, all right. And I don't know what came over me, either. At least you have an excuse. You're on an emotional roller coaster at the moment. You've just lost the most important person in your life, you're in a muddle, you said that. You hardly know what you're doing . . .'

196

'Don't I?' he responded quietly. 'No. No. You won't make me feel better. I have no excuse at all, just a lot of reasons why I should not have done that. Look, I really had better go.'

She felt almost as emotionally drained as she was sure he was. Certainly, she had no energy left to try to further rationalise either his behaviour or her own. She just wanted to be left alone, to at least try to come to grips with what had happened. Or rather, she supposed, what had nearly happened.

'Yes,' she said quietly. 'I think you better had go.'

She made no effort to see him out. He knew the way well enough. And he went at once, without saying another word. Perhaps, like her, he did not know what more to say.

She remained standing at the window and watched as his little MG pulled out of the car park and began to move slowly along the seafront road.

Sophie was at her feet, brushing against her, trying to wind herself around her legs. It was funny how, on the one hand, she was a typically selfish cat and, on the other, so sensitive to Karen's moods that she almost invariably seemed to know when her mistress needed comfort.

Karen bent down and picked up the cat, scratching the back of her neck as she lifted her against one shoulder. Sophie's more or less constant purring grew louder and louder in her ear.

'You know what, Sophe,' Karen murmured. 'Your Uncle Kelly and I very nearly did something extremely stupid.'

Karen realised she was almost in a state of shock. Fond as she was of him, she had never considered Kelly in any sort of romantic or sexual way before. It had just never occurred to her.

And she was grateful that they had both come to their senses before that extraordinary moment had developed into something more. She was extremely glad they had stopped. But only because she had felt it was wrong. After all, the timing had been just terrible.

But the man, when his arms had been around her and his body pressed against hers, had not felt wrong at all. He had been both tender and exciting at the same time. As for the kiss, well, the kiss had been fabulous. Quite fabulous. She didn't want to admit that, but it was true.

197

She could still taste it, still feel it. It had been a very special kiss indeed, and she was quite astonished. She had never thought there could be anything like that between her and Kelly.

None the less, it must go no further. She did not need any more man trouble, and Kelly was always, always, trouble. Also, she valued their friendship a great deal, and romance – or perhaps she really meant sex – was, in Karen's experience, all too often inclined to render friendship dead in the water.

'There's only one thing for it, Sophe,' she muttered to the still-purring cat. 'Your Uncle Kelly and I just have to forget all about that little incident and go back to exactly the way we were before.'

Fifteen

Kelly's whole body was trembling as he drove home. Like Karen, he had found their kiss very special. It had woken up his senses again. He had always found Karen attractive, but in an abstract kind of way, and it had simply never occurred to him before that their relationship could ever become anything other than it was. And now, like Karen, he believed that what had happened between them had been very wrong, particularly at this time. The fact that he had so actively enjoyed kissing Karen, just one day after he had buried his partner, made him feel quite sick. In effect, what he had done was little more than to make a clumsy pass at Karen Meadows, quite possibly destroying a friendship he cherished. And then there was their professional association. Had he destroyed that too?

Normally, even at a difficult time like this when he was coping with grief, he would be feeling elated to be on the threshold of an investigation like the Hangridge one. And, indeed, he had been truly excited by the information which Karen had handed him on a plate. It was, after all, potential dynamite. This was the kind of story the old hack in him lived for. And now he had spoilt it all. Not only had he killed the thrill of it for himself, but also, for all he knew, Karen Meadows might not even be prepared to continue with the information-sharing scheme she had presented to him. At the very least she must consider him dangerously unstable, he reflected.

He muttered a few expletives as he parked the MG. Why was he such a fool? But then, perhaps he had always been dangerously unstable.

The house looked particularly dark and empty that night. He hurried to unlock the door, get inside and switch on the lights. It was almost as cold in the house as it had been outside.

He checked the central heating boiler. The timer had been playing up. The system had closed down a good couple of hours earlier than it should have done. Cursing some more, Kelly switched it on again, made himself a mug of tea and wandered upstairs to check his answering machine.

There was a message from Margaret Slade. Brief and to the point.

'Neil Connelly has just phoned. Whatever you said to him worked. He's come round in a big way. I think he's going to join the campaign. Call me.'

Kelly smiled. At least this would give him something else to think about. Still marvelling at the change in the woman, he returned Margaret Slade's call at once.

'I told him all I knew and I reckon he's prepared to go all the way with us,' she said. 'He's a solid sort of man, too, I think. It's just journalists he doesn't like.'

'I'm not a journalist.'

'Yes, well that's the sort of prevarication that puts him off 'em, I should say.'

Kelly chuckled.

'You've got an answer for everything, all of a sudden, Margaret. And, by God, you're going to need to have, taking on the military. You should know that the police, although aware of a big question mark hanging over these deaths at Hangridge, are not going to be investigating. Not at the moment, anyway. The official view is that these deaths have already been properly investigated by the SIB.' Kelly paused. 'Even though we now have four deaths to consider. I've found out about the squaddie called Trevor. And what you were told has turned out to be absolutely right. His death was another alleged suicide, very similar to your Jossy's, as it happens. His full name was Trevor Parsons and I have his last civilian address.'

'That is progress, John.'

'Yeah. Look, you should know that I do have a very good long-time police contact, Margaret.' Kelly paused again. The thought continued to lurk in the back of his mind that Karen Meadows might no longer be quite such a good contact. Not after what had happened that night. But he certainly had no intention of discussing any of that with Margaret Slade.

'I'm not going to tell you who it is, but, suffice to say, we are talking about a senior police officer who has basically been refused permission to pursue matters with the army, and that this officer is actually angry enough about that to be prepared to pass on information to me.'

'Wow! You are good, John, aren't you?'

'Umm. We'll see. But what about you? I think I'm only just beginning to get the hang of you. No doubt, you've got your next move planned?'

'Well, sort of. We're going to call for a public inquiry. You have to be focused, don't you, and it's no good making a lot of noise without knowing what you're aiming for. We thought we might march on the House of Commons, or something like that, but I'd like more ammunition.'

She broke off. 'If that isn't an unfortunate choice of words under the circumstances,' she said.

Kelly smiled again. Black humour. All the best fighters, in any kind of battle, were inclined to indulge in black humour, he reckoned.

'Anyway, I don't think we've got enough to throw at Parliament yet, do you, John?'

'Probably not. We need to co-ordinate everything, find out all we can and then make our move. The march sounds great. And I'll handle the press side, when you decide to do it. I'd like to have a proper story ready to drop simultaneously. I do already have something to go on.'

He told her then, in some detail, about the inquest reports, and the various anomalies. 'I also have an address for a young man who was called as a witness at the inquest into Jossy's death. The other sentry. James Gates. Didn't you go to the inquest, Margaret?'

'I did, yes. But I was drinking then, wasn't I. I hardly remember anything about it. Don't forget, it never occurred to me to query that Jossy had killed herself.'

'So you don't remember Gates' evidence.'

'Vaguely. Now you mention it. Very vaguely.'

'Well, it seems the coroner was more than a little vague too.' Kelly gave Margaret Slade a summary of James Gates' evidence. 'It should have rung extremely loud warning bells. But the coroner challenged nothing and passed a suicide verdict, almost as directed by the army. Fucking disgrace, actually.'

'Ah. So your next move is to talk to Gates?'

'Absolutely. Him, and Trevor Parsons' family, of course. I may find you some more campaigners there, Margaret. James Gates could be trickier, though. It'll be a question of whether or not I can get to him, I reckon. He's probably still a serving soldier. If he really thinks there was anything dodgy about those deaths, he's likely to be pretty nervous about speaking to me or anyone else.'

Kelly thought for a moment.

'I will tell you something I want from you, Margaret. A signed letter authorising me to act on behalf of the families. I'll certainly need something like that if I'm going to get anywhere with the army, and it could be useful to show to all kinds of people. I suggest you list the other families involved so far, mentioning briefly what happened to their sons, and, of course, include your own details. Can you do that?'

'Of course. I'm a drunk, not an idiot.'

'A permanently sober drunk, I hope.'

'So do I.'

'Indeed. So can you fax it to me? Have you got a fax machine?'

'No. But there's one I can use at an office equipment shop just down the road. I'll send it as soon as they open in the morning, at eight, I think.'

'Good.'

'John, reassure me, we're not just imagining some kind of conspiracy, are we?'

'No, Margaret, I'm damned sure of it. Actually, I get more and more sure with every step we take. And, for what it's worth, my police contact, who is someone with very well-developed intuition in these matters, is damned sure of it too. Otherwise, I wouldn't be getting anything like this level of co-operation. Something's going on, and it's very nasty indeed.'

'It's pretty hard to get your head around, isn't it? I mean, I keep going over and over in my mind what we are talking about here. If it really is murder, who on earth would want to kill a load of young soldiers? And why?'

'I don't know, Margaret. And, if I'm honest, I don't know if we'll ever know. But there is no doubt that the army has successfully covered everything up so far, and one thing we can do is blow that cover-up wide open.'

'You've said it, John. And how!'

Kelly found he was smiling broadly again as he ended the call. Margaret Slade was turning out to be some woman. He liked feisty, intelligent women who were not afraid of a fight. And that thought led him back to Karen Meadows and the somewhat disastrous end to their evening together, which caused him to stopped smiling at once.

Karen had been right. He was on an emotional roller coaster. He just couldn't sort his feelings out at all.

Margaret Slade was as good as her word. The fax came through shortly after eight. Kelly folded it and tucked it into the top pocket of his suede bomber jacket. He had been waiting for it. He was all ready to leave the house and drive to Exeter to visit the last civilian address listed for Trevor Parsons. Once he was involved in an investigation, Kelly didn't waste any time.

The drive to Exeter took little more than forty-five minutes, and it was still only just nine when Kelly pulled up outside a big, rambling, old house on the outskirts of the town. Two small boys, scruffily dressed but somehow well-scrubbed-looking, rosy-cheeked and apparently brimming with good health, were squabbling over a broken tricycle on the pavement right outside.

As Kelly stepped out of his MG, a large woman, in her early fifties, opened the front door.

'Inside, you two, before you have an accident out there in that street,' she ordered.

There was a chorus of 'Oh, Mams' and a pleading to stay in the street for just a bit longer, but the two boys none the less obeyed readily enough. They looked about the same age or thereabouts, and although Kelly wasn't very good at guessing children's ages, he was pretty sure this pair were both under five. That, of course, was an educated guess. It was term time after all. If they were any older than that they should have been at school. And glancing at the woman they had called Mam, Kelly didn't think she would be someone who would take any nonsense on such matters. It did occur to him, though, that she was a little old to be the mother of these two small boys.

He became aware that the woman was studying him curiously now, which was hardly surprising. After all, a strange man had parked his car outside her front door and was now standing on the pavement, staring at her shamelessly.

'Mrs Parsons?' he enquired.

She looked puzzled

'Who?'

'You're not Mrs Parsons?'

The woman shook her head. She was tall, broad rather than plump, and had long greying-brown hair which framed a strong kind face.

'Oh. Perhaps I have the wrong address. I wanted to talk about the death of Trevor Parsons.'

'Trevor? But I thought that was all over. I mean, it was more than a year ago that it happened, wasn't it . . .'

The woman's voice trailed away.

'So you are Trevor Parsons' mother?'

'No. No. Not his mother.'

'Well, you knew him, anyway?'

'Oh yes. Of course. Look you'd better come in.'

Kelly followed her into the lofty hallway of the old Victorian villa. Inside the house was not unlike the two little boys who were now playing in the small front garden – a bit scruffy but well scrubbed. The tiled floor shone, although several of the tiles were chipped and broken, and the once white paintwork was scuffed and tinged with yellow, but none the less spotlessly clean.

'Come into the kitchen,' said the woman, leading the way into a big square room dominated by an old gas cooking-range and a huge wooden table covered with a flower-pettled plastic tablecloth.

'Sit down,' she said, gesturing towards any one of a selection of ill-matched chairs. 'Are you from the army? There's nothing more I can tell you about Trevor, that's for sure. It was a tragedy, his death, but I didn't think anyone was all that surprised.'

'You didn't?' Kelly queried, as he chose the chair nearest to him.

'Well, no. Look, who did you say you were?'

Kelly, glad that he had had the foresight to ask Margaret Slade for that letter, produced it from his pocket.

'There've been some other deaths in the Devonshire Fusiliers, and I have been asked by the families of some of the young people involved to investigate a little further. There are some unsolved mysteries in certain cases. I'm looking into it, that's all at this stage.'

Kelly held out Margaret Slade's letter towards the woman and she took it from him.

'I see,' she said.

Kelly waited in silence while she read it. When she had finished and looked up at him questioningly, he spoke again.

'Forgive me, but I wonder if I could ask who you are and what your relationship to Trevor Parsons was. I thought you were his mother at first, because, you see, yours was his last civilian address.'

The woman nodded. 'I'm Gill Morris,' she said. 'I was Trevor's foster-mother, but only quite briefly . . .'

There was a crash as if a ton of bricks had been thrown against the kitchen door, which swung open to allow the two small boys to burst through, pushing their tricycle before them like some kind of battering ram. Not for the first time, Kelly marvelled at the amount of noise and commotion the very youngest of children could create.

'No, you don't. Out!' commanded Gill Morris. And without even bothering to dissent, the two boys swung around, still pushing the tricycle before them with dangerous force and speed, and crashed through the door again.

'They're at the worst age,' said Gill Morris, casting her eyes heavenwards. 'They're already quite big and surprisingly strong, but they have little or no brain at all to go with their physical power. And no control, either. They're like miniature loose cannons.'

She smiled indulgently. Kelly raised one eyebrow in silent query.

'Yes, I'm fostering these two, too,' she said. 'My Ricky and I, that's what we do. We're professional foster-parents, I suppose. He inherited this great big house from his parents and it just cries out to be filled with children, doesn't it? We had three of our own, and then, when they started to grow up, it seemed natural to take in some more.'

'I see,' said Kelly. 'So Trevor was one of them. What can you tell me about him?'

'Not that much, really. We only had him for seven or eight months. He'd had a hell of a life as a youngster, poor kid. Knocked around by his dad. Neglected by his mother. He'd been in and out of care since before school age, and it had certainly affected him. He was a difficult kid, no doubt about that, but who could blame him? He was fifteen when he came to us and hadn't seen either of his parents for years. And he was about sixteen and a half when he walked out one day. He always said he wanted to join the army, but we didn't even know he'd done it until they came to tell us he was dead. Apparently, he'd joined up as soon as he was allowed to, at seventeen, but we didn't know.'

'So, what about the six months or so between when he was with you and when he was able to join the army? Why didn't he give that address?'

'I'm not even sure that he had an address. We heard through social services that they'd found him staying with a mate at one point. I don't know anything for certain. We never saw him again after he left us. Funny really, some of the kids do get to be almost like your own, however much you fight against it, and a lot of them come back and visit. We're surrogate grandparents a couple of dozen times over now, you know.'

As she spoke, Gill Morris sounded like any proud grandmother. He thought what a special person she must be. And her husband, come to that.

'But Trevor, once he'd gone, he'd gone. And like I said, he wasn't with us that long. Ricky and I even thought that it was quite possible that he may have slept rough for a bit. He always fancied himself as joining the SAS, you know. But there wouldn't have been much chance of him getting into a regiment like that. To be honest, Ricky and I were a bit surprised that he got into the army at all.'

'Really, why?'

'Well, like I said, he was pretty screwed up by all that had happened to him. He liked the idea of playing soldiers, but he wasn't exactly stable. I wouldn't have put a gun in his hand, I can tell you that for nothing.'

'And from what you said, it wasn't a shock to hear that he had killed himself.'

'Well, it was a shock, but when you thought about it, poor Trevor was so messed up that he had to be a likely candidate for suicide. You couldn't imagine him coping with army life. You couldn't imagine him coping with any sort of life, really. We just hoped that as he got older he'd settle down, sort his head out a bit. But he never got the chance, did he?'

'It would seem not.' Kelly was thoughtful. Maybe Trevor Parsons' death had been a genuine suicide, after all. It still didn't mean that Jocelyn Slade had killed herself, or that the deaths of Craig Foster and Alan Connelly had been genuine accidents.

'So, you honestly have never thought that there was anything suspicious about Trevor's death?'

'No. Not at all. Should we have done?'

Kelly didn't know quite what to say. 'Probably not,' he responded eventually. 'It's just that the parents of three other dead Devonshire Fusiliers are very suspicious indeed about the way in which their children died.'

Gill Morris nodded her head slowly. 'I grasped that from your letter,' she said. 'But all I can tell you about Trevor, Mr Kelly, is that the poor kid had probably been a tragedy waiting to happen for many, many years.'

Kelly left quickly after ascertaining that Gill Morris could help him no more. And what she had told him, while not necessarily having any relevance at all to the other deaths, had sown the first seeds of doubt in his mind. Back behind the wheel of the MG, he told himself that was no bad thing. It was important for him to keep as open a mind as possible in order to conduct a proper investigation. If he was too convinced that the deaths were suspicious, then his enquiries could end up being just as perfunctory as he was sure the army's had been. He needed to be very sure of himself before coming to any conclusions. He owed Karen that, because he knew she was sticking her neck out probably more than ever before.

He checked his watch and, as he did so, cursed his luck that the home of the witness in the Jocelyn Slade case, Fusilier James Gates, was in London, and East London at that, which meant that when approaching from the west the whole of the city centre had to be crossed. After all, the Devonshire Fusiliers still considered their home county to be their major source of recruitment, and Kelly already knew from his days as an *Evening Argus* reporter that approximately sixty per cent of the regiment's strength were native Devonians. Yet so far his investigations had taken him to Scotland and to Reading, and now he needed to travel to London proper. It was, however, only just gone ten o'clock. There was therefore plenty of time to make the return trip that day, and as he was already in Exeter, Kelly decided to pick up one of the Plymouth or Cornwall to London expresses from St David's station.

He parked in the station car park. The next train, due just half an hour later, arrived at St David's on schedule. For a change, the journey passed without incident and the train also arrived at Paddington on time. Kelly took the tube to Mile End, having already checked the London *A–Z*, which he always kept in his car, to plot the short walk necessary to take him from the tube station to what he believed to be James Gates' family home. He no longer had the money for cross-London taxis, and in any case he hoped that the tube would actually be quicker. Certainly, on this occasion, his entire journey turned out to be a surprisingly efficient one.

His walk took him through a fairly rough part of London to a council flat in an uninviting tower block. A legacy from the sixties, he thought. A sullen-looking young man, with close-cropped orange hair and a sprinkling of freckles, answered the door. He looked about the right age to be Gates himself. Kelly wondered if he had struck really lucky.

'James Gates?' he ventured.

The young man scowled. 'Is that some kind of a sick joke?' he asked.

'Uh, no.' Kelly was puzzled. You never knew what sort of response to expect in a situation like this, but the reaction of this particular youth was highly curious, at the very least.

'I'm looking for James Gates,' Kelly persisted.

208

The young man's eyes narrowed.

'Well, you'd better try the cemetery, then, hadn't you.'

Kelly felt his pulse quicken.

'What do you mean by that?'

'It's pretty obvious, isn't it?'

'I'm sorry?'

'My brother's dead.'

'Dead?' Kelly repeated the word. It was all he could manage. He was totally stunned. He felt as if he had been hit by a thunderbolt.

'Who the fuck are you?'

Kelly struggled to overcome his shock. He knew he had to explain fast. 'I'm investigating the deaths of a number of soldiers at Hangridge barracks, on behalf of their families.'

'About time,' said the young man.

'Could you spare me a few minutes?'

'Are you police?' The young man stared at Kelly suspiciously.

'No.'

'Then you're army?'

Kelly opened his mouth to reply, but was prevented from doing so when the young man answered his own question.

'No, you can't be, or you'd have known Jimmy was dead.'

'Absolutely right. I'll explain everything if you'll give me the chance. Look, what's your name?'

The young man seemed to consider for a few moments. 'It's Colin,' he said eventually.

'Right. Well, Colin, if I could come in just for a few minutes, then I'll explain exactly why I'm here.'

Colin stood in the middle of the doorway, square on, staring at Kelly for several moments more, before abruptly stepping back and gesturing for him to enter.

Gratefully, Kelly followed Colin Gates through a dark hallway and into a sparsely furnished but spotlessly clean and tidy sitting room. Colin threw himself almost full length across a sofa rather unattractively upholstered in vivid red leather, which clashed with his hair. The only other chairs in the room were the four upright ones positioned around a brightly shining, wooden dining table. Kelly pulled one of those across the room and sat down facing Colin.

'I had no idea your brother was dead,' he said. 'Would you tell me what happened to him?'

'They posted him to Germany. He died only five days later. An army chaplain and a major came round in the middle of the night to tell us.'

'But what happened exactly, Colin? Do you know?'

Colin Gates shrugged. 'We know what they said happened. They found our Jimmy dead in a paddling pool. He was pretty tanked up, allegedly, and fell in and drowned. So they said.'

'You're not convinced?'

'No. I was never convinced, but who was going to listen to me?'

Kelly studied Colin Gates more carefully. He was long and gangly and, upon reflection, Kelly realised that he was probably no more than fifteen or sixteen. But there was something in his manner that made him give the impression, at first, of being older. He was, thought Kelly, a lad who had had to grow up fast.

'Your parents didn't agree, then?'

Colin Gates sniffed in a rather derisory, dismissive sort of way.

'Me dad said I'd been watching too many bad movies. But then, he did twenty years in the paras and came out a staff sergeant. He's army through and through, me dad. The military police investigated, over there in Germany. They showed Dad their report, a tragic accident they said, and Dad accepted it.'

Another one, thought Kelly. Army families lived by a different code, it seemed. The habit of obeying orders and accepting what those in authority told them sometimes stayed with them, Kelly was beginning to realise years after they actually quit the military. For ever, probably.

'But you didn't accept it?'

'No.'

'Any particular reason?'

Colin shrugged again, and this time said nothing.

Kelly changed tack.

'Shouldn't you be at school?' he asked. 'How old are you, anyway?'

Colin shrugged again. 'I'm sixteen. I've just left school. I've got a temporary job in a hotel kitchen, but I hate it. I've taken a sickie today. Don't tell me dad, that's all. Jimmy was the golden bollocks round here. I'm the little bugger nobody listens to.'

Colin grinned. Kelly thought there was something rather likeable about him in spite of the aggressive front he affected.

'I won't,' he said. He glanced round the room. There were a few family photographs on a shelf above the fireplace, and that was about all. Most of those seemed to be of a young man in uniform, whom Kelly assumed to be James.

'What about your mother?' he asked. 'What does she think.'

'She buggered off when I was a baby,' said Colin. 'Dad said she didn't take to being an army wife. Me nan brought me and Jimmy up, but she died a couple of years back.'

'Colin, will you tell me, please, why you didn't believe the army version of your brother's death?'

Colin drew his knees up to his chest and spent what seemed to Kelly to be an inordinately long period of time staring at his trainer-clad feet. 'If you like,' he said eventually. 'Jimmy and I was always mates, you see. He told me all about it. About how he'd been on duty with that girl, who they said killed herself. Jimmy never believed that. He said he knew she hadn't. Just knew it. He said there were all sorts of things wrong. He gave evidence, didn't he, at her inquest, and he told them how he and the others had searched where her body was found, and it just hadn't been there. Jimmy reckoned she must have been moved. Also, there was some drunken Irish bloke trying to get into the officers' mess without any proper identification that night. Made quite a commotion, apparently. Then this Rupert came out and said to let him by. Jimmy said sentry duty was a joke at Hangridge. They didn't have a clue who was coming and going half the time, he said.'

'Did he ever find out who the Irishman was?'

'No. At least, I don't think so. He never told me, anyway. There was something else, though. He said, after he heard the shots the night the girl died, he saw someone running across the playing field away from the perimeter fence. He called out, challenged like – you know, the way they're supposed to.' Colin Gates paused and looked directly at Kelly. '"Who goes there?" Is that what they really say?'

Kelly found himself grinning. 'I don't have a clue,' he said. 'Go on. Did Jimmy tell you what happened next.'

Colin Gates nodded.

'Yeah. Apparently, this person kept running and just dis-appeared out of sight. Our Jimmy didn't even know whether it was a man or a woman. He said he thought it was a man, though, but he wasn't sure why.'

Kelly was fascinated. 'Why didn't he say all that at the inquest?' he enquired.

'He said he wasn't asked anything like that, that it was all sort of cut and dried, really, and he never got the chance to say anything except answer the questions he was asked.'

'But he had told the military police about seeing someone running across the playing field, away from the scene?'

'Oh yes. He said they kept pushing him about identifying whoever it was, but he hadn't a clue.'

'So it would be in the MP records.' Kelly was thinking aloud.

'How do I know?'

'No, of course not.'

With the elasticity of extreme youth Colin Gates suddenly swung his legs off the sofa and straightened himself, so that he was suddenly sitting bolt upright and staring quite directly at Kelly.

'Do you think my brother's been murdered, then? Is that what all this is about?'

Kelly found that he was quite disconcerted by the young man's blunt approach.

'Colin, I didn't even know your brother was dead until ten minutes ago,' he responded rather lamely, he thought.

'Right.' Colin continued to stare at Kelly for what seemed like another long period of time. 'How many deaths have there been up at Hangridge, then?' he asked eventually.

Kelly reckoned then that the young man before him was probably considerably more astute than he looked.

'I'm not sure that I know the answer to that,' he replied truthfully. 'Every time I move I seem to discover another one.'

Karen was in her office at Torquay police station. Her mobile was on the desk before her. And it was ringing. But she made no attempt to pick it up and answer it. Instead, she sat staring at it as Kelly's number appeared on the display panel.

'Damn,' she thought. What was it about her life? Everything in it seemed to get complicated. And it was invariably her own fault. Her relationship with Kelly had never been complicated before. In addition, although they had had their ups and downs over the years, their rather unusual friendship, which she so valued, had always remained strong. Until now.

Unaware that Kelly had exactly the same misgivings, she feared it would never be quite the same again. She finally reached for the phone just as it stopped ringing. She knew that Kelly had been planning to visit the families of both Trevor Parsons and James Gates, and she wanted to know what he had learned. She wanted to know that very much. Which meant, she realised, that she had to overcome the embarrassment she felt and talk to Kelly at once.

She punched in his number.

'Good afternoon, Karen,' he said quietly. And the sound of his voice caused her whole body to react, as she involuntarily remembered that forbidden kiss and how it had made her feel. She wouldn't think about it. She just wouldn't.

'Look, about last night—' she began, after a short pause.

'I know, it was an apparition,' he interrupted.

'Damned right,' she said, instantly relieved, but at the same time, in spite of her better judgement, just a tad disappointed to hear those words from him. 'You're almost certainly still in shock from Moira's death, and as for me, well . . .'

'I know. I'm so sorry. Look, can we just forget about it, go back to how things were before?'

It was exactly what she had wanted, of course. So why did it also make her feel rather sad? She gave herself a mental shaking. What was wrong with her sometimes?

'Of course we can,' she replied.

'Good, because I've got something to tell you.'

'Right, fire away.'

'OK. Just listen to this.' Kelly sounded excited now. And tense. 'Look, I'm in London. I came up to try to find James Gates. Now, it could be that the death of Trevor Parsons really was a suicide. It's impossible to say for certain, but it at least seems that he was a likely candidate. But, well, you're not going to believe this – Gates is dead too. Gates is dead,

Karen. And if you want my opinion, the way he died absolutely stinks.'

'Jesus,' said Karen, finally genuinely forgetting all about the events of the previous night. 'Not another one!'

'The fifth,' responded Kelly. 'And wait till you hear what happened to him.'

He told her then everything that he had learned from James Gates' younger brother.

Karen was quite incredulous. 'He died in a few inches of water, in a paddling pool? And in Germany, so there aren't any inquest records over here. And, coincidentally, he was a key witness at the inquest into one of the most suspicious deaths of all. You're right, Kelly, it stinks. And, quite frankly, if I can't get permission to open a proper police inquiry now, I think I'll tell the arseholes where to stick this fucking job.'

'Hang on, Karen. Hang on. You still have the situation where the army doubtless has plausible explanations for each individual case, even if we think that those explanations look thin when you consider the whole picture. So why don't you let me have a go at Gerrard Parker-Brown before you do that. I have quite a dossier now to put to him, and I am representing the families, don't forget. I don't see how he'll be able to ignore me. If I turn up unannounced first thing tomorrow morning, I might get something out of him. The surprise approach so often works, as you know . . .'

'And you might pre-warn him, Kelly.'

'He's warned already. He's met you, got to know you a bit. I can't believe that he was left in much doubt that you would not step back from this without a damned good fight. That's the sort of copper you are, and, from what you've told me, he's no fool. He would have grasped at once what he was up against. After all, he went straight to Harry Tomlinson, didn't he? The old pals act and all that. They're natural allies those two, aren't they? So, do you honestly think Parker-Brown doesn't know every official move you make? Let me have a go, first, please.'

Karen thought for a moment. 'OK, Kelly,' she said eventually. 'I don't know if it will do much good, but I can't think it'll do much harm.'

She put the phone down thoughtfully. If she was honest, she

214

quite liked the idea of Gerrard Parker-Brown being given the third degree by Kelly, who was, she knew, an excellent interviewer. It still rankled that Parker-Brown had, she was sure, deliberately set out to handle her. And, even worse than that, she admitted reluctantly to herself, he had initially succeeded rather well.

Also, she did need to be absolutely sure that when she went back to the chief constable, her case for an investigation would be so strong that he would have no choice but to agree. And Harry Tomlinson was a stubborn man. Furthermore, he was not the sort of policeman who would ever want to be involved in any kind of showdown with the military. Karen knew all too well that Tomlinson would only consent to her putting a formal police investigation in place, if the case she presented was so overwhelmingly strong that she gave him no choice.

She was well aware that she needed all the help she could get. In particular, she needed support from within the force. Karen did not really want to be put in the position where her only hope of taking matters any further was to inform the chief constable that the Hangridge affair was about to be blown wide open by the families of the dead soldiers, led by John Kelly. In the first place, Tomlinson would probably take that as some kind of threat and might react with increased bloody-mindedness. And in the second place, Tomlinson had always viewed Karen's close association with Kelly with deep suspicion, and had even dared, on more than one occasion, to hint at the station gossip, which she knew had been going on for years. There had long been a rumour that she and Kelly were having an affair, which was pretty ironic really, she reflected. Because there had never been even a breath of truth in that – until the previous night, when it had very nearly become a fact. Even though that now seemed rather unreal.

On the other hand, something that was very real, was the existence of one man within the police force whom she trusted totally to confide in concerning Hangridge and the Devonshire Fusiliers, and of whose support she was confident. However, he was somebody she had had an affair with. And he was a junior officer at that.

'Damn,' she said out loud, as once more she cursed herself roundly for creating her own complications.

Phil Cooper had been her sergeant when they had investigated a particularly complex and emotionally draining case, full of twists and turns. And one of the twists had been that somehow along the way she and Phil had begun an affair. No. It had been much more than that. For her, at least. She had fallen deeply and irrevocably in love, although she was no longer quite so sure of his true feelings.

Phil had recently been promoted to detective inspector and had rejoined the Devon and Cornwall Constabulary, after a brief spell with the Avon and Somerset. And Karen was well aware that his new job would be right up his street. Phil was now with the force's Major Crime Incident Team. The unit operated in a clandestine way, from an anonymous warehouse on an industrial estate on the outskirts of Exeter, unmarked and unheralded. Karen knew that the team thought of themselves as the elite, SAS-like, front-line troops of the police force, and there had always been a boy-soldier side to Phil, who was a big, rugby-playing, very physical sort of man. And although solid and reliable on the one hand, he was also the kind of policeman who enjoyed the unorthodox and, like Karen, was unafraid of taking risks – which may have been one of the reasons they had always got on so well.

Anyway, one way and another, in a professional sense she trusted Phil Cooper absolutely, even if personally she had grown to have her doubts.

He had called her not long previously to tell her about his new appointment and he had also made it quite clear that he was still available to her. Indeed, that he would very much like to re-open their relationship.

'Things would be different, I promise you, Karen,' he had said.

But she had asked just one question. 'Are you still married, Phil?'

'Well, yes, but—' he had begun.

'But nothing, Phil,' she had interrupted. 'Just fuck off, will you.'

And that had been their last conversation. Karen smiled wryly. Complicated or what? Well, she wasn't going to let it be. Not as far as the job was concerned, and not as far as Hangridge was concerned either. Resolutely she punched out Phil's mobile number.

'Cooper,' he replied, in that slightly sing-songy way of speaking with which she had once been so familiar.

'Hi, Phil . . .' she began.

'Hello, Karen, I'm so glad to hear from you,' he responded at once.

'Let me say from the start, this call is purely and absolutely professional,' she told him sternly. She felt rather pompous, but was none the less determined to make her position on that clear at once.

'Yes, of course,' he replied, backing off instantly. However – and she couldn't have explained why – she felt that he didn't entirely believe her. Typical, bloody arrogant man, she told herself.

Out loud she said: 'Look, Phil, I've got something big on. It's a very hot potato and I need some help. Just you and me, quietly. I don't want to talk about it on the phone, so I was hoping we could have a meet. Soon as you can.'

Phil asked no questions.

'I won't be able to get away this evening because we've got a big job on here, and it's likely to hang over into tomorrow, but what about tomorrow night?' he replied, with obvious eagerness, and she hoped it wasn't just that he was keen to see her. He would know, of course, that Karen must be referring to something very important indeed.

'I could drive over to the Lansdowne, if you like?' Phil continued.

Karen opened her mouth to say no. She didn't want an evening drinking session with Cooper. That was, after all, how their affair had begun in the first place. On the other hand, the quicker she met up with him the better. And as she was absolutely adamant that she never wanted to rekindle their relationship and that she was totally over him, then what possible reason could she have for avoiding an evening meeting with him?

'That would be ideal,' she said casually. 'But let's make it another pub, shall we?'

She didn't want the entire station knowing that she had been

217

drinking with Cooper. The word that their affair was on again would be round the nick in about five minutes, if they met in the Lansdowne. And that had caused enough problems first time round. But as Cooper replied, she almost wished she hadn't made the request for a different pub.

'Of course,' he said, sounding quite conspiratorial. 'How about that quiet little boozer we used to go to out on the Newton Abbot road.'

Oh, God, she thought. That had been one of their regular haunts during their affair. But she was determined not to show him that it meant anything to her one way or the other to go there again.

'Sure,' she replied, even more casually. 'See you there about seven? All right?'

'All right,' he replied, with rather more enthusiasm in his voice than she would have liked. And warning bells were ringing in her head as she ended the call.

But she needed Phil Cooper's help, she told herself. She really did.

Sixteen

The following morning Kelly spent an hour or so at his computer, checking a few facts on the Internet. Before confronting Colonel Gerrard Parker-Brown, he wanted to familiarise himself with any statistics he could find concerning non-combat deaths in the military, and also to bone up on the history of the Devonshire Fusiliers.

He already knew that this was a long-established regiment, and indeed learned from its website that it had been founded during the Napoleonic Wars, in 1812, just three years before the Battle of Waterloo. Kelly thought for a moment. Of course. The then newly formed regiment had served with distinction at Waterloo, and its part in Wellington's historic victory was recorded on the towering stone monument to the Iron Duke, which had been built high above the little Somerset town which bore his name. Kelly had several times visited the unique 175-foot phallic tower because its site, on the highest point of the Blackdown Hills, just two or three miles from the Devon border, presented one of the finest views in the West Country. On a clear day, you could see for miles right across the lush Taunton Vale to Exmoor and the Bristol Channel beyond.

He read on. The Devonshire Fusiliers also appeared to have served with distinction in every major war since, and when Britain's other four English fusilier regiments – the Royal Northumberland, the Royal Warwickshire, the Royal Fusiliers, City of London, and the Lancashire – had been united in 1968 to form the Royal Regiment of Fusiliers, only the Devonshire had retained its autonomy.

This was one of Britain's premier fighting units, with the proudest of histories. It was pretty obvious that a regiment with that kind of tradition to look back on would not take kindly to having its affairs scrutinised by any outside agencies.

And, as Kelly logged off the Net, he found himself wondering just how far even the most decent of men within the Devonshire Fusiliers would go to protect their regiment's hard-won reputation.

He eventually set off at about 10 a.m. to drive across the moors to Hangridge, a journey he reckoned would take around an hour, or maybe a little more depending on the traffic. He had to negotiate the busy market town of Newton Abbot in order to hit the moorland road, and that was rarely easy. But as soon as he pulled away from his parking space, he became aware of a familiar, unhealthy banging sound at the rear of his car. It was, of course, the exhaust, and broken exhaust pipes were the curse of MGs because the cars were built so low. Kelly couldn't even remember hitting the exhaust, but it was extremely easily done, and, whatever the cause of the problem, the entire system now sounded as if it were about to fall off. He certainly could not drive the car over Dartmoor. Cursing, he took a detour to his regular garage, Torbay Classic Cars, where Wayne, the rather morose young man who ran the place, expressed his dismay with characteristic gloom, said the car wasn't going anywhere and he wouldn't even be able to look at it for two days. But he did, at least, immediately offer Kelly the big old Volvo which passed for Torbay Classic's courtesy car.

Kelly didn't like the Volvo, which he thought was slightly less manoeuvrable than your average bulldozer. He was, however, grateful for any transport because he was determined to get out to Hangridge somehow, in order to confront Parker-Brown.

Having visited the barracks once before, as an *Evening Argus* reporter covering its 25th anniversary celebrations, Kelly had the advantage of Karen, in that he knew exactly where Hangridge was. He was pretty sure Colonel Gerrard Parker-Brown had already been in command at the time of the anniversary, but he did not remember the officer at all. However, the press had been safely corralled well away from the top brass, who had been seen only briefly, alongside their visiting minor royal, commander in chief, when assembled for a photocall. Kelly, like the rest of them, had only had direct contact with an army press officer, down from the MoD in London for the day.

Kelly had worked on a lot of army stories and, by and large, got on well with soldiers. Journalists usually did, in Kelly's experience, as they did on an individual basis with police officers. All three of these tough professions had a lot in common, Kelly reckoned. They provided more than a measure of excitement, tinged on occasions with fear, they involved crazy hours and confrontation with sides of life most people living in a halfway civilised society were fortunate enough never to have to face. And all three were run in a thoroughly autocratic way. Indeed, Kelly sometimes suspected that the unquestioned, absolute control an editor had over his newspaper and its staff probably made the newspaper world the most autocratically governed of the three. One way and another, soldiers, journalists and police officers routinely faced their own individual kinds of firing line at the discretion of their top brass. It was, perhaps, not surprising that the individuals concerned were inclined to be extremely comfortable in each other's company, sometimes even those who rather thought they should not be.

A light drizzle was falling as Kelly approached Hangridge. The headquarters of the Devonshire Fusiliers loomed on the hillside, a sprawling development of low angular buildings within a wire perimeter fence that snaked over the rolling terrain almost as if it had been drawn on in pen and ink. And, even when you were expecting it, the barracks, with its curiously suburban aura, still came as a surprise in the remote heart of one of Britain's wildest moorlands.

Kelly motored slowly to the sentry point, taking careful note of every possible detail as he did so. After all, this was where at least two of the young people involved had allegedly killed themselves. Wide verges of springy moorland grass flanked the big gateway. It occurred to Kelly that there was no cover of any kind. Anything going on in that area could be clearly seen from most parts of the camp.

He drew the big Volvo to a halt alongside the open gates to Hangridge, and handed his letter from Margaret Slade to the sentry who had immediately approached the car.

'I wonder if you could pass this to Colonel Parker-Brown and ask him if he has a few minutes to spare to see me,' he said.

The sentry nodded his assent and directed Kelly to park to one side, clearing the gateway for other traffic. There was not another vehicle moving anywhere in sight, but presumably this was the correct procedure. Kelly found himself smiling as he watched the young soldier then use the phone in his sentry box. Within a minute or two another soldier, a corporal judging from the stripe on the uniform sweater he wore over his khaki trousers, hurried out of the main administrative building and across the quadrangle, hunching his shoulders against the drizzle. Glancing curiously towards Kelly, he took the letter from the sentry and began to make his way back.

Would Parker-Brown call to a higher authority for guidance, or might he simply refuse to see Kelly? Kelly didn't think the colonel would do either. Everything that he had learned about the CO of the Devonshire Fusiliers indicated a man who made his own decisions, a high-flier who was not afraid of responsibility and taking control. Kelly could picture clearly in his mind the officer reading his letter and pondering what to do. He settled more comfortably into his seat as he waited, but he somehow didn't think he would have to wait long. Parker-Brown was, after all, trained to make fast decisions under pressure.

After just a minute or two more, Kelly was proven right. The sentry answered his phone and then beckoned Kelly forward, telling him that the colonel would see him shortly, and directing him to the visitors' parking bays just to the right of the main administrative building.

A sergeant, sternly uncommunicative, was waiting to escort Kelly into the CO's office. The Devonshire Fusiliers were taking no chances with him, he thought. He found his heart was pumping in his chest. He felt that a lot rested on this meeting.

Parker-Brown was sitting at his desk when Kelly entered. He rose to his feet at once, greeted Kelly warmly and invited him to sit in one of the room's two armchairs, as he lowered himself into the other, just as he had done when Karen had made her first visit only a couple of weeks or so earlier.

'Anything I can do to help, I will,' the colonel said at once. 'I do feel for these families, you know. I'm a father myself.'

It was an innocent enough remark, but for once in his life Kelly was rendered speechless. It was not the words, but just meeting the man which had had a devastating effect on Kelly. Parker-Brown did not seem to realise, but he had already

222

shocked Kelly rigid. Still standing, Kelly found that he could not stop staring at the commanding officer of the Devonshire Fusiliers.

Parker-Brown's soft brown eyes, which gave so little away, returned Kelly's gaze steadily. Kelly remained standing. The colonel, looking puzzled, glanced at him enquiringly.

'Do sit down, Mr Kelly,' he said.

Still without speaking Kelly sat down on the second armchair, trying desperately not to stare any more.

'So, what would you like to ask me, Mr Kelly?' Parker-Brown smiled easily and leaned back in his chair, stretching his long legs before him. He looked totally relaxed. Well, maybe he was relaxed, thought Kelly. He was, after all, quite patently, a pretty cool customer. Kelly still said nothing.

The colonel looked even more puzzled.

'So?' he queried. 'Please fire away, Mr Kelly.'

Kelly made a big effort to pull himself together.

'The families want some answers, they are very concerned, Colonel Parker-Brown,' he began eventually, struggling to keep his voice calm and controlled. 'There have now been five deaths in a period of just over a year, at least three of them highly questionable—'

The colonel interrupted smartly.

'Allegedly questionable, Mr Kelly. As I said, I do understand how upset the families that you represent are, but sadly what we are talking about are the kind of deaths that do happen in the army, even in peacetime. There is nothing sinister here, Mr Kelly, if that is what you are insinuating. In addition to the obvious danger of handling guns in potentially volatile situations, the pressures on our young recruits, some of whom do not always come from the most helpful of backgrounds, are immense. We do try to give all the help and support we can, but sometimes they simply cannot cope. Military life is not without its perils, and peril comes in many guises, not just when you are facing the enemy.'

'We agree on that, Colonel,' responded Kelly quickly. 'Within the past ten years there have been around a hundred non-combat deaths through firearm incidents in the British armed forces, and, according to the latest figures I could find, a further

223

one hundred and fifty-six suicides. Don't you think that is rather a lot?'

Parker-Brown frowned and tapped the fingers of his right hand on the arm of his chair, in what Kelly thought was probably a gesture of impatience.

'I couldn't possibly comment on those figures, as I don't even know whether or not they are correct. That kind of thing is a matter for the MoD, not a regimental CO. All I can do, Mr Kelly, is repeat what I have just told you. Army life is not without its dangers, even in what passes for peacetime.'

Unexpectedly, Parker-Brown stopped tapping his fingers, held out his hands in a conciliatory manner and flashed a big grin at Kelly, crinkling up his whole face as he did so. The man was a charmer, and quite obviously knew it. It appeared to be his first line both of defence and attack. He was, Kelly suspected, pretty used to his charm getting him whatever he wanted.

However, the charm offensive was wasted on Kelly, who leaned forward, once more locking his gaze on the other man.

'Don't you think that at the very least the army must be guilty of a breach of its duty to care for these young people, Colonel?'

'The utmost care is taken, Mr Kelly, I can assure you. Every new batch of recruits is the army's future. Beyond that, again, I cannot possibly comment. I can only discuss matters over which I have direct responsibility.'

Very deliberately Kelly settled back in his chair, stretching his own legs, trying to appear considerably more relaxed than he actually felt. To his great relief, however, his brain did appear to be working again.

'OK, so let's concentrate on events concerning Hangridge, shall we, and perhaps you will allow me to throw a few facts at you, Colonel,' he said. 'Shall we begin with the case of Jocelyn Slade? She died after suffering five gunshot wounds to the head. Now I know just a little about the SA80, and what it is capable of, the damage it can do in literally just a flash. But I put it to you, Colonel, that even with a volatile, fast-action automatic weapon like the SA80, it is highly improbable that anyone attempting to take their own life would be physically able to shoot themselves *five* times, would you agree?'

'That would be a matter for a pathologist and for a ballistics expert, Mr Kelly, not for me.'

'Precisely, Colonel. So perhaps you could explain to me why, according to the records of the inquest which I have seen, it appears that no ballistics expert was asked to examine the circumstances of Jocelyn's death before the military police decided so arbitrarily that she had killed herself and then managed to persuade the coroner's court to go along with their conclusioin.'

The colonel grinned again, but in a rather more forced fashion. 'Persuade the coroner's court to go along with their conclusion?' he repeated. 'I rather take exception to that, Mr Kelly.'

'Well, perhaps then, you could tell me why the SIB investigation did not include any reference to a ballistics expert, particularly when the military is presumably full of them.'

'That is a matter for the Royal Military Police, in particular the SIB itself, Mr Kelly, who, I am sure, conducted their investigation thoroughly and quite properly.'

'All right, Colonel.' Kelly had forgotten everything now except concentrating on the job in hand, and he was in full flow. 'Perhaps we can switch to the case of Fusilier James Gates, who was on sentry duty the night Jocelyn died. His evidence at her inquest indicated, did it not, that her body had almost certainly been moved—'

'Look, Mr Kelly,' Gerrard Parker-Brown interrupted. 'I agreed to see you out of courtesy to the families of dead soldiers from my regiment, and in addition to assure you, and therefore hopefully them too, that we have nothing to hide here at Hangridge. Indeed, I will do everything in my power to further reassure these families, and I am quite happy to meet any of them who might wish to see me. But I cannot – and will not – go into the kind of details you are asking for, Mr Kelly. Young lives have been lost, after all.'

'I'm all too aware of that, Colonel, and indeed that is why I am here,' said Kelly. 'But please, the case of Fusilier James Gates is particularly curious and there are certain events, which occurred that night, which apparently Fusilier Gates knew about but which were not revealed in the coroner's court. You are aware, of course, Colonel Parker-Brown, that Jimmy Gates is also dead?'

'Well, yes. I am. But his death had nothing whatsoever to do with Hangridge.'

'Really? Well, it could all have been an extraordinary coincidence, of course, but Gates was posted to Germany two weeks after the inquest, and then died in, to say the least, rather unlikely circumstances five days later.'

'Soldiers work hard, and play hard, Mr Kelly. They are inclined to get drunk sometimes, and sometimes they get far too drunk. Then freak accidents happen. Or they simply fall under a lorry. Which I believe is what started all this, is it not?'

Kelly detected a distinctly patronising note in the colonel's voice, but decided to ignore it.

'Speaking of drunkenness, Colonel,' he continued levelly. 'Fusilier Gates said that he confronted an Irishman, who he said was drunk and had no identification papers, trying to get into the base on the night that Jocelyn Slade died, and that an officer came out of the officers' mess to OK his entry. He also said that he saw a figure running across the playing field away from the perimeter fence, just after he heard the shots fired. Now, none of this was brought up in court. Don't you find that at least curious?'

'I really have no idea whether it is curious or not, Mr Kelly. To begin with, perhaps you could tell me how you could possibly know this? After all, as you point out, Fusilier Gates is dead.'

'I was given this information by someone Gates talked to about it before he died, someone very close to him.'

'Then it's hearsay, Mr Kelly. Nothing more than hearsay. And it gets you nowhere. I do remember, now I come to think of it, that we had some civilian building contractors on site at the time and I believe a couple of them were Irish. We can all make a mystery out of almost anything, if we choose, Mr Kelly. And it is upon hearsay and rumour, and nothing else, that this whole matter hinges, is it not?'

'Colonel, I am told that Fusilier Gates faithfully related all this to the military police during the initial inquiry, in which case it should be on record somewhere. And that is not hearsay, is it?'

226

Abruptly, the colonel rose to his feet, and when he replied, his voice was much louder.

'Mr Kelly, I have repeatedly told you that I have agreed to talk to you today merely out of respect for the families you are representing, and that I cannot and will not go into details concerning events which are not only military matters and quite probably classified, but also involve loss of life . . .'

At that moment Kelly, who was sitting with his back to the door of the colonel's office, heard it open behind him. Parker-Brown, still standing and directly facing the door, almost imperceptibly shook his head. Instinctively, Kelly turned around and glanced over his shoulder but saw no one, just the door closing again.

The colonel barely paused.

'I can only repeat that yet again,' he continued equally loudly. 'And as you seem unable or unwilling to accept it, then I must ask you to leave now and request that you make any further approaches to me or to anyone else connected with the Devonshire Fusiliers through the proper channels.'

Kelly stood up at once. He was almost exactly the same height as the colonel, albeit in comparatively pretty dreadful shape, and he didn't want the man looking down at him. No way.

'Colonel, I too will repeat what I said earlier. Five young soldiers serving in your regiment and stationed at this barracks have died in questionable circumstances. Their families are demanding to know the truth about their deaths, and if you won't talk to me, then, frankly, they and I will move forward to the next step. They are demanding that a civilian police investigation should be put into operation and that a public inquiry should be held. And they are planning to march on Parliament, within the next few days, to make their demands in public. If you think that by refusing to discuss this matter with me you are going to make it go away, then you are very much mistaken, Colonel.'

There was no longer any sign of Parker-Brown's big grin. His charm offensive had failed and he was now every inch the soldier. Stern, and more than a little forbidding. Kelly, however, had never been particularly impressed by authority in any form. And he had his own reasons for being even less impressed by Gerrard Parker-Brown than he might have been by any other army officer trying to browbeat him. As the colonel began to reply, Kelly glared at him defiantly.

'Mr Kelly, all I am trying to do is to make it quite clear to you that I prefer to accept coroners' verdicts based on information provided by the SIB, to this mishmash of regurgitated hearsay which you have brought to me today,' Parker-Brown countered, the note of anger clear in his voice. 'And I'm pretty damned sure that every agency of law in this country, right up to government level, would back me up on that. These deaths have all been properly investigated by the correct authorities. There is absolutely no need either for a civilian police investigation or any kind of public inquiry.

'Now, I have told you once. I really think you had better leave, Mr Kelly.'

Kelly glared at him for a second more. There was something different in Parker-Brown's eyes, which no longer looked warm at all. Kelly suspected that he had really shaken the army officer. And he liked the thought of that. He liked it a lot. But he had no idea whether it was what he had actually told the colonel concerning the families' plans, or if it was something else. None the less, he was sure that the real reason Parker-Brown had agreed to see him was exactly what he would have expected it to be. The colonel had wanted to find out what Kelly knew. Well, Kelly had been deliberately frank in many respects. But he had not revealed everything. Not by a long way.

Certainly, he could see no benefit in attempting to prolong the interview. Instead, and without saying anything further, not even goodbye – after all, the time had passed, he reckoned, for any pretence of pleasantries between him and the colonel – Kelly merely swung round and headed for the door. But as he reached for the handle, Parker-Brown spoke again.

'Who told you about what Fusilier Gates allegedly claimed to have seen, anyway?' he enquired with a kind of studied nonchalance.

Kelly looked back over his shoulder. He was beginning to like Gerrard Parker-Brown less and less, and to distrust him more and more.

It was Kelly's turn to force a big grin. After all, it wasn't only Parker-Brown who could pretend to turn on the charm.

228

'You have to be joking,' he said.

But as soon as he was outside the door, he stopped grinning at once. His legs felt shaky and he realised that he was trembling from head to toe. He could not wait to get away from Hangridge, to assimilate his thoughts.

'Shit,' he thought. 'What is going on?'

Once in his car, Kelly drove as fast as he could along the Hangridge approach road, right through the valley and up on to the moor at the other side. He swung off into a tourists' parking area, empty at this time of year, and drew the borrowed Volvo to a halt.

He switched off the engine and jumped quickly out, drawing in big gulps of the heady moorland air. It was several minutes before he felt he was breathing normally again, and only then did he remove his mobile phone from his pocket and dial Karen's number.

She answered at once. But then he didn't think she would be playing call-dodging games with him for some time to come, or at least until some significant progress had been made in solving the mystery of the Hangridge deaths.

'I've seen Parker-Brown,' he announced. 'And I have something extraordinary to tell you. I can't get over it, to be honest.'

'What?'

'No. You were right before. Not on the phone. Can we meet tonight?'

There was the briefest of pauses.

'Later on. I've already got a meeting at seven. How about 9.30-ish?'

'Great. Where?' Kelly didn't know what venue to suggest. He would much prefer their liaison to be private, but wasn't sure that he dared suggest that after what had happened the other night.

Again there was a brief pause.

'Come to my flat again, if you like,' she said eventually.

He hesitated. 'If you're sure?'

'Of course I'm bloody sure, Kelly. We are grown-ups, aren't we?'

229

Kelly found that he was smiling as he ended the call. That had been typical Karen Meadows. She had made him feel much better. Much more normal. And suddenly, John Kelly craved normality like nothing else in the world.

Seventeen

On his way home from Hangridge, Kelly made a detour and stopped off at The Wild Dog. It was interesting to revisit the place where all this had begun. Charlie, the landlord, was his usual taciturn self and if he was aware that a young man had been killed on the road not far from his pub, the last time Kelly had been there, he obviously did not wish to discuss it. And that suited Kelly fine. He wanted to think. He ordered his customary pint of Diet Coke and a pasty. Charlie's pasties, he knew, were made at a rather good local bakery in Moretonhampstead, and Kelly reckoned they were almost as good cold as hot. Certainly he knew better than to allow Charlie to turn his pasty into a soggy mess by heating it up in the blessed microwave.

Kelly sat on the same bar stool as he had on the night when Alan Connelly had been killed. His head was still buzzing from his meeting with Parker-Brown. His brain was in turmoil. He felt more than a bit peculiar, and it was almost as if he could sense Alan Connelly's presence, still see him, ghost-like, slumped on the bar stool next to him.

Such a lot had happened since that fateful evening when Alan Connelly really had been sitting there alongside him. The muscles in the back of Kelly's neck were so tense, they felt as if they had been forged together. It was actually quite painful to move his head. Kelly had to force himself to eat his pasty slowly and to order a second pint of Diet Coke. He suspected that the next few hours of his life were going to feel as if they went on for ever. He was even more eager to see Karen Meadows than he had been the last time they had arranged to meet in her flat. And what he had to tell her was weighing so heavily on his mind, that he had virtually forgotten altogether the potentially tricky development in their personal relationship, and the unexpected feelings which had been aroused in him.

When he eventually hit Torquay around mid-afternoon, he stopped briefly at a news-stand on the outskirts of the town, as he almost always did, to buy a copy of the *Evening Argus*.

He wasn't that interested, actually, but it was habit. And habits were always good to cling to when you felt the world was going mad. He had to force himself to make a pot of tea, which he carried to his chair by the sitting-room window. He needed to relax. To gather his thoughts. He knew all too well that the hours were going to drag until his meeting with Karen at 9.30 p.m.

He switched on his radio, tuned in as usual to Classic FM, and started leafing idly through the newspaper, making himself study each page carefully in order to pass the time. Suddenly he stopped turning the pages. His attention had been caught by a piece which was little more than a filler towards the back of the book, on a section on one of the pages that Kelly knew was reserved for late news.

Not only would the *Argus* have only been able to compile a sketchy report in the time available, but this particular incident was of a type that was no longer considered to be big news. Unless you knew what Kelly knew, of course.

'A local soldier on leave has been fatally stabbed as he walked along a street in East London.

'Police believe that eighteen-year-old Robert Morgan, of the Devonshire Fusiliers, may have been attacked by a gang of youths in a bid to steal his mobile phone, which was missing from the scene. Fusilier Morgan, who was stationed at Hangridge Barracks, his regiment's Dartmoor head-quarters, was stabbed several times in the neck and chest with a long-bladed knife.

'Detective Inspector Michael Drewe, of the Metropolitan Police, said yesterday: "This was a brutal and, as far as we know, totally unprovoked attack. However, there are indications that Robert fought back valiantly against his attackers and this may have been why he was ultimately stabbed to death so mercilessly."

'Robert's body was discovered in the early hours of this morning in Penton Street, East London, a tough part of the

232

city and not a district where people would be recommended to walk alone at night, particularly strangers.

'It is not known why the soldier, whose family run a general store in Paignton's North Road, was in the area.

'Said DI Drewe: "We are appealing to any witnesses to come forward, and also to anyone, who knew Robert, who may be able to supply us with information concerning his movements on the day he died."'

If Kelly hadn't been so methodically going through the paper from cover to cover, he may well have missed the relatively insignificant story on page seventeen.

As it was, two facts jumped off the page and hit him straight between the eyes. The first, of course, was that Robert Morgan had been a Devonshire Fusilier stationed at Hangridge, and the second was that he had been murdered in East London.

Kelly found that he was trembling again as he ran upstairs to his office and reached for the copy of a London *A–Z* on the shelf above his desk, where he kept the books he used regularly in his work lined up in a row – a couple of dictionaries, a thesaurus, a selection of telephone directories, a *Who's Who* and a Debrett's *People of Today*, a gazetteer and a number of other maps and atlases.

He quickly found the appropriate page and studied it carefully. Yes, his hunch had been right. He felt his pulse quicken. Penton Street was just a couple of streets away from Jimmy Gates' family home.

Willing himself to stay calm, Kelly picked up his hands-free phone and dialled the Gates' number. He was in luck. Colin Gates answered.

Kelly had no time for small talk, no time to soft-soap the young man, even though he knew that he should really proceed with more care and caution than he was able to muster.

'Do you know about the murder near you last night?' he asked.

'No,' said Colin.

Kelly was mildly surprised. It was quite likely that he wouldn't have seen an evening paper, but news of the stabbing would have been on the regional TV and local radio news, and surely everyone in the neighbourhood would have been talking about it.

'How could you not know?' he asked.

'All I've done in the last twenty-four hours is sit in front of my computer,' replied Colin. 'I've got this new game, it's fucking great. I'm already up to level four.'

Sad bastard, thought Kelly, then remembered his own predilection for computer games when he should be working. It was just that his were inclined to be less sophisticated, that was all, because, apart from backgammon, he had so far avoided loading any further games on to his computer beyond the standard package supplied by Windows.

'What's it go to do with me, anyway?' Colin asked.

'I just wondered if you knew the victim, or if your brother may have known him. He was a Devonshire Fusilier, a squaddie stationed at Hangridge. His name was Robert Morgan.'

'Rob?' Colin sounded shocked. 'Rob Morgan? I met him once. With Jimmy. They was best mates. Jesus. What was he doing up here?'

'I wondered if he might have been coming to see you. Or your father?'

'No. Well, I don't know. He hadn't phoned nor nothing.'

'There doesn't seem to be any other reason why he would be in your area. I mean, you don't know of anything, do you? A girl, perhaps?'

'No. I mean, I wouldn't. I told you, I only met him once. But I don't think he'd ever been up here before. He'd never been to ours, anyway. And our Jimmy used to go on about him being a real Devon yokel. He was only having a laugh, though. Jimmy was always talking about Rob. They were really good mates. I met him in Devon. Dad and I took Jimmy back there once, after he'd been home on leave, and we met up with Rob in a boozer.'

'Could he have wanted to tell you something, you or your dad? Something about Jimmy's death, perhaps?'

'Jesus,' said Colin. 'And I'm the one who's supposed to have been watching too many crap movies.'

'This is serious, Colin. More serious than you can possibly imagine, and more serious probably than even I imagined until today. I think perhaps you should contact your local police and tell them about your connection with Robert Morgan, and, come to that, tell them all that stuff your brother told you about Jocelyn Slade as well.'

'You're joking, aren't you? I don't have nothing to do with the filth, nothing more than I have to. That's the way things are around here. Anyway, I thought you were sorting all that out.'

'There's been another death, Colin. A young man, who may have had all kinds of knowledge concerning your brother and the death of Jocelyn Slade, has been murdered. That's no joke.'

Kelly paused.

'Look, Colin, it is possible that you are in danger, too.'

'Oh, come off it.' Colin Gates sounded totally incredulous. 'How could I possibly be in danger. Are you some kind of nutter or something?'

'No, Colin. I'm not. It's just that I don't like playing games with other people's lives. I've done it before, although I never meant to. I don't want to do it again. I think the time has probably come for all of us to put our cards on the table, to try to get some official help in all this. To make sure there aren't any more of these mysterious deaths. And, in your case, that means going to the police.'

'But I haven't got anything to tell them. I don't know nothing about Robert Morgan, not nothing. He could have had all sorts of reasons for being round here. Drugs. That'll be it. Drugs. I mean, if you're stationed at some barracks in the middle of Dartmoor, how the hell do you get yourself some gear, eh?'

'With consummate ease, if he was that way inclined, Colin. What do you think? That drug culture only exists in inner cities? Don't you believe it. I'm calling from Torquay, an hour's drive from Hangridge, and I promise you there's not a drug that's been invented that you can't pick up in this town, if you know where to go. No. Drugs wouldn't have brought Robert Morgan to your part of London, I'm sure of it. And what else would have led to him ending up stabbed to death in Penton Street? The only obvious link is your family, living, as you do, just a stone's throw away.'

'Well, I don't bleeding care what he was doing in our manor, to be honest. And I'm not fucking going to the filth. No fucking way. Anyway, I thought you was going to handle it all. I didn't think I'd have to do anything.'

'Please, Colin. I'm worried about your safety.'

'You really are a nutter, you. My bleeding safety, my arse. You got some imagination, you have. Apart from anything else, I don't know nothing about nothing.'

'Is your dad still away?'

'Till Saturday.'

'Look, I really, really think you should go to the police?'

'For what? So they can have a good laugh at me too. You can take on the British army if you like, Mr John Kelly, I'm not fucking doing it. I don't want to know whatever crazy conspiracy theory you've got into your head. I'm staying out of it. I shouldn't have talked to you in the first place, should I? I ain't got nothing else to say. I don't want ever to talk to you again.'

The line went dead. Kelly sighed. Perhaps he should tip off the Met about Colin Gates. Karen had indicated to him that she thought as much pressure as possible, from as many different angles as possible, would be the way to open up the whole affair. On the other hand, Gates was probably right about one thing. It seemed highly likely that the Met really would do little more than have a good laugh.

Kelly pondered his next move. He wondered if he should talk to Margaret Slade and the other relatives of the various dead soldiers, and suggest that they all get together to help him cobble up a story straight away, thereby rocketing the whole shenanigans into the public domain once and for all.

Kelly found that he really didn't know what to do, and that he was extremely worried. He knew that he was meddling yet again with matters he did not fully understand, and he was beginning to fear the consequences. Already, a sequence of events was unravelling in all sorts of unexpected directions.

Whether or not the death of Robert Morgan was connected with all the other deaths, it was at the very least highly discon-certing. Kelly didn't want any more blood on his hands. He had hoped to keep everything under wraps a little longer, and indeed to be able to delve into the mystery considerably more before hitting the printing presses with it.

But he was now beginning to feel that maybe he could not

wait. That none of them could wait. And he was beginning to think that when he told Karen Meadows all that he knew, and, even more, all that he suspected, she would agree. Indeed, this latest development might play into her hands. After all, she believed that a formal police investigation into the Hangridge deaths should be the next step, and the death of another Hangridge soldier, however unconnected it might at first sight seem to be with anything military, would surely have to be regarded as a significant factor in her campaign to be allowed to launch such an operation.

Kelly checked his watch for the umpteenth time. It was still not quite six o'clock. The hours really were dragging. But less than four hours to go now before his meeting with Karen, and maybe they could then reach a decision together about their next move. He would just have to be patient. Meanwhile, he amused himself by thinking about how Karen would react to the most important piece of information he had to give her. Something that he had yet to come properly to terms with himself. She would, he thought, be even more amazed than he had been.

He wandered downstairs again to make a fresh pot of tea, which he once more carried into the living room and set, with the sugar bowl, of course, on the little table next to his chair in the bay window. As he did so, his telephone rang. He answered quickly, half expecting it to be Karen. Automatically, he checked the display panel on his phone, registering that it was indicating that his caller's number was not available, which meant that it could well be her, phoning from her office in Torquay police station.

'Hello,' he said tentatively.

'I understand you're investigating the deaths of soldiers up at Hangridge,' responded a muffled voice. It was so distorted, no doubt deliberately, that Kelly could not even tell if his caller was a man or a woman.

'Well, I have been looking into various incidents at the barracks,' he replied cautiously.

'I have information that I believe could be of interest to you.'

'I see.' Kelly could feel the hairs standing up on the back of his neck. This was far from the first time in his life that he had received a call like this. Sometimes they were from total nutters.

More often than not, they were from people who thought they knew something important, but actually didn't. And once in a blue moon they were dynamite.

One thing Kelly knew for sure, this was the kind of investigation that was crying out for a deep throat. Because if he was honest, without something of that nature – some anonymous source of crucial inside information – Kelly did not see the truth ever being fully revealed.

On the other hand, there had now been yet another death which could be connected to the others. And there were other disturbing factors, notably the most important and the most potentially explosive aspect of his meeting with Colonel Parker-Brown earlier that day, when he had been confronted by something totally unexpected, something only he could possibly know about, and something he really could not wait to share with Karen. The sensible part of Kelly urged him to tell his caller to contact Karen Meadows and then to hang up. He was getting into extremely deep water. He should merely put together the best story he could from the information he already had, and then step back from the whole affair. After all, obsessive though he might be when embroiled in an investigation, he was not a totally stupid man. And he was becoming aware that even he could be in some danger, if he continued to delve into the affairs of the Devonshire Fusiliers. However, he quickly dismissed the thought from his mind. Of course, he wasn't in any danger. And even if he was, well, there was absolutely no chance of him stepping back from this investigation. If this caller had information for him, then Kelly wanted it, and Kelly would probably do almost anything to get it. So, he wasn't going to back off. Not now. Not yet. No way.

'Who are you?' he asked instead.

'Never mind that,' said the voice. 'I'm just somebody who has a great deal of information that you might want. You and the families of those dead soldiers. I know what happened to them all, you see. What happened and why. I know the truth.'

'I see.' Kelly didn't know what else to say.

'So, do you want to know the truth too?'

Kelly sat down in his window armchair with a bump. His

238

knees had suddenly seemed in danger of giving out, and he realised that he was sweating.

'Of course I do,' he said.

'Right.'

'Well, go on . . .'

'Are you off your trolley, man?' The remark sounded so incongruous when delivered by someone who appeared to be speaking through a thick wedge of cotton wool that Kelly found he was smiling in spite of himself.

'I'm sorry . . .' he began.

'Yes. You should be. I'm not telling you any of this on the phone.'

'Right.'

'No. We'll have to meet. And somewhere we won't be seen.'

'Right.'

'Do you know Babbacombe beach?'

'Yes.' How strange, thought Kelly. It was one of his favourite haunts, that and The Cary Arms. He had been up there – well, on the road above the small secluded beach, anyway – on the day of Moira's funeral. It had been a refuge for him then, and he didn't really regard it as quite the place for a clandestine meeting. But he wasn't going to argue.

'I'll see you there at midnight tonight. And come alone.'

'Yes. Of course. Right. Where exactly?'

'You just start to walk along the beach, from the direction of the pub. I'll be there. You won't see me at first. I'll find you. Don't worry. Just walk up and down the beach, until I do. Oh, and no torch. You don't need to see me, you just need to listen.'

'OK. But, tell me. Why are you doing this?'

'They were mates of mine. Alan Connelly, Jimmy Gates, Robbie Morgan. They were all my mates.'

The caller hung up then. Straight away. Leaving Kelly looking at a buzzing handset.

Shit, he thought. Connelly, Gates and Morgan. His mysterious caller was indicating a link between those three deaths at least, already backing up Kelly's own suspicions. And the most significant aspect of that was that he had included Morgan in it. Morgan, whose involvement had remained something of a long-shot until that moment. Morgan, a local lad whose death probably hardly anybody in Torbay knew about yet. But Kelly's anonymous informant knew. Less than twenty-four hours after Morgan had been murdered, he knew. He could have seen it in the evening paper, of course, just as Kelly had. And, indeed, maybe it was that which had prompted him to contact Kelly.

Kelly took his tobacco and skins out of his pocket and began to roll himself a cigarette. He was both excited and thoughtful. He had no idea how his caller even knew that he was investigating the deaths at Hangridge, but, apart from his dealings with the various families involved, he had now actually visited the barracks of the Devonshire Fusiliers and done his best to interview the regiment's commanding officer. He suspected that gossip in an army barracks was probably every bit as rampant as he knew it to be in newspaper offices and police stations. And he was in the phone book. A lot of journalists, Kelly knew, were ex-directory. But Kelly thought that was nonsense. It you want to gather in information, you need to make it as easy as possible for anyone who wishes to supply you with some to be able to do so. Whatever inconvenience that might cause on occasions.

Anyway, one way and another, his unexpected phone call changed everything. Absolutely everything. No way would he now be making any sort of move at all, and certainly there would be no question of breaking the story to the press, not until after he had met his mysterious deep throat.

He lit up and took a deep drag, forcing himself to remain calm. He was at a crucial stage in an investigation which was beginning to pull in all sorts of unexpected directions, and it was essential that he kept as cool a head as possible.

So much now hinged on whatever he might learn that night from his anonymous caller who, he was quite aware, of course, could still turn out to be a nutter. But somehow, and maybe it had been something in that muffled voice which had already convinced him, Kelly didn't think so.

Either way, Kelly certainly didn't want Karen Meadows to know about his deep throat, at least not until after he had met up with him. Assuming it was a him. For a start, she would only interfere, and Kelly wanted to handle this alone. Dealing with informants was always, in his opinion, a one-person job.

However, Karen Meadows would be sure to try to stop him keeping his lone midnight assignation. She would never take on board any responsibly for something like that. She was, after all, a policewoman. At the very least, she would insist on some kind of police back-up, and Kelly somehow felt absolutely certain that his caller would know if he did not turn up alone as promised. After all, he was probably military and probably trained in surveillance. Kelly reckoned he had no choice but to find some excuse for avoiding this evening's meeting with Karen, because she knew him too well not to glean at once that there was something big going on that he wasn't sharing with her. He did not even want to speak to her on the phone. Not now. Not until after that midnight assignation.

Instead, he decided to email her. And he used Moira's daughters as his excuse, telling Karen that they had arranged a special supper on their last evening together, before Paula returned to her home in London and Lynne went back to university in Bristol. The girls had wanted Kelly to be there, and he had naturally accepted their invitation, he wrote. However, he had totally forgotten his commitment to join them when he'd made his appointment with Karen, which he would now like to put off until the following day. He was very sorry, but he couldn't let the girls down, could he?

He read the message through several times, tweaking the odd word. It was good, he thought. Nothing at all in it to rouse Karen's suspicions.

He pushed 'send' and made himself another roll-up. He felt a complete rat for using the girls as an excuse in this way, so soon after their mother's death, but he told himself they would understand. The truth, of course, was that whether or not they would understand actually made no difference. Any kind of commitment to Moira's daughters was currently the best excuse available to Kelly. And Kelly was a very determined man. When he had an aim in his life, he was inclined to use any means at his disposal to see it through.

When she arrived, Phil Cooper was already sitting in what had been his and Karen Meadow's favourite corner table in the quiet little pub on the Newton Abbot road, that they had so often visited together. There was a pint of bitter in front of him. He beamed at her as she walked across the bar to him, and rose to his feet, his arms open in a welcoming gesture. Not for the first time, Karen marvelled at his cheek. What was it with men, she wondered? However badly they behaved, they just expected to be allowed to bounce back into your life.

'God, Karen, it's good to see you,' he said warmly.

'Phil.' She manoeuvred her way past him with some care, avoiding the physical contact he seemed to be inviting, and sat down. She intended to keep the entire evening strictly business-like and to be as brief and to the point as possible. She very nearly started to remind him again that their meeting really was business and no more than that. But she stopped herself just in time, reckoning that even to make the comment raised the possibility that she might be considering an alternative.

Instead she looked Cooper directly in the eye without smiling, and asked for a Diet Coke when he offered her a drink.

He looked at her questioningly.

'I am driving,' she said.

'So am I,' he responded. 'One glass of something won't do you any harm, Karen.'

'Diet Coke, please, Phil,' she repeated. She wasn't sure enough of herself to take any chances with this man. She watched him amble to the bar in that gangly way of his. It felt strange to be with him again. He had been so very important to her.

'And dinner,' he said, when he returned from the bar, dropping a couple of packets of crisps onto the table alongside their drinks. 'Smoky bacon flavour,' he said, grinning his familiar crooked grin.

She felt very slightly irritated. Smoky bacon was her favourite, in fact the only crisp-flavouring that she liked. Had Cooper deliberately set out to remind her of how well he knew her? She wasn't sure. And, in any case, she had neither the time nor the inclination to waste on such considerations. She made herself concentrate on the job in hand.

'Look, Phil, like I told you, I think I might have stumbled across something very big indeed,' she began. 'And Harry Tomlinson certainly thinks it's too hot to handle. It's military,

242

and it's sensitive, and if we don't do something about it pretty smartish, I reckon the whole thing is going to blow up in our faces and we're going to look extremely stupid. A number of deaths are involved. At least some of them could be murder. And all but one, that I know about so far, has happened on our patch, albeit mostly on army premises.'

She realised from the way the expression on his face changed that she'd caught his attention. But then, whatever else he was, Phil Cooper was a good copper, and that little build-up would have had any good police officer on the edge of his seat. Phil's manner had been vaguely flirtatious before, she thought. But not any more.

'Army, eh?' he remarked, the curiosity strong in his voice.

She nodded. 'Yes. And I can't handle it alone.'

He raised both eyebrows.

'I don't think I've ever heard you admit that before, Karen,' he said.

'I'm not sure it's ever been true before,' she said. 'Well, not about the job, anyway.'

As she spoke, she realised that the latter part of her remark could be taken in all kinds of ways she would prefer it not to be, and certainly not by Phil Cooper, of all people. But he appeared to be far too intrigued by what she was telling him to have even noticed.

She continued then, with the whole story, grateful that probably the one good result of her otherwise disastrous affair with Cooper was that she had become close enough to him to really learn the kind of man he was, and the kind of police officer he was. She knew absolutely that she could trust him, at least in a professional sense.

'Shit,' he said, when she had finished. 'That's big, all right. And how like Kelly to be involved.'

'Could you imagine him not being? A story like that breaking on his patch. He's not supposed even to be a journalist any more, but his nose started twitching before he even had a clue what it was twitching about.'

Phil giggled. He had always been a giggler.

'So, what do you want from me?' he asked.

'I'd like MCIT to get involved, but I want you guys to come

243

in from a different direction. I don't want the information coming from me. Hopefully, we'll have double the impact that way.'

'I think I see.'

'I'm sure you do, Phil. If someone from your team were to call on the chief constable to get a police investigation authorised, based on information that has come his way from sources totally independent to mine, then I think it would add an immense amount of weight. Even Harry Tomlinson can't take us all on.'

'That's the trouble, though, isn't it?' remarked Phil. 'He doesn't take anyone on, does he? He just sort of wriggles until it all goes away.'

Karen laughed. Phil had always made her laugh.

'With this one, though, what we have to do is to make sure it doesn't go away,' she said. 'It's too important, I'm sure of it.'

'Yes.' Phil was thoughtful. 'I'm not usually a great one for conspiracy theories. All too often the truth is something quite simple and straightforward. But you might have begun to uncover something quite extraordinary here, Karen, and I must admit I'd really like to have a crack at solving it. It's intriguing, isn't it?'

'It certainly is.'

'Yeah, well, you know something, Karen, I reckon I'll probably get an anonymous call tomorrow, from some frightened young soldier giving me almost all the information on Hangridge and the Devonshire Fusiliers that you've just given me.'

'Really, Phil? Now wouldn't that be an amazing coincidence?'

'Absolutely amazing, Karen.'

'Thanks, Phil.'

'My pleasure.' His eyes were fixed on hers and there was no mistaking the look in them.

'I've missed you,' he said.

'And I've missed you too,' she replied honestly. 'But that's life, isn't it?'

'Well, I suppose so, but . . .'

'Look, Phil, I'm sorry. But I do have to go.'

'Right.' He finished his drink and stood up. 'I'll call you, then, as soon as I have any news.'

'Do that.' She stood up too. 'And thanks again.'

244

They left the pub together and it wasn't until she was back behind the wheel of her car that she was able to reflect on the personal implications of her meeting with her former lover.

Something extraordinary had happened. Something she found she was extremely glad about. She hadn't felt anything. She really hadn't felt anything.

She realised then that when she had arranged to meet Phil, she had actually been much more worried about her reaction to him than his to her. She had not only fancied him rotten, she had loved him to bits. But she doubted he had ever really considered making the kind of commitment to her that she had wanted.

And now she didn't want it any more. She took a deep breath. She felt a huge sense of relief. It was over. She neither loved not lusted after him any more.

And she supposed she'd had to see him again to know that.

Suddenly, she was overwhelmed by the feeling of being at peace with herself for the first time in a long while. She so wanted her life back. And in a strangely insidious sort of way, her affair with Phil Cooper had taken it from her.

Eighteen

Karen arrived home just before 9 p.m. and embarked on her usual round of last-minute tidying before Kelly's arranged visit half an hour or so later. However, most of her flat was already moderately clean and tidy. After all, her recently acquired cleaning lady, Shirley, an out-of-work actress whose impecunious state had forced her to move in with her mother a couple of streets away, had made her weekly visit only the day before.

The bedroom, however, was its usual tip. Although Shirley was undoubtedly a good and thorough cleaner, and had even informed Karen that she was going to convert her house-cleaning activities into a proper business which would transform her finances, Karen was not entirely sure she was cut out for the job. Shirley – who had taken to wearing black T-shirts with the words DUST BUST emblazoned in white across her ample bosom, in order, she said, to attract attention to her new enter-prise – had attitude. A lot of attitude. Unless Karen's bedroom was in at least some kind of order, Shirley wouldn't even go into it.

However, as she stood in the doorway looking at the mayhem within, Karen had to admit that Shirley probably had a point. The pile of clothes on the chair at the foot of her bed had once again spread onto the floor. And entangled among the various items were at least a couple of pairs of old knickers.

Karen set about putting shirts and trousers on hangers, throwing casually abandoned shoes into the bottom of her wardrobe, and gathering up the more unsavoury items destined for the washing machine. Then she stopped. What on earth was she doing? There was absolutely no way Kelly was going anywhere near her bedroom. That was just not going to happen. So why was she so frantically tidying the room?

'For God's sake,' she muttered to herself. Sometimes, she wondered what on earth was going on in her head.

She abandoned the rest of the mess at once, made her way into the sitting room, flopped onto the sofa and switched on the TV to Sky News in order to catch up on the day's events. Yet another major royal scandal appeared to be breaking, and Karen, while actually something of a closet republican, had a real weakness for royal gossip – the more scurrilous the better. The British royal family were, after all, the world's greatest soap opera, she thought.

And in spite of all that was on her mind, she quickly became embroiled in the latest revelations, which cast almost inarguable doubt on the paternity of a major young royal. Indeed, she was so engrossed that she was surprised, when she glanced at her watch, to find that it was already ten minutes to ten.

She checked both her mobile phone and landline for messages, in case she had missed any calls. Her only message was from the irritatingly persistent Alison Barker.

'Such a pity you couldn't make dinner with Sally, but she's coming down again in a couple of weeks and I just wondered . . .'

Karen pressed delete. She was even less interested than usual in Alison Barker. She was puzzled. Kelly was normally punctual and she had realised when he'd phoned her earlier in the day that he'd had something he was dying to tell her, which made it all the more unlikely that he would be even five minutes late. She tried both of Kelly's numbers, but was merely switched straight to voicemail on each.

She wandered around the flat, picking up books and magazines and putting them down, periodically looking out of the window, watching for Kelly's car to turn into the car park. Ten o'clock came and went, and still Kelly had not arrived. A thought occurred to her then. Perhaps he had emailed her. Karen had left her police station office just after six thirty and she thought she had last checked her email about half an hour before that. Surely Kelly would not have cancelled that late in the day, would he? And surely he wouldn't have chosen email to do so, at such short notice.

None the less she logged onto her computer, which she kept hidden away in a Victorian roll-top desk in a corner of her big, high-ceilinged living room. And, indeed, there was an email from Kelly, timed 6.12 p.m., apologising for having to put off their meeting. She must have just missed it.

Karen read the message over two or three times. She was more than a little puzzled. The email, crucially she thought, made no mention at all of how important their postponed meeting might be, something Kelly had already made clear. In fact, it gave very little away, and that in itself made her deeply suspicious.

She could not imagine what could have happened to make Kelly back out of a meeting he had been so keen to arrange. But something had happened, she was quite sure of that.

More than that, John Kelly was up to something. She knew him well. She just knew he was up to something and, whatever it was, he had been quite determined not to tell her about it.

She logged off her computer, shut it away in the desk and, completely preoccupied, made her way into the kitchen where she opened a bottle of red wine. Unusually, although she hadn't eaten anything except Phil Cooper's crisps since lunchtime, she wasn't hungry. But she could do with a proper drink.

Thoughtfully, she wandered back into the living room and flopped down on the sofa again. The television was still on. Karen didn't even glance at the screen. Instead she reached for her cordless phone, took her palmtop computer out of her handbag, looked up a phone number and dialled it.

'Hello, Jennifer?' she queried. 'Karen Meadows. I was just calling to see how you and your sisters were getting on?'

'Oh, that is kind of you,' said the voice at the other end of the line, making Karen feel like a total rat. She didn't know it, but one way and another Moira's daughters seemed to have a habit of unwittingly doing that to people. Or to her and Kelly, anyway.

'We're fine. Well, we're coping. I mean, we were expecting it, after all. But it's always a shock, isn't it . . .?'

'Yes, of course. And your mother was just such a lovely person.'

Karen paused. As ever she was too impatient to keep up small talk for long, even under these circumstances.

'Don't suppose Kelly is with you, by any chance, is he?' she enquired casually.

248

'No,' responded Jennifer, sounding slightly puzzled herself. 'Should he be?'

'No, no, of course not,' Karen responded swiftly. 'I haven't been able to raise him at home or on his mobile and it occurred to me that he might have been visiting you.'

'No. We haven't seen him since the day of the funeral, actually.'

Jennifer spoke without a note of criticism. Typical, thought Karen. And she was now behaving just as badly as no doubt Kelly was.

'Oh, well, I expect he's very busy,' she responded lamely, and managed one or two other platitudes before ringing off, slamming the receiver quite violently back on its charger.

She had known it. She really had known it. Kelly had been lying. That meant he was keeping something from her. And that was sure to mean trouble. Because, with Kelly, it damned well always did.

Meanwhile, Kelly had decided, mainly because he was so on edge that he just couldn't sit at home waiting, to go out to Babbacombe early and eat in The Cary Arms, the lovely old pub built into the cliffside just above beach level, which was one of his favourite hostelries in the area. He arrived around 8.30, ordered steak and chips and a Diet Coke, followed by a couple more Cokes and a coffee in order to while away the time until closing. At around 11.20, aware of the landlady starting to fidget demonstrably, he made his way to the borrowed Volvo, parked in the car park down by the beach. It was a completely dark night. No moon and no stars were visible. The lights from the couple of houses to one side of the beach and the pub above them, barely cut through the cloak of blackness which seemed to have wrapped itself around Kelly. He shuffled across the car park to the Volvo, moving unnaturally slowly. It had, of course, been raining earlier in the day, and Kelly suspected there might be a shower again at any moment.

Once inside the Volvo, he rolled a cigarette and sat smoking with the window wound down, looking around him as best he could. Apart from what were now the relatively distant lights of the pub and the two beach houses, Kelly could see nothing at all.

Every few minutes he flicked on his lighter in order to check his watch. It was almost like a nervous tic. At exactly midnight, he opened the car door and stepped out.

The night was surprisingly warm for the time of year, even though he could feel the dampness of the sea air around him. As he shut the car door he took a long deep breath, savouring the salty seaweedy smell.

Both the sea and the beach were as black as the sky. He shivered, even though he was not cold, as he peered around him, screwing up his eyes in the hope that they might adjust a little to the lack of light. He could still see absolutely nothing. With extreme care, he again proceeded across part of the car park, raised just above the beach alongside the deserted beach café, which opened only in the summer, and then just during daylight hours, and attempted to negotiate the small flight of steps which led down to sea level. At the bottom he stumbled. He had somehow expected one step more. He fell almost to one knee and had to use the iron railing flanking the steps to haul himself upright again.

He had decided to obey all his instructions meticulously, including not bringing a torch, but he could really have done with one. He just hoped he didn't break his neck before even encountering Deep Throat.

There was barely a breath of wind, which was why the night was so unseasonably warm. Yet visibility was so bad he thought that the darkness of the night was probably being intensified by a sea mist. He really did feel as if he were engulfed in a slightly clammy blanket, a feeling he thought was unique to the coast, particularly in foggy conditions. Certainly, he had experienced nothing like it inland anywhere in the world. It was strangely disorientating. Momentarily, Kelly lost his sense of direction, and only the sound of the waves gently lapping on the shingly beach told him that the sea was to his right, and the wooded hill leading up to Babbacombe proper and the main drag into Torquay was to his left. There was no other sound at all. You could hear no passing traffic noise down at Babbacombe beach, of course, and the lack of wind made the night almost eerily silent.

Kelly stood for a minute listening. Was there someone else

already on the beach, he wondered? Not only could he not see anything, but neither could he hear anything. He began to pick his way over the shingles, straight along the beach as he had been instructed, startlingly aware of the rhythmic thumping of his heart, which, in the otherwise intense silence, seemed unnaturally loud. He slid each foot cautiously in front of the other. Once, a particularly large pebble cause him to stumble for a second time, but this time he righted himself immediately and continued to move painstakingly forwards.

Visibility was so poor that he almost walked into the cliff at the far end of the beach, unaware that he had even reached it. And he paused for a moment before adhering to his instructions once more, turning on his heel and shuffling back along the beach.

Twice more he repeated this manoeuvre, and, just as he had almost reached the far cliff for the third time and was beginning to wonder if he was the victim of an elaborate hoax, it happened.

Suddenly he sensed that someone was behind him. He had neither heard nor seen anything, but all his senses told him that there was another presence on the beach and that it was threateningly close to him. The beat of his heart not only seemed extraordinarily loud now, he was also aware that it was much faster than usual, indeed his heart was racing. He tried to turn around, and opened his mouth to speak, or maybe to scream. He wasn't sure. It didn't matter. He was not given the chance to do either.

With no further warning, an arm locked around his throat and he felt the pressure of a large, strong body against his back. The crook of his assailant's elbow locked beneath his chin, crushing his larynx. Kelly raised his own arms and lashed out with them frantically in all directions, desperate to make any kind of contact. A second arm from behind knocked his down to his side and pinned them there. The grip around his throat felt like steel and was tightening. He was being choked. Then he was aware of his attacker shifting his balance.

Oh, my God, thought Kelly. This is it. This is really it. I am going to die. This time, I really am going to die.

He forced himself to think. He realised he probably had only a few seconds of life left. Kelly knew a bit about unarmed combat. Certainly enough to be aware that his assailant was a professional. And Kelly reckoned he knew exactly what was coming next. He steeled himself for the sickening thud of a knee in the small of his back, before his head would be jerked back and his neck broken. Swift, silent and brutally efficient.

He struggled to clear the black fog inside his head, which was now every bit as dense as that outside.

He had once, briefly, undergone self-defence training with an elite para unit. The purpose had allegedly been to write a feature for his newspaper, but Kelly at the time was travelling the world seeking out the worst trouble spots. He had already been kidnapped by guerrilla forces in a remote part of a war-torn African state, and had had a narrow escape. So he'd paid close attention to his brief experience of military training, reckoning it might one day save his life. But he had never before had occasion to use any of the manoeuvres he had learned, and had no idea whether, even if he could remember what to do, he would stand a chance of executing any of it. Particularly against a professional. Kelly was twenty-odd years older, and carried a couple of stone more weight, almost all of it around his belly, than he had back then. And there was also the little matter of not one, but two drug and alcohol detoxes along the way.

Never mind, he told himself. He knew it was brain power which counted for most, in these situations, rather than brute force. He forced his brain to work. To remember. To maintain the discipline not to lose control even as death looms. To tell his body what to do. But the fog inside his head was already impenetrable.

So instead, he abandoned all thoughts of conjuring up some magical move of self-defence from the distant past, and merely struggled mindlessly, trying to slide his body down and away from the steel-like grip. Quite frantic now, he wriggled and kicked with all his might. One thing he did remember, was that a moving target was always more difficult to dispatch, not that he could move very much.

However, his terror seemed to give him a kind of frenzied strength, and he thought he actually managed to kick his assailant sharply on one shin – certainly, the grip around his throat suddenly slackened just enough for him to be able not only to breathe but to do the only other thing he could think of by way of a counter-attack. He yanked his head downwards and twisted his lower jaw as best he could in order to find his target, then buried his teeth into a section of what appeared to be exposed wrist, using all his strength to drive them into the bare flesh. The grip around his neck slackened totally then. Kelly realised two things. One was that he was no longer being strangled and, the other, that this slight reprieve would not last. After all, the grip of the second arm, the one pinioning his own arms to his body, had not slackened at all.

However, he took advantage of the brief, partial respite to cry out with all his might. Even in this moment of abject terror, logic told him that there was no one around to hear him – the pub and the pair of houses below it would both be tightly shut against such an unpleasant night and, in any case, were at the far side of the beach, but he didn't know what else to do. And, curiously, he found that just the sound of his own voice, which he had thought he might never hear again, gave him some fleeting comfort.

'No, no,' he yelled as loudly as he could manage. 'Help, help, help!'

But the moment was over in a flash, as he had expected it to be. The steel-like grip of his assailant's arm locked around his throat again, once more crushing his larynx, not only making any further sound impossible but also again making it extremely difficult to breathe. Kelly could only gasp for air. His legs had turned to jelly. He felt his body begin to go limp, his eyes start to glaze over, and all reason begin to drain from his brain.

He prepared to die. And with what remained of his strength, he braced himself against the sickening thud he expected to feel at any moment in the small of his back.

But, instead, the grip around his arms and body slackened. It made little difference, however, and he was sure his assailant would have known that, because he had no strength left to put up any further fight. And he was certainly not able to even attempt to break free and escape. In any case, he knew he had no chance at all of getting away. Instead he half stood, half leaned against his attacker, barely breathing, like an old, broken, rag doll.

Then suddenly he was aware of a bright light shining in his

face. He blinked rapidly, half strangled, half brain-dead, desperately trying to work out what was happening. It was a torch. Of course. A torch. And for some reason his attacker was shining it directly into his face. Why? Why would he do that? Even in Kelly's befuddled state the answer came quite quickly. Just to double-check. To be sure that he had the right man. That would be it. Yet again Kelly prepared to die.

The torch remained shining straight into his face for several seconds. Then, as abruptly as it had arrived, the blazing light was gone. The torch had been switched off. Kelly could hear his heart beating even louder and faster than ever, and was absolutely sure it would not be doing so for long. He was also aware of a warm wetness between his legs. Somewhere, deep in his subconscious, he registered that he must have involuntarily urinated.

Then the arm around his throat was abruptly withdrawn. Instinctively, Kelly tried to turn around, his legs buckling beneath him, to face whoever was attacking him.

Before he could do so, the dull thud he had been anticipating came. But there was no knee in his back. Instead he felt the torch smash into the side of his head. Obscurely, as he sank to his knees on the beach, the thought occurred to him that it must be a rubber torch or else the blow would have been much more brutal. Perhaps even lethal.

Neither could he have been hit with as much power as he would have expected, because he had not been caused to collapse totally nor plunge into full unconsciousness. Instead, swaying only slightly, he remained kneeling almost upright for a moment, the rough edges of the shingle digging through his thin trousers into the flesh of his knees. Then, needing more support, he toppled forwards onto his hands.

His head felt as if it belonged to somebody else, and somebody else that he did not know, at that, but he still remained just about conscious, even though a million coloured lights danced before his eyes.

Then, just as he had earlier been aware of the close proximity of his assailant immediately before being attacked, Kelly realised that he was once again more or less alone. He heard the crunching of shingle to his left and peered into the gloom. He

254

could just make out a shadow heading for the cover of the densely wooded hill.

His head felt as if it were taking a ride on a fairground roundabout without him. And suddenly he was not aware of his heart beating at all. Although, as he was still breathing, he assumed it must be.

He straightened slightly and sat back on the beach, bringing his knees up to his chest and resting his head on them. His head was still spinning. He recognised that he had concussion. He had experienced it once before when he had taken a nasty fall ranch-riding in Arizona. On a story, of course. Kelly had never had time for hobbies. And he had had no more opportunity to fully master the art of horse-riding than the art of self-defence.

He wrapped both his hands around his head in an effort to soothe it, tentatively fingering the bruise which was already beginning to form on his forehead, and remained there, sitting on the stony beach for several minutes. The shingle was icy-cold and slightly wet, probably just from the mist and the dampness of the sea air, yet Kelly barely felt it as he struggled to regain normal consciousness. But then, his trousers were already wet. And as his mind and senses began to function again, even if only marginally, he became aware of the stench of urine mixing with the salty tang of the air.

After a bit, and with extreme caution, he raised his head from his knees and moved it slowly from side to side. It no longer spun for England. And although there was already considerable swelling on his forehead where he had been hit, it seemed that there was no blood. Apparently, the skin had not been broken and the blow had missed the more vulnerable spots. The potentially lethal spots. The parts of a man's head and neck with which Kelly somehow felt sure his assailant would be thoroughly familiar. It was almost as if he been hit with care. That didn't make sense, of course. But Kelly could think of no alternative, not in the state he was in, anyway.

Obliquely, the story of John Lee, the man they couldn't hang, drifted across his muddled mind. Towards the end of the nineteenth century, Lee had been employed as a footman in a house secluded in the hillside woodland above Babbacombe beach, the woodland into which Kelly's attacker had just disappeared. Lee had been condemned to death for the murder of his mistress, but had always denied the crime. When sentenced, he had predicted: 'The Lord will not let me hang.' And, indeed, when he was taken to be hanged in the courtyard of Exeter's forbidding old walled castle, now the regional crown court and in those days home of the assizes, the trap beneath the gallows had, quite extraordinarily, failed to open three times. So, as was customary, after the third attempt, nineteen-year-old Lee's death sentence had been repealed.

Crazy, violent images coursed through Kelly's dazed brain. He was still unable to think rationally and there were still bright lights dancing around before his eyes, not unlike the symptoms of a very bad migraine.

He could, however, think clearly enough to register one thing.

He should be dead. Like John Lee more than a century earlier, he really should be dead. He was sure of it. Somebody had come onto that beach that night to kill him. Somebody skilled in the art of death. And yet, at the last moment, his attacker had backed off and left him.

Kelly was alive. He was still alive. And he didn't know why.

Nineteen

Eventually, Kelly staggered back to his car. It took him several seconds of fumbling to unlock the door before he was able to fall gratefully into the driver's seat. In spite of his shaky condition he switched on the Volvo's engine straight away. He had no wish whatsoever to spend a moment longer than necessary in the deserted beach car park. It was, after all, not remotely beyond the realms of possibility that his attacker might regret letting him live and return for another go. Kelly did not intend to give him that opportunity. Clumsily, he jerked the Volvo into gear and took off as fast as he could up the steeply winding hill past The Cary Arms. His head was still swimming alarmingly and he could barely focus. Swinging the big, cumbersome vehicle around the near-vertical right-hand bend, part way up the hill, almost proved beyond him. His first two attempts to tackle the bend in the big car failed. Each time, he ended up having to slip the clutch and allow the car to run backwards, before slamming it into forward gear and having another go. He succeeded on the third attempt, and, although functioning so inadequately, he eventually reached the main road at the top of the steep winding hill, where he pulled to a halt in the first lay-by and slumped over the steering wheel. And he remained there for another ten minutes or so before he dared try to drive again. He was well aware that he still should not be driving, but he just wanted to get away from Babbacombe and to get home as soon as he possibly could. He had absolutely no intention of calling the police, not even Karen, until he was able to think more clearly.

So instead, when he felt recovered enough to at least make the attempt, he drove very slowly home to St Marychurch, keeping the driver's window open, partly because he thought fresh air might help clear his head, and partly because he couldn't stand the acrid stench of his own urine.

257

As he drove, he tried not to think about anything except getting home safely. He needed every ounce of concentration he could muster. He reckoned it would probably be several hours before the effect of his concussion fully departed. And then there was the shock to consider. He knew that he was definitely in shock. He had expected to die, after all.

The five minutes or so that it took to reach his home were just about the longest of his life. His little terraced house, high above Torquay's town centre, suddenly seemed like the most desirable place in the world. He desperately wanted some time there alone, to change his clothes, perhaps to have a shower, and to rest and recuperate a little before doing anything else. He knew he should probably drive straight to the casualty department of Torbay Hospital, but he didn't intend to do that, either. For a start, he wasn't yet ready to even attempt to explain what had happened to him.

Gratefully, he pulled up outside his house, vaguely aware that he seemed to have parked at an acute angle to the pavement but totally incapable of doing anything about it. At his first attempt to step out of the Volvo, he almost fell over. His knees gave way. It seemed that his legs were still not fully capable of supporting him. He leaned against the car for a minute or two, before taking a cautious step across the pavement and grabbing hold of the gate post. He realised that he was trembling from head to foot.

Once safely inside, he peeled off his soiled clothes as soon as he had closed the door behind him, dropping them in an untidy pile on the tiled floor of the hall, and made his way uncertainly upstairs to the bathroom, being careful to hold on to the banister.

He stepped into the shower and turned on the water to very hot and full power. His head was beginning to ache unpleasantly, but no longer seemed quite so strange. In fact, the shower helped even more than he had expected, and when he stepped out of it onto the bathmat, he was already a little less shaky than he had been when he had arrived home. He wrapped a couple of towels around his dripping body, and rummaged in the bathroom cabinet for the packet of Nurofen he knew was in there somewhere. As he closed the cabinet's mirrored door, he caught a glimpse of his reflected face. It was not a pretty sight.

He was white as a sheet, apart from the swollen, multicoloured bruise on his forehead. And it also looked as if at least one black eye was beginning to form. Wincing – as much at his own sorry image as because of his headache – he struggled to control trembling fingers in order to remove three of the small white pills from their foil container. He put them in his mouth and washed them down with tap water which he brought clumsily to his lips in cupped hands, spilling half the water over his front as he did so.

Thankfully, his legs felt much steadier. He made his way along the landing to the bedroom he used as an office and settled into his big leather swivel chair, where he sat perfectly still, breathing as deeply and as rhythmically as he could manage. He was only just beginning to realise fully how terrified he had been on that beach. He had been frightened, quite literally, out of his wits, and it was going to be some time before he would function normally again.

He leaned back in his chair and closed his eyes, which proved to be something of a mistake, because it brought about a return of the dancing lights. Swiftly he opened his eyes again, and sat waiting for the lights to disappear and, hopefully, for the Nurofen to start working on his splitting headache.

Eventually the pain in his head did begin to lessen and he started to think about what he should do next. He had a feeling he should tell Karen Meadows about what had happened as soon as possible. He did not yet have any idea exactly what he might have stumbled on at Hangridge, but he had certainly learned that he was now personally involved in a highly dangerous situation. There had been a string of deaths of young soldiers, almost all of which were at the very least highly suspicious, and now he too had almost died. Almost been murdered, in fact. Even Kelly knew that the time had come to step back and hand over everything he knew to those who, hopefully, were professionally qualified to deal with the consequences.

Impulsively he reached for the telephone to call Karen Meadows, but his vision was still suspect and his hands were still trembling so much that he realised it would be difficult for him to dial the number. He decided to wait a little longer. He would very much like a cigarette, but doubted he was capable of rolling one.

Then, just as he was desperately trying to remember if there was a packet of ready-made cigarettes secreted anywhere in the house, his mobile rang. In the hall downstairs. He remembered that it had been in the pocket of his suede jacket, which he had so unceremoniously dropped onto the floor just inside the front door. He had earlier dodged the calls that he knew Karen would be bound to try to make to him, but now he desperately wanted to know who could be calling him at such an hour.

Cursing under his breath, he jumped quickly to his feet, without thinking, in order to hurry to retrieve the phone. But the sudden movement set his head whirling again and he had to promptly sit down once more.

By the time he had managed to make his way downstairs and then delve in all the wrong pockets, his mobile had long since stopped ringing. When he finally found it, he at once the checked the display panel, half expecting his caller to have been Karen again. After all, he had stood her up.

Nick's mobile number showed up on the little screen. Kelly was mildly surprised. He peered at the clock on the wall to the left of the hallstand. As he had thought, it was nearly 1.30 a.m. A little anxiously, he checked the message service. There was one message from Karen asking him where the hell he was, but nothing from his son. What could Nick possibly want at this time of night, he wondered.

While he was contemplating this and trying to gather the strength to return the call, the phone rang again and again the number of Nick's mobile flashed up on the display panel. Kelly answered at once.

'Oh, hi, Dad, sorry to be so late, but I know you rarely go to bed much earlier than this, in spite of pretending to be an early-bird writer.'

'Yeah, well, you're probably right, and don't worry, it's always nice to hear from you.' Kelly realised as he spoke that his words were very slightly slurred. His head was not yet completely clear. It was actually quite an effort to speak.

Nick seemed to pick up on that too, which was probably not surprising, thought Kelly.

260

'Are you all right, Dad?' he asked. And Kelly could detect the note of anxiety in his voice.

'Yes, of course, I just fell asleep in the armchair, that's all,' lied Kelly, concentrating hard on his diction. He might well choose very soon to tell his son what had happened that night and would probably have already discussed the Hangridge affair with him, had he had opportunity. But Moira's funeral had certainly not been the occasion. He had not seen Nick since and neither had he wished to discuss any of it on the phone. Now this, once more, was certainly not the moment. After his brush with death that night, Kelly was even less likely to discuss any aspect of Hangridge on the phone, and in any case he still couldn't think clearly.

'Oh, I did wake you, then. I'm sorry.' Nick responded.

'That's OK. It's fine.' It was Kelly's turn, in spite of his fuzzy-headedness, to feel anxious. 'But what about you? I'm bloody sure you must have a good reason for calling me at this hour.'

'Yes, sorry, Dad. I just wanted to pick your brains actually . . .'

Not a good moment for that, either, thought Kelly, whose brain still felt as if it were coated in thick gooey mud, but he did not interrupt, preferring to preserve what little energy he had left.

'I'm working on something big,' Nick continued. 'I've been at my computer all night. There's a bug that's got into the system at the MoD and it's causing mayhem, hence the urgency. I've traced the source to Washington D.C. and I've just found an article on the Net – about exactly the same bug – written by that mate of yours over there who you often talk about. You know, Terry Wallis, the *Times* man in Washington, isn't he? Apparently, it nearly brought down the entire Pentagon network and Terry seems to know an awful lot about it. I desperately need to compare notes with him, and if I have to wait until morning it will be the middle of the night over there. I wondered if you had a phone number for him?'

'Um. So you thought you'd rather wake me up in the middle of the night than Terry Wallis, did you?'

'Well, you are my father. I thought you'd be more likely to forgive me.'

Kelly smiled in spite of himself.

'Smooth bugger,' he said. 'Hang on, I'll look the number up for you.'

Kelly and Terry Wallis, one of his few old Fleet Street friends still in the employ of a major national newspaper, kept in quite regular touch. Terry's Washington number was scribbled in the back of his desk diary, and it took Kelly only a moment to look it up and relate it to Nick.

'Thanks a million, Dad. You may have saved the MoD, as well as my life.'

'Jolly good.' Kelly didn't want to discuss lives being saved, right then, and was quite grateful to end the call, which at least seemed to have helped him to function a little better. The effort of making conversation, however perfunctory, appeared to have done him good, he thought.

He reckoned his speech was almost back to normal, and he now felt that he could just about cope with calling Karen Meadows. Even though he knew she was not going to be exactly delighted to hear from him at this hour.

He dialled her home number, his fingers still trembling but at least more or less doing what he told them to, and at around the tenth ring she answered very sleepily and not a little grumpily.

'Yes,' she growled.

'Karen, it's me. I'm so sorry to call so late . . .'

'So you fucking well should be . . .' She mumbled something else that Kelly couldn't quite understand, before rounding on him in language he understood perfectly.

'It's not fucking late, Kelly. It's fucking early. It's a quarter to two in the fucking morning!'

Kelly ignored the outburst. He just wasn't up to it.

'Look, something's happened. You ought to know about it, really you—'

'What? Now? In the middle of the night? Are you off your head? Anyway, I thought you didn't want to see me till tomorrow. I thought you were having dinner with Moira's girls tonight.'

Kelly knew he couldn't play games any more.

'I lied.'

'Yes, you bastard. I know, actually.'

'You do?'

'I phoned Jennifer.'

'Checking up on me?'

'Bit late for that, really.'

'I'm sorry, but, believe me, I did have a good reason.'

'Don't you always?'

'Maybe. But this time I really did.'

'Ah.' There was a brief pause. 'Are you all right, Kelly.'

Kelly had thought he'd been managing his speech rather well. What had she picked up on, he wondered. Kelly supposed he should not be surprised. It was quite possible that Karen Meadows actually knew him better than his only son did. In any case, he probably was still slurring his words a bit, although he couldn't be certain because there was an echo inside his head, which made everything sound slightly distorted.

'Yes. Just about. But there has been an incident, something I never for a second expected. I need to talk to you about it.'

'At this time of the morning?'

'Yes. Honestly, Karen, it can't wait. It really can't wait.'

'Look, it's nothing to do with . . .' she paused. 'You know, what happened the other night, is it?'

'What?' For a moment he didn't know what on earth she was talking about. Then he realised. She must be referring to their misguided kiss. For God's sake, he thought.

'Nothing, absolutely nothing, could be further from my mind,' he answered honestly.

'OK. OK. You'd better come over, then.'

'No.' Kelly shook his head as he said the word, and a shooting pain darted from somewhere around his eyes, right through his nervous system, down to the base of his spine. He really couldn't do any more driving. For a start, his vision remained far from normal.

'Look, I don't think I should drive. Could you come over here to me?'

'You haven't been drinking, Kelly, have you?' she asked suddenly, and now she really did sound alarmed.

'No.' He managed an attempt at a dry laugh. 'I haven't been drinking, Karen. But something has happened which could have even more disastrous consequences. And not just for me.'

There was a brief pause, and when she replied she did not

prevaricate any more. He was aware that while she knew him to be capable of some quite extreme moments of madness, she would also know that he would not ask her to visit him in the middle of the night without a very good reason indeed.

'I'll be with you in half an hour, maximum,' she said.

She pulled on jeans and an old sweater and then delved into the back of the wardrobe for her old and much-loved, quilted denim Armani coat, with its distinctive metal badge. She needed comfort clothes for this jaunt, she thought. And, preoccupied as she already was by her brief conversation with Kelly, the faded blue coat, which she reckoned oozed quality, still gave her a bit of a satisfied feeling as she pulled it on. 'They don't make 'em like this any more,' she muttered to herself.

On the drive along the front and through a deserted town centre, Karen tried to imagine what on earth could have happened to induce Kelly to call her at 1.45 in the morning and demand an audience. Particularly, as whatever he had been up to earlier – and she had been right, of course, he had most definitely been up to something – he'd, apparently, at first been quite determined to keep it from her.

He had sounded quite peculiar, too. She wished now that she hadn't referred to their little emotional lapse, but she had a feeling that the whole incident was in any case about to pale into insignificance.

In St Marychuch, she had to park a little down the road from Kelly's house, mainly because of the large Volvo already parked outside, and at such an angle to the pavement that it blocked part of the road. He answered his front door before she even had the chance to ring the bell. She could only assume that he must have been looking out of the window for her to arrive and she had various lines of banter ready for him, all of which went completely out of her mind as soon as she saw him.

There was now a large, very sore-looking bump towards the upper left of Kelly's forehead. It was a nasty, yellow-reddish colour and there were signs of residual bruising all around it. In addition, both of Kelly's eyes were puffy and discoloured and he seemed to be having difficulty in focusing. She was genuinely shocked.

'Good God,' she said. 'What the fuck happened to you?'

'It's a long story,' he replied. 'Come in. I've made fresh coffee. I think we're both going to need it.'

He led the way into the living room, gestured her to a chair by the fireplace, and poured coffee from a steaming jug into two big mugs. She waited with unusual patience. After all, she needed a few minutes' grace to recover from the shock of his appearance.

'Well?' she enquired, when Kelly finally sat down across the fireplace from her.

'As you can see, I've had a bit of a going-over.'

'I certainly can see. Don't you think I should take you to casualty?'

'No, I'm all right, really.'

'What the fuck happened?'

'I think somebody tried to kill me,' he began. 'And I really have no idea why he didn't go through with it.'

'Shit,' she said.

Kelly nodded his assent. 'Shit, indeed,' he said. 'I'm scared, Karen, and I don't mind admitting it.'

He began to tell her everything then, deliberately leaving the best bit until last. Even in the sorry state he was in, Kelly retained the tabloid journalist's sense of the dramatic when it came to a good story. First of all he asked Karen if she had seen the article in the *Evening Argus* about the death of yet another young Hangridge squaddie, murdered in London on a street close to the family home of key witness James Gates, also dead.

'No, I didn't see the *Argus* yesterday,' she admitted. 'I was too busy.'

She thought for a second.

'That's shocking enough, but I get the feeling it's not the half of it, is it, Kelly?' she enquired. 'And you've yet to tell me how you ended up looking as if you've just completed ten rounds with Mike Tyson.'

Kelly tried to smile. It obviously hurt. He told her about his anonymous tip-off and the arranged midnight meeting on Babbacombe beach, which he was now convinced had been a set-up. In graphic detail, he explained how he was attacked by an assailant he was convinced was a professional killer, and how he had been let off but could not begin to explain why.

265

'Like John Lee,' he said. 'And just as unlikely an escape, I promise you.'

Karen was shocked. Kelly didn't need to explain the analogy to her. She was, after all, a local girl, and, like almost everyone from the Torbay area, had been brought up on the tale of John Lee, the man they couldn't hang.

She cupped her chin in her hands and leaned forwards in her chair.

'Right, Kelly,' she began. 'I don't think we should even go into why you are still alive. I just want to make sure you stay that way. So, let's get one thing clear, shall we? You must pull back from the Hangridge affair at once. I'll call the nick straight away and set up an investigation into the attack on you. I don't need anybody's authority to do that. On the surface, at least, this is a straightforward case of an innocent civilian being assaulted in a public place, and if that leads into military matters, then all for the better. I'll get the SOCOs out to Babbacombe straight away, just in case they can pick up on something, and I'm afraid whether you like it—'

'Karen, please, I haven't got to the most important bit yet,' Kelly interrupted.

'Look, Kelly, we must move as fast as we possibly can in order to protect all remaining evidence. Whether you like it or not, you'll have to come back to the nick with me now. You mightn't want to go to casualty, but you do have to be seen by our police doctor, we may be able to get some forensic evidence off you.'

'Oh, shit,' said Kelly, 'I've had a shower.'

'I don't believe it.'

'I just wasn't thinking straight.'

'OK. Well, we can still go over the clothes you were wearing. Or have you destroyed them, too?'

Kelly managed a wan smile, apparently without too much pain, and shook his head.

'Good,' she continued. 'And you said you managed to bite your attacker, so if you made a halfway decent job of it, there may be some fragments of skin in your teeth. You haven't brushed them, have you?'

Kelly shook his head again.

'Thank God, for that. We'll want a statement too, but that can

266

wait until later on in the morning if you don't feel up to it. I'll probably ask Chris Tompkins to interview you, because I shall go to Exeter first thing. Or as soon as I recover from this middle of the night assignation, anyway. Whatever comes out of this attack on you—'

'Look, Karen,' Kelly interrupted again. 'I've been trying to tell you. There's something else you should know, before you—'

But Karen still wouldn't let him finish. She was on a roll, putting an investigation together, planning her next move. It was what she did best. And just knowing that she now had a valid course of action to follow was making her feel so much better.

'Yeah, yeah, but first, Kelly, let me explain. Whatever comes out of this attack on you, that, coupled with this murder of James Gates' mate in London, should really get things moving. In fact, if it doesn't force frigging Harry Tomlinson to give the go-ahead for a full scale CID inquiry into every one of these deaths of Devonshire Fusiliers, I don't know what the fuck will—'

'Karen!' Kelly raised his voice to a shout and Karen could see that he had really made his head hurt. He screwed up his face in pain. She studied him anxiously. In addition, there was something in his voice now that absolutely demanded her attention.

Yes?' she queried quite meekly.

'Karen, please, please, listen. Do you remember I told you about the two men who came into The Wild Dog looking for Alan Connelly, the night this all began?'

'Yes, of course I do.' Karen was mildly irritated. Did he think she had turned into an idiot?

'Well, one of them, the one who did all the talking. I think I know who he was. Actually, I am quite sure I know who he was.'

'Really?' Karen was puzzled. Why the big build-up, she wondered.

Out loud she said: 'Well, spit it out, then.'

'I-I met him yesterday,' Kelly continued. 'And I recognised him. At once.'

'What?' Karen was even more puzzled by the air of mystery Kelly was creating. 'Not the man who attacked you on the beach? I thought you said you couldn't see him.'

'I couldn't. No, not him. Well, not as far as I know, anyway.'

He paused again. Infuriating man, thought Karen. Even in the state he was in, he was still playing to his audience, going for the biggest possible dramatic effect. She realised the quickest way to be put out of her misery was to play along with him.

'Well?' she prompted, expressionlessly.

'It was Gerrard Parker-Brown. I am absolutely sure of it. Really I am. Colonel Parker-Brown.'

Twenty

Karen felt as if she too had been run over by a truck.

'Kelly, no,' she said. 'It couldn't have been.'

'I'm telling you, Karen.'

'But, for God's sake, those E-fits you and Janet Farnsby came up with, neither of them looked a bit like him.'

'You said yourself that they are hit and miss. I did my best, but I knew they were both pretty terrible likenesses. And, anyway, Parker-Brown and the other man were wearing woolly hats and had their coat collars turned up.'

'So, you couldn't see his face properly?'

'Quite enough, I promise you. I could see his eyes, Karen. I didn't really think about how special they were until I saw him at Hangridge. Then it hit me. Big brown eyes, with long eyelashes. They're like a woman's eyes. You must know how distinctive his eyes are.'

Karen knew. She also knew how attractive they were. And that she had very nearly fallen for their appeal and, indeed, for Gerry Parker-Brown's all-round charm. It seemed that she could have had a very narrow escape, indeed. Thank God, that for once in her life, a degree of common sense had triumphed over her natural impulsiveness. 'Like a woman's eyes', Kelly had said. And that had to be the clincher. She had, after all, thought the same thing herself.

'Shit,' she said. 'And when you met him yesterday, do you think he recognised you? You went in as an investigator representing the families of the dead soldiers, didn't you? Do you think he realised that you had been in The Wild Dog with Alan Connelly? That you were probably the witness I had told him about.'

'I have no idea. But if he did, he gave absolutely no sign of it, I can tell you. Even though I stared at him all the time. I couldn't help it.'

269

'Well, maybe you gave yourself away, then?'

'Maybe. I hope not. I tried not to.'

'But he gave no indication of recognition?'

'Not at all. I mean, for whatever reason, he and his side-kick were obviously extremely relieved to find Connelly that night. It's quite possible he barely noticed who else was in the pub.'

'Maybe. I'll tell you one thing, Kelly, I've had enough to do with Gerrard Parker-Brown to come to the conclusion that he is some performer in every sense of the word. He's a devious manipulative bastard, actually, and more than likely, I'm beginning to have to accept, quite an actor. A much better actor than either you or I, that's for certain.'

'You could be right.'

'And if I am, if he did recognise you from The Wild Dog, well, then, he would consider you to be one hell of a threat to him, wouldn't he? Do you think it could have been Parker-Brown out there on the beach? Don't tell me the thought hasn't occurred to you?'

'Of course it has.'

'And?'

'I just don't know. Anyway, do senior army officers like Parker-Brown do their own dirty work?'

'No idea. But, if you're right, Parker-Brown was doing his own dirty work, and very possibly murderous dirty work at that, the night Connelly died, wasn't he?'

'Yes, he was.'

'So, could it have been Parker-Brown who attacked you?'

'Yes, it could. But I have no way of telling. I told you. The bastard approached me from the back, half strangled me. Then he shone a torch in my face. I never got a look at him. It was pitch-black . . .'

'Think, Kelly, think. Why did whoever attacked you shine a torch at you? Why did he back off like he did, run off into the woods?'

'I don't know. I've been trying to work it out ever since . . .'

'Think, Kelly. I know you've been bashed over the head, but you've got a really good brain when you choose to put it into operation . . .'

270

'Good God, a compliment to my brain? Have you been knocked over the head too, Karen?'

'Get on with it, Kelly. Think!'

'Well, it was like he was taking a look at me when he shone the torch at me. But why would he do that? After all, presumably he damned well knew who I was.'

'None the less, your attacker shone a torch at you, full in your face, presumably took a look, and then he hit you with the torch. How did you describe it? Carefully. He hit you carefully. And then he buggered off.'

'Yes. That's it, exactly. And no, it doesn't make any sense to me either.'

'OK, let's go back over it all. I mean, for a start, are you absolutely sure it was a man who attacked you?'

'Yes, well, I think so.' Kelly was initially slightly hesitant, but sounded quite decisive when he spoke again. 'Yes. I am sure. I couldn't imagine any woman being that strong, and I'm also pretty sure, somehow, that it was a male arm I bit. Muscle tone, that sort of thing. And I have a vague memory of body hair, too.'

'Right. Good. So, again, could it have been Parker-Brown? I mean, how tall was he? At that close quarters you must at least have got some sense of your assailant's height and build, surely? Concentrate, Kelly.'

'Yes, I suppose I did.' Kelly's voice was thoughtful. Karen could tell he was really concentrating. 'Yes. He was a tall man. Probably about my height, six two. But thinner than me. Definitely thinner, and much fitter. Does it sound crazy that I'm so sure of that? It was the way he moved – the stealth, the power. The way he grabbed hold of me. He was strong and fit and he knew what he was doing. I was convinced, somehow, as soon as he got hold of me that he was a pro. Somebody military, I'd bet anything you like on that. So yes, I suppose it could well have been Parker-Brown.'

'Jesus,' she said. 'Then let's get the bastard, shall we?'

Karen took Kelly with her back to the station, just as she had said she would before Kelly had dropped his bombshell, and arranged for him to be seen by a police doctor.

By around half past three in the morning, she decided there

was little point in bothering to go home to bed. Often, when her night's sleep was interrupted, she fared better dosing herself with coffee and staying up than returning to her bed for a further snatched two or three hours.

Instead, she began straight away to set up the initial investigation into Kelly's attack. She organised a SOCO team to go out to Babbacombe, and when Kelly decided, after his medical examination, that he'd rather carry on and give his formal statement then, Karen interviewed him herself, along with a young, uniformed, woman constable on night duty. By the time she had done that and finished setting up the rest of the investigation, it was getting on for 6 a.m. In view of having had her entire night's rest disrupted, she allowed herself the rare treat of a full fried breakfast in the canteen, and, shortly after 6.30 a.m., set off for headquarters in Exeter to confront the chief constable.

She knew that Harry Tomlinson was an early bird, who was often at his desk at Middlemoor by around 7.30. She had also been told that he was frequently in a better mood at that hour than he was inclined to be later in the day, although it had always seemed to Karen that Tomlinson was never in anything remotely resembling a good mood when he had to deal with her, whatever time of day she chose. The two of them were like chalk and cheese – Karen, the sometimes reckless maverick, who knew that she could be inspired on occasions but whose police career was not without a smattering of perhaps unnecessary errors, and Tomlinson, a neat, dapper, by-the-book, little man with a bristly manner that matched his bristly moustache, a jobsworth and a paper-shuffler, in Karen's opinion. And a police officer promoted way beyond his station. She also had a pretty good idea what Tomlinson thought of her. Indeed, she reckoned it was something of a miracle that, with him in charge of the Devon and Cornwall Constabulary, she had ever made detective superintendent.

None the less she had no choice but to deal with Harry Tomlinson, and certainly, if she was going to get the result she was looking for from him, on such a sensitive matter as Hangridge, she had to tread with extreme care.

She did not see, however, how Tomlinson could have any

choice now but to authorise a full-scale investigation into Hangridge. And, as she drove herself to Exeter, she was cautiously optimistic that at last she would be able to do something really positive towards finding out what had happened to all those young soldiers.

Her mind was racing. Ever since Kelly had dropped his bombshell, she had been trying not to think about Gerry Parker-Brown and what a narrow escape she had had. She would not have needed many more dates with him to have willingly jumped into bed with him, she suspected. After all, he was extremely attractive, and he had, quite calculatedly, she was absolutely sure now, set out to charm her. It had been, of course, a highly sensible decision to back off almost as soon as she had any doubts about him, but that could be regarded as having been somewhat out of character for Karen. When it came to matters of the heart, let alone of the flesh, she had rarely shown much sense before.

At least one half of her still couldn't believe that Parker-Brown really was involved in the mysterious deaths connected with the barracks, but he was now certainly a prime suspect.

Karen arrived at Middlemoor at almost exactly 7.30 a.m., and, just as she was locking her car, she saw the chief constable's black Rover saloon, driven by a uniformed PC, pull up outside the main doors.

She hurried across the car park, calling out to him as she did so. This was no time to stand on dignity.

'Sir! Sir!' she cried.

He turned at once, eyes wide with what she thought was probably ninety per cent affected surprise.

'Good God! What on earth are you doing here at this hour in the morning, DS Meadows? I always had you down as a night owl, going by the trouble you usually seem to have keeping early morning appointments, anyway. Couldn't you sleep?'

She smiled wanly, ignoring his sarcasm. This was no time to be petty, either.

'I had to see you urgently, sir,' she said.

'Really? So urgently that you couldn't make an appointment in the proper manner?'

She had known that would annoy him, of course. To a man like Tomlinson, his diary was a bible.

'Sorry, sir,' she persisted. 'But yes. It is that urgent.'

The chief constable's small mouth puckered up. His eyes looked even more as if they were likely to pop out of his head than they usually did.

'Very well,' he said eventually. 'You'd better come into my office, then.' He checked his watch. 'I can give you fifteen minutes, maximum. I have a breakfast meeting at eight with the chairman of Exeter Chamber of Commerce.'

'Yes, sir.'

She followed him meekly. Once inside his office he did not even bother to invite her to sit down, but she did so anyway, automatically choosing the upright chair opposite his desk, in much the same way as she had during her last meeting with Parker-Brown. She didn't want Tomlinson looking down at her, either. After all, the CC couldn't be much more than five foot five or six, and the only time he could come close to looking down on her was when he was sitting in a higher chair.

'Well?' he enquired tersely.

'It's Hangridge, sir,' she began. 'There have been some further—'

'Oh, please, Detective Superintendent,' Tomlinson interrupted brusquely. 'Not again!'

'Sir. Do let me explain. There have been some further incidents, important incidents, the death of another Devonshire Fusilier which could well be connected, and an assault on a member of the public—'

'A member of the public?' Tomlinson interrupted. 'Who exactly?'

Damn, thought Karen. She hadn't wanted to go into that at this precise moment, but the chief constable had given her no choice.

'On John Kelly, sir . . .'

'John Kelly?' The words came out like a small explosion. 'Why am I not surprised. That man is a total loose cannon. He should not be allowed to get involved in something like this. When will you ever learn, Detective Superintendent?'

'Sir, John Kelly was assaulted, in such a manner that he thought he was about to die, and the incident occurred after he

274

had discovered some rather extraordinary information concerning Hangridge,' she persisted grimly.

She told him everything quickly then, before he could find an excuse not to listen. She told him about Jimmy Gates and Jimmy Gates' friend, Robert Morgan, who had been murdered in London, and about how Kelly had recognised Gerrard Parker-Brown as one of the two men who had come looking for Alan Connelly on the night he died.

'Can Kelly be sure?' responded the chief constable. 'I saw those E-fits. I wouldn't have recognised Parker-Brown from either of them, that's for certain.'

'I know, sir. Kelly admits they weren't a good likeness, but yes, he really is quite sure. And, of course, it was right after he confronted the colonel that he was attacked. It could well be that Parker-Brown also recognised Kelly from The Wild Dog that night and realised what a danger he could be . . .'

'Oh, come, come, Detective Superintendent. 'You are not suggesting, surely, that it was Gerry Parker-Brown who attacked John Kelly last night?'

'Well, sir, it must be a possibility—'

'Actually, Superintendent, no, it isn't a possibility. Gerry and I had a late supper together at my club here in Exeter last night. And it was after midnight when he left. Indeed, it was the clock striking midnight which made us both break up the party. Such good company, Gerry. So I'm afraid you will have to take him off your list of suspects, after all, Miss Meadows.'

Karen winced mentally. She might have known it. What a clever bastard Parker-Brown was. Supper with the chief constable at his club, just when Kelly was being attacked. Obscurely, it went through her mind that she hadn't been aware that Tomlinson had a club, or even that the kind of club she somehow imagined he was referring to existed in Exeter.

'Sir, don't you think that is just a tad convenient?' she ventured.

'It was an engagement that has been in my diary for nearly two weeks,' responded the chief constable, as if that answered everything. Karen waited for him to continue and to clarify exactly what he thought that proved, but obviously Harry Tomlinson didn't think it necessary, so she decided to try again herself.

'Look, sir, a man like Parker-Brown is not really likely to do his own dirty work, is he? It is rather more possible, I feel, that someone – a real professional, Kelly thought – was instructed to dispatch Kelly on his behalf.'

'Really? In which case, if the attacker was so professional, why is John Kelly not dead?'

'That is one of the many mysteries of this case, sir.'

'It certainly is.' The chief constable stood up and walked to the window so that he had his back to Karen.

'All right, Karen,' he said eventually, in a resigned sort of voice. 'I do see that there are now a number of unanswered questions here . . .'

And at that inappropriate moment, just as Karen began to believe she was about to get the go-ahead she was seeking, the chief constable's desktop phone rang. Someone else who understood the advantage of getting to the boss early in the day, she thought.

'Good morning, Detective Inspector,' said Tomlinson into the phone, peering over it at Karen in a particularly curious manner, she thought.

'Yes, yes, I see,' he continued. 'Well, well. You had an anonymous caller, did you? Well, would you believe, DI Cooper, that I have one Detective Superintendent Meadows here with much the same story to tell, but with a few additional literary details. Different source, of course. Now isn't that a coincidence?'

Shit, thought Karen. Another most unhappy coincidence was that Phil Cooper had chosen to contact the chief constable just when she was with him. She remembered then that Tomlinson had made comments in the past which had indicated that he had known about her relationship with Cooper. But, of course, it would have been hard for even him to have missed it. After all, she suspected that the whole of the Devon and Cornwall Constabulary knew about their ill-advised affair. And now Tomlinson had put two and two together, and quite correctly come to the conclusion that she and Cooper had conspired in their attempts to persuade him that there should be a major police investigation into the Hangridge deaths.

Karen waited for him to finish the call, wondering how he

would react. The really annoying thing was that the death of Robert Morgan, combined with Kelly's additional information concerning Parker-Brown, and indeed the very fact that Kelly had been assaulted, meant that it had probably been quite unnecessary to bring in Phil and his Major Crime Incident Team. But she hadn't known that last night.

Tomlinson had a broad smile on his face and now looked as if he were thoroughly enjoying himself, thought Karen, who was not actually surprised by the pleasure he seemed to be getting from watching her mounting embarrassment.

'Right. I'll need to talk to Detective Superintendent Meadows, and I'll get back to you in a few minutes,' were his last words into the phone.

He turned to Karen.

'Well, well, Karen,' he began, and as ever when he used her Christian name it made her feel all the more uneasy. 'It seems that your former b—'

He paused. Karen looked at him in amazement. Had he really been about to say boyfriend?

'Your former sergeant,' the chief constable continued eventually, 'shares your opinion that it is time we staged a full-scale police investigation at Hangridge. And, amazed as I am at the many coincidences between your two, doubtless, totally separate approaches . . .' He paused again to peer at her quizzically and she couldn't help wincing a little. '. . . I must come to the conclusion that I have no choice but to give my authority,' Tomlinson went on. 'In view of the serious nature of this investigation, I think it should be a joint operation between you and your team, Detective Superintendent, and the MCIT. I will inform DI Cooper of that at once, and you, of course, will be the senior investigating officer, in view of your rank.'

There was something in Tomlinson's voice that left Karen in no doubt whatsoever that he had only put her in charge with some reluctance. But then, what was new about that? She really didn't care. She had got her own way, more or less, and that was all that mattered.

'Thank you, sir.' Karen jumped to her feet at once and headed for the door. She was buzzing now. She had work to do, and at last her hands were no longer tied.

'Just one moment.'

Karen stopped in her tracks and looked back over her shoulder.

'Don't make a balls of it, will you, Karen? And do keep John Kelly out of all of this, if you can.'

'Yes, sir,' said Karen out loud. Under her breath she muttered to herself something entirely different. 'Chance would be a fine thing.'

Kelly was taken home in a police car just before 6 a.m., little more than half an hour before Karen set off for Exeter. She had wanted to provide him with protection.

'Somebody has tried to kill you once, Kelly, it could happen again,' she told him.

He had declined quite forcibly. He needed time to himself to think. He was horrified by the very thought of a police minder.

'I'm not going anywhere except bed, I promise, and I'll keep all the doors and windows locked,' he said.

They had compromised. No minder, but a police patrol car would call round periodically to check on him.

Kelly felt absolutely terrible. His brain hurt, his face hurt, his eyes ached, and the whole of his head still felt as if it belonged to someone else. He was also totally exhausted. He took himself off to bed straight away, and yet he feared he would not be able to sleep at all. However, after taking another two of the blockbuster painkillers the police doctor had given him, he went out like a light, and was astonished to find when he eventually woke up that it was gone three in the afternoon and that he must have slept for nearly nine hours.

However, the long sleep did not seem to have helped that much. His head ached for England, the bump on his forehead was now truly multicoloured and he had two rather splendid black eyes – the left one, directly beneath his bump, only marginally more spectacular than the right.

Everything he did upon waking up, like making his tea, dressing, brushing his teeth and shaving, seemed to take much longer than normal. It wasn't just his head which was causing him pain. His whole body seemed to be aching in sympathy.

He was just wondering whether he might as well write off the rest of the day and return to bed, when his phone rang. He glanced at the display panel. If it had been anyone but Jennifer, he may well not have answered. But he couldn't ignore Moira's younger daughter.

'John, I just called to say hello and check you were OK,' she began.

'I'm fine,' he lied. Kelly was sometimes disconcerted by the ease with which lying came to him.

'It was only that Karen Meadows called last night. She'd been trying to get hold of you. I was afraid you might have shut yourself away and be moping. You're always welcome to come over here if you're down, you know that, don't you? It's what Mum would have wanted.'

Kelly felt his bruised eyes moisten. Jennifer had a knack of tugging on his heartstrings, and he knew that she did it totally unwittingly too. He felt ashamed, though, that the truth was that he had barely thought about Jennifer's mother at all since the day of the funeral.

'Thank you,' he said. 'Maybe I'll pop over tonight. Or tomorrow.'

As he spoke, he realised that might not be a good idea even if he did feel so inclined, because he would be forced to come up with some kind of explanation for his damaged face.

'That would be great,' responded Jennifer warmly. 'Oh, by the way, John. How's Nick? You didn't tell me he was down again.'

'What?' Kelly was completely taken aback. His astonishment must surely have sounded in his voice, but Jennifer did not seem to notice it. Unlike him, she probably was still preoccupied with her mother's death, he thought.

'I was in town yesterday evening, for the late shopping, and I saw his car parked just off Fleet Street,' Jennifer continued. 'You didn't tell me he was here. It's always nice to see him,' she said somewhat accusingly.

'Uh, no. Sorry.' Kelly stumbled for words, automatically seeking refuge in another lie. 'It was only a fleeting visit. He was on a business trip and just stopped over. He didn't have time to see anyone.'

'Right. He's gone back to London already, then?'

'Yes,' replied Kelly promptly. The truth, of course, was that he didn't have a clue, but that seemed the only appropriate answer. He strove for a way to find out more from Jennifer without giving himself away.

'Didn't know you were such an expert on cars,' he commented lamely.

'I'm not. But you can't mistake that special silver Aston Martin of his, can you? Even at Mum's funeral, you could see everybody was admiring it.'

'I'm sure you're right,' he said.

'Well, give him my love when you speak to him, anyway,' concluded Jennifer.

Kelly's hands were shaking again when he hung up. He told himself that Jennifer may have been mistaken. Nick's customised Aston Martin was indeed very special and it was a limited edition, but there was sure to be a number of others not unlike it around, and there could well be at least one other currently in the West of England.

None the less Kelly was experiencing a horrible feeling of dread, as if some unspeakable monster was being hatched in the pit of his stomach. Once before he'd found himself doubting his only son, wondering what he might be capable of, but then had at once dismissed the thought. Now the doubts were back.

On impulse he picked up his phone again and dialled Nick's home number. The reply was almost instant.

'Nick Carter.' Kelly, grateful for having had the call-identification feature removed from his line, hung up straight away. As he did so, the thought fleetingly crossed his mind how often over the years he had regretted allowing his ex-wife, justifiably bitter at the way Kelly had treated her, to change their son's surname from Kelly to her own maiden name. He hated to think that there was even a chance that he might one day cease to regret that his son did not bear his name.

He forced his thoughts back to the present. Well, Nick was in London now, he mused. But what did that prove? As far as Kelly could work it out, Nick had built a whole career, both in the army and outside of it, around his ability to move fast and to think on his feet. He could easily have been in Torquay the previous night and back in London by now. Kelly may just have dragged himself out of bed, but it was mid-afternoon. In any case, Nick thought nothing of driving for several hours when other people were sleeping. He was that sort of young man.

Or, at least, that was the sort of young man Kelly thought he was. But, and not for the first time, he was beginning to wonder if he really knew anything much about his only son.

Twenty-one

As soon as she left Middlemoor, Karen's first impulse had been to drive straight to Hangridge and to confront Gerrard Parker-Brown face to face. But she also knew that this was now the time for consolidation. So instead she headed back to Torquay in order to assemble her troops and to study fully every jot of the potential evidence gathered so far.

In addition there was just a chance, in spite of Kelly's conviction otherwise, that there might be some evidence gleaned from the Babbacombe crime scene, or at least some meaningful forensic evidence gathered from Kelly's clothing.

She already knew that the doctor had found some tiny fragments of what appeared to be alien skin in Kelly's teeth, but it would be several days before she would receive a DNA profile from the scraps of skin, and even then, unless Kelly's attacker had a criminal record, it would not be much use to her without a suspect to compare the DNA with. And whatever part Gerrard Parker-Brown may or may not have played in the deaths of Hangridge soldiers, it appeared that he could not have been guilty of attacking Kelly. Not personally, anyway.

There were other lines of inquiry to be followed up. She managed to acquire a photograph of Parker-Brown from the chief constable's commendations ceremony the previous year, and dispatched an officer to The Wild Dog to see if the landlord might also be able to identify him as having visited the pub on the night that Alan Connelly died.

Then she spent the rest of the day making sure that she was up to speed on every development, while at the same time sending off teams of detectives to interview the families of the various dead soldiers. In cases where the families lived out of the Devon and Cornwall Constabulary's area, in particular Alan Connelly's family in Scotland, Jimmy Gates' brother, Colin, in London and

Jocelyn Slade's mother in Reading, she liaised with the various regional forces so that statements could be taken as soon as possible by officers already on the spot.

She also rang Phil Cooper and suggested that they stage a joint blitz on Hangridge the following morning, by which time, hopefully, several other lines of inquiry would have been followed up.

'I suggest we get there early, about seven a.m., and hopefully take them by surprise,' she told him. 'And we'll go mob-handed, Phil. I don't know quite how you put the fear of God into the arrogant, bloody British army, but let's give it a damned good try, shall we?'

'Yes, boss.' Cooper's response was short and sweet. He really was a good man to have on your side, and she was glad that she was no longer troubled by confusing personal feelings about him.

'You and I will confront Parker-Brown first of all, and then we will systematically work through the whole damn camp, if necessary,' she continued. 'The place is no doubt a hotbed of gossip, and I intend to make the most of that. It must be full of people in the know. And I want to know what they know, even if we have to talk to the lot of them.'

'Yes, boss.' No nonsense. No arguing.

She ended the call swiftly, as soon as she had said all she needed to. There was still a lot of work to be done that day. Then she had to make sure she got a good night's sleep, in order to be fresh for that early-morning confrontation with the commanding officer of the Devonshire Fusiliers.

And for once in her life she couldn't wait for dawn to break.

Kelly knew that he should phone Margaret Slade to keep her in touch with developments. Or at least those developments which he was prepared to share with her. But somehow he just didn't seem to have the heart or the energy to do it.

He still didn't feel at all well. There was something he desperately wanted to do, something which involved a long journey, and he still didn't feel capable of driving, or indeed embarking on a journey of any kind, by any mode of transport.

He decided that he may as well return to bed and was just

about to make a move, when his phone rang again. He checked the display panel and saw that this time his caller was Margaret Slade. He still didn't want to speak to her, but reckoned he owed her that much, at least. She sounded extremely excited.

'John, I've had two local CID round, sent on behalf of your mob down in Devon, apparently. They wanted to know everything about my Jossy and how she died and about what people said to me at her funeral, absolutely everything. They've launched a full-scale police investigation. Isn't that great, Kelly? Isn't that great?'

Kelly was so preoccupied, and so worried by his preoccupation, that he just couldn't keep up with her enthusiasm.

'It certainly is, Margaret,' he said eventually, as warmly as he could, 'It certainly is.'

'Yes, it's a real result,' she went on. 'They also told me about that other soldier who's been killed in London. I'm dreadfully sorry for him and his family, of course, but it's another reason why the authorities can't pretend any more that there isn't something very wrong at Hangridge. And we haven't even had to use our people power yet. You must have really stirred things up, John, you really must have.'

'Yes, I think you can say that safely enough,' responded Kelly, with absolute honesty.

'So, what should we do? You must be itching to get some stories into the press. It speaks for itself now, doesn't it? Devon and Cornwall police yesterday launched a major inquiry into the suspicious deaths of a number of soldiers, all stationed at Hangridge barracks, HQ of the Devonshire Fusiliers. It writes itself. I think even I could do it.'

'I think you could too,' said Kelly, managing a small smile. She was right. The story would write itself. But at that moment, possibly for the first time in his life when confronted with such a thoroughly cracking yarn, Kelly couldn't bring himself to write it.

'But I still think we should hold off on the publicity front,' he continued, sounding pretty pathetic, he thought. 'Let's see what the next few days bring, eh? We don't want to screw things up after such a grand start, do we?'

'Well, OK, if you say so.' Margaret Slade sounded both

284

disappointed and surprised. Kelly understood that. He supposed it must be a little surprising to listen to a journalist trying to justify why he *didn't* want to publish a story.

'But the whole thing could break at any moment now, couldn't it?' she continued. 'I thought you'd want to make sure you got your story in first. After all, you've done a good job for us, John, really you have.'

'Thank you very much. But I still think we should hold back for a day or two.'

'Right.'

Margaret Slade rang off sounding much less excited and somewhat bewildered. Kelly's head was swimming again, and still aching for England. He was relieved that Margaret hadn't asked him if he knew of any fresh developments, other than the murder of Robert Morgan, because he didn't want to go into all that with her. Not at the moment, anyway.

He made his way into the bedroom and took two more of the police doctor's blockbuster painkillers. He couldn't even think straight, and he certainly could take no action of any kind until he felt a whole lot better. But he hadn't wanted to discuss any of that with Margaret Slade, either. There were, in fact, a number of aspects to this investigation that he intended to keep entirely to himself – at least until he was able to draw some conclusions of his own. And he thought that the only constructive thing he could do was to crash out again and hope that he woke up considerably recovered.

He checked his watch. It was nearly five o'clock now. Time for bed again, he thought. His beleaguered brain was buzzing and once more he did not think he would sleep easily. Yet, within seconds he was deeply asleep.

Karen was not so fortunate. In spite of being exhausted, and in spite of her determination to be rested for her early-morning raid on Hangridge, when she finally went to bed just before 11 p.m., she was barely able to sleep at all. She had arranged to meet the three officers she had decided to take with her out to the barracks, Detective Sergeant Chris Tompkins, Detective Constable Janet Farnsby, and Micky Turner, a young uniformed constable, at the station at 5.30 a.m., but she actually got there herself before five. She really hadn't been able to wait.

Just before six, the four police officers set off in a marked squad car driven by Constable Turner, and met up with Phil Cooper and his team, as arranged, at a crossroads on the top of the moor, a couple of miles from Hangridge. There were two cars already parked at the designated spot. Karen recognised Phil Cooper's own four-wheel drive, and there was also a second police squad car parked just off the road.

Phil had brought with him an MCIT detective constable, a huge man who made his tall and well-built inspector look a bit on the small side, and, travelling in the squad car, two uniformed constables, whose services he had apparently obtained from Exeter's Heavitree Road police station.

'Well, it's the army, isn't it, boss?' Cooper remarked laconically. 'All they understand is muscle and uniforms, right?'

'I'm beginning to think you might be right,' she responded wryly.

The three vehicles set off in convoy for Hangridge, with Karen in the lead car. She instructed PC Turner to approach the gates to the barracks as fast as he could, an order the young constable was more than happy to obey with enthusiasm, and, with a satisfying squeal of tyre rubber, the squad car jerked to a fairly dramatic halt alongside the sentries.

Karen wound down the window and flashed her warrant card at the young soldier peering in at her with an air of considerable bewilderment.

'Detective Superintendent Karen Meadows, Devon and Cornwall Constabulary,' she announced with deliberate formality. 'I am here to see your commanding officer. Now!'

With that, she instructed PC Turner to drive on, without even waiting for any kind of reply, and all three vehicles swept through the gates past the sentries, who patently did not know what to do. They were doubtless all too aware that they should not let civilians pass like that, but on the other hand, what were they supposed to do when confronted with three carloads of police officers? Shoot them? Karen watched in the wing mirror, with some amusement, as both sentries ran into their sentry boxes and picked up phones.

She directed PC Turner to park right outside the front door of the main administrative building, ignoring the designated parking area beyond.

A sergeant, doubtless alerted by the sentries, opened the door to the admin building as Karen and her team climbed out of their cars.

'Can I help you?' he enquired, his face giving nothing away. But then, soldiers were trained to give nothing away in their facial expressions, weren't they, reflected Karen, thinking obscurely of the troops of the Household Cavalry sitting on their beautiful horses, staring straight ahead, in spite of suffering all manner of indignities from tourists, while on guard duty in London.

'Detective Superintendent Karen Meadows,' she announced again. She had noticed that the sergeant, presumably employed as an administrative clerk, was not the same one she had encountered on her previous visits.

'I want to see your commanding officer, at once.'

'I see ma'am. Well I believe the colonel is having breakfast at the moment. Would you like me to contact the officers' mess?'

'I most certainly would.' Without waiting for an invitation, Karen led all seven police officers accompanying her straight past the sergeant and into the reception area of the admin block. There was nowhere to sit, except at the one desk which Karen remembered being occupied by the other sergeant on her former visits. However, the new sergeant retreated to an office, presumably to use the phone, and shut the door behind him, leaving Karen and the team standing around rather awkwardly. Karen did not care about that, but she was mildly irritated that she could not overhear his call.

However, she was kept waiting only seconds before he returned.

'The CO will be over straight away, ma'am. And I've been told to ask you to wait in his office, ma'am. You'll be more comfortable there.'

Karen stepped forward, gesturing to Cooper, Chris Tompkins and DC Farnsby to follow her. Four officers, two men and two women, somehow felt like just the right number for this confrontation. The others could continue to make their presence felt just by standing around in the reception area.

Inside the familiar room, Karen tried not to think about her previous dealings with Gerrard Parker-Brown, particularly their outings together to the Cott Inn and to that antiques fair. But once again she did not have long to wait.

The door of the CO's office swung open and a man she did not recognise, with the pips of a half colonel gleaming on the shoulders of his khaki uniform sweater, strode into the room.

'Good morning,' he said. 'I'm Lieutenant Colonel Ralph Childress, commanding officer of the Devonshire Fusiliers. And what can we do for you here at Hangridge, at this hour of the morning, ladies and gentlemen?'

Karen, who had been on something of a high, felt as if she had been poleaxed. For a few seconds she just stared at the square-set, sandy-haired man standing facing her, apparently oozing self-confidence. His blue eyes returned her gaze levelly. She was shocked and alarmed.

'Where is Colonel Parker-Brown?' she snapped.

'I have no idea,' replied Ralph Childress coolly. 'He is on special duties. It was a sudden posting, but Gerry was in command here for more than two years, which is a normal tour of duty. Exactly where he has now been posted to is classified information, I'm afraid.'

'Is it, indeed? Well, we will see about that,' snapped Karen. 'Meanwhile, could you please tell me exactly when Gerrard Parker-Brown was relieved of the command of this regiment, Lieutenant Colonel Childress, and when you took over.'

'I wouldn't use the term "relieved of his command",' Ralph Childress responded quickly. 'That sounds in some way critical, as if Gerry left under a cloud. Nothing could be further from the truth. He is an exceptional officer whose services were urgently required elsewhere, in a highly specialist capacity, that is all.'

'Please spare me the commercial. I asked you when Gerry left and when you took over.'

'Yesterday. I arrived here yesterday afternoon and he had already gone. I told you, he was needed urgently elsewhere.'

'How convenient.'

Lieutenant Colonel Childress ignored Karen totally then and

more or less marched straight through all four police officers. DC Farnsby stepped aside to let him pass, and Karen made a mental note to give her a rollicking for that, later. Meanwhile, Lieutenant Colonel Childress sat down behind his desk, clasping his hands neatly before him. Karen found her gaze drawn to his short stubby fingers. Obscurely, she noticed how well manicured his nails were.

'So, please, how can I help you?' the lieutenant colonel enquired, flashing a brief, empty smile which went nowhere near his eyes.

'Could I ask you if you have been stationed here at Hangridge at all in the last year, in any other capacity, before taking command yesterday,' Karen asked.

'Not at all. For the past five years I have been employed in various jobs at the Ministry of Defence.' Ralph Childress flashed the empty smile again. 'I cannot tell you what a joy it is to be at Hangridge and to have taken command of my regiment. It's like coming home.'

'Really.' Karen thought she had rarely heard such insincere tosh. 'As you only arrived here yesterday, Lieutenant Colonel, you personally can help me very little. You should know, however, that I am now setting up an investigation into the suspicious deaths of a number of young soldiers stationed here at Hangridge, and an assault on a member of the public. I will therefore want at least three rooms set aside for my officers where they can interview as many of your soldiers as we feel the need to. And I shall expect all personnel to be made available for interview instantly, upon the request of anyone in my team. We are quite possibly investigating more than one murder here and I will no longer tolerate anything other than full co-operation from the military. Is that clear?'

The commanding officer nodded his assent, and it gave Karen some small satisfaction to see that he no longer looked quite so self-confident.

'Right. I should also like you to get on to your high command or whoever it is that regimental commanding officers take their orders from, and I want you to tell them that I require immediate access to Colonel Parker-Brown. Straight away, and wherever he might be. He is currently under suspicion of involvement in these deaths, and I will not tolerate all that rubbish about special duties. I need to interview him fully, and I do not intend to allow army protocol to get in my way. And neither do I care whether or not his whereabouts are classified. I am conducting a murder investigation and I will not be obstructed. Is that also clear?'

'Perfectly,' The new CO's voice was totally controlled, but Karen could see that she had rattled him, which she couldn't help finding rather satisfying.

Long before Karen even arrived at Hangridge, John Kelly set off for London. He had slept for another nine hours or so and woken just before four in the morning feeling much better than he could reasonably have expected. He certainly felt well enough to drive to Newton Abbot and catch the first fast train to London. Even if he had not felt so well, he would probably still have gone. He just couldn't wait any longer.

He arrived at Paddington just after 9 a.m. and took an expensive cab across London. He still didn't feel able to cope with the tube. The cab journey, into the heart of the new trendily reinvented docklands of London, took around forty-five minutes, which was considerably better than he might have anticipated at that time of the morning.

When he arrived at his destination, he paid off the cab driver and stood on the pavement for a few moments peering up at the impressive riverside tower block, which was home to his only son. Nick lived in the penthouse, and his apartment, which Kelly had visited several times before, boasted picture windows, a huge terrace and panoramic views up and down the Thames.

Kelly was not expected and had no idea whether Nick was in or not, but Nick ran his business, whatever that was, from home and Kelly reckoned he had a fifty-fifty chance of catching him in, possibly more at that hour of the morning. It was quite simple, anyway. If Nick was not there, he would wait until he returned. There was nothing, absolutely nothing, more important for him to do.

He walked across the sweeping expanse of pavement which led to the entrance of the apartment block, and rang the appropriate bell on the intercom. Nick answered at once.

'Hi,' said Kelly. Just the one word.

'Dad?' Nick sounded astonished, as well he might. Kelly lived over two hundred miles away and had never arrived unannounced before. 'Good Lord! What on earth are you doing here?'

'I wanted to see you. So I thought, to hell with it, and jumped on a Cornish flyer.' He tried to make his voice as light as possible. 'Hope you haven't got anyone with you. Not an inconvenient time, or anything?'

'No, no. Of course not. Come on up. Open the door when you hear the buzzer. You know your way, yeah?'

'Yeah.'

Kelly took the lift to the fifteenth floor. Nick was standing in the doorway of his apartment. He looked as tanned and fit as ever, and was wearing a long-sleeved, pristine white shirt – cuffs neatly buttoned at the wrists – which hung loose over well-ironed, faded blue jeans.

'Good God, what have you been up to?' he asked as soon as he saw his father's damaged face.

'It's a long story,' replied Kelly. 'I'll tell you later.'

'But you're all right?' There was concern in Nick's voice, and Kelly was sure that much at least was genuine.

'Fine. Honestly. It looks much worse than it is.'

Nick stepped back and ushered his father into the apartment. Kelly stood for a moment in the middle of the huge ultra-modern living room, with its polished maple floors and just a few pieces of big, expensive-looking, leather and chrome furniture, very minimalist. A dazzling morning sun was blazing directly into the apartment, making everything look bright and shiny, and as he looked out, briefly taking in once more the stunning views across the river and South London, with the dome of the Maritime Museum at Greenwich in the distance, Kelly had to squint in order not to be blinded by its glare.

When he heard the click of the front door, as Nick closed it, he swung round, smiling, to face his son.

'Well, I've come all this way. Don't I get a hug?'

Nick's face was instantly split by a big grin.

'Of course, Dad,' he said, and, stepping forward, began to wrap his long arms around his father.

Moving again with unexpected speed for a man of his years

who had lived his lifestyle, Kelly grabbed hold of the cuff of Nick's right sleeve and ripped it violently upwards. The button popped off at once and Kelly was able to pull the cuff back in one smooth movement, revealing his son's bare lower arm.

A line of angry red indentations ran right across his right wrist. The skin had been broken in several places and one or two of the indentations were still oozing a watery puss. They were clearly toothmarks.

Kelly let go of the sleeve at once and stepped away from his son's attempted embrace.

'You fucking bastard,' he said very quietly. 'Who the fuck are you, and what is it that you do?'

Nick had turned white. He looked down at his wrist, then up at his father's damaged face again. Suddenly his whole body language became threatening. He stepped forwards, arms hanging loosely at his side. For a moment Kelly thought he was going to attack him. And that this time he would not stop.

But, quite abruptly, Nick did stop. He turned away from Kelly and sat down on one of the big, black leather armchairs. Kelly stared at him, willing him to speak.

'I don't know what to say,' Nick managed eventually.

'Well, at least you are not denying it,' said Kelly.

Nick shrugged.

'You came to Babbacombe beach two days ago to kill a man, didn't you, and when you realised that that man was me, you backed off, isn't that right?'

Nick shrugged again.

'You had been employed by somebody to kill me, only you didn't know who your mark was. You had no idea you had been sent to kill your own bloody father. Isn't that how it was, Nick?'

'You seem to have all the answers . . .'

'Don't fuck with me,' said Kelly, raising his voice to a shout. 'Just don't fuck with me. Because I do have all the answers. Not only do I know it was you on the beach, and you were sent there to kill me, but I can also prove it. There were fragments of your skin in my teeth. These are currently being examined in a forensic laboratory and DNA will ultimately be extracted. The police will be able to prove extremely easily that it was you who attacked me.'

292

With a carefully executed sense of the dramatic, Kelly removed his mobile from his jacket pocket.

'One call. One call, Nick, to my old friend, Detective Superintendent Karen Meadows. That's all it will take. The police would then arrest you and take a DNA sample from you, and if it matches with the bits of skin in my teeth, which it will, of course – well, that's it, isn't it. All the proof any court of law would need. A foolproof case.'

'Oh, come on, for fuck's sake, Dad . . .'

'No. Don't you even fucking talk to me unless you are going to tell me what I want to hear. I want to know exactly who set you up for this. Was it Parker-Brown, was that who it was? I want to know, and I want to know exactly what has been going on up at Hangridge, and don't damned well tell me you don't know. I want the lot, Nick, and I want it now.'

'I can't tell you, Dad. It's army stuff . . .'

'Nick, you're not in the fucking army. You left several years ago, and the more I think about it, the more I think you didn't leave at all. You were chucked out, weren't you? That's what happened to you. So just tell me all of it. Or I make that call.'

Nick attempted his knock 'em dead grin again, but it merely made him look vaguely skeletal. 'Come on, Dad, if I'm half of what you seem to be making me out to be, what gives you the idea I'd let you make that call? You can probably guess how easily I could kill you.'

'You had the chance two days ago, and you didn't take it then.'

'No. Maybe I underestimated you, though, underestimated just how dangerous you can be.'

'Maybe you did. But I'm still your father. I don't want to shop you any more than you wanted to kill me. I just want the truth. Please.'

Nick narrowed his eyes and appeared to think long and hard.

'You'd better sit down, then,' he said.

Kelly did so at once, never taking his gaze off his son. It seemed that, as he had hoped, Nick might be prepared to gamble that his father would ultimately be unable to harm him, just as he had apparently been unable to harm his father.

'It was Parker-Brown who sent you, wasn't it?' Kelly enquired.

Nick nodded. 'Yes. Of course.'

'And he had no idea that he was asking you to take out your own father, because we don't even have the same name.'

'That's right.'

'Why, for God's sake?'

'Because he thought it was necessary. Look, Dad, there aren't all that many men I'd kill for without question. Not without a bloody great pay packet, anyway.'

Kelly turned his head away. He had been unable to stop himself wincing and tears were pricking the backs of his eyes. He did not want Nick to see. He did not speak.

'You don't understand, Dad. Gerry was SAS too, and he was my squadron leader when I was in the regiment. He was the best. The fucking best. He was always on your side, Gerry. And you were half right, I didn't actually get chucked out of the regiment, but as near as damn it. They asked me to leave. I'd got involved in a bit of freelancing, working alongside some mercenary outfits, and the brass wouldn't have it. But Gerry understood. We all did stuff like that. It wasn't the money. That was only half of it. It's just that you can't do much about cleaning up the world, getting rid of the real scum, if you only play by the rules.'

Kelly tried to keep the astonishment off his face. He'd had no idea that his son held such right-wing views, for a start.

'Anyway, Gerry was promoted to half colonel and eventually went back to the Devonshires as CO, and I became a sort of freelance military consultant. The world's full of people who want my skills.'

Nick grinned again. Kelly thought it looked like a leer.

'So, when this spot of trouble they had at Hangridge came to the boil, it was natural enough for Gerry to turn to me,' Nick went on. 'He told me there was this guy, who'd been employed by the families – who could finger him, someone who'd seen him when he'd been looking for a squaddie who was out to cause trouble because of what he thought he knew—'

Kelly interrupted. 'Alan Connelly?'

Nick nodded. 'Yeah, that was his name. Gerry just said he

294

thought this man may have recognised him, and he needed taking out.'

Kelly was mesmerised. So Parker-Brown had remembered him from their brief confrontation in The Wild Dog. And he had not given himself away, by even a blink, that day at Hangridge. Karen had been right. Parker-Brown certainly was a smooth operator and one hell of an actor.

'It didn't seem like any big deal,' Nick continued.

Kelly could hardly believe his ears.

'Just a job. That's all. And I had no idea who I was taking out. We work on the basis of need to know, you see. I didn't need to know. Gerry set it up and just told me the instructions you'd been given, to walk up and down Babbacombe beach at midnight, until you were approached. You got a phone call, didn't you, an anonymous call?'

Kelly nodded.

'That was Gerry. He's quite an actor.'

'I know,' said Kelly flatly.

'Well, I hightailed it down to Torquay and out to Babbacombe. Like I said, Gerry had no idea, of course, that I was your son. And it didn't occur to me to think you might be involved. I suppose it should have done in a way, with your history. But with Moira just having died and everything – well, it simply didn't occur to me. Not until you managed to break away from me a bit – I guess that was the first time I underestimated you – and started yelling your head off. I recognised your voice, didn't I? I recognised the sound of your voice. I was gobsmacked. Absolutely gobsmacked. I shone the torch in your face to make sure, and then, well, I didn't know what to do. I couldn't kill you. Not my own father. Not you. I love you, Dad.'

Nick looked across at him appealingly. Kelly felt absolutely nothing. He knew that Nick loved him, had loved him since they had become so joyfully reconciled a few years previously, in spite of the fact that Kelly had been such a neglectful father. Kelly had always thought it a miracle that Nick had still been prepared to accept him, and had never failed to be deeply moved when Nick expressed his love for him. Until now, he thought grimly.

'So, you knocked me senseless, instead,' said Kelly flatly.

'What else could I do? I had to be able to make a clean get-away. I couldn't let you find out that it was me. My torch had a rubber casing, so I knew that if I chose the spot carefully, I should be able to stun you without doing any lasting harm.'

'So you tried to knock me out carefully, is that it?'

'Well, that's one way of putting it, I suppose.'

It was exactly what Kelly had thought at the time, of course.

'And then you rang me up in the early hours of the morning with some spurious excuse, in order to make sure that you had been careful enough.'

'Well, yes, I suppose so. I watched from the woods too. I saw you get in your car and drive away. What were you doing in that bloody great tank of a Volvo anyway? If you'd been driving the MG, I'd never have gone near you. I'd have known it was you.'

'The exhaust went.'

'Ah, just for a change, eh?'

Nick understood about MGs. Kelly wasn't interested.

'But if it hadn't been me, you would have killed whoever happened to be walking up and down that beach without question?' he persisted. 'Is that it?'

'Well yes. I suppose it is. But you don't understand, Dad. Really, you don't. There was good reason, you see . . .'

'Try me, Nick. Tell me your good reason for being prepared to strike down and kill a quite possibly innocent stranger, just because your former squadron leader asked you to?'

'Look, Dad, Gerry and I were in Northern Ireland together. And we both felt extremely strongly about what was happening over there. You have to see it to believe it, Dad . . .'

'I saw it, Nick, you know that,' said Kelly.

'No, Dad. Not the way we did. And the IRA is like any other organisation. At the core of the worst atrocities, there is an extremist minority. Most of them call themselves the Real IRA, nowadays, whatever that means. Now we allegedly have peace, but there are all too many bastards who don't even want it. Gerry, well – when things needed sorting Gerry was prepared to go that bit further than most, even within the SAS. His father had been an NCO in the Devonshires and had died in Northern Ireland. Did you know that?'

296

Kelly shook his head. He neither knew nor cared, as it happened.

'He didn't give a shit, actually, Gerry. When balls were handed out, Gerry got given a pair the size of fucking footballs.'

Kelly, who could see the pride in Nick, even under these circumstances, was becoming more and more starkly aware of just how deep into some other murky world his only son had become immersed. He said nothing.

'We had this man over there, undercover. His information was dynamite. Always. He was an Irishman, but he was British army through and through. Trained in the Marines. He spent years there undercover. Gerry and I, well, we ran him. The man was amazing. A real hero. Last year they had to get him out, his cover was about to be blown. Gerry was determined to find a new life for him. He got him into the Devonshires, made up some story for him, gave him a new name and a whole new phoney background. You know what they say, if you want to hide a lump of coal, then put it in a coal bunker with lots of other lumps of coal. The Irishman was a soldier. So they slotted him into the Devonshires and made him a sergeant, and Gerry took him under his wing. But, well, he was never an easy man to handle. All that time undercover. It had done something to him. To his head. He was a bit of a monster with women, it's true.'

Kelly found himself thinking back to when he had been sitting in Parker-Brown's office at Hangridge. He had a small bet with himself that it had been the Irishman who had opened the door and then quickly closed it again after Parker-Brown had shaken his hand in warning.

'So he was sent to a barracks where vulnerable young women were being trained? Brilliant.'

'Well, anyway. Apparently, he'd come on strong to this girl—'

'Which girl?'

'Her name was Jocelyn Slade.'

'Just strong?'

'Well, she claimed he'd raped her.'

'Oh, dear God, Nick.'

'Look, the Irishman had lived too long under different rules.'

'Oh, yes. I know the type. And he'd think young women soldiers were fair game, of course.'

'I don't know. I don't really know what happened. Just that it all snowballed. Jocelyn Slade had a boyfriend, didn't she? She'd told him all about it.'

'Craig Foster?'

'Yes. Well, Gerry tried to calm it all down, but Slade and Foster were apparently telling people that they were going to go to the newspapers. Eventually, the Irishman sorted it himself. Slade and Foster. A suicide and a tragic accident. Unfortunately, the other sentry – what was his name?'

'Gates, James Gates.'

'Well, he was suspicious of what had happened. The Irishman thought he was a loose cannon, him, and Alan Connelly. They'd been mates with Foster and did a whole lot of talking. Big talking. Anyway, Gerry arranged for Gates to be posted abroad, to Germany.'

'And then had him killed over there.'

Nick shrugged. 'I have no idea. Could have been a genuine freak accident, for all I know. But Connelly didn't think so. So when Connelly went AWOL, Gerry knew he had to find him.'

'And kill him?'

'I've no idea about that, either. It was an accident on a filthy night, wasn't it?'

'Oh, spare me, Nick. I was there. I saw how frightened that boy was. Out of his mind with terror. And no wonder. It was his CO who walked into that pub, and Connelly already believed that soldiers were being killed. It must have been so damned easy to throw him under a truck, make it look like an accident.'

'Well, I don't know about that.'

'I do. I did from the beginning, somehow. Parker-Brown and his sidekick – who was that, then, the Irishman?'

Nick shrugged.

'I'll bet it was.' Kelly paused, thinking back. The second man hadn't uttered a word that night in The Wild Dog. If he had done, his Irish accent would have been evident.

Kelly's head was swimming almost as much as when his son had nearly killed him two days previously, but for an entirely

298

different reason. He knew he was experiencing an acute emotional reaction to all that he had been told.

'And what about Robert Morgan, the soldier knifed in London, on his way to the Gates' family home? He knew things, too, didn't he? And he had probably decided not to stay silent any longer. I'd bet my house on that. Am I right?'

Nick shrugged. 'I think I've said enough.'

'Did the Irishman kill Morgan as well, then? Take his mobile phone? Make it look like a mugging? Was that the Irishman?'

Nick looked away and said nothing.

'Does this Irishman have a name?' asked Kelly.

'Several. But none that I'm telling you. Anyway, he's gone with Gerry. He'll have another name today.'

As Nick spoke, Kelly was suddenly hit by another revelation.

'Oh, my God,' he said. 'It wasn't the Irishman who killed Robert Morgan, was it? It was you, Nick. That was you, again. You murdered him.'

Nick continued to avoid his father's gaze. 'I've told you all I am going to . . .'

'Fine. It doesn't matter, really.' Kelly's voice was very flat. 'You've told me all I need to know.'

'I told you you wouldn't understand, that's for sure.'

'Damn right, I don't understand. You're a cold-blooded murderer, Nick, aren't you? You're prepared to kill a man on request, an innocent man, and to you, it seems, it's little more than swatting a fly. You . . . you, you're the lowest of the low. You're inhuman, Nick.' Kelly paused, and he could feel the tears pricking more incessantly at the back of his eyes. He had to fight to stave them off. 'Damn right, I don't understand,' he repeated.

It was then as if something snapped in Nick. He jumped to his feet and strode across the room towards Kelly, jabbing a pointed finger at him, his lips drawn back over his teeth in an unpleasant snarl. But Kelly wasn't afraid. He was beyond fear.

'You wouldn't, would you?' Nick shouted. 'The army was the only family I ever had, Dad.' And the word 'Dad' came out heavy with sarcasm. 'When I was growing up, you were off all over the world, allegedly on stories, actually cheating on your wife – my mother – at every opportunity, fucking everything that moved, drinking yourself into a stupor and ultimately sticking God knows what up your nose.'

Kelly recoiled. It felt as if Nick had hit him again.

'Gerry Parker-Brown is the finest man I know, and when the army didn't want me any more, he turned out to be my best friend. He never let me down. I'd do anything for him and for his regiment. As for the Irishman? I couldn't begin to tell you what he has done for his country, and *his* country, Dad, is Great Britain, not fucking Ireland. We owe him. All of us. Everything he has done is down to the British army and what we put him through. Gerry was determined to protect him, and that's why he came to me. Unfortunately the whole thing got a bit out of hand . . .'

Nick stepped back, more controlled now and no longer behaving threateningly. Kelly, wondering at the understatement, managed a wry smile.

'It did, didn't it?' he said. 'But Gerry wasn't really protecting the fucking Irishman, was he? Not in the end. And neither were you. The more out of hand it all got, the more he was trapped into protecting his regiment, and both of you were protecting yourselves. I dread to think what you two lunatics had done in Northern Ireland. But the Irishman knew, didn't he? If he went down, you two would go down with him, wouldn't you? That's why you were prepared to kill for Parker-Brown, Nick, not for any fucking altruistic reason. You both had so much to lose, too, didn't you? Parker-Brown had his whole fucking glorious career, and you, and you . . .' Kelly looked around the luxurious and expensively furnished apartment, with its breathtaking river views. 'You had your fancy lifestyle to lose, didn't you? All of this, your flash cars and your holidays in the Caribbean.'

Nick sat down again, apparently quite calm again.

'Think what you like,' he said.

'I don't like my thoughts,' replied Kelly, forcing himself to focus. There were still aspects of all of this that puzzled him.

'If life is so cheap among you, Parker-Brown and the rest, why didn't you take out the Irishman himself, when he started to cause so much trouble?' he asked.

'To begin with, it was loyalty to him, whatever you think. Then, after he'd dealt with Slade and Foster, it became too

300

dangerous. If he'd come to sudden harm, the colonel reckoned it would come back on us and blow out the whole Irish operation we had overseen. There could have been mayhem. It seemed easier to let the Irishman do it his way.'

'And sacrificing those young people was not a problem?' Kelly found the detached way his son discussed violent death quite chilling.

'National security was involved, Dad.'

'Absolute bollocks.'

Nick looked down at the ground.

'Well, we never expected it to snowball like it did, never expected it to involve so many . . .'

'So many murders, Nick? Is murder the word you are seeking?'

Nick shrugged.

Kelly felt ill, really ill. He stood up, concentrating hard. The room seemed to be moving.

'I'm going to leave now,' he said. 'I can't stay here with you any longer.'

'I didn't want you to know, Dad. Not ever.'

'I don't suppose you did.'

Kelly moved shakily towards the door. He had to hold on first to the back of the sofa and then to the edge of the table to ensure that he did not fall. Nick did not appear to notice.

'How did you know?' he asked. 'What made you think it was me? I didn't think you'd ever suspect me.'

Kelly studied his son sorrowfully. 'I suspected you once before,' he said. 'There was that other murder, wasn't there, more than two years ago now, that I, just for a moment, came to believe you might have committed. But I told myself I was crazy, plumb crazy . . .'

Kelly let his voice trail away. Nick looked startled, but made no response.

'And there was something else,' Kelly continued. 'Just a coincidence, a very meaningful coincidence. Jennifer saw your car parked in Torquay on the same night that I was attacked. A customised Aston, so distinctive that she spotted it at once. Careless of you, Nick.'

Nick's eyes widened. 'I didn't drive my own car to Torquay,' he said. 'I'm not an amateur, for God's sake. I'd never have done that. I know my motor is distinctive, but it's not the only one in the damned country. There are some others very nearly the same. Jesus! She didn't see my car, Dad, no way.'

Kelly managed a wan smile. This, surely, was the final irony.

'Well, there you go,' he said quietly.

Nick stood up again, his handsome face creased in a frown.

'What are you going to do now, Dad?' he asked.

'I'm going to get some fresh air,' said Kelly. 'I need it.'

'I mean, are you going to the police?'

Nick reached out and put a hand on his father's shoulder. Kelly shrugged him off. He couldn't bear to be touched by his son. Not any more.

'I haven't decided,' he said, leaning against the front door for support. 'What would you do if I told you that I was going to the police – kill me?'

'You know I couldn't. I have already proved that.'

Kelly opened the door. Suddenly, he really could not stay in the same room as his only son for a second longer. As he left, he had the last word.

'Yes, well, I haven't made up my mind what I am going to do yet. So, you'll just have to live with that for the time being, won't you? Which is, of course, a luxury your various victims have been permanently denied.'

Twenty-two

Meanwhile, at Hangridge, Karen left Cooper, Tompkins and the rest to methodically interview the entire barracks, if necessary, and headed back to Torquay police station, driven as earlier by PC Mickey Turner.

On the way, she tried to call Kelly but both his phone at home and his mobile were on voicemail.

'I hope you're still sleeping, Kelly, and not doing anything daft,' she said in her message. 'I just wanted to touch base with you. Guess what, Parker-Brown has flown the nest. Call me as soon as you can to let me know you're all right. Let's keep in touch.'

Back in her office, she learned that the patrol car which had just made a routine check on Kelly had reported that his borrowed Volvo was no longer there and his house appeared to be empty.

'Damn the man,' muttered Karen. He undoubtedly was doing something daft, and she was worried. His life could well still be in danger.

But, after instructing uniform to continue to look out for Kelly, she did her best to put him out of her mind. There was nothing more she could do.

She then contacted Tomlinson to bring him up to speed. Her call was double-edged. Parker-Brown had been transferred out of immediate harm's way with extraordinary swiftness, she felt, and with interesting timing – just as she had been given the go-ahead to launch a full investigation into the Hangridge deaths.

Karen suspected that he had been tipped off. And she had a pretty good idea that Harry Tomlinson, under those damned clubby, all boys together, rules again, had called Parker-Brown and told him what to expect. She was pretty damned sure, though, that the chief constable would not for a moment have considered the possibility of Parker-Brown promptly doing a runner. After all, that was not playing the game. And, even if it was a bit childish, she was somewhat looking forward to telling Tomlinson about that.

And indeed, when she explained to him the situation which had confronted her at Hangridge that morning, he sounded both shocked and let down.

'What? He's just gone? And without telling anyone?'

Karen knew that what the chief constable meant was that Parker-Brown had not notified him that he was about to stage a disappearing act. And that, of course, no doubt broke all the rules of Tomlinson's damn silly code of honour.

'That's right, sir,' she responded expressionlessly. 'And, naturally, a top priority of this investigation now is to find Parker-Brown. All I have been told so far is that he has been transferred, that he's on special duties, and that his whereabouts are classified. The whole thing stinks of a cover-up, quite honestly, sir. Anyway, I was hoping you might be able to help, put some pressure on the MoD to tell us where he is, that sort of thing.'

'Umm. I'll do my best.'

For once, the chief constable did not argue. Karen reckoned he probably didn't dare. He certainly wouldn't want it ever to become public knowledge that he had given Parker-Brown any kind of warning about the impending investigation, as Karen suspected he had.

'Thank you sir,' she said.

'He could already be a long way away, of course. We've still got dammed near a war situation in Iraq, after all, and that would certainly put him out of our grasp for a bit.'

'It's possible, sir. Yes.'

'On the other hand, he might have gone nowhere at all. If you're right about all this being another military smokescreen, well, he might just have gone home to put his feet up for a bit.'

'Yes, sir.'

Karen sat very still for a few seconds after she ended the call. The chief constable had the previous day guessed straight away that she had set up Phil Cooper and the MCIT to support her bid for a formal investigation into Hangridge, and now once again she may have underestimated Tomlinson. Of course. Parker-Brown could well be at his home. Why on earth hadn't she thought of that?

Within seconds of hanging up she patched herself through to Middlemoor again, on the line which she knew would connect her directly with Tomlinson's secretary.

Joan Lockharte was her normal cool self. Karen responded merely by being brisk and businesslike.

'I wondered if you happened to have a home address for Colonel Parker-Brown?' she asked.

'I might have,' replied Joan.

Karen counted to six. 'Could you look for me?' she continued pleasantly.

There was a silence lasting little more than thirty seconds, while Joan presumably checked her computer database.

'The Old Manor, Roborough,' she recited crisply, when she picked up her phone again.

Karen may never have liked the woman, but she had always admired her efficiency. And had she been in the same room instead of on the end of a telephone line, she might have been tempted to give her a big hug. As it was, she settled for a very genuine thank you.

She was a little puzzled, though. Roborough was a village on the outskirts of Dartmoor, conveniently just a few miles from the centre of Plymouth, which had become extremely fashionable in recent years. And the Old Manor sounded a fearfully grand address to Karen. Parker-Brown had told her that he had married a rich wife, but he'd indicated that since the break-up of his marriage, his finances had been drained. Also, while she and Gerry had somehow never got around to discussing where he lived when he wasn't in residence somewhere with his regiment, the Old Manor did not sound like the sort of house a man on his own would choose.

Kelly did not pick up his messages, not from Karen, not from anyone. He kept his mobile switched off while he was travelling to and from London and did not bother to check his answering machine when he finally arrived home.

It had been a nightmare journey. He still felt far from well.

Kelly had been fortunate enough to pick up a cab almost immediately upon leaving Nick's apartment block and stepping out into the street, which had been all for the best, because he had feared that he might be about to collapse.

He had recovered slightly on the drive across London to Paddington railway station, but none the less had been in something of a daze throughout the train journey to Newton Abbot. Appalling images of death and destruction, some that he had experienced during his long years as a globetrotting journalist, and some which were merely the product of a feverish imagination, kept flashing across his mind.

Somewhere around Taunton, he had finally fallen into a fitful sleep but that had brought no relief. Instead, he had dreamed that he was back in Northern Ireland in the 1970s, and that he had been taken blindfolded to some secret destination in order to interview an IRA leader.

But when the blindfold was removed, his son Nick stood before him, holding an automatic rifle aimed straight at Kelly's head.

'You don't fucking understand,' shouted Nick, but he spoke not in his own voice but in a broad Ulster accent. Then there was a huge bang and a blaze of light, and Kelly woke up in a cold sweat, just as the train pulled into Newton Abbot station.

Yet again Kelly had driven, although only the few miles to the station, when he knew he really shouldn't have done, and now he had to drive home – very aware that the effects of that bash on the head remained a long way from wearing off. And to make matters worse, he was still driving the big cumbersome Volvo because he had not had the time or the inclination to swap it for the MG, even though he knew his little car was now ready. He had to concentrate very hard merely on focusing, as he made his way slowly to St Marychurch.

Once back in the comfortingly familiar surroundings of his home, he slumped into his armchair in the bay window and closed his eyes. He was neither asleep nor fully awake. The phone rang several times. He ignored it. There was nobody in the world he wanted to talk to. Nobody at all.

His doorbell rang. He peered out of the window. A police patrol car was parked outside and two uniformed constables stood at his door. Kelly sighed. He knew that if he tried to ignore them they wouldn't leave him alone.

'Are you all right, sir,' asked the older of the two PCs when he opened the door.

'Fine, yes.' Kelly was abrupt. He just wanted them to go away.

'Do you mind if I ask you where you've been, sir?'

'Oh, just some shopping.'

'Quite a long shopping trip, wasn't it, sir?'

Kelly shrugged.

'Right. Well, just don't go out again without letting us know, OK, sir?'

'I'm not planning on going anywhere, Constable,' said Kelly. And this time he meant it. He had nowhere left to go.

Little more than an hour or so later, Karen and Mickey Turner arrived in Roborough. The Old Manor turned out to be a huge granite pile on the outskirts of the village, with sweeping views across the moor. Karen had been right. The house, with its tree-lined private driveway and apparently extensive grounds, was extremely grand indeed. It also looked well cared for. Indeed, it stank of money.

Karen looked around her with interest. A property like this must surely have been acquired thanks to Parker-Brown's wealthy wife, she assumed. You certainly would not get even close to this place on an army officer's salary. But what kind of woman would walk away from all this and leave her husband *in situ*, she asked herself? In any case, hadn't Gerry Parker-Brown indicated that his marriage break-up had left him in some financial difficulty.

Still studying the imposing surroundings as she and Turner approached the tall, porticoed entrance to the house, she stood back to allow the young PC to ring the doorbell.

A tall, elegant woman, quite possibly in her early forties, but meticulously well preserved, answered the door.

'Yes?' she enquired coolly, flicking a strand of coiffured blonde hair away from her face, and apparently completely unconcerned by the presence of a uniformed police officer on her doorstep.

Karen, who had been even further taken aback by being

confronted by a woman, allowed Turner to do the introductions.

'We're looking for Colonel Gerrard Parker-Brown, madam,' he announced.

'My husband? Is he expecting you?'

Her husband? Not for the first time during the course of this investigation, Karen felt as if she had been kicked in the belly by a mule. If the truth be known, she had begun to suspect such a possibility from the moment Joan Lockharte had supplied her with Parker-Brown's address. But, my God, that man had done a number on her.

'Is he here, Mrs Parker-Brown?' she interrupted sharply.

'Well, yes . . .'

'In that case, please get him at once, will you?'

Within a couple of minutes Gerrard Parker-Brown arrived at the front door. He was wearing jeans and an England rugby sweater. He looked as handsome as ever, and if he was anything like as disconcerted by her unexpected visit as he should have been, then he was not showing it. But then, Karen remembered that the man was a consummate actor. Or that was one word for it. She was beginning to prefer words like charlatan and con man.

'Karen,' he began, smiling at her. 'What an unexpected pleas—'

'Detective Superintendent, to you,' she snapped. 'I'm here to formally interview you, Colonel, concerning a number of suspicious deaths within your regiment.'

'Ah. I'm afraid you're too late.'

'I'm sorry . . .' Karen was about to blow her top.

'Yes. As soon as I heard that a police inquiry had been set up, I realised that I would have to make a statement. So I sorted it out through the top brass and I gave a full statement to two officers from the National Crime Squad, who drove down here early this morning. Apparently, there has been rising concern at the Ministry of Defence regarding the number of suicides at certain army bases, and an inquiry has been set up to look at the problem as a whole across the country, which is why the National Crime boys are already involved. As I told you, Detective Superintendent, we do take the welfare of our soldiers extremely seriously. No doubt, that statement will be forwarded to you in due course. They told me that was all that would be necessary.'

I bet they did, thought Karen. She had never heard of an inquiry anything like the one Parker-Brown had referred to, and she rather suspected that it had probably been set up within the last twenty-four hours. In as much as it existed at all. Aloud, she said:

'I see. None the less, Colonel, I am the senior officer in charge of this investigation here in Devon, and I'm afraid I am going to have to ask you to go through that statement again, right away, with myself and PC Turner, and to answer any additional questions we may have. So perhaps you would invite us in, please.'

Parker-Brown did not move an inch from the doorway. As so often with him, she now realised, his face and eyes were giving nothing away.

'I'm so sorry, Detective Superintendent. I have been instructed by my superiors at the MoD to give no further interviews to the police. It is felt that I have already fulfilled my every obligation.'

'I'm afraid I do not agree with that, Colonel, and I must insist.' Karen struggled to keep her voice calm. She was absolutely furious.

'Oh. Are you planning to arrest me, Detective Superintendent?'

Parker-Brown was so cool that Karen wanted to slap him.

'Not at this moment. No.'

'In that case, Detective Superintendent, I am sure you will forgive me if I prefer to follow the orders of my superiors.'

Karen stared at him for several seconds. If she had thought there was any way she could have got away with it, she really would have hit him. She was trapped and she knew it. Gesturing to Turner to accompany her, she turned on her heel and began to walk away from the house.

'Do not think this is the end of the matter,' she commented rather lamely, she thought, over her shoulder. 'We will be back.'

'I look forward to it,' he responded, his manner teasing, his voice displaying more than a touch of arrogance, she reckoned.

It was too much for her.

As Turner stepped into their squad car, Karen returned to Parker-Brown, who had not moved from his position in the doorway of his home.

'I met your wife,' she told him quietly.

'Ah,' he said. She waited to see if he would make any further comment. He didn't.

'Why?' she asked.

He understood what she meant at once.

'I didn't think you'd have anything to do with me if you thought I was married.'

He could have no idea, of course, how ironic she found that remark. He didn't know about Phil Cooper. Married men, unfortunately, had not always been off her agenda. Congenital liars were.

'You're a grade A bastard in every direction of life, Gerry,' she told him, her eyes blazing with anger. 'And I am going to get you, I promise.'

He said nothing, but she thought there may have been the merest flicker of concern in those strangely feminine brown eyes. And with this man, she thought, as she turned away from him again, even that was a result.

Kelly stayed in the armchair in the window for the rest of that day and the whole of the night, going over and over everything in his mind.

There had been a total of six sudden deaths of young soldiers stationed at Hangridge: Trevor Parsons, Jocelyn Slade, Craig Foster, James Gates, Alan Connelly and Robert Morgan.

Parsons' death, it seemed, could well have been a genuine suicide after all. Jocelyn Slade and Craig Foster had, according to Nick, both been murdered by the monstrous and mysterious Irishman. James Gates' death remained unexplained, although Kelly strongly suspected he had been murdered too, probably on the instructions of Parker-Brown. Connelly had almost certainly been dispatched by the Irishman and Parker-Brown. And Nick's silence when his father had accused him of killing Morgan made Kelly quite certain that he was guilty of that final murder.

It was mind-blowing. Kelly felt sick. He sat staring into space,

310

desperately trying to come to terms with it all. The phone rang several more times but he continued to ignore it.

He did not sleep properly all night, only occasionally dozing fitfully.

In the morning, still feeling nauseous, he decided to check his messages, even though it was highly unlikely that he would do anything about them.

There were several from Margaret Slade.

'John, things are really starting to happen. We're planning to do our bit, too, just to make sure this investigation doesn't get swept under the carpet as well. We're going to march on parliament at the end of the week and we want to publicise that. We also want to announce that we are calling for a full public inquiry. The papers already know there's something up. People talk, don't they? Neil Connelly has apparently told his local rag in Scotland that he now thinks his son was murdered and that he might not be the only one. I've had the *Sun*, the *Mail*, the *Mirror* and the *Guardian* on to me already and so far I've stalled, because I need to know what you are planning. Please call me.'

'John, where are you? I think I've now had every paper in the country on the phone. They're all champing at the bit. John, it has to be time to make our move.'

'John. Please call me.'

'John. If I don't hear from you tonight, I'm going to try to handle everything myself. I'm going to have to start giving interviews.'

Kelly stared blankly at the machine. He knew he should call Margaret Slade back. She didn't deserve to be suddenly abandoned. He just didn't feel able to do so. He couldn't tell her any of what he had learned. Not yet. But worse than that, unless he did something, unless he did tell Karen Meadows all that Nick had told him, unless he shopped his only son, he had a dreadful feeling the truth was never going to come out – even if the families did force a public inquiry.

There were also several messages from Karen Meadows.

'I do hope you're there, Kelly. I heard from uniform that you did a disappearing act. Will you please pick up the phone. I still need you on the case. You'd never believe the wall that the army are building round this little lot. One thing is certain, this investigation is only just beginning.'

The final call was from Jennifer.

'I've also left a message on your mobile, John. I thought you were planning to come over? I've got some news.'

He switched off the answering machine, pulled the telephone socket out of the wall, and sat staring into space for several minutes. Eventually, he went up to the bathroom and removed the packet of Nurofen he always kept in the cabinet. Then he went downstairs and raided the cupboard in the kitchen, where he kept the rest of whatever other medical supplies he had. There was some Paracetemol, some more Nurofen, and, best of all, a three-quarters-full bottle of sleeping pills that had been prescribed for Moira when she had first begun to feel ill. And the remains of the blockbuster painkillers, which the police doctor had supplied him with, were still in his jacket pocket. He piled the lot of them into the wicker basket on the worktop which Moira had used for bread. Then he went to the other cupboard in the kitchen, which served as a bar. Kelly knew that an alcoholic who can only refrain from drinking by avoiding all contact with alcohol was unlikely to succeed in his aim, and he had, so far at least, not been tempted to start drinking again simply because he kept alcohol in the house. He had always felt that visitors to his home should not be deprived of alcohol, just because he was no longer able to drink without destroying himself. He rummaged through the contents of the cupboard and at the back found an unopened bottle of Glenmorangie, which, ironically enough, was Nick's favourite malt whisky. And when Kelly had been a drinker, it had been his favourite too.

He took the bottle from the cupboard, found a suitable glass, picked up the little basket of pills and headed for the living room. He switched the radio on. Something by Mozart, he was sure, though he didn't know quite what it was, was being played on Classic FM. He turned the radio up as loud as it would go. He didn't want to be able to hear himself think.

He drew the curtains on the bay window that overlooked the street, and sat down in his favourite armchair, leaning back, trying to relax. For the second time in three days, he prepared to die. But this time it would be by his own hand.

312

There was a pen and a notepad on the table by his chair, and for a moment he considered writing some kind of letter. But he had absolutely nothing to say. And for the first time in his life, just as he was about to end it, Kelly understood why only twenty-five per cent of suicides leave a note, a statistic he had always previously thought surprising.

For a few minutes more he let the music wash over him, hoping that it might help to numb all of his other senses. Then he sat upright in his chair, opened the bottle of Glenmorangie and began to pour the whisky into the glass tumbler alongside it on the table. He filled the tumbler to the brim. Then he took the bottle which contained Moira's sleeping pills, emptied the pills into his hand and counted them. There were twenty of them, surely enough to do the job. He glanced at the other packets of medication on the table. He thought he might take the Paracetemol as well, just to make sure, but decided to begin with the sleeping pills.

He put two in his mouth, picked up the glass and prepared to drink a big mouthful of the whisky to wash them down.

Then the doorbell rang. Instinctively, Kelly put the whisky glass down. Then he picked it up again. It didn't make any difference who was at the front door, he told himself. In any case, it was probably his police watchdogs, and he certainly didn't want to be confronted by them. He would just carry on with what he had planned. He could think of no reason at all why he should want to remain in this world.

The doorbell ran again. Kelly took a gulp of whisky and swallowed. The first two pills disappeared down his throat. He was about to take two more when she called through the letterbox.

'John, John, are you there? We're worried about you. I've phoned and phoned. Answer the door, John.'

Damn, thought Kelly. It was Jennifer. The one person he could never easily ignore. He still didn't intend to answer the door, though. But he did put down the whisky glass and empty the pills from his hand onto the table.

Jennifer continued to call through the letterbox.

'John, I told you, I've got some news. Good news. Paula's pregnant again, John. And she's going to have a girl. She's had

the scan and she's going to have a girl. Mum's second grandchild, and so soon after her death. It's like it was meant, John.
Isn't it wonderful?'

Kelly put his head in his hands. It was aching, of course. But
then, it had been aching for three days, ever since his only son
had tried to kill him.

'John, John.' The voice was more plaintive now, as if Jennifer
were giving up on him being there or at least on him answering
the door. He heard the letterbox snap shut. He imagined her
turning and trudging off down the little garden path, disappointed at not having been able to share her news, and
probably still worried about him.

Suddenly Kelly found himself on his feet and hurrying out of
the living room, almost unaware of what he was doing, acting on
some kind of autopilot. He flung open the front door just as she
was stepping out through the gate and onto the pavement.

'Jennifer,' he said.

She turned smiling, but the smile faded when she saw his face.

'Good God, Kelly, what on earth has happened to you?'

'Uh, I had to stop suddenly in the car and I bashed my head on
the windscreen,' he lied fluently. 'That bloody Volvo, I hate it.'

She smiled again.

'I'm sorry,' he continued. 'I was lying on the bed. I don't feel
all that hot.'

'I'm not surprised. Oh dear, John, are you sure you're all right
here on your own? Have you seen a doctor?'

'Yes, I have, and I'm fine. Just tired and a bit sore, that's all.'

She nodded.

'John, did you hear what I said?'

'About Paula? Yes. That's really great news, Jennifer.'

He found that he meant it too. It was great news.

'They're going to call her Moira, after Mum. She'd have liked
that, wouldn't she?'

'Yes, she would.' Kelly felt his eyes moisten.

'Do you want me to come in and make you something to eat
or anything?'

'No. No, thank you. I just need to sleep, I think.'

'Paula and Ben are coming down at the weekend. Will you
come over for Sunday lunch? To celebrate their news.'

314

Kelly hesitated.

'We'd really like you to be with us.'

'Yes,' he said. 'Of course. I'd love to.'

'Great.' Jennifer left with another smile and a wave.

Kelly closed the front door and went back into the living room. He scooped all the pills back into the wicker basket, picked it up along with the bottle of malt whisky and the still nearly full glass, and made his way upstairs to the bathroom.

There, he poured the contents of both bottle and glass down the sink, and flushed the pills – all except the packet of Nurofen and the remaining few blockbuster painkillers, which he still had considerable need for – down the loo. Then he closed the lavatory lid, sat down on it, and proceeded to cry his eyes out.

Twenty-three

Six months later, Karen was sitting at her desk in Torquay police station, disconsolately leafing through some of the numerous files and reports which had by then been compiled on the Hangridge affair. She feared she had little choice except to put it all behind her now, but the case remained one of the most frustrating she had ever been involved with.

The police investigation she had fought so hard to put in place had so far been spectacularly unsuccessful, and although it was officially still ongoing, in fact most lines of inquiry had now been completed and there seemed scant chance of taking matters much further.

Karen had done her best to make sure that every possibility had been fully explored, every piece of evidence meticulously followed up and recorded. However, her highly unsatisfactory confrontation with Parker-Brown, and the contents of his statement to the National Crime Squad, consisting almost entirely of denial and evasion, had rather set the trend for the entire investigation. It had led nowhere. And the involvement of the NCS, throughout, had compromised her autonomy as senior investigating officer, as she had known that it would, and indeed suspected had been the intention of those in authority, both in the military and the police, who had involved the NCS in the first place.

No evidence at all had been found to indicate that Trevor Parsons' death was anything other than suicide, and Karen had been forced to accept that the death of the unfortunate young squaddie really might be no more than a coincidence.

The body of Jocelyn Slade had been exhumed and an independent ballistics expert employed to study the gunshot wounds she had suffered. His findings, however, had not been conclusive. He reported that in the case of at least two of the five

316

wounds Private Slade had suffered, the bullets had entered from an angle suggesting that the SA80, which had killed her, had been held considerably higher than he would have expected in a self-inflicted shooting. However, all five bullets had been fired from a distance which was consistent with a suicide attempt. And similarly, the ballistics expert found that while it was perhaps surprising for as many as five bullets – even fired from a fast-action automatic weapon – to have found their mark in a suicide bid, it was possible.

No evidence had been found to prove that the deaths of Craig Foster and James Gates were anything other than tragic accidents, although there were some particularly suspicious circumstances surrounding Foster's death. The logbook of his SA80, which would have contained the rifle's entire history, had inexplicably disappeared soon after Foster was killed, and the clothes Foster was wearing on the fatal exercise had since been destroyed.

In the case of Gates, the peculiar manner of his death remained questionable, but the level of alcohol in his blood system, almost four times the legal driving limit, countered that. Indeed, because of his extreme drunkenness, the German authorities argued that there was no cause to re-open the investigation into his death.

The death of Robert Morgan, knifed in a London street, had definitely been murder, of course, but no evidence was found to suggest that the military might be involved, or indeed to link his killing with the other Hangridge deaths in any way.

The inquest on Alan Connelly, finally held three months after the launching of the formal police investigation, had been the worst moment of all for Karen. Kelly was called as a witness, and freed from the restrictions of libel laws by courtroom privilege, he could have made any allegations he wished against Gerrard Parker-Brown. Virtually the entire British press, alert by then to the possibility of a major scandal involving the military, had been represented at Torquay Coroner's Court. And if Kelly had voiced his suspicions about the colonel, and explained how he believed him to have been one of the two men he'd seen escorting Connelly out of that Dartmoor pub, just minutes before the young man had been killed, media speculation would have run riot and could have led to all kinds of further developments.

But Kelly chose not to do so.

When asked if he recognised either of the two men who had come looking for Connelly, he'd merely replied that both men had been wearing woolly hats pulled down over their foreheads and had had their coat collars turned up, and that it would not be fair to make any kind of guess.

Karen had been surprised and had felt let down. After all, if it hadn't been for Kelly's various claims and accusations, not to mention his constant pushing, there quite probably would never have been a police investigation in the first place. It was all so infuriating. She remained absolutely convinced that Parker-Brown was up to his neck in some kind of nasty, and thoroughly sinister, conspiracy, but, to her immense irritation, she was no closer than she had been six months ago to finding out exactly what. And the way in which Kelly had backed down had not helped at all.

She'd had little choice ultimately but to accept the somewhat simplistic explanation he had later given her, which was that, upon reflection, he really couldn't be absolutely sure that Parker-Brown had been one of the two men in The Wild Dog. And that he preferred to keep silent, rather than make a mistake in court on something so vital.

Karen had been unconvinced, and had commented that it was not really like him to suddenly have doubts about something he had at first seemed so certain of. Kelly had merely shrugged. Privately, Karen later came to the conclusion that Kelly must have been frightened off, that he didn't want to risk further involvement, and she couldn't entirely blame him for that. He had thought he was going to be murdered, after all. None the less, that wasn't like him, either. It was totally out of character for John Kelly to run scared, even when he had good reason to be.

The separate investigation into the attack on Kelly at Babbacombe beach had proved no more successful than the Hangridge investigation. The team had made no progress at all in finding out who had attacked Kelly. As he had predicted, there seemed to be no evidence except the fragments of flesh

318

they had managed to extract from his teeth, but even they were no help unless there was a suspect with whom to compare the DNA. And there was no suspect. Neither had it even been possible to conclusively link the attack on Kelly with the Hangridge affair. His mystery caller's claim that he could provide information on the Hangridge deaths strongly suggested such a link, but there was no proof. The attacker could have been someone with an unconnected grudge against Kelly.

Karen was extremely fed up and disappointed. It was late afternoon, almost 5.30. She thought she might try to find an excuse to go home early for once. She fancied curling up on the sofa with Sophie, her cat, and having a good sulk. Along with several large gin and tonics. There seemed little more that she could do.

Then, just as she had started to clear her desk, the door to her office burst open and in bounced the normally morose DS Chris Tompkins, his face unusually animated.

'They've done it, boss, they've bloody done it,' he cried, waving a thin sheaf of A4 paper at her. 'The Hangridge families, they never gave up, did they? They've done it, boss. There's going to be a public inquiry, after all. It's just been announced.'

Karen's spirits immediately lifted. There was just a chance that her ongoing police investigation, even if it had not been a very successful one, may also have played a part.

'That's great news, Chris,' she said.

'Isn't it?' the normally long-faced detective continued, with unaccustomed enthusiasm.

The relatives of the dead soldiers, led quite splendidly by a reborn Margaret Slade, had campaigned with tireless energy for a full public inquiry into the deaths of their loved ones. Karen knew that they'd gained the active support of more than a hundred Members of Parliament, and their various demonstrations – staged at Parliament, at the Ministry of Defence, and with relentless regularity outside Hangridge itself – had ensured that they'd rarely been off the front pages of the national press throughout the last six months.

Now it seemed that the British establishment had finally caved in. A victory for the people, thought Karen. The families would be absolutely delighted. She just hoped the enquiry proved to be genuinely independent, that was all.

'There's more, boss,' continued Tompkins. 'The Standing Orders to the Land Army are going to be changed to ensure that nothing like Hangridge could ever happen again. It's all in a statement from the MoD, that's just come through on email from the chief constable's office.'

He slapped the sheaf of paper he had been waving onto her desk. Karen picked it up eagerly. In future, a civilian police investigation into all sudden non-combat deaths within the military would be standard practice, and a new protocol was about to be issued to UK police forces to ensure they properly investigated all deaths on army bases, rather than the previously accepted practice of only becoming directly involved in obvious cases of murder. In addition, both the Royal Military Police and military base commanders would be banned from taking an active part in investigations into suspicious deaths, except to act as witnesses.

Karen read the statement again, more slowly, after Tompkins, still bouncing, had left her office. Then she continued to clear her desk. She would still leave early, but she no longer wanted to go home to curl up with Sophie. No. Her mood had changed dramatically. On an impulse, she decided she would drive round to Kelly's house to share the good news with him. She understood that the contents of the MoD statement were not public knowledge yet, and she was sure Kelly would be as pleased as she was. After all, he must surely be unhappy with the lack of progress so far in the police investigation, just as she was, and also with his own failure to deliver, Karen suspected.

She had barely seen Kelly in the last six months, except briefly at Connelly's inquest when he had seemed like a changed man. And she had barely heard from him either, which was highly unusual. She had wondered once or twice whether he was still embarrassed by the incident in her flat when they had kissed, although her own embarrassment had faded considerably with the passage of time, and, as ever, had been overtaken by a succession of other anxieties, mostly concerning her work. In any case, instinct told her that it was something else.

She arrived at Kelly's house just after six. He opened the front

320

door straight away, and as he led her into the living room, she at once blurted out her news.

'So, the police investigation may be continuing to draw a blank, but this is a real result, Kelly,' she enthused. 'The families have got their public inquiry, and, regardless of whatever that produces, there's going to be a new directive to the civilian police which will hopefully ensure that nothing like Hangridge will ever happen again.'

'Great,' said Kelly. But Karen noticed that he wasn't smiling and there was little enthusiasm in his voice.

'I should say so,' she said.

He smiled wanly. She studied him carefully. He had lost a lot of weight, but that rather suited him. His paunch was gone for a start. He didn't look ill exactly, just weary. He seemed totally devoid of his usual energy.

'Kelly, is something wrong?' she asked. 'You really pulled back from this one, didn't you? And that's not like you at all.'

'Yes, well, maybe I got scared. I did think I was going to get killed.'

'I know.' Karen ventured to put into words her thoughts on the way Kelly had backed down at Alan Connelly's inquest. 'That's what I reckoned it must have been. But it's not like you to be scared, Kelly. In fact, I have never known you to be frightened of anything. You usually just get all the more pig-headed and determined.'

Kelly smiled more easily at that.

'Perhaps it's about getting older,' he said. 'You scare easier as you get older.'

'Perhaps,' said Karen, still staring at him. His eyes looked tired and his hair was considerably thinner than when she had last seen him. She considered again what he had said – you scare easier when you get older. Perhaps it really was as simple as that.

Anyway, she knew Kelly when he was in this kind of mood. He wasn't going to give anything away. She decided she may as well change the subject.

'How's Jennifer?' she asked. 'And the other two? Paula's new baby must be due soon.'

Kelly hadn't even been aware that Karen knew Paula was pregnant again. 'They're fine, the baby's due in a couple of weeks, and it's a girl. Paula and Ben are going to call her Moira.'

For the first time since she had arrived, Karen could see some life in Kelly's eyes, and when he smiled his whole face lit up. She found she was extremely pleased to see that. Karen really was fond of John Kelly. And, in spite of her resolution to forget it, she had given some thought over the past few months to their one, long, lingering kiss. The timing had been dreadful, of course, but the kiss itself, although it had come as something of a shock, remained a special memory.

'That's lovely,' she responded warmly. 'I'm so pleased. And Nick? How's that handsome son of yours?'

Kelly turned away. 'He's fine too. I think.'

'You think? Don't you know?'

'I haven't seen him for a while.'

'Is he abroad?' Karen knew that Nick was a high-flying entrepreneur who travelled the world, but just like Kelly – until he had so recently learned the unpalatable truth – she had absolutely no idea exactly what he did for a living.

'Yes. Has been for some time.'

Kelly did not seem inclined to offer any more information on that subject, either, and Karen was not that interested. She had always thought that Kelly's son, although undoubtedly hand-some and obviously highly successful, was rather an empty young man. But, naturally, she had never told Kelly that.

He turned to face her again and the life had gone from his eyes. God, he really did look tired. And, upon reflection, he was now too thin.

'You look as if you could do with feeding up,' she blurted out, on impulse again. 'How do you feel about joining me for dinner?'

She was aware of Kelly hesitating. Maybe, unlike her, he really was still embarrassed by their kiss. And maybe he wasn't pre-pared to risk any situation that might lead to a repeat performance. Or maybe he just didn't want to have dinner with her. She waited.

Eventually, he smiled at her again. 'I'd love to,' he said. 'What a good idea. Just let me change my shirt.'

Upstairs in the bathroom, he splashed cold water over his face.

What he had told Karen about Nick was very nearly the truth.

322

Nick was in Baghdad, which seemed starkly appropriate to Kelly. There was still so much murder and mayhem going on out there that his son would fit like a glove, no doubt. Kelly did not like to think about what Nick might actually be doing in Iraq. He didn't like to think about anything Nick might have done in his adult life. Indeed, he didn't like to think about his son at all. Not any more.

And that broke his heart.

Nick had called several times from Baghdad. A couple of times Kelly had inadvertently answered, but had hung up at once when he heard Nick's voice.

Several times Nick had left messages. They were all the same. Slightly anxious for his own skin, no doubt. Slightly whining. And calling, although only in the most general terms over the open air waves, for his father's understanding, for a resumption of their previously warm relationship.

There was absolutely no chance of that. Kelly never wanted to see Nick again for as long as he lived. It did occur to him once or twice that he might still be in danger, but not directly from Nick, he didn't reckon. As his son had said, he had already proved that he wouldn't harm his father. Or more or less. And Kelly thought that the moment would have passed, as far as Parker-Brown was concerned.

Nick had not told him how Parker-Brown had reacted when he'd learned that Nick had failed to kill Kelly. And Kelly had not asked. He assumed that the army officer had taken it as part of the fortunes of war, or something like that. From what Karen had told him at Alan Connelly's inquest about Parker-Brown's attitude, the colonel remained pretty convinced of his own invincibility.

Meanwhile, Kelly had not yet been able to come to terms with the consequences of revealing the truth about Nick. One half of him, John Kelly the man, John Kelly the journalist, John Kelly the human being, had already wanted many times to tell Karen Meadows all. But the other half, John Kelly the father, had been unable to do that, unable to face the prospect of standing in court and giving evidence against his only son. Even though, in allowing his son to – quite literally – get away with murder, he was aware that he was also letting off a host of other murderous bastards. Including Gerrard Parker-Brown. Not to mention the monstrous Irishman, a man still without a name.

Kelly was not impressed by sweeping statements about protecting national security. He didn't give a damn what had initially provoked Parker-Brown, the lunatic Irishman and his own son to embark on a course of action he considered to have been quite evil. He had never subscribed to the view that the end can always justify the means.

But neither had he so far been able to throw his own son to the wolves, send him almost certainly to jail, to life imprisonment. He had chosen instead to withhold evidence in order to protect Nick, and it was that really, perhaps oddly, rather than what Nick had actually done, that had led him to so nearly take his own life.

He splashed more water on his face. The bruising and discoloration on his forehead and around his eyes had long since faded, but the mental scars would last for ever.

He thought about Karen and her honest, old-fashioned enthusiasm for catching criminals. He thought about Margaret Slade and how the campaign to seek justice for her daughter, and the other dead young soldiers, had turned her into a whole new human being. He thought about Jocelyn Slade, killed with her own rifle and earlier raped, something her mother had yet to learn about. He thought about Craig Foster, James Gates, Alan Connelly and Robert Morgan, the oldest of them only nineteen, and how their lives had been summarily snuffed out.

And then he thought about how he had let them all down.

Coming face to face with Karen that evening, knowing that so much still rested with him, knowing that he was one of the very few people alive who had any idea what had really happened at Hangridge, and that he was certainly the only person alive even remotely likely to do anything about it, made Kelly realise that the time had come to act.

Perhaps it was inevitable. Having taken the decision not to end his own life, he could not live for ever with his terrible knowledge. He would have to sacrifice his son, and only now did he feel able to do that. It cut to the core, even though he knew that Nick did not deserve any better. His son was a cold-blooded murderer, and in Kelly's opinion, a truly wicked man. Kelly

324

could no longer cover up for him. He could no longer cover up for any of them. The moment had indeed come.

He could only imagine how it would feel to give evidence in court that would condemn his own son, and in so doing quite possibly be forced to reveal his own failings – the way in which he had abandoned in childhood the boy who grew up to be a killer. But he was prepared to do so now.

He felt much stronger than he had at the time of Alan Connelly's inquest. He had at least come to terms with Moira's death, more or less. And, although his spirits were low, he was certainly no longer suicidal.

Kelly dried his face and hands very deliberately, and then made his way downstairs again. Karen was standing in the hall waiting for him. She looked up at him expectantly. His heart gave a little lurch. She was quite probably his best friend and he had missed her over the last few lonely months. Like her he remembered their one kiss with considerable pleasure, and he couldn't help wondering if perhaps one day, with better timing, just perhaps . . .

No. Yet again this was not the moment, not the moment to even think about such things.

Kelly had something to say, and he could no longer put it off. He came straight to the point.

'I think we should forget dinner, Karen,' he said. 'There's something I have to tell you. Indeed, there's an awful lot I have to tell you. I think you'd better sit down again.'